Cruel Poetry

Vicki Hendricks

First published in this edition in 2007 by Serpent's Tail
4 Blackstock Mews, London N4
www.serpentstail.com

Typeset by Martin Worthington
Printed by Mackays of Chatham

10 9 8 7 6 5 4 3 2 1

Vicki Hendricks lives in Hollywood, Florida, where she teaches English and creative writing. She enjoys dangerous sports, having started sky-diving to research *Sky Blues*. Since then she has completed close to 600 skydives, learned to dogsled in Finland and birded in the jungles of Costa Rica.

Serpent's Tail publishes Vicki Hendricks' earlier novels, *Voluntary Madness*, *Iguana Love* and *Sky Blues*.

Praise for Vicki Hendricks

Voluntary Madness

'I never miss a book by Vicki Hendricks. No one on the current scene is writing supercharged, erotic, real noir novels like these. Think Jack London, James M. Cain, and Colette' **George P. Pelecanos**

'The toughest female writer on the block... This is an unflinching look at the potential madness of unconditional love... Funny, colourful and erotic, it is an adrenaline-drenched love story for those who like to walk on the wild side' **Jack Baxter,** *Sunday Express*

'*Voluntary Madness* is that rare creature, a book you don't want to finish, but when it does, it leaves you with an ending that doesn't disappoint' *Time Out*

'The relentless, reckless nihilism is enough to make your head spin' *Guardian*

'If you missed it, I fervently urge you to acquire it... Hendricks certainly knows how to devise an enthralling, eminently original, page-turner of a book that adds lubricious noiresque eroticism to the thriller genre. Crazy, sexy and very cool' *Crime Time*

Acknowledgements

Since it has taken me over five years to complete this novel, I hope I haven't forgotten any of the help along the way. Working backwards toward the start, thanks to my agent David Hale Smith, my editor John Williams, and my publisher Pete Ayrton for everything they did to get me here. Much appreciation to Michael Connelly for his encouragement and recommendations and to my readers: Betty Owen, Brian Sullivan, and Mary Anne Costello, and also to Elisa Albo for checking my Spanish slang and David Beaty for the knowledge of the phrase "pasa gato." For continued ego reinforcement and comments on early parts of the draft, many thanks to Crime Dogs Anthony Neil Smith, Victor Gischler, and Trev Maviano.

Thanks to Lisa Carroll for the inspiration of Renata's physical representation. Much appreciation to playwright Janyce Lapore for inspiring conversation and e-mails on characters and scenes, and for the title. Your crazed energy kept me going!

The highest esteem to Harry Crews for his genius in literature, and gratitude for allowing me to use the line "Que Encuentres un cono a tu medida!" from *The Gypsy's Curse*.

For Brian

"As everything in the world is but a sham, death is the only sincerity."

— Yamamoto Tsunetomo,
from *Hagakure: The Book of the Samurai*

CHAPTER 1

September 1, 10:00 am, Miami Beach, 86 degrees,
seas at a light chop

Tropical Moons Hotel, Room 2-B

Renata

Sunshine penetrates the salt-streaked window above
Renata's bed, sliding across the peeling paint of the sill to a
stain on the mottled purple bedspread crumpled around her
feet. Flecks of silver gleam on her aqua toenails among the
dark folds, and the walls reflect amber light filtered through
the canvas awning that runs across the east face of the cheap
South Beach hotel.

There's movement beside her – Francisco, her lover and
business partner, who has spent the night. A grin widens across
his face, and he rolls against her, burrowing his nose into her
neck, snorting sounds that tickle. She turns her head to meet
his mouth and lets it cover hers. His lips are toned muscles like
the rest of him. The bite of cigarettes and last night's beer turn
her on like a switch, familiar accompaniments to the hard
cock.

He straddles her hips, his head lowers to her neck, and his lips make a slow nibbling journey from her shoulder to her mouth. She reaches for his cock and slides it inside her. Sensation drains from the rest of her body as she grips and pulls. Hearing is muffled. Her vision, hazy and narrow, focuses on Francisco's face shining inches above her, thick black lashes feathered against his cheeks, one thin drop of sweat tracing the corner of his jaw as he pumps her, slow, full, and hard.

She grazes the moist toffee skin of his throat with her fingernails, running them through the loose black curls, across shoulders worked to a smooth hardness, silk over steel, like his cock. He's hot, eye-candy by the hunk, pure energy that never runs out. Thunder rumbles inside her head, pleasure clouds colliding, as an orgasm builds deep in her abdomen. Her clit numbs with tension, and the rush drops her into delirium, spreading her mind over the universe in one long wave, like oil on water swept clean to the horizon. The far-off place where fucking takes her is as good as drugs.

Her mind refocuses. Francisco is still moving inside her. For no reason she thinks of Richard – Professor Dick, the poet – and how last time they fucked he said that her eyes were the opaque green of the ocean on a stormy day. She told him that was poetry, but he'd meant he couldn't read her – that it's bad never to show feelings. But she has none – no love, no pain. Richard is a paying customer, and she wants to make him happy, but there's no person she would drown in – not anymore – she's full of energy and free of compromise. Her deepest feelings are below the navel. Life is safe when nothing matters.

Another orgasm takes hold and she lets out a long sigh, tightening on Francisco. The sound of her own voice brings on another surge, and she slams her hips against him and comes again and again, hot and wet. Practice makes pleasure so easy. The muscles used for a smile make you feel happy, so can fucking coax you into love?

Renata returns to this time and place, as Francisco slips to her side. She's comfortable, lying flat and naked, legs slightly apart, arms behind her head. She thinks of herself as a portrait, aglow in the amber light from the window, with her bright copper hair and freckles, carved cheekbones, and soft, full curves. Yet she realizes her lack of importance, one more insignificant detail in the cycle of life. Being happy and making others happy is the key. The lifestyle requires her to spread herself thin and charge a price, but she's good at it.

CHAPTER 2

10:20 am, Tropical Moons Hotel, Room 2-A

Jules

She moves from her spot at the wall where she's been listening into Renata's room next door, through the old space-heater hole. She picks up the beach picture used to cover the hole on her side of the wallboard, and re-hangs it. She studies the beach scene, knowing that the print hanging on Renata's side is the same. Over the years, smoke has discolored the azure waves and sky until they look real, like the true South Beach Jules has come to know. The cheerful art deco colors are bleached gray by the brightness, the fun sucked right out of them. When she moved into the motel a couple of months before, she thought the scene was depressing. Now it suits her.

She wipes sweat off her face with a paper towel, pushing the bangs off her forehead and the flat brown hair behind her ears, and opens the laptop. She watches it boot up, still thinking about Renata and Francisco. At some point she lost the feeling of guilt for listening in on Renata and the men. She remembers that she first started doing it for the novel, to get some germ of an idea when suddenly she had none. The atmosphere of the beach wasn't helping her as she had planned. Her big chance to redeem herself, to show her father that she is an interesting person, is starting to fizzle. Her romantic vision of cultivating a spare life, with all her earthly possessions in one room, and all her time to write, has turned to a feeling of deprivation. Her weakness for comfort is undeniable. She expected to be in the hotel for three months, tops, while her parents were in Europe. It sounded so satisfying, spending her days in the excitement of pounding out a first draft, something to show for herself back home, so everyone, her old classmates, even her adventurous sister, would admire her. Now there's little hope. Her time is wasting away, again. She recalls her father's angry face, as he proclaimed that writing a novel was a silly idea, warning her she would fail, as in everything else.

Admittedly her teaching career is over, after quitting the high school at mid-term. Three months of uncontrollable and disrespectful adolescents brought on blackouts that saved her from continuing. She doesn't have the guts for the freelance journalism grind either, yet writing is what she does best, something she can do alone.

She swallows her fears for the moment and perches her fingers on the keyboard – write the goddamned book and get out of here. Make Dad proud so she can go home and fit back into her family of overachievers. Get a life. "Get a fucking life!" she yells. That's what Renata would tell her – she did tell her that, last time they went drinking, more than once. Jules is trying – trying with all her heart, but she can't concentrate. She goes back to the wall and removes the picture.

CHAPTER 3

10:40 am, Tropical Moons Hotel, Room 2-B

Renata

Francisco sits up. "You got something live inside there, girl?" he says, chuckling. He touches her clit with one finger.

Renata opens her eyes and smiles slowly. She smells the tangy odor of their come.

He stretches, nods toward the wall, and whispers, "She listening? That lady?"

Renata shrugs, the smile lasting. She whispers back, "Jules? Hope so. She needs some excitement."

"Ought to charge her – we charge for lookers, so maybe a discount price for listening."

"Put a bill under her door."

She knows Jules can hear them, wonders if she would like to watch – or participate. Doubtful. Pale, thin, shy Jules, a friend by location, on the other side of the wall, scared and lonely girl in her early thirties – sometimes Rennie mentions the sex just to see her face bloom into pink.

No reason to get up. Renata turns her head and relaxes her muscles one by one, starting with her thighs, letting tension drain like water and her mind swirl into roses and jewelry — luxuries she's never needed — how she's taught herself to fall asleep quickly.

The snake, Pepe, comes from under the bed and glides across her thigh, to rest his hard, square head lightly on her shoulder. Renata opens her eyes. His body nestles into her armpit, running diagonally across her stomach downward from crotch to ankle. He's come for warmth, the sun across her side, and she lets him stay. She's fond of Pepe, just a baby, only four feet long. She strokes him, his warm, shining yellow and pearl skin, patterned like a skirt she once owned, but the skirt was cheap. It faded and she threw it out. Pepe is genuine.

Francisco yawns and runs his fingers down her arm. "Takin' off in a minute. Gotta see some *pendejos* about a deal. Don't forget tonight."

She turns to him and smiles her sweet grin. "Bring me a piece of cheesecake — white chocolate macadamia nut. For later — I'll eat it off you."

He gets up and lights a cigarette, then clicks on the TV, finds cartoons. "*Space Monkeys* — it's a good one. You wanna watch?"

Renata shrugs.

He turns up the volume and slips on his khaki cotton pants and black t-shirt. He smiles at Renata. He's trim, bold, and satisfied. "Why you want white chocolate when you got the rich cocoa?"

Renata yawns and stretches her legs toward the ceiling, straight and wide. They glow golden in the light. "Variety."

He opens the refrigerator, takes out the last beer. "Anything for you, *mamita*."

Francisco bends to give her a kiss, but she puts her hand on his cheek and holds him off. "Careful of Pep."

He stands back. "What do you do with him when I'm gone? Eh, chickie? What do you do with the fucking snake?"

She turns her head and kisses the side of Pepe's head, where an ear would be if pythons had ears. He doesn't move.

"When you getting rid of it?" Francisco asks.

"Not till I have to." She looks at him, laughing and holding up the bird finger on her left hand, a half finger, cut off at the second knuckle. He shakes his head and goes into the bathroom. She closes her eyes and strokes Pepe's perfect head. When Francisco comes back out, she's too sleepy to move, but she smells the cigarette and hears his quiet steps as he closes the door and walks down the hall.

She's thinking she should hide Pep when Luiza comes back from Brazil to claim him. Say he worked his way out through a wall and was spotted in Mangoes – a bar on the beach – drinking *cachaça*. Luiza will laugh and Rennie will laugh, and she'll keep repeating the story, no matter how many times Luiza says gimme my snake.

CHAPTER 4

11:00 am, Tropical Moons Hotel, Room 2-A

Jules

She thinks about what she's just heard. Can she get a scene from it? Renata's lovemaking is the center of the novel – a beautiful girl conducting her men like an orchestra, a symphony. Jules has come to know the two regulars – Francisco, the play-toy, and Richard, the foolish poet, who thinks he can make Renata love him. He'll come around in a few hours, unless he has a meeting at the university or his wife surprises him for lunch. Then there are others who come and go, unidentified bumps and groans in the night. Jules has learned to sleep through them.

She opens the file and takes a look at what she has from the day before, the raw material converted into the character of Renata.

> I climbed onto Richard's lap, resting my trim ass
> on his solid runner's legs, using my hand to push
> his cock up my wet slit. I pulled off his designer
> shirt, already sweaty, and dropped it like a rag on

the stained linoleum. He started to move inside me, his jaws quivering like a panting dog, an old dog.

He closed his eyes as he worked me, held back, worked some more. I reckoned he was trying to reach my soul with his penis. Poor Dick. It wasn't long enough. I clutched him with my pussy, once, twice, and he came, his body shuddering. The tears ran down his face.

"You're killing me, Rennie. I'm a dead man."

I smiled and put my arms across his shoulders. "You don't have to work so hard, baby."

He took my hand, the one with the first finger cut off at the knuckle. The stem is still beautiful without a rose, he's told me. He pressed the tip to his mouth. "It's not that. I want you to love me. I'm dying for you to love me."

I pretend I don't understand. "I just did."

"You know what I mean. I want you to show me you love me from your heart."

"Why? It doesn't matter. Really. What could be any different for us?"

"We could create our own world."

"Your world," said Rennie.

Jules wonders if she can use Richard's real words, as she remembers them. Can he sue? As if anybody will ever read this. Should she take out the "panting dog"?

What does Rennie want with him? She doesn't want his world. That's been clear from the first time Jules heard them talk, but Richard doesn't see it, the dick. Renata, what makes her so cold?

Maybe Jules should put in a gun. Francisco could have one – or a knife. She goes back and reads from the beginning. It's all sex scenes with Renata, all stolen reality. There's no plot and she hasn't got the imagination to create one.

Someone knocks. Sure to be Renata. Jules closes the laptop, happy with the excuse for a break, and goes to the door. Renata is wearing a big grin and a tiny black crocheted bikini top that's open-weaved enough to show the pink of her nipples. Jules' eyes go on down to the cut-off jeans that don't quite cover Renata's pubic hair.

Jules looks up. "I had a top like that when I was nineteen. My father never let me wear it."

"Probably this one. I bought it at a thrift shop. Perfect fit – small!" She stretches the straps, pulling the cups all the way down and showing her freckled breasts and nipples. Jules blinks. Renata adjusts the top so the edges of her nipples are showing. "Feel like a beach walk before it gets too hot?" she asks.

Jules looks into her eyes, the only place where nothing is showing. "I'm working. I shouldn't."

Renata steps inside and grabs Jules' hand and presses it against the crocheted top, teasing, in her warm, sexy way. "Come on, you. Take a walk on the beach with me – don't make me fucking beg. You know you'll go. You said it's good for you to break up the day."

Jules shrugs in agreement and turns to the laptop, faces it away from Renata, opens it, and closes the file. "Break it up? I haven't done any work yet this morning."

"Writers write in bars, on cocktail napkins, don't they? We can stop in a bar."

"It's only ten o'clock."

"Whatever you want. Hell, makes no fucking difference to me. I just wanna get out of here – talk for a while."

"Let me find my purse."

"You don't need that – I'm buying. Probably nothing in it anyway."

"Not much." She looks at Renata. No place for money in that outfit. She had to have cut off the lining of her pockets to make the pantlegs that short.

"Come on, fuck it," Renata says. "The afternoon thunderstorms will start soon."

"Okay. A short walk."

Jules and Renata cut over the next block to the beach and walk in front of the sidewalk cafés. There's a breeze still, cool enough to keep Jules from sweating. There's the friendly sound of silverware clanking and people talk loudly with the freedom and good feeling of the morning. Across the street, the ocean sparkles, and Jules gets that vacation feeling, as always, no matter how bad her life is. It could all change so quickly. If she were walking with a lover and had the book written, life would be perfect. She watches the men in the sidewalk cafés, sees the looks that Renata gets from many of the men and some of the women. Even in South Beach Rennie's beauty stands out.

Renata stops at the doorway of Mangoes, gaudy and exotic-looking, even in the morning. "I feel like a drink. Come on."

Jules follows her in. "I'll just have a club soda or I won't be able to write."

They pass empty wrought-iron tables and a mural of tropical birds sipping drinks that runs the length of the room. A few guys are sitting along the cool back end of the bamboo bar, tourists, probably, from the style of pastel shirts, shorts, and sandals.

Renata takes a seat in the middle of the bar. Jules sits on her left toward the outside. She can see the beach, and the men can watch Renata.

Renata pats her pockets, as if something could be in there. "Forgot my cigarettes. *Coño!*"

Jules looks around, but there's no machine.

The bartender comes up. He's good-looking, tall, and worked-out, sun-streaked hair with an earring on the left side. He stands there and looks at Rennie. Keeps looking without a word. Jules feels her face getting warm, but Renata is cool. She grins. "I'll take a little Sex on the Beach. How 'bout you, Jules? One for my friend too."

"No. Please. Just a club soda with lime."

He looks at Renata, no expression on his face. "You really want a little one?"

"No – just being cute. I want a nice big one."

"Nice too? No problem." He kisses the tips of his fingers and floats them toward Rennie. He smiles, showing very white teeth. "I'm Brent."

"Renata. This is Jules."

"Pleased to meet you both."

Rennie pats her left breast then feels her hips. "Damn, no cigarettes. Can I bum one off you, Brent?"

"I don't smoke, but wait a sec. What kind?"

"Anything with a filter."

He returns in a minute and puts an unopened pack of Cools into Rennie's hand. "How's this?"

"Sweet. What do I owe you?"

"Stop in later."

She shrugs. "Maybe."

He lifts his eyebrows. "I'll get your drinks."

Rennie turns to Jules. "Cute, huh? Girl, you're blushing."

"It's hot." She glances to see if the guys down the end are watching. They are. "I'm not used to flirting in bars."

"Best place for it."

Jules watches the flow on the sidewalk, mostly young people, skaters and joggers, tan muscular bodies, tiny swimsuits or over-large pants with the crotch nearly to the knees, the variety of a circus. It's like vacation, living on the beach, with Rennie around to drag her out.

An older woman starts to walk past, but hesitates, squinting as she looks inside. She's dressed in a loose white linen dress with pastel butterflies, her hair short and curled, face perfectly made up, despite the heat. She stands looking very small, clutching her straw bag, undecided for a moment, but then she smiles and steps into the bar.

"You look beautiful, honey," Rennie says. "Can I help you?"

Jules turns to see that Rennie is holding the woman's hand,

magnetism somehow having drawn her to where Renata's charm transforms her shyness into a glowing spirit.

"Thank you so much."

The woman explains that she's looking for a restaurant where she used to eat with her husband, but she can't remember the name. Jules realizes that the husband is deceased. Renata recognizes the description of the restaurant and gives directions. "Great food there," she says. "Enjoy." The woman walks out, smiling back as she turns down the street.

"You know her?" Jules asks.

"No. I waved her over. She needed a lift – not used to being on her own."

Jules is touched with admiration for such quick kindness and the ability to put it into action, a sensitive facet of Renata that she would never have expected. "That's so nice. But how could you tell?"

Renata shrugs. "I don't always think. Just do what's natural."

"I can't be that friendly. I don't know how."

"Maybe you're afraid. No reason to be."

The bartender comes back with two drinks, the same, and sets them down.

"Oh, I asked for club soda!"

He looks up surprised. "Sorry, I thought you both wanted the Sex."

Renata starts laughing. "She wants it. She just doesn't know it."

"Rennie!"

She keeps laughing. "She'll drink it. Or I will."

The bartender takes out a lighter and holds the flame against the tip of Renata's cigarette. The guys from the end are calling him over. He gives Renata a big grin and goes.

Rennie clicks her glass against Jules'. Jules looks at her in wonder and picks up the glass. "What a con you are."

She wrinkles her freckled nose. "It's fun." The wispy ends of her hair float in the breeze of the ceiling fan, and her collarbone and shoulders are a delicate painting of shadow and light. Her eyes are bright as a child's.

Jules sips from the straw. It's a strong drink. Rennie tosses down a gulp. "Umm. Knows how to pour. Think he's got a big cock? Acts like it."

"No idea."

Renata takes a big slurp. "So, Jules, I know you're writing, but I don't know how you can stand it in that room all day. The place is a dump – outside there's paradise."

"You don't mind living in The Moons."

"No, but that's me – I go out a lot."

"I have to stand it," says Jules. "That's why I came to Florida."

"You need a break – get out, find some company."

"You're my company, okay. Here we are."

Rennie puts her head closer. "Speaking of that, you know I have a lot of company. You hear me through the wall – me and my – "

"I don't –"

"I'm not saying you sit there with your ear glued – I mean, the walls are fucking thin, and there's that hole."

"I hear you sometimes. I'm sorry – "

"It's okay. I don't mind."

Jules takes a big drink. The condensation from the glass runs down her hand and she wipes it off with a napkin. "You have a lot of boyfriends."

"They're not boyfriends. Well, maybe Francisco and Richard. Or just Francisco. I'm with him the most." She takes a drag off the cigarette. "Depends on your definition of a boyfriend."

"The one you love?"

"None of them. That's why there're so many."

"Francisco stays with you most nights, doesn't he?"

"If it's convenient. Me and Francisco are in business together. We run ads in the *New Times* off and on. Couples massage. You know what I mean? Outcall."

Jules takes another long drink. "Yeah. I know." She takes

another drink. "Aren't you scared of . . . things – violence and . . . you know . . . diseases?"

Renata lights another cigarette. "Hell, I don't let those jokers inside me without a condom." She inhales deeply and tilts her head back to exhale toward the ceiling. "We're careful. We mostly do people we know."

"You and Francisco – do Richard and his wife?"

"No, no, not his wife. I met Richard by himself about a year ago – when he was depressed." She finishes her drink and puts it on the back of the bar to signal for another. "It's not always couples – and sometimes I just do the wife while the husband watches."

"Oh. Uh huh." Jules isn't surprised, but the cool way that Rennie gives the information is hard to get used to. She looks down at her drink to hide the blush she knows covers her face and neck.

The bartender comes back from a big group. The lunch drinkers are starting to jam in. He sets two drinks on the bar. "Anything else I can get you?"

"Maybe later," Rennie says. She winks. He gives her a look and goes off.

Jules looks at the full glass in panic. "I can't drink another one."

Rennie laughs. "Oh, yes you can! You'd be surprised what you can do."

Jules shakes her head, moves the drink closer. "So these . . . customers pay you?"

"Yeah. But we limit ourselves to a few, like I said. Francisco has other businesses to take care of. Richard supports me partially – what he can with his side income, and what I'll allow. He wants me to quit altogether, break it off with Francisco and be with him only. His fantasy – I can't live like that."

"He loves you."

"Some men just want pussy and others want your soul along with it. I'm only selling pussy – and it's expensive." She takes a drink and runs a hand through her thick curls. "It's that obvious? Through the wall?"

"No – I've seen you downstairs with him – at the bar in our building."

"Well, he has a wife and kids, a nice house with a pool – he's shown me pictures. I don't want him fucking it all up to be with me. I'm a bad influence. I don't love anybody."

"You're still in your twenties. You will."

"Think so? By the time I'm your age? A few more years?" She laughs. "Have you?"

"Not sure. It didn't last." Jules takes a drink, sets the glass down, and picks it up again. "How did you meet him? I can't imagine Richard calling . . ."

"No. He's never seen the ad. We met on the beach. I was playing with him – for something to do. He was sitting on a bench, all sweaty from running – and so sad. So sad. Sadness was all over his face. I wanted to see if I could make him feel good."

"I guess you did."

"Oh, yeah." She stubs out her cigarette on the bottom of her sandal. "Maybe it wasn't such a good idea."

Jules nods. "I don't even know him, but Richard scares me."

"Jules, you scare too easy. I saw you looking scared at the bartender. I wanted to tell you that. It's not good to be scared all the time – it's even worse to let people see it."

"He's desperate."

"We're all desperate," Renata says. "You're desperate."

Jules motions to her with the glass. "You're not."

"Oh, yeah. Why do you think I'm always laughing?" Rennie laughs, swirls the drink and flips her cigarette butt toward the garbage can behind the bar. It misses. "*Coño.*"

"Why are you desperate?" Jules asks her. "You don't act desperate."

"Fuck. I'm not. I just said that. All I wanna do is stick a poker up the ass of the world." She licks the side of her mouth and bites her bottom lip. "Actually, Jules, I am desperate – for excitement. I'm fucking desperate not to be bored to death — and maybe I would fucking fall in love if I knew what it was."

"You haven't found the right person."

"Bullshit," she says quietly. "My kind are all over the place — I just don't have that need, those strong feelings. Maybe it's better like that. What do you know about it?"

Jules can't answer. She shakes her head.

"I never told anybody that before," Renata says. "You open me up, girl." She puts her hand over Jules' and squeezes it.

Jules focuses on the half-finger. She thinks of the pain Renata must have felt. Sometime she'll ask her about it.

Renata motions to Brent for the tab. She gets up. "I'm gonna pee. Be right back."

Brent comes and puts the check down in front of Jules.

"Oh . . . Rennie will get it. She'll be right back." As she says the words, she hopes they're true. Surely Renata wouldn't take off out a back door? She feels panic building. Renata might do anything. She looks at Brent washing glasses across the bar. "She'll be right back."

He looks unconcerned. Jules drains her glass. Maybe he'll cover it. It's not her fault if she can't pay. Fuck, she didn't even want the damned drinks. Now she's drunk before lunchtime. She looks toward the back. No Rennie. She notices that her face feels a little detached, like a mask, and she knows she'll have to be careful when she stands up and tries to walk.

The guys in the back are getting noisy. Jules looks around. They're standing, crowding into a huddle, laughing. Jules is uncomfortable. Come on, Rennie. She fishes a piece of ice out of her glass and sucks on it.

"Let's go." Rennie is standing by her side pointing the half-finger toward the beach. She looks at Brent. "The guys in back will handle our check."

He nods. "Stop in later — any afternoon. I get off at five — take you out somewhere nice."

Jules follows her out blindly, like she followed her in. Now, instead of worrying where the money will come from, she's wondering where it came from. "Those guys bought our drinks?"

"Yeah."

"We didn't even talk to them." Jules looks at Rennie. No clue.

Rennie laughs. "I showed 'em my tits. No big deal. It's fast that way. No need for conversation. There's always some *chupaculo* who'll pay."

"I don't get it. They could walk out on the beach and see all they want."

"Not as nice!" She smiles. "Things are more valuable when you have to pay."

CHAPTER 5

Noon, Atlantic Shores University, Coral Gables, Florida

Richard

The sun angles through the window in a hot streak across the back of Richard's neck. Despite the cold air conditioning of the office, he's beginning to overheat. He scoots his chair closer to the desk to skim the last essay. He'd shuffled it to the end of the stack, in case he might die and never have to grade it. His worst student – a D paper, undoubtedly – and the kid will throw it directly into the trash without reading the comments. He's given up on the freshmen comp students. He can't help them. They come in exactly as they go out, with a few exceptions. He could probably assign a course grade after the first essay and save time for everybody. This boy drives a Ferrari at age nineteen – what interest does he have in a fucking B.S.?

The poetry students are different, all heart and guts, struggling to reach the peak of their possibilities, regardless of the minor rewards. He's not sure which classes are more painful, but he's been at it too long to be teaching freshmen.

He looks at his watch. Since he hasn't heard from Linda, he'll be free from one until six-thirty when she gets home from work and picking up the twins. He calls Renata and leaves the message she's expecting on a Friday — he'll be there at one-thirty or so, depending on traffic.

He finds a parking spot easily and walks the block past other cheap hotels and apartment buildings. South Beach — the enigma, a mixture of exotic decadence and cheap sleaze. Renata falling somewhere outside of it all, in her own category. Wherever she falls, he'd like to catch her. There's nobody like Rennie — beautiful, bright, innocent, cynical. She's a free bird. Having removed herself from the unlucky circumstances of her birth, she makes her own way. If only she were less independent.

He asks himself again and again what he's doing with a prostitute, when he has an interesting, voluptuous wife at home. Although Linda's drinking has gotten a little heavy, she still amazes him after all their years together — recently making her way to the top of her company, while managing the household perfectly with little help from him. After all their years together, she still caters to him as an artist, making sure he has free time for his poetry — although it's been months since he's been able to write a line.

He knows Linda so well he could pick out her toes in a line-up — or the smell of her shit — but familiarity is not a problem. He's weak beside her, and every time he cheats, he feels weaker and guiltier, for all he's done and all he hasn't. There's minor comfort, knowing she'd do fine if he were gone. Without the burden of his bouts of depression, she'd be happier and probably drink less.

No matter how ridiculous and foolish, something steers him back to this squalid and forbidden place. It's beyond the natural attraction of Renata's uniqueness — something within himself that he can't name. How can he possibly entertain the fantasy of giving up his job and family and running away with Renata? What he needs is psychiatry, but he'd rather have Rennie.

He opens the door to the barely cool lobby and bar and

wipes a drop of sweat from his eyebrow. It's warmer still, upstairs in Renata's room, but she likes it that way, hot and moist. He's rarely seen her sweat – except for the trickle that runs down her backbone when she has an orgasm.

He passes the two patrons of the bar, a bleached blonde dangling a thin sandal from her toe, her head propped with her elbow on the bar – a hooker he sees there often. She's talking and pursing her lips at a young guy with bleary eyes, who's smoking and watching her tits. Richard walks up the stairs. He hears the sound of computer keys as he passes the first door, open about a foot to get some cooler air from the hall. It's Renata's friend, the woman Jules, trying to be a writer. He can't imagine that a woman living at The Moons could write anything, but who knew? Maybe a female Charles Bukowski – frightening thought. He hopes she never asks him to look at her work.

He knocks on Renata's door and feels the surge of heat down his body. He's already excited, but half-afraid that she won't be there. He can never be sure of anything with her. The door opens slowly. Renata appears at the edge of it, her soft pink cheek touching the dark green painted wood. She smiles halfway, slowly, then more. Her eyelids are heavy. "Hey, you. Wanna come in?"

Richard feels her run through him and his legs get weak. He wonders how many men get to the point where they'd choose death, rather than give up a woman. He never knew this extreme before. The door opens wide enough for him to squeeze through and he pulls her from behind it and puts his arms around her neck and fills his hands with her hair. He's already had enough moments for a lifetime, no regrets, no matter what happens. The rest of his life is non-existent.

"Mmm, baby," she says. She puts cool lips, tasting of alcohol, against his and her hot tongue inside his mouth. He feels himself drawn to the bed in dreamy movements, pulled against her naked skin. His legs are rubber, but he doesn't need them. He's floating, drugged, only his lips and hands working, as she sits on his lap. The curtains are closed and it's dim. He thinks of the attic from his childhood in upstate New York. He masturbated up there after school when he was supposed to be doing homework.

She pushes him down onto the bed, and he stretches his arms above his head in surrender. His shoes hit the floor, his belt opens, his pants slide off. He closes his eyes as Renata takes his hard cock into her hot mouth, running her tongue on the underside, pulling at the head with her lips, sucking, slurping. She's off and then she's back, sliding the hot wet lining of her pussy up and down, gripping all the way as she reaches the top and rides back down the shaft. His cock hits bottom with every push, the deepest he's ever been inside a woman.

He can tell from Renata's vacant eyes and deep groans that she's coming and coming, so he holds on while she shudders and clenches, her juice making the pushing more slippery. Finally, she goes still, deep inside herself. He keeps moving, but he can't come now. Something in him wants to save, to savor, and he can't let go.

He stops thrusting and she gets off. In anguish, he pulls her down to his chest, holding her head with his hand, pretending that he won't ever have to let her go. But his eyes wander to the dresser, to the little wooden box where he will deposit two fifty-dollar bills, a reminder of his limits. He closes his eyes hard.

A minute passes and he feels himself get soft inside her and slip out. She pushes herself up and out of his arms. She stands and stretches her sleek, firm body.

He gathers himself and props his head up. "How do you come so much − and so fast? Even for a woman −"

"I learned from the nuns."

She plops beside him, her shoulders rounding as she crumples inward, laughing deep down in her stomach. The sparkle in her eyes intensifies and her mouth puckers, her frame vibrating with pleasure. He marvels at the way she loses herself, bubbling, at the slightest trigger. "Nuns?" he asks.

"Catholic school — you know." She giggles. "I'm teasing — there was no clit-licking. They told me I'd go to hell for fucking — 'impurity'. I figured if I was already hellbound I'd enjoy every bit of the ride. I trained myself to come fast. Faster means more."

"You're amazing." He can feel the shine in his eyes, thinking of her in a prim little uniform and knee socks. "I didn't know you went to Catholic school."

"Not for long — my last set of foster parents put me in, but I got thrown out. The nuns were convinced that my mind was a devil's workshop." She raises her arms at her sides. "Not my fault."

"An idle mind is the devil's workshop?"

"Yep. I thought I had a tiny workshop inside my head, like Santa's place, not filled with elves, but cute little red guys with horns and tails, sitting around a miniature table hammering and sawing. I was only fourteen." She vibrates with the stomach laugh. "I was never on the right track."

He crooks his arms behind his head. "When I was in high school, I dreamed of myself as a samurai — with a beautifully embellished sword. I believed I was skillful, strong, and unyielding." He bites his lip on the inside, in the nearly unbearable sweetness of revealing himself to Renata. "The samurais were often poets, and deeply concerned with the idea of death, as more important than life. The philosophy suited me perfectly as an adolescent. People think of them only as fierce warriors, but they were the most literate and intelligent men of the 16th century." Renata's eyes become glassy, and he thinks he might finally have touched a romantic glimmer in her soul. "My fantasies are gone," he says, "but I would give my life for you. I am your samurai."

She settles down beside him and cuddles. "Oh, baby." She runs her fingers through his hair. "My samurai? Like in the movies?" Sunrays from the slit in the curtain pick up copper flames in her lashes as she tilts her head to look into his eyes.

"Your personal samurai, to guard and protect you. The samurais were bodyguards for their rich masters, giving up their lives to protect them, if necessary. Sometimes they killed themselves once their master died because they had no reason left to live."

"I don't know much about things that happened before I was born, except from the movies. Then I never know if they're real or not." Renata smiles. "I don't need you to protect me – good thing, since I'm not rich."

He sits up, takes her hand, and pulls her toward him. "Oh, yes, you are rich, the richest – and you do need me." He chuckles. "You'd like my long sword, my real sword." He strokes her shining pussy. "I would fight for you. Doesn't every woman want that?"

"No. For sure not. You might get hurt. You have a real sword?" She straddles his thigh on the bed, the wetness between her legs cool on his skin.

"Yes – two. They're antiques, a *daisho* – one pair of long and short swords, *katana* and *wakizashi*. They're mounted on my living room wall. I bought them almost twenty years ago, but I never knew the real reason I needed them. They were for you. They're symbolic – of my pledge to you."

"You don't need to pledge anything for me. I'm not worth it. Trust me, Richard." Her trickle of laughter reveals to him that her lack of value for herself is a source of comfort, as if she's got nothing to lose.

He takes her close and crushes her face to his shoulder, feeling her delicacy. He wants to say how precious she is, and how he'll take her away to a wonderful life, protect her, give her the finer things . . .

She pulls away and bends forward to kiss him lightly. "Sorry. I have an appointment this afternoon." She picks up his wrist with the watch still on it. "You have to be out of here in half an hour. Want me to make you come?"

He knows she means a blow job, and he'd almost rather hold her and talk, but she's done talking. He knows he can't come inside her pussy because his cock won't want it to end. He nods and lets the warm idea of an orgasm take over. She lies across his leg, in her usual position where she can rub her pussy on his calf, her nipples on his thigh, and take his cock into her mouth.

CHAPTER 6

4:00 pm, Tropical Moons Hotel, Room 2-A

Jules

She's been listening for too long. Tears run down her cheeks. Richard pounds his heart out on that battered bed, despite Renata's complete lack of feeling. He accepts Francisco and the others because he has no choice. It's frightening, how his feelings allow him to live on such small return. There's something in Renata that takes control. Jules feels it, knows what it means to be Rennie's samurai, to have a single overwhelming and primitive purpose to live by, a spiritual purpose. Choices become easy.

Jules puts the seascape back on the wall and lies down in the musty-smelling bed. For some reason, it's easier to think lying on her back than sitting at the laptop. She should tell Richard to give it up, before he destroys his family, but he won't listen. She feels herself relaxing. It's just too hot to move. She's thinking, half-dreaming of Renata, her soft thick hair, nipples innocently showing through the loose crocheted top, and light red pubic hair feathering out, the thin denim crotch barely covering the tiny triangle. Richard must crave to touch her always, as every man who sees her must. Touch her and put their fingers inside, feel her heat and moisture, always ready for them. Kissing, touching, tonguing . . . soft, slippery, hot . . .

Jules wakes to sounds from Renata's place. She lifts her head. Unusual sounds — thumping and gasping. Not right. The rasps of a whisper, but she can't understand the words. Fear slices through her and she's instantly awake.

She jumps up and pulls the picture off the wall. Rennie's voice is muffled, like a squeak, like she's screaming under something heavy — or something is stuffed into her mouth. What could Richard be doing? Jules looks at the clock. He's gone by now. This is somebody else. Francisco? She throws the picture on the bed and puts her head inside the wall as far as she can get. She can't tell what's happening. She should call the police. Run down to the desk. She doesn't know. If something is happening, there's no time. The bed squeaks violently. She can't risk it.

She looks around for her pepper spray, grabs the purse, dumps it. Rennie might be dead and now he's raping her body. She can't find it — the pepper spray is gone. She has Rennie's key. The scissors are on the table. She grabs them tight in her palm and throws herself into the hall. She turns the knob. The door is unlocked and she rams it wide open.

His back is to her and he's kneeling over Renata on the bed. Naked white ass, dark hairy testicles, thick thighs. He turns enough that she can see his hands around Rennie's neck with something, a thick cord cutting into her throat, Renata's face ruby, sickly, like red construction paper, eyes bulging, her legs thin white sticks under his big thighs. Jules shifts the scissors in her hand and runs straight at him. No stopping, no thinking. His hands are still on the cord as she jams the scissors into the side of his neck. He slips sideways onto one knee and grabs her arm, but she pounds the blade in farther with the other hand before he can push her away. She kicks him in the knee. He goes down, and she kicks him in the ribs. The scissors falls out and blood spouts like a water fountain, a strong, startling, intermittent pulsing stream. Jules' arm is drenched. He makes an animal noise, a growling scream, and tries to get up, holding his neck, blood running in a river down his arm. She grabs an empty bottle from the table and cracks him over the head. It doesn't break, but he goes back down, all the way, and she stands there holding the bottle, ready to hit him again, watching the blood flow around her feet. All she can think is that there's so much more blood than in the movies.

She becomes aware of Renata moving toward her from the bed, gasping. Renata drops the cord from around her neck and puts her arm around Jules. They stare at the man in the widening puddle. "Shit! Shit!" Renata says. "Motherfucking shit."

Jules' eyes are locked on him. He doesn't move. "He's dead," she says. Her stomach lurches, and she swallows bile.

She feels a tremor pass through Renata. "No shit. No fucking shit."

Jules turns and presses the clean side of her face to Renata's. Renata hugs back. "Are you okay?" Jules asks her.

She nods, looking at the body. "You're stronger than I would've thought."

Jules is shaking. "I don't think I can dial."

"Dial? Grab some towels. Blood might seep through the floor."

Jules runs into the bathroom and grabs the mat and the two towels from the rack and runs back out. Renata motions to the floor and Jules drops them into the puddle and starts moving one around with her foot. She's dazed.

Renata dials the phone, lighting a cigarette, sucking hard. "Yeah. Make it fast."

"Did you give the address?"

"Huh?"

"The ambulance. Can they find us?"

Renata puts her hand on Jules' shoulder and motions her to the far end of the bed. "Julie, we don't need any ambulances. He's dead. If we call an ambulance, the fucking police will get here first. We definitely don't want them."

"He would have killed you. We need the police while the marks are around your neck. I don't want to get into trouble." Jules looks at her neck. Already the red lines are fading.

"Listen, sweetie, I don't know much about the law, but this guy's a hot-shot lawyer, so he probably has a lot of hot-shot friends who would like to prove that I'm a piece-of-shit hooker that gets off on oxygen deprivation – making you the cold-blooded murderer of an upstanding citizen and devoted husband." She grits her teeth, grimaces at Jules.

Jules gasps. "No?" She stares.

Renata nods. "Maybe not such a devoted husband."

"Jesus. Jesus! What am I going to do? I never knew you did that."

"I don't – much. You did the right thing – for all you knew I was dying. You would have saved my life. But we're in a bad spot. We can't take the chance. Not only the prostitution charge – they'll look for drugs – who knows what? They'll think of some kind of murder motive for you, just seeing this place. I don't know – jealous lesbian girlfriend."

Jules hangs her head and shakes it. The room is hot and seems to tilt. "We have to call the police."

"Nope. The law is not your friend, Julie, honey. Trust me. Francisco is on his way over. He'll help us."

Renata yanks off the bedspread and starts mopping. The blood has stopped gushing. Jules can't move.

Renata lifts his arm to wipe the floor under it, pushes him on his side. "Damn. He's an ugly fucker when you really take a look at him, so pasty white. Thanks, man," she says to Jules. "I might've fucked him again if you hadn't've killed him." She starts into a high-pitched laugh, hysterical, but contagious. Renata grabs Jules' shoulders and they hold each other, shaking and laughing. Finally, out of breath, they stop. Fear flashes across Renata's eyes and fills Jules' chest.

Renata smiles. "Truly, girl. You did right." She smiles wider, stretching her cheeks with her fingers, trying to get Jules to join her. Finally, she presses her face hard against Jules', the tears sealing them together. Rennie lets go, and Jules stands limp, her arms hanging.

Renata bends and tilts up the lawyer's face, showing moles and hairs standing vivid against the bluish, pockmarked skin. She shivers. "Seriously – I'd rather be dead than fuck this asshole again."

Jules know they're both losing their minds. But in a weird way, it's not the worst kind of horror she would have imagined. She feels something warm about being in it with Rennie, in anything with her. Renata puts her arm around Jules' neck. "Don't worry. We'll handle him." Underneath the tough words, Jules feels her trembling.

Rennie straightens up and points to Jules' blood-soaked shirt and shorts. "You should get out of those clothes."

Jules looks down at herself and nods. She goes into the bathroom to wash up and puts on Renata's robe. It's flimsy but she doesn't dare cross through the hall in her bloody stuff. As she's coming out of the bathroom, the apartment door opens and Francisco walks straight across the room to the body.

"*La madre que lo pario!* What happened? Mother-fucking shit! I knew it was something like this."

Renata stands there with the python across her shoulders, tail wrapped around her arm. His head sits on top of hers, like he's listening, guarding. "What do we do?" she says to Francisco.

He puts his palms over his ears. "Don't fucking ask me. Not my *puta* deal." He swipes across his jaw. "Why you fuck such a big one? So much blood. *Coño.*"

"Come on, Francisco. You know people that can take care of this kind of problem."

"Not really – and nobody does it for free."

"He's a prominent lawyer," Jules tells him. "We have to get rid of the body."

Francisco throws his head back. "Jesus Christ, Renata. I'm not in the mafia. I just run a little weed. Why'd you do a lawyer?"

"He sounded nice and had the bucks," she says. "What else? You can't help? – then fuck off. Don't come back."

"Let me think." He smooths his hair and holds it behind his ears. "*Que encuentres un coño a tu medida!* It's a curse. Women!" He takes a breath. "All right. Let's get him into the bathtub, so you can clean this place." He stares at Renata. "Get rid of that fucking snake."

"I did it," Jules tells him. "I'll clean up." She bends toward the guy and grabs his hand, thinking she'll drag him. She drops the hand, runs into the bathroom and throws up into the toilet. She comes back and tries again, straining, the arm seeming to lengthen, the body stuck to the floor.

Francisco puts his hand out and stops her. "You can't move him. You're just gonna make a bigger mess. Hang on while I get my clothes off. I'll take him in there."

Francisco strips off his shirt, hangs it on the chair, and steps out of his pants, no underwear. Jules stares. She hasn't seen a naked man so smoothly muscled except in the movies, the clear toffee skin, his dark hairy pubic area so obscenely large. She can't help watching as he folds his pants neatly at the creases and turns to place them on the chair. She would rather look at him than a dead man. She shudders at her inappropriate thoughts.

Francisco motions to the guy's clothes on the floor, half in the puddle. "Renata, get his wallet. He better have some cash. I'm gonna need a down payment to get rid of him."

Rennie bends down and lays the snake gently on the bed. "Go, Pepito." He slithers under the sheet as if he understands. She searches through the pockets of the pants and shirt and takes out a wallet, keys, cigarettes, and lighter. She puts them on the dresser. "Have to do something with this stuff, huh?"

Francisco arranges the guy's arms on his chest. "Keep it. He don't need it and we do." He kneels and levers the body onto his thigh, hoisting it up halfway off the floor, grunts, and grabs under the armpits. "Fuck, he's heavy. Hold up his legs, ladies."

Renata and Jules each take a knee and thigh, and Francisco

lifts higher. Balls and dick hang between them. Jules' hair drags into the blood on his hip and she gags. Francisco motions with his chin, "Go." The three of them shuffle through the puddle, creating a slippery path. They bend his knees to make the turn into the bathroom. Francisco lowers the body and lets it thump into the tub.

"You girls clean up the blood. There's somebody that owes me – not this much, but we'll see. For a little money maybe he'll do it."

"I hope so," Jules says.

He turns to Rennie. "You owe me big time, *chiquita*."

"Oh, yeah? You owe me plenty, bud. This might almost make us even."

He shakes his head, as if to say there's no hope with her, then gets on the phone. Rennie and Jules soak up blood with the two towels and take turns rinsing them in the sink. Francisco hangs up twice and dials somebody else. He mentions the Everglades. Jules stops listening and concentrates on keeping her stomach down.

Francisco hangs up. "Okay. Finish it and then we're out of here for the night. I have to see this guy about the details. Rennie, I'll meet you at the diner – we have our appointment."

She nods.

"What's your name – Julie? You go somewhere. You don't wanna hear these kind of noises through the wall tonight."

Knives and chainsaws run with rivers of blood in her head, but she breathes an okay. She remembers she has to go to work. She drags the bedspread into the bathroom and drops it over the body, gagging. She and Rennie wipe up the last of the blood. Finally, the floor looks the same stained color it did before. Jules goes into the bathroom, trying not to look at herself in the mirror, her face and hair again sticky with blood, more on her arms and legs. She has to wash. She tosses the flimsy robe into the sink and steps into the shower carefully, slitting her eyes to blur her vision, straddling the bloody hump. Her stomach wrenches and she has to step out. She shoves her face low to the toilet and lets go the acidic lumps remaining in her stomach. She gags until her throat aches. Finally, the gagging stops. At least, there's an end to everything, she thinks.

She climbs back across the body, careful not to touch, but feeling better, her jitters gone. She turns the water on hot and lathers up in the clean scent of soap, scrubbing her arms and face with a washcloth, and rinsing her hair until the stream of water loses its pink tint. She cracks the door and calls to Renata, who hands her a thick white robe. It's soft and comforting.

When she walks back into the room, Francisco is still naked, hand on a hip, looking out the window, smoking. Rennie is drying her arms by the sink, with her hair turbaned in a towel. She takes a cigarette and lights it off his.

"How much green in the wallet?" he asks.

"About $300," Rennie says. "Two hundred's mine for the fuck. Lots of credit cards."

"Piss on yours," Francisco says, his lip curling at the idea. He stubs out his cigarette in an ashtray on the windowsill and puts out his hand. "We need enough to pay for his plane ride."

Renata hands him the money and credit cards. "Take it then. That's it."

"Won't cover it."

"Don't you have any money?" Renata asks him.

"I have some money," Jules tells them. "Be right back." She opens the door a crack and looks out before she goes to her apartment. She has $500 that she's been saving for an emergency. This is it.

She hands the money to Francisco. He counts it. "Eight hundred might cover expenses for tonight. I'll let you know. This isn't my field."

Jules' stomach lurches. "There's no more − I just waitress part time, make enough for food and rent. When I finish my book −"

"Okay, Julie. It'll do − for now."

CHAPTER 7

5:30 pm, South Miami, 89 degrees

Richard

With all the extra time, Richard stops to hit a bucket of balls on his way home. This way he'll be hot and sweaty with good reason. No way to take a shower before he sees Linda, and he needs to burn off some of the energy he's got left over from Renata. The fire and frustration rekindle every time he leaves her. He lets himself fantasize about the life they could have together, how good he could make it, if he were free to show her what love truly is.

You fool, he tells himself again – wonderful wife, smart and healthy twin boys, an easy, prestigious job – he'd never find another university job if he quit to run off with Renata. His father-in-law, even retired, could make sure of that – if there ever was a creative writing position offered for a middle-aged poet with a minimal reputation. Richard remembers the day the Dean of Humanities introduced him to his daughter, Linda. She was gorgeous. It was his first year of teaching at Atlantic Shores University. Love at first sight expanded his exuberance until the world was his. He remembers the feeling, but it makes him sad. Even now, there's still love between them, but eroded over the years, the peaks worn level with the valleys, sea level like the entire state. No escape. He wonders whether Linda would leave him, if she weren't such an honorable person and so devoted to raising the boys in the best way. She's still beautiful and full of life, while Richard sucks all positive energy from the relationship. What would he do without Linda and the boys? He feels passionately that he should stay. He's desperate to go.

He tries to set the ball on the tee, but his hand is shaking – with fear? Desire? He stands to regain composure. The conflicted thoughts tear at his stomach – ridiculous, since he has no power to choose, and might never. He tees up and hits, watches it hook. He'd move to Moosehead, Alaska, and live on *muktuk* and homebrew in a yurt, if Renata would go. But she won't. More likely she'd rather he go there by himself. He's getting old, on top of it all. Not long until it really shows. By the time she's ready to settle down, he'll be – who knows? He has to do something now, to show her what kind of life he can give her.

He whacks the plastic grass and the ball barely goes a hundred yards, bouncing into the fence on the right. He flattens the piece of plastic back where it goes. She has to realize how much better her life can be. Somewhere in her lost soul, she must want to get out of that business – stop risking murder and dismemberment and live around respectable people, enjoy the finer things. He needs to sweep her off her feet, but that's tough on his salary. He's not sure a woman like Renata can ever be swept away.

He tees up and hits one ball after another without a pause or a practice swing. It's too hot, and he's not enjoying it, but he's paid for the bucket, so he lines them up and finishes them off. He hooks. He slices. When the balls are gone, he's relieved. He can get a quick beer or two at the neighborhood bar down the street to help dull his feelings. Guilt is starting to creep up on him. Linda is such a good sport, so loving. If she ever found out about his feelings for Renata, her pain would kill him. If only he could stop taking the risk.

He opens the black painted door and takes off his sunglasses in the cool dark room. The loud obscenities of construction workers make him feel like he's somewhere he shouldn't be, and it feels good. The seedy sports bar is a man's world, and power is as thick as the cigarette smoke.

He orders a longneck Bud and looks up to see what sport is on the TV. It's women's softball. He has very little interest in the game, but he scrutinizes the players, comparing them to Renata, noting how they all fall short of her in beauty. The batter almost has her chin, but not really. Can't he forget about her for a second?

A bald guy walks up and motions to the TV with his bottle. "Got a favorite?" He points to the batter taking her swing. "Good team. Ever see so much nice pussy?"

Richard shrugs and takes a drink of his beer.

"Some guys say these athletic girls are all dykes, but I don't believe it." He laughs and taps Richard on the arm with his bottle. "I'd give any one of 'em a try."

"Can never tell."

"I liked the little gymnasts in the Olympics this year. Bet if you get ahold of a little gymnast when she's celebrating – I don't mean the real young ones – remember that Russian? You could toss her in the air and she would slide right down your dick every time." He puts his arms out straight from the shoulders, to demonstrate the splits.

"You bet," Richard says. He raises his beer in a toast, but his thoughts are caught in the memory of Renata and how he couldn't come, for all her sliding up and down. She'd make a good gymnast – if she ever took anything seriously. An uneducated small town girl, with no money and no legally marketable skills, owning nothing – why is it so difficult to win her heart? He offers her his world and all she does is laugh.

The guy wanders off. Richard gets another beer and looks

around the bar. It's crowded with all types of men from various levels of affluence and education, lawyers to blue collar and no collar types, all drinking for something to do, watching pussy on the giant screen. Despite the guilt, he feels superior with his secret, the hidden gem in his life. He takes another look around. He's in better shape than any of them. Age hasn't done him in yet. It's only been in the last few years that women have stopped staring at him on the street. He still gets the occasional proposition from a sexy stranger, as well as his young female students – dangerous business that he has always left alone. He finishes the beer in a few gulps and puts the bottle down on the bar.

He pulls into the driveway and moves the boys' bikes into the garage next to Linda's car. She'll probably be cooking out on the grill. Fresh tuna steaks, he hopes. He passes the sliding glass doors and sees her in the back, turning on the gas grill. She doesn't see him and he heads right for the shower. He can get a quick one while she's scraping the grate. Then he'll be back to himself with all traces of the afternoon erased, nothing to make him feel guilty and taint his dinner with the family.

"Hi, sweetheart." He walks into the kitchen where Linda is unwrapping thick tuna steaks so fresh they're neon pink. She tilts her cheek toward him and he kisses it. "Just what I was hoping for," he says.

She laughs. "It's what you're always hoping for. Fish oil and lots of protein."

He sniffs. "Do I smell sweet potatoes baking?"

"No."

"I'd like to."

"Not tonight – corn and salad."

He nods and goes toward his desk to look at the mail.

Linda looks back at him. "Would you mind husking the corn for me? The water is already boiling and I need to get this fish on the grill."

He makes a face and points to his eye, "Would I? *Wood eye*?" The nonsensical phrase of an old joke they've repeated over the years since they were newly married still makes her laugh.

"Hare lip, hare lip — get a move on."

Richard goes to the brown bag of corn on the counter. He knows that more than anything his wife is his pal, and that says a lot for their marriage — if only it were enough. He watches her putting the tuna steaks gently on the center of the grill, respectful of their $20 a pound. Behind her, the gate opens and Eddie and Bill come running from next door with their friend. They cannonball into the pool and Linda laughs and wipes her forehead, a few drops having sprayed her. Richard smiles. He remembers how happy he was when he learned he was to be the father of twin boys.

The twins start a game of catch in the pool — so innocent and unsuspecting of the boredom that will come into their lives as adults. He strips the ears and picks the thin silks from between the kernels, careful to get every strand. What if he were to leave them, leave Linda? If a miraculous change came over Renata? He would see the boys on weekends, of course, maybe the same amount of time he normally does. But not live with them? He can't reconcile his thoughts. His stomach wrings itself into a knot.

CHAPTER 8

7:30 pm, South Beach, Tropical Moons, Room 2-A

Jules

The long shadows of palms stripe the beach as the sun drops behind Tropical Moons, tracing the clouds in red. Fear creeps over her, fear that alcohol can't drown. She sets her vodka on the sink and gets into the shower, washing her hair again, thinking about the bloody corpse next door, once a man, perhaps with a family. She needs to get out of there soon before Francisco's druggie friends arrive, but her body can barely move. The chainsaw comes back into her mind. Too much noise. How else can they get the body out of the building? She doesn't want to know.

Renata has already left – Jules heard the door slam and her nighttime heels click down the stairs, so there's only the body on the other side of the wall. She finishes drying her hair and notices how pale her face is. Renata would let her borrow some blush, but she doesn't dare go over. She'll look like death at work, but she'd better get moving, before the horror starts.

She drags herself out the door and down the stairs. She holds tightly onto the rail, nervous that she'll see something she shouldn't. She weaves her way between the tables to the lobby door. She stops. Two men are outside the glass windows, each carrying a large suitcase. They're normal-looking guys, a little on the grungy side, like many residents of the hotel. Their hair is too long for most types of employment, but both are wearing dark t-shirts and jeans that fit in with the South Beach crowd. Jules imagines them without their clothes, dripping with blood . . . on their chests, in their hair — chopping and sawing, joints snapping . . . She grabs the back of a chair for support and waits, head down and hair blocking her face, as if she's staring at a drink ad on the table. The suitcases don't seem large enough to hold the body parts and their hatchets and saws. Bags inside bags? Whatever. She turns toward the empty side of the room and her stomach convulses. They pass within a few feet, heading toward the stairs. She won't be able to forget their faces, ever. She hopes they had no reason to look at her.

CHAPTER 9

7:35 pm, South Beach, 83 degrees

Renata

There's a misty breeze off the ocean as Renata clicks down the open sidewalk, hot sun flashing in short bursts as she passes openings between buildings. Only a year-round Floridian without good AC could tell the change in season, but she feels some relief from the summer heat. The humidity will drop in a month or so. She walks into the inside section of the News Café where she'll meet Francisco, noticing someone's pie and thinking of the piece of white chocolate macadamia nut cheesecake he was supposed to bring her. Not his fault since she called him early, but she'll mention it just for fun. Good that he took care of the body. Jules, Jules! The trouble she could have caused. As it was, they all got their adrenaline going, but everything turned out fine. The guy was an ugly, nasty motherfucker. She guesses somebody will miss him — some desperate woman maybe — but not for long. It's unlikely that he told anybody where he was headed for the afternoon. She won't spend time worrying about it. She has to keep Jules from worrying too. Poor sweetie.

Francisco motions to her from a dark back table – on time – his face shining smooth like the polished wood that surrounds him, a cigarette hanging loose in the corner of his mouth, two beers on the table. Renata slides across the red leather cushion to sit next to him, and he removes the cigarette to take her by the chin and kiss her hard on the mouth. She puts her hand down between his legs and gives a light squeeze as her greeting. He pulls his head back to smile.

"Well?" Renata asks. She takes a long drink off the beer.

He takes a drag of his cigarette and exhales. "It'll be taken care of before we get home tonight. I'm gonna need more money outta Julie in a couple weeks. I could only cover a small down payment."

"Jesus, Franco. I don't think she can come up with more cash. Don't those guys fly out there to make their drops anyway? What's the big deal?"

"I don't know where the hell they fly. Fuck. I had to make the deal. They named the price – no room to barter."

"Okay. Whatever. Richard will give me extra. Let me know how much." Renata takes out a cigarette and lights it off Francisco's. "Let's have a drink and then get on our way."

"Suits me. I don't have much money till after the job tonight."

"Oh, no money for cheesecake?"

He makes a face then picks a curl from Rennie's shoulder and twists it, takes the cigarette out of his mouth and exhales. "You okay for the job? After all that."

"Yeah. I'm okay. If you're gonna be stupid, you gotta be tough."

"Stupid? Wasn't your fault."

"I should have finished my date with Professor Dick. The lawyer was freaky. Julie did save me."

"Professor Dick. Where'd you find him? Not in your neighborhood."

"I have to do business without you, you know?"

"Yeah, make them all fall in love."

She blows smoke toward the ceiling. "It just happens. It doesn't bother you, does it?"

"No, *mamita*. It's fact – scientific law. Just making light conversation. I don't worry about something I can't change."

The car is parked on a side street and they drift toward it, past tourists and early locals starting their rounds at the bars and restaurants. Renata catches a whiff of coconut oil, the vacation smell that reminds her why she came here. She's never regretted leaving her home town. Nobody there for her anyway. The wind is picking up, and the air feels wild as it whips off the water. Renata points out over the ocean. "Full moon."

"Not the best night to get rid of anything," Francisco says.

"I keep picturing the meaty parts floating around the tall grass, gators lurching in on top of each other, snapping up chunks. They would float, wouldn't they?"

"Chunks of the body? I guess so – or lay on the grass. How do I know?"

Francisco drives to the house in Coral Gables, and Renata thinks about the routine that follows – pleasant enough to take her mind off the other thing, she hopes. Single malt scotch first, with blues in the background and the stories from the couple's latest trip. Then Dahlia will take Francisco out to the pool to smoke dope, while Renata takes off her clothes and massages Daniel, then sits on his lap feeding him sushi and letting him drizzle wine on her tits and snatch and lick it up, before it runs onto the Turkish rug. They'll fuck and maybe sit in the hot tub. Then they'll drink some more, and she'll play with Dahlia while Dan watches, until he's ready again. Francisco will finish up the snacks by the pool. Something like that. She can handle it. Francisco will say he can smell Dahlia's cunt all over Renata's face. Renata will say it's the best perfume.

They turn onto the street. It's bright with the full moon, every house huge and unique, among tall palms and exotic foliage. "Remember to keep your pants on with Dahlia, no matter what she says, Franco."

"I know. I know. Dickweed Dan reminds me every time. It's okay with me. The customer is always right."

"Poor Dahlia. She needs you to fuck her brains out. Surprised she doesn't call you when Dan's out of town."

"She has morals." He flicks his tongue. "I take care of her fine."

"Better not take care of her too well."

They pull into the drive. The two-story Spanish-style house is set far from the street, the misty glow of the porch light visible behind the trees, a signal that Dahlia and Daniel are ready for them.

Francisco turns off the engine. Renata puts her hand on his thigh. "What if Daniel asks you to suck him off?"

"Why would he?"

"He mentioned it last time."

"Me? No."

"Hey, they're our best customers, and they're always right."

He takes a deep breath. "For $200 extra – he can blow me, but that's it – only because we need it right now. I'll close my eyes."

"Don't insult him. You never see me draw the line."

"There's nothing you don't like, girl. Don't give me that."

Renata laughs. "I'll think of something – just so's we're even."

Francisco lights up a cigarette and takes a drag. "I'm not putting his dick in me anywhere. If he has to blow me, you set it up ahead. I'll wear a blindfold." He twitches. "That's enough about it."

"Pretty squeamish for a whore, ain't you?"

"I protect your ass, Rennie."

"Don't need to." She looks at the tight frown on Francisco's forehead. He's still holding the car keys.

"Fuck, Franco. You musta done that before? What's the big deal?"

He purses his lips and shakes his head. "I'm Cuban."

"Don't give me that. You were born in New Jersey.

Everybody mixes it up — whatever feels good."

"I'm Cuban — my roots."

"Daniel likes your root." Renata laughs at her own joke, laughs and laughs. "Just teasing. Daniel never said a word about a blow job." She pats Francisco's cheek. "I make him come — he'd never get to you."

"You do that. I took care of the body for you."

"Yeah, Christsakes. Quit reminding me. Let's get in there and make some money to pay it off, *maricon*!"

CHAPTER 10

September 14, 11:00 am, South Beach, 90 degrees,
seas at a light chop

Jules

It's been two weeks, but the incident is still clear in her
mind. Body parts haunt her dreams and she can't look at meat.
Her stomach is sour. Her skull aches. She sits in the harsh glow
of the computer, willpower keeping her there, but nothing
will come.

Why is she doing this? What's the sense of torturing herself daily? She took a life, so she owes one. It's much easier to
kill herself. So many people have died, all kinds – if they can
do it, she can. A few seconds of pain. Not as horrible as living
a life where everything goes wrong. What the hell is she supposed to do anyway? She's tried one thing after another, put
her heart into everything, and failed, and failed, and failed. The
only thing she's succeeded at is murder! Death might be one
more big fat disappointment, but the final one.

She thinks of Sylvia Plath, her favorite poet, and the gas
oven. She understands, feels the temptation. She looks at the
stove – there's no oven, just electric burners. She never

noticed. What about drugs? Renata must have some. If you take enough of anything it will probably kill you – but it might take a lot. If only she had those swords of Richard's. One quick slice on the wrist. She goes to the drawer and pulls out a paring knife, tests it with her finger. Dull. The pain will stop her before she can do enough damage. She's given up her soul, why won't her body just die?

She looks around at the mismatched table and chairs, the worn floral curtains, and the cheap bedspread she purchased to replace the germ-infested, roach-burned, shredded one. Why did she come here? If only she could have kept her teaching job. Maybe the blackouts would have stopped – she wouldn't have killed anyone. If only, if only. The phrase sums up her whole life.

She grabs a plastic bag from the cabinet and pulls it over her face, holding it tight around her neck. She throws herself on the lumpy sofa and smashes her face into the cushions, sucking the plastic into her mouth, wedging her arms under her to hold the bag. Holding, counting, kicking her legs not to let go. She gasps. Pulls off the bag. Flings it. She's a failure at suicide, no surprise! She presses her face back into the disgusting piece of furniture and tries to cry herself to death, pressing her face so hard into the corner that her teeth cut into her lips. She wears out. There's no one to care or stop her. She has cried every bit of emotion out of her body. She still wants to be dead. She wants many things.

She gets up and looks at her face in the mirror. Horrible. Swollen. Who cares? She gets the bottle of vodka and takes a gulp, then pours a half of a juice glass full. It's going to be slow self-destruction, but it will work. Meanwhile, she'll punish herself with the writing. It's all a coward can do.

She takes the vodka to the computer and reads. None of the books she's read can help her. Okay, so what? Just write crap. Nobody will ever see it. She remembers something, Chekhov's advice – if there's a gun on the wall, fire it. She's got Richard's samurai swords in the book – but no way he'd use them . . .

The only ideas she has are from real life. She knows what blood looks like, a lot of blood. Her stomach threatens to heave, but she holds it down. The hotel is made for murder, a perfect setting of gloom and despair, dirty dealings, more like a film set than reality. Killing – she knows every disgusting detail of how to do that. She should write it, put her ruined life to good use.

She gets up for another splash of vodka. Just a splash. Down to the level of the next line of printing on the bottle. She takes a mouthful and sits down at the computer again. If she writes the bloody scene maybe she can move it someplace outside of her head. How would it have felt to Rennie? She loses herself in the words, sweating, drinking, pecking the keyboard.

Renata gave up the struggle as the breath left her chest. Her throat became numb and her eyes lost focus. Her arms dropped limp to her sides.

Bang! Like gunshot. She looked up. The door had been flung wide, hitting the wall. Her vision was cloudy, yet bright, with the surge of energy against death. Jules appeared like an angel. Her eyes burned with blue flame, and rays of orange light silhouetted her tall form, cutting the darkness as she leapt across the room. The lawyer, still clenching the garrote around Renata's neck, gasped. She felt his cock pull out of her and saw the gleaming scissors blade, solid in his throat, then blood spurting out like a puncture in a hose, as Jules pulled it free and stabbed again. His hands fell. Jules' fist came close into view, yanking the scissors from the gash, plunging them again . . . yanking . . . plunging. He fell off the bed onto the floor and lay in the puddle of his blood.

Renata couldn't move, but Jules sat down facing her, and her fingers slipped the leather from

Renata's neck and touched the red ridge left
there by the noose. Renata had no words. Love
swept over her for Jules, her beautiful savior. She
hugged her to her bare chest. Wrapped in Jules,
she felt the comfort and glow that she recognized
as something missing from her life. She wanted
Jules now, always, more than any man, like a delicacy to taste and savor and never share.

Jules rereads. There's something worthwhile there, the feeling. She would like Rennie to feel that way. She continues:

Renata put her hand on the back of Jules' head,
feeling her soft hair and drawing her close. She
opened her mouth –

The door opens and Renata sticks her head in, the snake
draped across her shoulders. Jules quickly saves and shuts the
top of the computer. Renata steps inside. "Girl, got a minute?"

Jules picks up her glass. "Sure. I'm not burning up the keyboard here."

Renata walks across the room, barefooted. She adjusts
Pepe's tail so she won't sit on it and takes a seat on the bed.
"You been crying?"

"I guess."

"Well, stop it. Damn it." She motions to the vodka bottle
with her half middle finger.

"Can I join you? A half-finger of that for me, please."

Jules jerks her head up. She's not sure whether it's a joke.

Rennie widens her wicked grin. "Great line, huh? Feel free
to laugh." She laughs. "I know I have a half-finger, Jules, and I
know you know it, so we don't have to act like it's perfectly
normal."

"I don't think it's funny. How did you lose it?"

"Sticking it some place I shouldn't've – the usual way."

Jules waits but she sees that no details are coming. She can't think of a usual way to lose part of a finger. "What's up?"

"I hate to tell you this – Francisco needs more money. You know, for that asshole. I got some from Richard, but it's still not enough."

"God! I only have about fifty dollars saved, Rennie. The tips aren't very good this time of year and my hours are short."

"We can earn it. Get a payment together tonight. I have a client you can help me with. Okay?"

"Have sex with a stranger? I can't. Really. Besides, I have to work at the restaurant."

"It's necessary, Jules. Call in sick. This is money we need to save our lives."

Jules shakes her head. "I can't imagine –"

"I have other friends who'd be happy to share the job – easy money – but we need all the money tonight. You don't want to owe these boys. Besides, you'll do great. The customer requested somebody refined –"

"I'd be too embarrassed. I wouldn't even know how to begin."

"You can have the wife. Just kiss – like you would normally. Then do some things that would feel good to you. No fisting or anything that hurts. She'll probably tell you what she wants. It's not even real sex – no cock – maybe plastic."

"Fisting? Don't tell me what that is." Jules finishes off her vodka in a gulp. "Me with a woman? I'm not a lesbian."

"I never thought you were – that's meaningless. Look, it doesn't matter to me who you pick. I'm trying to make it easy. You can have either one – unless they choose."

"They'll both want you." She's thinking of Renata's body in comparison to her own, her pouchy stomach and tiny breasts. She shudders.

"They want two. Are you in, or do you have some other way of getting five hundred bucks tonight? I'd rather not be chum."

"Chum?"

Renata gets off the bed and hoists Pepe tighter around her. She takes Jules by the shoulders and talks into her face. "They'll come after us, you know. We'll be the next gator feast. I'm not kidding. Francisco too."

Jules holds her face as far from Pepe as she can. "They'd just kill us for a few hundred dollars?"

"Not just. Beat us up first. Maybe send us to the hospital. Finish us off next week, my guess. I don't know what their deal is, but it's all part of a big operation. Not only drugs. They don't mess around."

"Rennie, I'm not a prostitute!"

"Fancy legal word. The money is to show appreciation. Listen, I hate to tell you, but we're all gonna be raped in the ass if we don't get the money, raped hard." She holds up the hand with the half-finger — "maybe tortured for extra fun. You're worried about a little lubricated fucking?"

Jules gasps and holds her mouth.

"Sorry, sweetie. I'm going over to get a shower. No use talking. Neither of us has a choice in professions tonight." She frowns. "No more crying and getting puffier. Francisco will pick us up in a half-hour or so."

She strides across the room with Pepe trailing head and tail from her back like a wedding veil, opens the door, and she's gone. Jules thinks how strong Renata must be to carry that heavy snake, how strong she must be to live this life.

Jules' legs go weak. She sits on the bed, drops to her side, and pulls up the sheet, snuggling down like in her childhood, when Daddy would fix all her problems. She never had to worry. Now she just needs to die.

She yanks herself up. She can't lie there, doing nothing, until there's nothing left to be done. If she doesn't sneak out of there before Francisco arrives, she'll have to go with them, have sex with a strange man, or a woman — or both. Jesus Christ. It could be somebody worse than the lawyer.

She hates herself for the thought that comes into her mind, but fear makes her hurry to dress. There is one possibility for her to get the money, although it's against all her principles. Her old principles.

She walks to the café and goes in through the alley entrance. The door is always open, so the staff can run back for quick smokes, standing half inside and half out, and hear their names called when the food comes up. Nobody around, no burning butts in the ashtray, but it's only a matter of time. She could easily get caught.

She listens. No sound from Patty's office to the left. She can hear the sizzling and racket of pans in the grill area and full-house noise out front – Patty's voice, thanking the customer, as she runs the register. Can Jules steal from someone who's always been kind to her? But so has Renata. Jules imagines Rennie's beautiful body, naked, bruised and bleeding . . . her face floating among the weeds . . . strawberry-blonde curls and dead eyes. It will be all Jules' fault. Jules will be next.

She moves fast to the office door and looks through the small window. Patty's purse is on the desk. Jules tries the door knob. She flinches. The office is unlocked as usual. Jules has heard Barbara, the day manager, warn Patty about her carefree habits and suggest she needed a proper safe. One day, you'll learn – Barbara said. Patty agreed, but hadn't changed her ways. Jules doesn't want Patty to learn. The world needs all the trusting people it can get, but right now there's no choice. Jules opens the door. If she could explain how much she needs it, Patty might even loan her the money, but she can't tell the truth, and she's not good enough to lie. Maybe the money is insured – a tax write-off, at least.

Jules glances out the window, sees no one, and grabs the purse. She makes a quick check of the wallet, a few twenties – she leaves them – a key is what she's after. She begins to go through the zippered sections. Patty would already have emptied the cash register and put the day's cash into the bank pouch and locked it in the cabinet. If Jules can get the money, leave and come right back to work, no one will know she's already been there. She finds the key chain and runs to the cabinet.

She listens. Still not a sound in back, but there are several keys. She tries them one by one in the padlock, her hand shaking so it takes twice as long. There's no excuse in the world for her to be in the office. Three left. Still no luck. Second last key – open. She grabs the bank pouch. Nice and full. If the day's lunch was a big one, there could be a thousand bucks, more than enough. She opens the pouch, stuffs the packets of bills into her purse, and puts the empty pouch back. As she withdraws her hand, she thinks about fingerprints. Could the police make each employee give prints? She uses the end of her shirt and wipes down the pouch, the padlock, the cabinet door. God, how many things did she touch? She runs to the desk to put back the keys. She has to wipe each key separately . . . then the purse, the inside compartments, the wallet, the inside doorknob . . . Sweat runs down her face as she listens and pushes open the door with her hand still gloved by her shirt. One swipe on the knob as she closes the door, and she sprints toward the exit, bursting into the alley, flying out to the street. She runs for the next two blocks until she has to slow down, gasping, a pain in her side. From there she can see the front of the hotel. No police waiting for her, yet.

She calms her breathing and enters the bar. One of the local street girls is having a beer. She waves to the bartender. Nobody else around. She can't believe she made it. She climbs the stairs slowly, her heart pounding, hoping Rennie is still home so she can hand over the money before they give up on her and go. The hall is empty and she walks to Renata's door and knocks. The knock pushes the door inward, and she opens it. She freezes. Renata and Francisco are staring at her. Francisco is pointing a small gun. He puts it down to his side.

"Christ! Where'd you run off to?" Renata says.

Francisco puts the gun in his pocket. "What's this shit?"

Jules is still panting. "I'm sorry. I got the money. It should be enough to pay them off."

"You got the money? How? How much?" Renata asks. Her

eyes are wide.

"I don't know, but it feels like a lot." Jules dumps her purse on the bed, several sleeves of fives, tens, and twenties. "I have to get back to work. Seems like this should be enough."

"Jules? You're leaving? Where'd you get the money?"

"Stole it. I'll pay it back."

"*Dios* – more trouble," says Francisco.

"I took it from work. Nobody saw me. I have to go back, so they don't suspect."

"Fuck! You'd rather get arrested than spend a cozy evening with rich friends?" asks Renata. "Jules, get some sense, girl."

"I just did it. I had to – for you."

Renata picks up a stack of bills and fans the money. She looks at Jules. "Did you go to Catholic school?"

"No, why?"

Renata drags her close for a hug. Jules smells her clean hair and feels the softness of her breasts pressing against her. "Your priorities seem a little skewed – choosing grand theft as the lesser evil." Renata steps back, looking into Jules' eyes, and laughs. "We'll have to work on that." She closes in again, kissing Jules on the mouth, pushing her tongue inside, and pulls away laughing. "Thanks, sweetheart. You just saved our lives."

Jules stares, her lips slightly open, heat rushing to her face. Francisco snickers behind her.

CHAPTER 11

September 15, 9:00 am, South Miami, 84 degrees

Richard

He's seated on a stool by the window at Starbucks, sipping his special Sumatran blend of the day and feeling eager for his after-lunch appointment with Renata. Linda comes in from dropping the twins off at school and orders her cappuccino, the usual Friday routine. He watches while she fishes for change in her purse, and he thinks what a slim waist and great ass she has in those black fitted pants. It flits through his mind to take her back home, throw her on the bed, and fuck her, but they both need to get to work. They have just a few minutes for coffee, a habitual early celebration of the weekend.

Linda brings her coffee and espresso brownie to the counter. She looks around the shop. "I was thinking about that incident last year when somebody was killed at the Starbucks in North Miami. It doesn't seem to fit — too cheery. You need a dark place that serves alcohol, for murder, some place with heavy curtains."

"The shooting? I guess if you're set on murder, the decor doesn't matter."

"I don't remember hearing anything afterward. Whether it was some loony or an illicit love triangle. Maybe drug-related."

"Don't know," Richard says. He's having a hard time concentrating on light talk, thinking of Renata – she cancelled his last appointment without an explanation, and he's worried she might do it again. He needs to find a way to give her more money. She's probably taking on new customers to fill in. He pushes a feeling of disgust aside.

"This isn't the kind of place I would choose for murder. I'd take that Italian joint down the street from us, with the candles and dark velvet cushions. At least give them half a chance that the blood stains won't show."

"Uh huh."

She pokes his ribs. "If I found out you were fooling around on me, I'd take you down there in a dark booth and shoot you."

"What?" He replays her words in his mind. A charge of fear runs through him.

"Richard, wake up!" Linda looks at him. "Am I boring you this morning? Sometimes I think you need another woman – to bring you back to life."

He senses a change in her tone. "Jesus Christ. Don't create an issue."

"An issue? I was *kidding*. Hey, that's probably what the guy said to his wife before she shot him – Don't create an issue."

"What guy?" Richard is irritated. "Let's talk about something else."

Linda's mouth is pursed, but she doesn't speak. A flash of guilt runs through him and he's afraid it's reflected in his eyes. Linda can always read his mind, and it's full of Renata, flashing in neon. He takes a sip of his coffee, rolls his eyes to imitate a gesture he often makes to indicate a joke. "What's the matter?"

Linda's eyes glint with points of steel. "Nothing was the matter when I came in here, but now I'm beginning to think there is an issue. I see it in your face."

"What?" He can tell that she's not going to stop and his face boils in the guilt. She can read it, he knows she can, but he might be able to convince her to distrust her feelings, if he sticks with it long enough. He looks down at the table to think, picks up his coffee, and snaps on the lid. "I'm sorry, I was only half listening. Work is getting to me — grading." He looks at his watch. "It's late. Let's get out of here."

"I wasn't going to bring it up, but I changed my mind."

He can barely breathe. He sits back down. "What?"

"I've called you several times when you're supposedly in your office, and you're not."

"When? You know I have meetings — department, faculty —"

"I've been married to you for a long time. Something's different now. It's been going on for a while."

"You're imagining things. When? Give me some times and I'll figure it out."

Instantly he knows he's said the wrong thing.

Her mouth hardens. "I haven't kept a log. Maybe I should."

He can't stand to lie and watch her have to take it. He stands up. "I'm sorry. Please, let's talk later. I have to get to work."

She leaves her coffee and follows him out. He feels her presence moving swiftly behind him as he crosses the parking lot to his car. He turns as he gets in. "What's the matter?"

"I know you too well after all these years. I saw it in your eyes."

He's shaking inside. She knows him as well as he knows her. He puts his arm on her shoulder, strokes her neck. "Sweetheart, please. What is it? It's me, your regular old Dick. Talk to me." His heart aches as he acts the lie. "I'm sorry. There's nothing going on. Let's talk about this later when I can think. I'm very tired. I didn't sleep well last night."

She's still staring at him with a burning distrust. She speaks softly, "Why not? Feeling too guilty?"

He takes a deep breath. She's beginning to make him angry. "Look, we can't discuss this now. You go to work – or go home and relax – whatever you want to do, and I'll call you later. Maybe we can work this ridiculous argument out in time to have a nice dinner. Okay?"

"I don't have any choice. I have a meeting this morning. As much as I enjoy it, I can't stand here in the hot sun and listen to your pitiful defense."

"We need some time together. Maybe we can go away next weekend? Over to the West Coast –"

"That sounds like a line from the movies." She shakes her head slowly and puts her hands on her hips. She's still staring into his eyes.

He looks at his watch. "I can't be late for class. I'll call you." He waits for her to move toward her car, but she stands frowning. He goes to his, gets in, and starts the engine. He looks in the rearview mirror. She's waiting off to the side, still watching him. He gets a chill.

He backs out and pulls forward. As he makes the turn out of the parking lot he can see her staunch silhouette, the sun hot and orange behind her.

CHAPTER 12

Noon, South Beach, 90 degrees

Renata

The room glows amber, heating from the outside, sizzling through the walls until the weak output of the air conditioner is nearly useless. By the time she wakes up, it's steamy. Sweat beads up between her breasts. The bed is damp under her lower back and thighs. She opens her eyes to orange light that tells her another morning has passed. Her stomach is queasy from all the wine she drank the night before, and she knows Richard will turn up soon.

She isn't in a mood to see him, but she can't cancel again, two in a row. She's sticky and her stomach is a ball of pain. She goes in to take a cool shower. Richard won't mind wet hair. Maybe she'll just let him talk today. He can keep on going, talking and touching her, while she dozes with her eyes open.

She dries off and wraps the towel around her hair. She reaches into the drawer to get the brush and sees the plastic baggie with the class ring that she sneaked off the lawyer's finger when Jules was washing up. She doesn't really know why she kept it — a kind of souvenir — but it might be useful. It needs to be better hidden for safe-keeping. She gets down on her knees and drops it in the back corner of the sink cabinet. It's a dark and dirty wooden shelf sprinkled with roach droppings. Nobody will feel around back there.

She goes out to get dressed. Pepe is sleeping in her underwear drawer. She takes his head and coaxes him around her shoulders instead of putting anything on. It's too hot. Richard won't care. He likes Pepe – for a second or two. She gets a beer and sits on the bed, stroking the snake's clean skin, leaning her head on the wall, with Pepe's cool head on her chest and his tail looped across her thighs, absorbing her heat. She wonders if Richard would care if she fell asleep while he was fucking her. Nothing she does ever puts Richard off. That's both good and bad.

There's a knock. "Come on in. It's too hot to move."

The door opens. Jules steps in – stops short. "Hi. Sorry. I didn't know you were undressed."

"Waiting for Richard."

"Oh."

"Too lazy to put clothes on and take 'em right back off."

"I'd better leave then," Jules says.

"No. Stay. He won't be here for a few minutes." She points to her naked body. "You don't mind? I don't want to move Pepe."

Jules shakes her head, but doesn't look directly at Renata. "I wondered if everything went okay last night."

"With the job?"

"No, the payment."

"I don't know. Francisco handled it. He went to meet them after the job. I haven't talked to him yet."

"Oh. Would you call me when he comes back? I need to know so I can quit worrying."

"Yeah, but I'm sure it's okay. How much fucking money can they want for one night's work?"

Jules looks at her with tight lips.

"It'll be okay. Francisco said so." Pepe raises his head toward

Jules. "He's saying hi to you, Jul. Come over here – give him a pet."

Jules steps closer and stretches her arm to touch Pepe's head, pets him a few short strokes. "I should be going before Richard gets here."

Renata sees Jules' eyes flicker over her breasts down to her pussy. "If you want. I'll catch you later when I hear something."

Jules goes out and Renata takes her beer from the windowsill. She's wondering if there's bad news and that's why Franco didn't come back last night. He never liked to tell bad news. Would let it go as long as he could. She takes a swallow of lukewarm beer and puts the can under Pepe's nose. He moves his head to the other side of her neck. She leans against the wall, stroking his body. "Good boy, Pep. Bad beer. No good for you."

The knob turns and the door opens. Richard's face changes from a smile halfway to a frown, then back again. "Master Pepe," he says, "the luckiest snake in the world." He has a bottle of champagne in his hand. Renata recognizes his favorite – the yellow label.

"Pepe makes his own luck," she says. She spreads her legs slightly. "Brought me a present?"

"Yes, my sweet naked lady. For us to celebrate the weekend." He comes close and gives her a quick peck on the lips. He sets the bottle on the counter and unwinds the wire. He picks up a towel and jumps back. A roach runs down the cabinet. "Palmetto bug!"

Renata laughs. "You disturbed his sleep."

Richard swats air as the roach disappears under the cabinet. He drapes the towel over the cork and works at it. "Too bad that damned snake doesn't take care of them."

"He's not damned. Snakes don't eat bugs. He eats rats. I thought you liked him."

"I do. I'm not in the best mood today. The champagne will fix me up. Just give me a second. I won't bore you with my problems."

Renata sighs into the back of Pepe's head. She wonders if he can feel her warm breath and if he likes it. "Go ahead, Richard. Tell me. It'll make you feel better."

"No, it's about my wife – I don't want to talk about her. I want to talk about us. How can I see you more often? If you didn't have to live on the beach, I could put you in a nice little cottage in the Grove – nearer to me."

"Richard, you can't afford that. I'm fine here." Renata uncoils Pepe from around her shoulders and chest and watches his graceful movement down the side of the bed and under it, thinking how beautiful he is, and hoping Luiza never comes for him.

Richard stops working at the cork. "I'm afraid my wife suspects something. I don't know what to do."

"If your wife is suspicious, you should stop seeing me. It's that easy. I'm only a hobby – one you can barely afford."

The cork pops and hits the wall. He shakes his head. "That's ridiculous. I'm not even considering giving you up. No use talking about it." He sets the bottle down while it foams over the top. He stands back and opens a cabinet. "Where are the glasses?"

"I got tired of washing dishes – threw them all out."

He looks at her. "You're serious?"

"Yeah – don't ruin your marriage for me. I'm not worth it."

He opens the other cabinet. "No. I mean about the glasses?"

"Yes – they were a pain in the ass. We can swig off the bottle."

Richard laughs. He brings the champagne to the bed and laughs some more. "That's what I love about you, my extraordinary dreamboat." He keeps chuckling.

Renata frowns. She never knows what will blow Richard's skirt up. "What? You love that I threw out the glasses?"

"It's the way society never touches you – hard to explain. You're not trapped by ordinary expectations." He laughs again.

"Fuck, Richard. I'll throw out something every week, if it makes you this happy."

"That's okay. I don't want to get here next week and the bed's gone."

She laughs. "How'd you guess what I was thinking?" She takes the champagne bottle from his hand and tips it for a long guzzle. She burps quietly, then smiles. "Nice. How 'bout you take some clothes off? We should be decadent while we drink this expensive stuff. It is expensive, right?"

"Yeah, fairly." Richard pulls the drapes and takes off his shirt, letting it land on the floor. "You know what would make me really happy?" He glances at Renata's innocent face. "If you would let me take you far away from here – somewhere up in the Northeast, where the air is crisp this time of year – I would treat you like a princess for the rest of your life, everything for your pleasure, comfort, and happiness."

Renata looks up and sighs. Richard's a respected professor at the university, smart and in shape – sort of a Robert de Niro type, like her father, or the vision she has of her father. She's certainly had worse in bed. She could depend on Richard's devotion and support as long as he lived. For a flicker of a second a vision of soft carpets and cuddling on the sofa near a fireplace dances through her mind and body – decorating a Christmas tree. Then summer, picnics with baskets of wine and cheese, a checkered tablecloth spread by a lake, like in the movies. She might like to be pampered and loved, even if she can't love him back.

He drops his shoes and socks, undoes his belt, slips off his pants and shorts, and stares at her. "Well? Think about it."

"Could I have a dog?"

The laughter rolls from Richard. He grabs her and pulls her face to his chest, and for a moment she catches the intoxication of his feelings, laughing against his strong body. He tilts her face up. "Of course, you can have a dog – any kind of animal you ever wanted. You wouldn't have to ask permission for anything. You're just a little girl at heart, aren't you?" He sits and puts his arms around her.

She wonders if Jules is listening to all this and what her feelings would be. She's shaking her head for sure. It pulls Renata back to reality. "No, I'm not — not a little girl in any way — really." She chuckles. She knows how to shock him. "What do you think I want the dog for?"

Richard clicks his tongue.

"Don't make the mistake of thinking I'm innocent. I can't think about running away with you —"

His face drops, but his voice is soothing. "Don't be hasty. Let it rest right there with thoughts of a puppy."

"Okay," she says. She smiles.

He hugs her, and she can feel his heart beating against her chest. Maybe there's something to be said for strong feelings, but she's not ready, probably never will be.

Over his shoulder she watches Pepe slither from under the bed into his pile of clothes. As Richard pulls back to stare into her eyes, she hands him the bottle and snuggles against his hip. In the dim light he looks strong and beautiful, with his square jaw and thick movie-star hair, a shining stroke of gray on one side. She runs her cold champagne-bottle hand down his thigh and makes him twitch. She giggles.

"Easy," he says. He kisses her shoulder. "Time to get serious."

She lifts her face to his and gives him a long kiss, sucking his lip and running her tongue inside the edges, pushing hard against his mouth as she grabs the back of his neck. She feels the rushes of pleasure and the softening in her chest. Such a nice man, so in love with a dream.

Richard sets the bottle on the windowsill and moves over her, kissing her forehead and trailing his lips over her nose and chin. His gentleness reminds her of butterfly kisses from when she was little, eyelashes fluttering against her face from her foster mom, sweet dreams that butterflies bring. She's almost in a trance while he kisses her tits and twirls his tongue around her nipples. He is a nice man. He moves down her stomach and nuzzles into her pubic hair, parts her thighs farther and gets in there with his tongue. She closes her eyes and drifts.

The door flies open. "Renata! Jesus Christ. They found a head!" Renata turns and Richard pops up like a slice of toast. Jules is standing there with a face to match the splotched white walls, staring at Richard. She's holding a newspaper. "Oh! I didn't hear you." She puts her hand half over her eyes. "I thought it was just Rennie with the snake! My God. Sorry! Sorry, Rennie!" She turns and runs out the door, slamming it behind her.

Renata's first instinct is to laugh, but Jules' words stop her. Richard is instantly dead serious. "What's going on?"

Renata chews her lip. "You don't wanna know."

"A head? Christ, Renata, a head? What kind of trouble are you in?"

"None that I know of."

"Then why did that woman come running over here?"

"It's not important. She gets upset easy."

Richard pulls her hair back away from her face, smoothing it and caressing her neck. "You have to tell me. I know you're in trouble. I can help."

"This is out of your line, honey."

"Someone found a head. A human head?"

She shrugs. "Somebody got killed. It happens."

"She killed someone?"

Renata sighs. "Yes, but it was an accident."

"And you're helping her. You would do that. I knew this place —" He squeezes her tight. "You've got to tell me all about it."

Renata holds still and feels how good it is to be comforted. It doesn't matter if Richard knows. "Yeah. Okay. She killed this lawyer that was over here — thought he was hurting me because he had a strap around my neck. Some people were supposed to get rid of the body."

Richard cringes. He takes a breath through his teeth. "I would have killed him too."

She fills in the details of Jules' actions. "He should've been gator shit by now – something's fucked up."

"Maybe the head was too –" Richard stops. "I don't know. Are they looking for her?"

Renata shrugs. "Jules and me are in this together. I have to tell you that. Maybe you shouldn't come over here anymore. It might get you into trouble."

"Quit saying that!" He stands up next to the bed and looks down at her. "Everything that happens – you try to use it to make me stay away. It's ridiculous. If I'd been here – or you'd have been with me – you wouldn't be in trouble now. You allow all this trash – this slime – into your life . . . What do you expect?" He holds his palm against his forehead, as if he's keeping his brain from exploding. "I bet this pimp friend of yours is in on it."

"I called him to help us."

Richard reaches down, moves her leg from the bed, and sits next to her, putting her calf across his thigh and stroking it, staring at her toes. He shakes his head and squeezes her foot. "I can't live like this – worrying about you all the time."

"Don't even go there. Francisco isn't slime and neither is Jules. She saved my life and I'll do anything for her. I take what comes," Renata says. "I don't expect anything. I don't worry about it." She stares at him, waiting for his fire to burn itself out.

"Okay. I don't know Jules. But, Rennie, I told you that I'd do anything for you. Remember the samurai? It's not just talk, like you get from all the other men. What has to happen before I can convince you to leave this fucking bug-infested druggie hangout and be with me? I'm afraid for you."

"Chill, Richard. I fit here – better than anywhere else. I can take care of myself. You have a wife and kids to worry about."

"Yeah? I'm not so sure. Linda has a temper. I might already have given up my home. I should just leave and take you with me. Right now." He bends and kisses her knee. He looks up, his eyes round. "Listen, beautiful – just for a minute. My brother runs a bed and breakfast in Maine. He took over when my mother passed away last year – my father's been deceased for a long time. That business is half mine. Right now I only make a small profit, but if I were to move up there and help out, I would have a place to live and enough money for both of us. It's beautiful too, rustic but luxurious."

There's the flash of determination in his eyes. If she said the word they'd be out of there, into Richard's corner of the world. Again, for a split second, Renata savors the thought. Just leave, be a new person, all taken care of – be Richard's person. She watches him stroking her calf, waiting for an answer, as if she can go to that world filled with elevator music and polite talk, where everything's safe and legal, a place for everything and everything's in its place – a boring road towards death, like an eternal ride through a golf course. She remembers the never-ending day when Richard took her to watch a tournament.

"It's fucking freezing up there. I'd die."

"Silly. Only for a few months in winter. You just have to put on enough clothes, layers. Keep your core warm." His eyes are bright. "There's ice skating and cross-country skiing. We'd build crackling fires and sip hot chocolate – roast chestnuts for our guests."

It's just too cozy. A chill runs through her. "Richard, get on top of me. I need to be fucked. Isn't that what you're here for?" She waits until the protests drain from his face. "If I let you take me away, everything would be spoiled. You need me here, like this. You don't need another wife. You already have a good one."

He scoots down on the bed next to her. "No. I need you. I swear to God, Rennie, I don't need anything on this earth but you, anywhere – the sweetest, most beautiful, most exciting woman alive. You save me from myself – from dying in the repetitious agony of life, the numbness and sameness, the emptiness of feeling all alone."

She touches his cheek and moves her fingers over his lips. They're trembling. She wants to tell him that he's badly confused about her, but it's useless, and she can't bear to carry on the sad conversation another second. "You've got me right now, and it's getting late." She rolls on her side and starts kissing across his chest, dragging her hair over his ribs, and stroking his sides.

"Sex isn't all I want, Renata."

She doesn't stop to hear his words of love. She wants to get him out of there while he can still go home and fix things up, and she can put it all out of her mind. She lifts her head and looks at his shining eyes and the tears on his cheeks. He would do anything for her, no doubt at all. "If I need you, I'll call you – promise," she says. She moves her face down to his cock and takes it into her mouth, drawing on it hard. She runs her nails down his hips to his thighs and lifts his balls, stroking them lightly and cooing in her throat until she feels him finally relax and melt into the feeling.

CHAPTER 13

4:00 pm, South Beach

Richard

He checks his watch as he closes Renata's door. He wasted enough time trying to get that snake out of his pants, and then finally had to wake Renata to remove it. He hopes Linda was busy all day, with no time to dwell on details of the morning conversation. He'll never be able to calm her down if she's spent the day dredging up suspicions. What would she do, if she really knew something? A wave of nausea passes through him at the thought. Maybe his guilt is making more of this than there is. He starts down the hall at a fast pace, but pauses outside the door of the next apartment. He can hear the TV so he knows the woman is home – Jules.

Renata sleeps through anything, but he's careful to knock softly on Jules' door, thinking he will influence her a little in his favor and she might pass the good feelings along to Renata.

The door opens and Jules stands there in the yellow light of a ceiling fixture. "Oh," she says. She blushes. She's a slender girl, but soft, with big brown eyes and dark shoulder-length hair. "I thought you were Rennie. But, I'm sorry about before. I get frightened by the violence around here, and Rennie and I are used to running back and forth to the apartments –"

"I already know what happened. Just let me in for a minute."

Jules steps back and opens the door wider, her face turning white. He hadn't noticed she was so pretty when she burst in on them. There's a laptop open on the table, and he sits in a kitchen chair opposite. "Oh, yes, you're a writer. Rennie mentioned it."

Jules closes the laptop and sits across from him, folding her arms. "Trying to write. I had some articles published. I quit my teaching job to write a novel."

"Good luck. It's tough. I'm a poet. I won't be quitting my teaching job any time soon – not to make a living on poetry anyway." He scoots his chair closer. "I thought I would stop by to see if I could help. You seemed very upset."

She lets out a sigh. "That's all? No blackmail? Everyone keeps asking me for money. I don't have any."

"No, no, of course not. I came to tell you that I understand. I won't say a word to anyone. I'll help both of you if there's anything I can do."

Jules lets out a sigh. "Thanks, but I don't see how you can help. According to the paper, they've identified him and figured out the time and cause of death. I'm thinking I should go and turn myself in."

"No – I don't think so. It's too late for that. You could get yourself into a lot of trouble – and Rennie. Don't even consider it."

"I don't know what to do."

"Nothing. There's no reason to do anything. No one's been here, right? The police?"

"No."

"They haven't made the connection then. It's not likely he told anyone where he was going. How many times have you seen him?" He notes recognition in Jules' eyes, realizes that she knows the motivation of his question.

"Never before — I doubt it anyway. Francisco's there at night and I'm here all afternoon." She blushes and looks at the table. "I hear a lot, and I've never heard anything like that before — Rennie said it was the first time with him. She was glad never to do it again."

He twitches. "Francisco's there every night?"

Jules hesitates. "Oh, no, he has his own place above Crunch."

"Crunch? The club?"

"Oh, wait. I think he moved."

He reaches and takes her hand, tries to steady himself. "Thank you for going to Renata's rescue. I wish I could have been here." He rubs Jules' hand. "You must know how much I love her."

She shakes her head. "I know how you feel, Richard. I hardly know you, but I can see what it must be like to be a man and . . . be with Rennie. I don't understand her, but I want to protect her too."

"I don't want to protect her. I want to give her the life she deserves —"

"She's not going to let you. She likes the way she lives. I feel bad to say this — but it's the truth. You're a customer over there. You should —"

He slides his chair out and doesn't hear the rest. "Are you sure you're capable of giving advice, Jules? Maybe you don't want Renata to have the kind of life that you're missing, and you want to keep her here so you can live off her energy." He walks to the door.

Jules' eyes fill with tears. "You're wrong. I love Renata's energy, but — but — mostly, I love Renata. I'd never take anything away from her."

Richard looks again, hard. He feels distrust for this woman. She says *love* like she means it. "You'd better be careful. You killed someone."

Jules laughs, way over the top, almost to hysteria. "Be careful? It's all so fucking easy. You try it, Professor Dick."

His head jerks with annoyance. He turns and walks. Her laugh echoes down the hall until the door closes. He'd hoped to win Jules' support, so she would help to convince Renata to go away with him. Now he realizes she's his adversary. Professor Dick. He's heard that one before. He wonders if Rennie calls him Professor Dick. Jesus, there's no time to think about any of it. He picks up his pace. Now he's got rush hour traffic and Linda home waiting – unless she's gone.

CHAPTER 14

4:30 pm, Tropical Moons, Room 2-A

Jules

She sits down behind the computer, opens the lid, and gets back up. Richard isn't what she expected. She hasn't seen him up close before to notice his attractiveness, his strong, tall frame and thick graying hair, the hardness of his jaw, those intense blue eyes. He doesn't seem the same person that she hears talking through the wall, so gentle and pleading.

She gets the vodka from the refrigerator where she put it to answer the door. She pours a little more into her glass and sits back down. She's on the verge of hysterics, but whether it's from fear of the law or of Richard as an enemy, she's not sure. In a way, she's glad he stopped by. Now she doesn't feel sorry for him anymore, the asshole.

If only she hadn't gone running over there, or bought the newspaper in the first place, or stabbed the fucking lawyer. Anger begins to heat inside her chest. She slams the glass down on the table and yells, "Fuck, fuck, fuck." She doesn't want to know about the head or anything else. She just wants to write her damned book. She slaps the top down on the computer.

"Fuck!" She takes a big drink of the vodka, while tears run down her cheeks. Until the past few weeks she could count on two hands the number of times she'd said *fuck*. Now it's the most common word in her vocabulary. Soon she'll be adding cocksucker and motherfucker . . . if she lives long enough.

The door opens. "What's the matter, Julie, baby?"

She wipes her eyes and takes another drink. "Richard was over here. I don't think he likes me."

"He's in a bad mood. Don't worry."

"Have you heard from Francisco?"

"No. He'll be over tonight. I think he's holding off with the news."

"Something could have happened to him."

"He's a big boy. Don't worry." She raises her eyebrows and smiles. "He's a real big boy. You oughta come busting in when he's got it smoking – instead of Richard."

Jules winces. "Sorry. I came straight from the store and didn't hear anything – it was so dark in there –"

"Hey, who cares? Not me."

"Now he knows about the lawyer."

Renata walks around the table and puts her arm across Jules' shoulder, kisses her cheek. "Lighten up. Professor Dick isn't going to say a thing. He'd rather wear his nuts in a vise than have me carted off to prison."

"He might think he can get rid of me."

"Why would he want to get rid of you? No. Uh-uh. No way I'd let him anyway. I have insurance, in case of trouble."

"What do you mean?"

"I kept a ring from the lawyer – a school ring from some-where. I hid it in the bathroom cabinet under the sink. I'll have to show you, in case you ever need it –"

"Why would I want it? Is that a good idea?"

Rennie shrugs. "Never know. It's a card to play – maybe – to shift the blame to someone else. Easy to get rid of, if nec-essary."

"I couldn't – you'd do that to Richard? Get him arrested

for murder?"

"No. Hell. I'm just trying to tell you that you're safe, no matter what. Anyway, it wasn't murder." Renata pulls her closer and talks into her ear. "Honey, you mean more to me than any of these men – it's true. You saved my life."

"I wish. Besides, any of the men would have done the same."

"They didn't." Renata touches Jules' chin and turns her face so their eyes are inches apart. Renata nods up and down slowly. "Read my lips, girl – it's true."

Rennie puts her hands on Jules' shoulders, and Jules can feel Rennie's warm breath on her lips. She feels the kiss coming as Rennie adjusts her face and moves in to press their mouths together more firmly than Jules is expecting, holding it for seconds before she pulls back. Rennie smiles at Jules with a teasing look. "You like kissing, don't you?"

Jules feels herself go red. She's not sure how to answer the question – does she like kissing or kissing Rennie? "I – yes – of course . . ." She never knows how to take Rennie, but there's a warmth, an excitement, no matter what. It scares her.

Renata picks Jules' glass off the table and takes a long drink. "Mmm. I was hoping this wasn't water." She smacks her lips and holds the glass to Jules. "Yeah, man. To us."

"Okay, to us," Jules says. She's confused, but takes a sip from the glass. "Let me fix us some fresh ones." She goes to the cabinet and takes out another glass.

"You have a lot of glasses," Renata says. "I threw mine away."

Jules looks at her. "Oh, do you need some?"

"No, thanks." Renata sits down on the bed and looks out the window. Jules puts ice in the glasses and fills them two-thirds with vodka. She brings them over. She's half afraid that Rennie will pull her down on the bed. She doesn't know what she'd do.

Renata sprawls against the wall with her drink. She's wearing a clingy beach dress, clearly without underwear, the thin shoulder strap falling down to expose the top of one breast, her legs far enough apart to see the darkness between them. She seems unaware. "Sit down, Jules. Tell me how your novel is coming."

Jules sits on the edge of the bed, her side toward Renata. "Not coming. I think I made a big mistake quitting my job."

"Did you like it — teaching?"

"No, I hated it. The classroom was a war zone."

Renata puts her hand on Jules' hip. The touch is light, but Jules can't help focusing on it. "Then why the hell are you thinking about that? You'll write your book or you'll do something else. There's a whole world of shit to do. I'll help you find what you're looking for."

Jules feels Renata's fingers move to her inner thigh and rest there, as if it's natural. It is natural, if Jules could stop thinking about it. "I guess I'll keep trying for a while longer. I don't mind the waitress job part-time."

Renata nods. "Whatever you think." She points to the door.

Jules hears footsteps passing by.

"Francisco," Renata says. She slides off the side of the bed, goes to the door, and opens it. "Hey, Franco — you *dulce de leche*." She glances at Jules and winks. "Eye candy with the huge dick — we're over here."

In a few seconds Francisco walks into the apartment. Jules gets up to greet him. His left eye is black and his nose is swollen. He has a bandage on his forehead. He hands Renata a bakery box.

"Fuck! What the fuck happened to you?"

"You thought I'd forget about your cheesecake, huh? I spent the night in the hospital. Concussion. I'm still not feeling that good." He looks at Jules. "Hey, Julie — how's it goin'? Mind if I have one of those drinks? Before my Percocet wears off."

"Sure." Jules goes to fix the drink. She tries to stop her hands from shaking.

"I'm fine. A little fuzzy. No big deal. I got into a fight with one of the assholes. I pay the guy, then find out this morning they didn't do the job — not right. So I drove back out there to get our fucking money."

"Did you get it?" Renata asks.

"No, but he's not going to have much fun spending it."

Jules hands him the drink. "Are we in trouble with the police?"

"Not that I know of. But I don't expect to pay for such sloppy work. They didn't take him far enough — or weigh him down. They should've known what to do."

"See, honey, we're fine," Renata tells her.

Renata looks at the bandage on the side of Francisco's forehead and touches it.

"Ouch, don't touch."

She touches lightly near it while he drinks the vodka. "Poor baby. Want me to make it feel better?"

He nods, a sheepish look in his eyes. "If you wanna try. I don't know what I'm good for."

She takes his glass and sets it on the table, then takes his face in her hands and kisses his mouth. Francisco reaches down and takes her by the waist, pulls her close into him. They stand there kissing, Francisco working his hands down to Rennie's ass. Jules watches, not knowing where to go.

"Come here, Jul," Renata says. "Help me make Franco feel better."

Jules walks around them where she can see Rennie's face.

"Help me feel better," Francisco says. He sounds dazed.

Renata reaches out her arm. "Come here."

Jules moves closer and she's pulled in with the two of them, arms folding around her. "Kiss us," Renata says. She kisses Jules with her mouth open, her tongue licking inside Jules' lips, moving around soft and hot. Francisco moves closer, kissing along her neck with his mouth, his hands moving down her body, caressing her back and moving down her breast. It's all a warm haze. They switch and she feels Francisco's larger rougher tongue in her mouth, Renata on her neck. Her legs are weak. She wants to pull back, but can't make herself move. She feels a tingle and moisture between her legs. Renata's hand begins rubbing her over the crotch of her cotton shorts.

"Do you want to make love with us?" Renata asks. "We're all together now – whatever happens. We have to take care of each other, make each other feel good."

Jules shakes her head. She can't think of taking off her clothes, letting both of them see her pale bony body. "No, no, I can't. You go. I'm fine here by myself."

Renata kisses her again. "Beautiful Jules, come with us."

Jules pulls back. "No, I can't."

Francisco tucks Jules' hair behind her ear. "Maybe another time." He picks up his glass. "Let's go, Renata. Julie's okay and I need to lay down."

"Remember, Jules, you don't have to be by yourself, honey. Anytime – come over."

Their hands move down her arms, caressing as they let her go, and the two walk into the darkness of the hall, Renata looking back, smiling. Jules feels the chilly air on the moist places where their hands and mouths have touched her. But she's warm inside. She knows Renata means it.

CHAPTER 15

6:30 pm, South Miami

Richard

He stops at the mailbox at the end of the drive. It's empty, so that means Linda was home after three when the mail was delivered, probably worked a normal day. He can hope. He rolls up the drive and presses the opener. There it is, her silver Volvo, parked where it should be. That's a relief. Now he just has to do some good talking.

He walks through the dark house into the bedroom. A glance around the room doesn't show anything unusual. "Linda!" he calls. He walks past the boys' rooms – nobody. The cat doesn't even come out from wherever she's sleeping. He makes the turn into the Florida room and looks through the sliding doors. Linda is in the pool. A good sign. He looks closer. She's not wearing any clothes. That's unusual. The wooden fence goes all the way around, but there are knotholes, and she's always said anybody could be looking in and she'd never know it. Richard opens the sliding doors and steps outside. He sees Linda's drink on the side of the pool.

"Hey, about time you decided to come home!" she yells.

"Get in. Water's great."

Richard sits in the chair and takes off his shoes. He can tell by her voice that she's drunk. "Where are the twins?"

"Gramma's. Get yourself a drink," Linda calls.

Her attitude makes him uneasy. He slips off his pants and shirt and puts them on the chair. He's thinking he should get into the water quickly to rinse away any smells. It occurs to him that he's just spent the afternoon with Renata on the day that he should have been home saving his marriage. He never even called. He's losing his mind.

He dives in at the deep end and stands up, wiping down his face with his hand, and flinging the water off his hair. Linda strokes toward him. Her arms are graceful, despite her drunkenness, and her delicate white neck has ringlets of wet hair plastered to it, a sweet young look. She grabs him around the shoulders and presses her body against him. Her full tits are firm and warm against his chest and he reaches down to take her ass in his hands. Even after the day with Renata his cock is aroused. He amazes himself as he becomes hard in seconds, and she lifts her body and slides down on his erection, the warmth inside her replacing the cool water. He moves against her soft hips. She's worked up, breathing hard, and in less than a minute he feels the shudders inside her and recognizes the familiar sound of her coming. He pumps into her several more times and loses himself in his own orgasm.

She pushes herself off when he's barely finished and swims back to her drink. He stands there, a little off balance, not sure what comes next. Linda finishes the drink, which looks like straight scotch from what he can tell.

"At least you can still get it up for me, huh?"

Despite his betrayal, his heart is breaking for her. "I love you. You're beautiful. You're my wife and my best friend. Let's go have dinner at the Italian place and forget all about this morning."

"I've been thinking about it all day. I can forget about this morning, but I can't forget what I know — what I saw in your eyes."

"You're wrong." He tries desperately to look at her without blinking, hopes the alcohol will blur her vision. "Nothing's going on – how can I prove it to you?"

She takes a drink and stares at him.

He stares back. "It's impossible to find evidence of nothing. How can I prove I'm not lying?"

"You can't. The truth will out, my scholar. Shakespeare? It always does. Meantime, don't worry, I'll give you plenty of rope to hang yourself."

Richard shudders. "It's chilly out here. Let's get a hot shower and eat. I'm starving. Are you hungry?"

"No."

"How long have you been in here? Time to get out."

"I'm feeling free and easy. Since you're cheating, I have plenty of options. I haven't decided what I'll do yet."

He holds back a response. Is she talking about finding a lover? Under the circumstances he's in no position to argue with her statement, but the idea drives a spike into his stomach.

She picks up her glass. "I need another drink. Get me one, Dick. Scotch."

She never calls him Dick, but he doesn't remark on it. He ducks down, swims underwater to her, and picks her up, feeling her smooth legs and back, slippery in his arms as the water pours off.

He walks to the steps. Linda is laughing. It's a wild drunken laugh. "You haven't done this for a long time. How do I compare? I mean, who would you rather be carrying, me or your girlfriend?"

He carries her out of the pool and into the house. Water drips all over the tile and then the white carpet, as he tromps through the Florida room down the hall – and he doesn't care if palmettos fly in through the open door. Strangely, he feels powerful. If he broke something right now – even the Tiffany lamp – it would almost feel good, because he doesn't need it.

He doesn't need objects to make a life. He's alive with the excitement of making love in the pool where the neighbors might be watching. He's excited by hauling Linda into the bedroom against her will. The passion in her accusations and the stimulation of taking strong action bring him alive. He's never realized the power of it before, a frightening and wonderful discovery worthy of a poem, but there's no need to preserve it on paper.

He sets Linda on the bed. She's soaking wet in the middle of the king-sized mattress. She crooks her arms under her head and starts laughing, looking up at him, legs spread, her naked body soft and full on the fluffy white down comforter. She stretches and smiles. He thinks of crawling back on top and doing her again. Then he's struck with a terrifying thought. Perhaps it's not Renata who brings him alive, but only the energy of his deceit and the lure of the forbidden – the impossibility of having her making it all more attractive. He shoves the thought aside, angry at himself for continuing to question his motives. No, it couldn't be that. It's Renata. He feels it. Renata – and his ability to give her a life – their life together.

He bends down to Linda and moves a curl from her face. "Do you want to go eat? You need something in your stomach."

"Think we can find a place where you haven't taken your girlfriend?"

"Don't be ridiculous, Linda. You're going to make me angry."

She starts laughing again. "That's very funny. See if you can put me on the defensive again, like this morning. I feel *sooo* bad."

He goes to the closet. "Okay, you're drunk and you need some food. I'm going to dress you."

"Hmm. This is getting interesting."

He glances back at her. She smiles a bright grin, then lies back and closes her eyes. He goes to the dresser first and gets his clothes, a comfortable shirt and underwear, takes some pants from the closet, and slips on his shoes.

He moves to Linda's side of the closet and pulls out a soft black knit dress with a wide neck that he can pull over her head. He's seen her wear it without a bra so that's less trouble. She looks sumptuous without a bra. He brings it to the bed.

She sits up looking woozy and raises her arms loosely over her head to let him slip the dress on. She tosses her hair with her hands and slides off the bed. "Ready," she says. She pulls the knit down below her smooth naked ass and straightens it on her hips. "Yes, I could eat some fettuccine Alfredo."

He goes to the closet for shoes and he holds her steady while she slips her feet into flat sandals. She looks at him. "Thank you, my dear. You're so considerate tonight. I think I'll get drunk more often."

He takes a deep breath. Her response isn't what he was expecting. Neither does he expect any of the feelings that make him half-erect again, as he stands there looking at his beautiful wife, without any idea of where his life is going — just that it's moving fast, something altogether new.

CHAPTER 16

September 30, 12:15 pm, Tropical Moons, Room 2-A

Jules

It's past noon when Jules hears the door slam at Renata's. She needs to discuss the conversation with Richard. She has a creepy feeling about him, even though she can't pin anything down.

She goes to the hole to listen, to be sure Francisco isn't still lounging around naked. She hears, "Sweet snake . . . yeah . . . good boy," Rennie no doubt cuddling Pepe, and Francisco gone. Jules closes the computer and goes over.

She knocks.

Renata yells, "Come in, Julie – if it's you. Anybody else – go away."

She opens the door and there's Renata on the bed in a sheer silvery negligee, reading a magazine, hair and snake shimmering around her in the sunlight. "Hey, big sis, you finished writing for the day?"

"I've written a sentence. That's probably it for today. Nice lingerie."

"Should be. Costs more than a month's rent. There's this

guy that buys stuff for me – all I have to do is model it for him at the store. We both enjoy it." She lifts the whispery fabric and lets it fall. "How many years does it take to write a novel?"

"A lifetime? Harper Lee only wrote one novel – a bestseller that became a classic, but I don't know how long it took her." She laughs. "I'd be happy with that." She pauses. "I came to talk to you about something."

Renata closes the magazine. Jules sees that it's *Playboy*. "You read that? Sometimes it has good stories."

"Fuck, no, Francisco reads it. I just look at the pictures. I might be in there one of these days, if I get my ass in gear and send them a nice shot." She spreads her legs and grabs the lacy panties for emphasis.

Jules blushes. "You're pretty enough."

"I get a kick out of you! Sorry – I can't help but tease."

"It's okay. I just never know what you'll do."

Renata puts Pepe under the covers, and slides off the bed. "It's fun that way, isn't it? Life."

Jules nods, but she's thinking a little calm would be a good thing. "You know, I can't stop worrying about my chat with Richard."

Renata looks in the refrigerator. "What did the old dog say to upset you?"

"He's not old. He's very attractive."

"I know – he can get it up good and hard too. It's just talk."

"He says he would never say anything to anyone, but he's so much in love with you – he makes me nervous. He doesn't like me."

"You're lucky. It's a lot easier that way." She opens a cabinet. It's empty. "I feel like a drink. You have anything?"

"Vodka. Nice and cold in the fridge. I'll get it."

She leaves Renata poking around in the dresser drawers. Jules empties an ice tray, puts two pieces in each glass, and fills them halfway with vodka. She takes a sip. It's a taste she's begun to enjoy any time of day.

Renata comes through the open door in shirt and shorts.

"What's taking so long, girl? Starting without me?"

"Drink alone? Not a chance." Jules laughs and hands her a glass.

"You sound like me – almost as sarcastic."

"Thanks," Jules says. She clinks her glass against Rennie's. "That's a compliment. I'm getting streetwise – like you."

Renata points to the laptop. "Can I see? I'd like to read something you wrote. English was my worst subject, but I admire people that write."

Jules represses a shiver of self-loathing. "Sorry, I can't show you. It's terrible. I'm not ready to show anybody." She unplugs the computer and moves it over to the counter. "I'll get this out of the way. I don't want to look at it."

"No problemo." Renata picks up her glass and motions to the bookcase on the far wall. "Have you read all those?"

"Yeah. Those are just the ones I have left – favorites. I gave away most of my books when I came here."

"I guess you always loved books."

"Oh, yeah. I'm obsessed. I get it from my father. The house – back home – is filled with every kind of literature, but he likes the tough crime novels the best. My dream is to write one and get it published – so he can be proud, you know?"

Rennie nods.

"But . . . it seems impossible."

Renata walks to the bookcase and fingers some of the bindings. She turns to Jules and drains her glass. "Let's get smashed and read some books."

Jules drains hers and takes the bottle to Renata. She fills both glasses back up. Getting drunk sounds good. She sets the bottle on the bookcase and picks out a book of Bukowski poems. "You might like this, Rennie. It's down to earth. This guy was just a drunken bum until he became a famous writer."

"Success made him stop drinking?"

"No! He became a famous drunken bum!"

"My kinda guy. What's he doing now?"

"Not much that I know of — dead, I think. But he held out a long time."

Jules opens the book and flips through. "Here we go: 'the dream of a man is a whore with a gold tooth and a garter belt, perfumed, with false eyebrows, mascara, earrings, light pink panties, salami breath — "

"Salami breath? You'd never get away with that. Yuck. Let me see the rest of the poem." She rests the book on her chest and reads.

Jules notices that she forms the words with her lips, a habit she would normally think of as meaning slow, but in Renata it has an endearing quality, like she's absorbing the meaning through her mouth, consuming, digesting, making it part of herself.

"This is good. This woman, he says, has warts and she's fat and drunk, but she'll do everything for him and leave after a week. Makes sense. I could do with a man like that!"

Jules watches Renata turn the pages with care, seeming to know the book is precious. Bukowski's poetry is a big part of what brought Jules to this section of South Beach — to live among working-class people where she would be an unnoticed observer. Not the way things have turned out.

"How 'bout if I get us some herb? I think we can improve on this with a little smoke."

Jules shrugs and takes the book from her hands. "Bukowski would be honored, although his drug of choice was cheap wine."

Renata goes next door and comes back with a cigar box. "Lost my pipe. I'm going to roll us a couple white boys." She sits at the table and takes out papers and herb. "Teachers always said reading poetry should be fun."

"It can be — unless you're reading Ezra Pound."

"Huh? Ezra? The name's familiar. I think Richard brought his book over one time."

"Makes sense. Did you like it?"

"Yeah. Now that I remember, I did. Richard was reading in

his soft, nice voice and I fell right to sleep, deep dreamy sleep. I don't think he noticed – I told him I like to listen with my eyes closed."

Jules and Renata laugh until Rennie stops to lick the paper and roll it up. Jules notices how evenly and easily she rolls it, even using the third finger in place of the missing half of her middle finger. She lights the end and takes a deep pull, hands the joint to Jules. She takes it and inhales. This is the first time she's smoked since her college days and she wonders why. She's smelled the sweet aroma many times, wafting through the hall.

Jules takes the book over to the bed and they lean against the wall. Jules finds a short poem and reads it to Rennie. Rennie reads one back. She reads smoothly. They each take another turn. Jules waits for sarcastic comments, but they never come. Rennie rolls a second reefer. A few more puffs. Jules can't stop laughing. Rennie puts it out with her fingertips and takes Jules by the shoulders, looking her in the eyes. "You're a little blitzed, honey." She leans toward Jules until their foreheads are together. They laugh.

"I'm nice, I'm nice," Jules says. They keep laughing.

After a while, Jules puts her head back and sits up. She touches Rennie's hair. "Can I ask you something?"

Rennie looks up with pink, glassy eyes. "Sure, anything."

Jules slowly lifts Renata's hand with the half-finger. "What happened to it?"

"Told you, I put it someplace I shouldn't."

"A meat grinder?"

"No – a door. You don't wanna know. It's boring. Let's read more poetry."

"Yes, I do. I want to know what you went through. I think about it all the time."

"Okay – don't tell anybody. I never told Richard or Francisco."

"Promise."

"I was married for a couple years. Toward the end he

started locking me in the closet so I wouldn't cheat on him while he was at work —"

"He locked you up? What kind of a monster — ?"

"He'd put food and water and a bucket in there. I was allowed my tape player and vibrator, a blanket. Around the end of a week or so I was fighting him and he slammed the door — just locked it and left me there with my finger caught all day, probably nine hours —"

"All day? My God, Rennie! Couldn't he see — ?"

"He knew."

"How did you stand it? My God!" Jules takes Rennie's finger and holds it, puts her cheek down on Rennie's hand and presses it there, trying to squeeze out the pain from the past.

Renata pats her hair. "Jules, I'm okay. It was six or seven years ago."

Jules raises her head, shaking it side to side. "How did you stand it?"

"I screamed like an idiot for a while. Then I must've blacked out. He took me to the hospital that night. Finger was too fucking dead to save."

"Nobody heard you?"

"We lived way out in the country."

"Jesus Christ."

"He was right. I was cheating on him every second I got."

"Didn't you report him to the police?"

"No. My lover killed him the next day."

"Good."

"I should've done it myself, but he never gave me a chance. I never even saw the body. Lured him out in the woods — shot him right in the head."

"Like a hunting accident?"

"Make us another drink, will you, sweetie? We need our mood back. No. Just walked him out there and shot him at close range. Went to prison for it — pleaded guilty. He's still there as far as I know. He figured he was saving my life — probably was — but that didn't help him."

Jules' eyes fill with tears and they run down her cheeks. She wipes across her face and gets up for more ice. The unfairness is sad — and frightening.

Rennie rolls another joint. Jules opens the poetry book, but her eyes are too blurry to read.

"Hey, get over it, girl," says Rennie. She reaches across the table and ruffles Jules' hair. "I got over it. Nothing can hurt me now."

CHAPTER 17

2:30 pm, Atlantic Shores University

Richard

He comes out of his comp class and realizes that in one hour he'll be at The Moons with Renata. An almost tactile aura of happiness comes over him, making him smile as he walks toward his office. Linda hasn't said anything more about his odd behavior. He hopes she isn't just giving him "rope to hang himself." In the two weeks since her intuition, things have been quiet, almost completely normal. Neither of them has mentioned the conversation at Starbucks, nor the dinner that never came to pass because Linda fell asleep in the car. He's been spending time around the house, helping out more with the cooking, and playing ball with the boys. He took Linda out for lunch the preceding Friday and the hostility between them seemed completely forgotten. In many ways he wishes he had never met Renata. In too many other ways, he's more alive than he's ever been.

As he crosses the hall near the secretary's area, Judy smiles and flags him over. "Your wife's waiting. I let her into your office."

His legs go loose under him. He tries to look pleased and at the same time remember if he's left anything with Renata's name on his desk, any schoolboy doodling or her phone number. He can't think. "Thanks. I'm headed that way."

As he walks down the hall, he tries to think of a plan. Can he tell Linda he has a meeting and send her on her way? She could always call and check on that later, now that she's suspicious. It's too dangerous. He can't think of any way to get to Renata's on time, and he won't have a chance to call her. His cell phone is in the office. He opens the door. Linda is sitting in the chair across from his desk, her legs crossed, voluptuous in her white satin blouse, a trim pair of black pants, and heels. "Hi, honey. I got the afternoon off. My turn to take you out."

Richard's stomach sinks to his knees. He smiles and brings her close for a kiss, trying to cover his true feelings. "Not much work today?"

"Fridays are slow in the afternoon. I'm thinking of making it a regular thing. I can go in early for a couple of mornings during the week and get things done on the computer when it's quiet. I don't know why I didn't think of this years ago."

Richard feels the blackness so thick in his head that he fears he might pass out. He sits down at the desk and straightens a set of papers. His vision is blurred. "I have a couple of hours of grading to do. If I don't finish it this afternoon, I'll have to bring it home for the weekend –"

"Oh." Linda scoots out her chair with a screech and stands up. "All right. I'm out of here. I'll find some way to fill up my Friday afternoons."

Richard is panicked. "No. Sit down. Please. It's just that I could have planned better if I'd known. I'll grade the essays on Saturday."

He thinks he sees her eyes narrow, a look of distaste and distrust. She sits down. "Well, okay, then. I just figured you had the time last week, so we could do it again."

"I planned ahead last week – but it doesn't matter. Just give me a few minutes to organize. Where do you want to eat?"

She names something, but he doesn't hear. He's trying to figure out how to get a call through to Renata, and when he'll ever be able to see her again. "Sounds good. Where are you parked?"

"I'm on the south side of the building, near you."

He nods. "That's convenient. I have to gather up here and stop in the men's room. Want to meet me at the restaurant?"

"You know where it is?"

He struggles to remember, somehow play back the words, but he'd been too far away. "What was it, again?"

Linda frowns. "Celebration. It's new — on Miracle Mile. Fusion cuisine."

He's trying to think of how he can get the cell phone into his pocket and go to the men's room. The restaurant almost doesn't register with him again, but he catches himself. "All right, I'll follow you."

He stands and puts the folder of papers into his briefcase and slips the cell phone into his pocket. He'll call from the restaurant. He ushers Linda out the door and locks it behind him. As they walk down the hall they pass two other English professors. He nods to them, and they greet Linda warmly, like an old friend, reminding him how much she's a part of every aspect of his life and how insane his colleagues would think he was if he left her.

The restaurant is lively and loud with bright colors and calypso music, but Richard can hardly sit there for the minute it takes Linda to look over the menu. It's impossible to live like this. He orders a bottle of red wine and excuses himself to go to the men's room. He feels her delving into his thoughts, and her eyes seem to follow him. He's conscious of trying to move slowly so she doesn't figure out his errand. It's ridiculous. He's only going to the restroom. But she knows him so well. Now that she's alert, he has to think of everything unless he's ready to give it all up in a moment.

He goes into a stall and hits the button to dial Renata. He realizes he needs to clear that little convenience before Linda finds it. It rings and rings, no answering machine, probably unplugged. He can't wait too long. Renata might be over with the woman Jules. He doesn't like that. He'd rather she didn't spend time with anyone else, and he has a bad feeling about Jules. Where is Renata? She should be in the apartment waiting for him. He stops the call and urinates, then washes his hands and tries again. Still ringing. He can't stay any longer.

Linda looks annoyed when he joins her at the table. "You should have told me what you wanted." She motions with her hand. "Now all these tables are ahead of us."

"We're not in any hurry, are we? We have the whole afternoon." He's thinking, we have the whole fucking afternoon, the entire fucking afternoon, and he can't do a thing about it. His stomach is one long, sharp pain – like a knife in his gut. He can barely stand to look at the menu. He watches their waiter who's moving in a hectic pattern across the room. "Next time we do this, we'll call for a reservation and have everything planned out."

"Why? Like you said, we have the whole afternoon. It's fun to be spontaneous."

The lunch drags on and he tries to be his normal self, but can't think of anything to talk about. He takes a few bites of the shiitake-encrusted sea bass, but can't taste it. Linda is less cheerful than usual too, although she eats everything on her plate. He drinks most of the first bottle of wine and orders a second one. Linda can see that there's something wrong with him, and if she hadn't already figured out that Friday was his day to meet with someone, she surely knows it by now.

He pleads restroom once more and hits Renata's number. This time she answers. "Where are you? I've been sitting here with nothing to do."

"I tried you earlier. You weren't there. Listen, I can't make it. I can't talk. I'm in the men's room, in a restaurant, and my wife out there waiting. I have to set up a different time. Fridays won't work anymore."

"You could have told me so I had time to fill in. Friday's a popular afternoon."

There's a knife in his heart now, whether or not she intended it. "Rennie, honey, I'll give you whatever you want to make up for it. You know that. I couldn't call. She surprised me at the office, and I've been stuck ever since."

"Richard, this is bad. You better take care of your wife. Call me later — I don't know if I should see you again."

"Renata, for Christsakes, you're my reason for living. Don't even say that. I have to go. I'm dying here. I'll get over there somehow."

"Richard, don't. I don't know when I'll be home."

"I'll call. Don't say anything else. I love you." He hangs up and tries to settle his breathing. What is wrong with him? His throat is tight. He feels tears in his eyes and goes to splash his face. Linda will be wondering what he's doing in there. No, she'll know what he's doing. He wipes his face with a paper towel and walks out into the restaurant.

He sits down and puts his napkin back on his lap. "I'm not feeling well," he tells her.

"You don't look well," she says. Her voice is flat.

"Let's get the check. I need to go home and lie down."

"I ordered coffee and dessert while you were in the bathroom. Sip some Pellegrino." He picks up his water and drinks. He doesn't know what he's going to do, but he must see Renata before the night is over, no matter what.

CHAPTER 18

5:30 pm, Tropical Moons, Room 2-B

Renata

She's still groggy after a long nap and goes back to sit on the bed thinking about Richard's call. Now what does he expect her to do, wait around for his mad dash over? She wonders if she can call it quits without him doing something drastic. What can she say to him before it's too late? He has a wife and kids, for Christsake, and a beautiful home. She doesn't want to cause Richard pain. She'll never have the deep feelings for him that he craves.

She looks out the window at the early evening sky, the sun having dropped behind The Moons. Francisco will be over in a couple of hours before their appointment, and she wonders if Richard will call or just show up. It could be interesting. He's never met Francisco, and even though Richard knows about him and their line of work together, seeing him up close might be a good reality check. It's up to fate at this point.

She takes Pepe in her lap and turns on the TV, but all she can find is news. She needs something funny. She decides to go down to the bar for a drink. Jules has left for work. Should be a few happy-hour people around.

She puts Pepe under the covers to keep him safe and slips on a thin leopard-print bathing suit cover-up. No bathing suit under it, but it's long enough that she won't get arrested – unless she stands in front of the light. She laughs to herself. Where did that saying ever come from? A skirt so short you'll get arrested. She's taken off all her clothes in a bar more than once, and nobody even asked her to put them back on, much less called the police.

She slides into her sandals and drapes Pepe around her shoulders – his mottled yellow and pearl skin goes nice with the leopard. Not like she has to be the center of attention, but it gives her something to do. Everybody appreciates something to talk about, especially if it's a little dangerous.

She leaves the door unlocked behind her, and takes nothing so she can keep her hands free, in case Pepe gets squirmy. She carries him down the stairs and makes the turn into the brightness of the bar with its picture windows on the street – not quite dusk yet. She covers Pepe's eyes against the glare and walks to an empty stool in the middle of the bar. She smiles. Oliver is bartending, one of the sweetest guys she knows, for real, since he's not interested sexually.

"Good afternoon, lovely Miss Rennie and company." He wipes the bar in front of her and lays out a cocktail napkin. "What would you like?"

She can't resist a little tease. She touches his chin. "Can I have anything I want – any way I want it?"

"I'm sure you may. Just not from me." He kisses her hand and then touches Pepe's head where it rests on her chest. "In another lifetime, darling. Save some for me."

She bends forward until their lips touch. "You bet I will. I guess I'll make do with a vodka and cranberry for now – on credit? I didn't bring any money down."

"We know where to find you." He pours the drink and sets it in front of her. "Anything for the lad?"

She laughs. "Nope. He's on the wagon."

Renata sips her drink and makes eye contact with the men seated near her. They smile. A blond guy in dress pants and a white shirt raises his glass to toast Pepe. He stands up and walks over. "Nice snake. Can I touch him?"

"Sure. Just be gentle."

"I always am."

"Oh, really?" Renata pretends disappointment.

He laughs. "Yeah. I used to have one like this – not quite so big."

She giggles. "Damn! What happened to it? Oh, are we talking about snakes?"

"Aren't you the cute one? And looking for trouble."

She's sliding her eyes down his front, thinking he might make for a sweet night sometime, if he wants to pay. "That depends how you define trouble."

"Are you a hooker?"

"Sometimes." No reason to argue over words with this guy.

He looks down her outfit. "Guess I should have known."

"I can be a nice girl, if I want. I'm busy tonight anyway."

He clicks his bottle against her glass. "Okay. Mind if I look?" His eyes roam up her body and back down and she knows he can see her silhouette through the thin fabric.

She feels a cool streak of wetness between her legs. "I enjoy being looked at."

He moves in closer, blocking her from anyone's view, and lifts her skirt a few inches, letting it fall lightly back across her thighs. She moves her legs a little farther apart, feels her breath get deeper. "You're getting close to a charge here."

"Any second I'll be handing you my wallet."

She finishes her drink. "You can buy me another one of these. Two, if you want. I haven't paid for this one."

He smiles. "Would you stand up, so I can see the rest of you?"

She holds Pepe close and slides off the stool to stand in front of him, her back to the light from the window, her legs apart so he can see she's wearing no panties. She turns to the side. "How's that?"

"Now I want to touch."

She moves closer and gives him a kiss on the mouth with Pepe looking over his left shoulder. He ignores the snake and his hands slide down her back over her ass.

Renata pulls back and takes his hand. She's about to ask him if he wants to come around after the weekend, when she sees two men walk through the door. Something alerts her, the way they carry themselves, the suits — something means cop. She watches them walk across to the desk clerk. They aren't the types to be looking for a room.

The blond guy turns to see what she's looking at. "Couple of boys from downtown," he says. "They here for you?"

"Huh? No. Who are they?"

"Plainclothes cops. I've seen them at the courthouse."

"You a lawyer?"

"Normally. Beach bum today."

Renata feels caution come over her — another lawyer. "You always drink in dumps like this?"

"I don't like the glitzy tourist places. Nothing wrong here. It's friendly." He looks at Rennie. "Very friendly."

She keeps watching the men. They're asking questions at the desk. Too many police and lawyers in one room to suit her.

He leans close. "Can I make an appointment to see you in the next few days?"

"For a date?"

"Yeah. You live here?"

She feels a warning fluttering in her stomach. Jules' nervousness is contagious. Caution is against her nature, but it seems necessary. "Sorry. No time. I have regular customers. It's getting late now." She picks up her fresh drink and drains it down to the ice.

He stands there frowning. "Next week?"

"No, sorry." He seems innocent, but she doesn't want him to know she lives there, just in case he's checking about a missing friend. There's no other way upstairs, and Francisco is due any minute. "Excuse me. Time for my appointment. Ciao." She hopes he thinks she's just visiting. She turns as she reaches the staircase and he's still watching her, as if he can see through more than the dress.

CHAPTER 19

7:30 pm, South Miami

Richard

He goes straight into the bedroom and flops on his stomach, diagonal on the king-sized bed. The orange light of dusk is projected on the wall in front of him, and he thinks of the growing shadows on the beach, and the darkness of Renata's room. He would be leaving there just now.

Linda walks into the Florida room and turns on the TV. He can tell she's not happy with the way the afternoon has gone. Normally, she would have called her mother to pick up the boys from school, so she and Richard could see a film. They would be in the theater now, maybe laughing at some romantic comedy or gripping the seats, transported by drama into another world. He remembers how they both enjoyed *Magnolia* together, sharing, without words, the bittersweet tragedy of life's absurdity, as revealed and deepened by the artfulness of the film. If they could watch *Magnolia* again and again, always seeing it for the first time, nothing more would be needed.

He rolls to his side and props his head. Why does he still

have so much goddamned energy at his age? This could be the problem with keeping fit – not aging and mellowing with the rest of them, not content to live a simple, comfortable life. He's part of the first fitness generation, and the old standards are still in place. It's incredible that he qualifies to retire at sixty with full benefits, when at forty-eight he's only beginning to live. He takes a breath and exhales loudly. Fuck the guilt. He can't watch *Magnolia* again for the first time, so he has to create new moments. Fuck the goddamned guilt.

He puts on a pair of shorts, a t-shirt and his running shoes, goes into the bathroom, brushes his teeth, splashes his face, and pulls the comb through his hair. He walks down the hall, hearing the news, knowing Linda is sitting in the chair, probably working a crossword puzzle while she watches. He stops. She's looking up as if it's what she expected.

"I'm going to drive down to the beach for a run."

"You're feeling better?"

Her calmness is spooky, but a relief at the same time. "Not great. The nausea is gone. If I run, I'll get back some energy. There's just enough time before dark."

She watches him as he waits for her to say something else. She looks down at the newspaper in her hands and fills in a word.

"Okay. Be back soon."

She doesn't say goodbye, so neither does he. He wonders how much rope she's going to give him. It's not like Linda to sit and do nothing. He has a sick feeling about leaving her like that, but he can't stop himself. He takes the cell phone out of his pocket as he pulls on to US-1.

As Richard touches the Renata button, he remembers that he should delete the quick dial. The machine comes on, the computer voice, so he can't even enjoy the sound of her voice. It doesn't matter. He's on his way there, even if it's just to leave her a note.

The last edge of daylight is about to be swallowed up by cloud cover as he feeds the meter on the side street near

Renata's building. His supply of quarters is running low, and he can only pay for a half-hour. He'll check to see if she's there first and then come back with change. It wouldn't do to have the car towed. Parking is just another of the irritations of her living on the beach. The sooner he gets her into a little cottage in the Grove and away from the sleazy bums she has around her, the better off they'll both be in many ways.

He looks around the bar – not there. As he walks toward the stairs he sees a blond guy watching him. It's a casual interest, not a gay come-on. Something about the guy makes Richard think he's been with Renata. He wonders if every man in the bar has been with her, the women too. He's losing it. He gives the guy a look before he gets to the hallway.

There's no light or sound from the Jules woman's apartment as he passes, but he can hear music coming from Renata's. He knocks. There's a short wait and Renata opens the door. The scent of marijuana rolls out like a wave, and she floats before him in a translucent animal print dress, her sleek silhouette almost aglow in the lamplight. His eyes catch a movement behind her. A young dark-haired guy without a shirt is sitting on the bed. Richard's throat tightens. His hands make fists by his sides and he digs his nails into his palms.

"Richard. I thought you were going to call?"

"I did. You didn't answer." He can't take his eyes off the guy on the bed, sizing him up, noting the muscled shoulders and arms, the thick black hair. The man looks at Richard, inhales from the joint he's holding, and leans back against the wall.

"Whatever. I'm just about out of here," Renata says.

He speaks low. "Who's that?"

"You know. Francisco."

"Just let me kiss you."

She puts her arms around his neck and stretches upward. He takes her shoulder and holds her away. "Not in front of him."

She pushes closer. "No problem. He's used to it." She tries

to aim for his mouth again, but he pushes her back.

"I'm not used to it. I'm not used to seeing you with another man in your apartment – period."

"Richard, fuck. You know what I do. If you drop in, what do you expect?"

He takes her wrist and moves her into the hall, away from the door.

"Yeah, this is much more private," she says.

He ignores her sarcasm and goes for her mouth, his lips sucking her in, his fingers grabbing her ass through the thin fabric, his pelvis pushing against her so she can feel how hard he is. All his energy – his essence, his soul – is concentrated right there between his hips, and it's so powerful that she should fall into his arms, clinging, never wanting to let go.

"Rennie, let's get out of here. I'll take you away, anywhere you want, buy you everything you need. You never have to walk back into that room again."

"You're losing it, Richard. This is where I live. I don't wanna leave, and I can't take everything from you." She pecks him on the cheek. "Go home."

He's desperate. He's wondering when the guy will decide to come out and see what they're doing. "Renata – listen – my wife is making more trouble. I don't know when I'll be able to see you again. Let's go. Please. Do something wild and leave with me right now."

"Have you been drinking?"

"No. Not since lunch. Listen to me. I love you. I'll do anything for you."

"Go home then. Call me next week and we'll work something out." She twists her wrist from his grasp and slips through the door. It closes. He hears Francisco asking her what's going on. He can't hear her answer. He stands until the music goes off and heels click across the floor. He dashes down the stairs. His eyes fill. There's nothing he can do.

He decides to run on the beach in the dark to get sweaty. He doesn't know if Linda believes anything he tells her now, but it's worth the run if there's a chance to keep things calm. If only he could keep running all the way to Key West, rather than going home to face her.

He runs from 16th down to 5th and back. He runs back again. It's crazy, but he can't stop. He's sweating so hard, he runs down to the water and takes off his shirt, wading into the surf in his shorts, feeling steam come off him. It feels good, but he's still not ready to go home.

He needs to run some more. He remembers that Crunch is just a few blocks away on Washington Street. A run past it seems like a good idea. The pimp is probably still at Renata's, and he can see what his building is like. As he slows down at the door, loud bass vibrates his chest from the club. He sees another entrance on the side and slips between the buildings to look through the small window. He opens the door and climbs the stairs. There's a smell of stale beer, and the bass is even louder. Cheap rent, for sure. So the pimp isn't raking in the money, probably keeps Renata mostly to himself. Richard can't decide if that's good or bad. He stops at the apartment door and knocks, for the hell of it, trying to think of an excuse, just in case the pimp got home early. He turns and heads down the stairs.

"Hey, dick, what do you want?"

Richard's head snaps around. "You know me?"

Francisco is bare-chested, wearing jeans. His face is swollen and bandaged. He yells loud above the thump of bass. "No, prick, you woke me up."

"My name's Dick – Richard."

"Richard?" Francisco laughs. "Professor Dick. I do know you. You're the prick that was at Renata's door tonight. You been trying to take her away, huh?"

"You're a pimp."

"Pimp? You think Renata works for me? Not a chance."

"You set up her appointments."

"That what she tells you? Man, you're way off. Renata does what – and who – she wants. Sometimes I'm in on it." He stares at Richard and laughs.

Richard feels the truth in it, but anger is building. The ass . . . He leaps the three steps to the landing, but Francisco is on him. Richard's head hits the wall. Francisco holds a gun close to Richard's mouth.

Afraid to move, he sucks in a breath slowly. "Please. I just want to know what's going on."

Francisco holds back, a sneer on his face. "You know what's going on, you stupid motherfucker." He drops the gun to his side. "I feel sorry for you."

Richard takes a breath. "What do you mean?"

"You're sliding fast, man, right over the edge. I seen it before."

"No. I'm waiting. It's only a matter of time until Renata is ready to go."

"It won't be with you."

"With whom? You? Is that your plan?"

"I don't have any plan. I'm just way ahead of you. Think about the facts, man." Francisco is too close, in Richard's space, insolent, like a student with a lousy poem who refuses to believe it.

Richard knows Francisco is referring to the age difference, but he's a punk. Shallow. Stupid. Richard walks to the bottom of the stairs. He turns. Francisco is still staring down at him, the gun at his side. Richard yells up, "Renata will leave with me. You and your gang, just leave her alone."

"My gang? What is that? Get this straight, Dick. I'm Renata's boyfriend, and we're in private business. Consider yourself lucky to be a client — while it lasts."

Richard bursts through the door to the cooler air outside. He's burning, but scared, by his murderous thoughts. He knows that if he'd been the one with the gun, the pimp would be dead. That cool exterior didn't fool him for a second — Francisco loves Renata, and nobody knows better than Richard what that means.

He takes off running again to cool his head. There's little

traffic and he keeps up his speed to the side street where he parked. At first he thinks he made a mistake. There's an instant of disbelief before the hot surge runs through him. He forgot to get change and feed the meter. The car has been towed, and now it will be late before he can get home, besides costing him a taxi ride and probably a hundred dollars to get the car back. He doesn't dare call Linda for a ride.

It's after midnight when Richard pulls up and parks on the drive at home. The house is dark and he'd rather keep it that way. In the past he would have shared with Linda the terrifying feeling of a gun in his face, and she would have calmed him, but he's broken that connection forever. He opens the door quietly, takes off his shoes, and walks down the hall and into the bedroom. He begins stripping off his clothes. As his eyes adjust to the darkness, he realizes that the bed is empty. He turns on the light. Everything is where it should be except Linda. He walks down the hall and peeks into the boys' rooms. Empty. He goes into the kitchen and turns on the light, walks through the Florida room, looks outside. No sign of anything. No note. He doesn't know if they've left him or gone to the movies. It's late for the boys, even on Friday night, but maybe. If only he'd gotten to Renata's before her . . . friend – her pimp. Maybe he could have convinced her to go away with him forever. Then it wouldn't matter where Linda was, or what she said to him, ever again. Of course it would matter, but he would have Renata. He goes back through the house turning off all the lights. *Maybe*s and *if only*s aren't getting him far. He decides to take a shower and get into bed, like everything is normal. They might be on the way home from the movies.

He turns on the TV and opens the folder of papers to grade. There's no chance of concentrating, but he can grade without thinking at this point. The students will be spared the subtleties. His hand takes out misplaced commas by rote, and he makes comments in the margins on the same errors over and over, while he wonders what will happen in his future. He grades until his head dips on his chest and the pen falls onto the sheets.

He wakes when Linda gets into bed. He can smell alcohol. "Are the boys in bed?"

"They're at my mother's."

"Where were you?"

"I'd ask you that, but it's not worth the bother," she says.

He breaks out in a cold sweat and lies there wide awake and still for hours.

CHAPTER 20

October 1, 9:00 am, Tropical Moons, Room 2-A

Jules

When she awakens that morning, the curtains are billowing into the apartment, a long-awaited cool breeze, somewhere below 80 degrees. Fall must be on its way at last, one thing to be thankful for, with the hangover building in the back of her head. It was a long night at work after drinking all day with Renata. Her clothes are scattered where she threw them before falling into bed. She sits up. She lies back down. There are no excuses for her not to write today. She closes her eyes and tries to think of something to get her started again. There's still that long sword on the wall. Maybe she can put Richard into a rage and have him come swinging it through the bar and up the stairs after Francisco. It gives her the chills. She decides to change all the names before she gets any farther. She can't identify real people as murderers. Time to "find" and "replace."

She's booting up the laptop when the phone rings.

"This Julie?" a man's voice asks.

"Who is this?"

"Friend of Francisco."

She feels panic rising into her voice. "Why are you calling me?"

"You're the money girl, and there's a money problem."

"I don't have any more money."

"You and your friend Renata. Get yourselves out here to Jimmy's, the airboat place. Jim's. She knows where it is. Don't bring Francisco. We don't want him out here again."

"We don't have a car – and no money. We'd be wasting your time meeting you."

He laughs. "Look. I know where you live. I been up there once – you know what night I'm talking about? Your turn to come see me. Rent a fucking car and get your asses out here this afternoon. We got unfinished business."

He hangs up and Jules stands holding the phone in shock. They paid all the money, so what does he want now? She shuts down the laptop. Not today. She finds some underwear and a shirt and long pants in case of bugs and snakes. She's never seen the Everglades. She can't imagine how she and Renata will get out there by themselves. Maybe Francisco can help. She rushes next door and knocks.

Renata opens the door. Jules looks inside. "Francisco here?"

"Gone. Come on in."

Jules gasps. "Renata, fuck. There's another fucking problem with those guys."

"Easy, girl. You're starting to sound like me."

Jules explains about the call. "Can you get ahold of Francisco? I don't even know where the Everglades is."

Renata lights a cigarette, takes a long drag, and puts it in the ashtray. "Francisco can't get 'em off his back. They're connected with some big shot assholes. Francisco did some work for them to make up the money. Now they won't let him quit." Renata pulls off the shorts she's wearing and squirms into a pair of cut-off jeans. Jules notices that she's wearing no panties and there's no bra under her t-shirt. It wouldn't be Jules' choice for meeting criminals in the Everglades. "You never mentioned more money," Jules says.

"We didn't want to scare you. There's been all kinds of problems with them. Let's just go. We'll find 'em and call their bluff. I know where they are. Francisco took me out there a couple times to pick up some weed."

"What can we do? I don't have any more money."

Renata goes to the bottom drawer and reaches under some clothes. Jules thinks she's looking for cash. Renata holds up a gun, black and square, dangerous. "We're not paying anything. They won't let Francisco alone — and now they're after us. It's blackmail. It will never end."

"Is that loaded?"

"Not yet." She gets out a canvas bag and puts the gun in and gets a box from another drawer. "I'll load in the car. You drive. I don't have a license anymore." She stuffs in a sweatshirt with the sleeves and neck cut off. "Don't worry, Jules, I know how to shoot."

"You do?" A jittery wave runs between Jules' shoulders and her stomach flutters. "What kind of gun is that?"

Renata is pulling on socks. "Glock, nine millimeter. Little one. Francisco got it for me in Georgia. We practice at the shooting range for kicks, but I always figured it might come in handy."

"You're really going out there to shoot them?"

"No, just to threaten them. We have to end this. Show them we can't be pushed around."

"Where do we get a car?"

"Downstairs."

Jules has no idea what Renata has in mind, but she follows her down the stairs and out to the bar. Oliver is washing glasses at the other end. "Hey, sweetie," Renata yells to him. He comes over. She leans toward him and kisses him on the mouth. "Can we borrow your car? We'll have it back by the time you're ready to leave."

He smiles, reaches into his pocket, and puts the keys on the bar. Renata throws another kiss and takes Jules by the hand.

The traffic is heavy. Renata directs and Jules jerks from one lane into the other. Her foot hovers above the brake, ready for a pedestrian to dart in front of them or somebody to stop suddenly. She would be scared to death to drive if she wasn't already out of her mind. She crosses the bridge and merges onto I-95 where the traffic is moving twenty mph above the speed limit. Jules has no idea where she's going, but she keeps quiet and follows Rennie's instructions until finally they get to US-27, a less busy highway. Open grassy fields spread out alongside them, and she lightens up, despite the fear. Rennie is a survivor, and Rennie is in charge.

"I told the guy we don't have any money. Why are they wasting their time?"

"They're assholes, local idiots that got big connections, and now they think they're tough. That's what Francisco thinks. He didn't know what he was getting into. Listen, Julie, they're planning on a payment of some kind – you know?"

"Sex? From me?"

"I'd say so. Maybe they're figuring on a regular payment schedule from now on. And if they get rough, who's gonna know? Way out here?" She shakes her head. "Chopping up a body – or two – it's all in a day's work."

Jules stares at the road, gripping the wheel, thinking this can't be happening.

Renata winks. "We'll fuck 'em all right. We'll fuck 'em up." She reaches over and pats Jules' thigh. "Don't worry, baby."

"Rennie?"

"Take it easy. I got the gun, and I know how to use it."

Jules opens her mouth to tell Rennie that she doesn't want to kill anyone – then closes it.

It's a long ride, yet not long enough, when Rennie motions Jules to take the exit. They head down a blacktop road and turn onto a stretch of gravel that becomes tire tracks with holes and bumps. The grass is up to the windows, a sea of light green and tan surrounding them.

"I thought the Everglades was full of water," Jules says. She peers ahead, hoping the road doesn't suddenly become a river.

"Some of it. You'll see. It's a cool place — too bad we have to waste our time on these cocksuckers."

"I thought there were alligators."

"Sure, lots. We just can't see them."

Renata points right. "Turn here."

There's no track, but Renata keeps motioning. Jules turns into the weeds and sees a wooden house to the far left. She can't imagine how Rennie remembered the location. Rennie seems to act on pure will and guts without any knowledge, and she always gets away with it.

Rennie points toward the cabin, then places the gun on her lap and covers it with the sweatshirt. "Drive really slow, Jules," she says, "we want to seem scared."

Jules looks at her, feeling bug-eyed. "We are."

Renata laughs. "Don't worry. I've got us covered."

Jules can hear the excitement in Rennie's voice. She can feel her own pulse in the side of her throat and her stomach fluttering.

"Park."

Jules looks at the shuttered windows. The cabin seems deserted. No vehicles.

"Hope we didn't drive out here for nothing."

"Jesus, I hope we did," says Jules.

Rennie is out of the car with the gun tucked into her waistband in back, before Jules can shut off the engine. She pulls down the loose shirt to cover the gun. "This makes my jeans tight." She unsnaps a button. "I'm no quick draw," she whispers, "but surprise is on our side."

Jules' chest tightens. "Please, don't say anything else."

They walk up the wooden steps and onto the rough porch. Cigarette butts are strewn over the surface and blown into piles in the corners. A small stinking rabbit skin covered with flies is nailed to the overhang. There's water behind the house stretching to the horizon, and a turquoise blue airboat is tied to the dock.

Tall grass bends and shines in the sun, along with flowering water plants, but no alligators. Having done some bird watching as a child, with her father, Jules recognizes a wading bird she always wanted to see. With a splash of brilliant coral on a pale pink body, and the strange flat bill, it can only be a roseate spoonbill. Its unexpected presence reminds her of pleasures she misses from those innocent days.

"Jules?" Rennie motions to her and knocks on the door. The spoonbill startles and lifts its pastel wings to take flight, flapping gracefully, entering the sky over the water. Jules watches, holding her breath, until it is out of sight.

Jules steps up on the porch. Renata points to the silent, rusty air conditioner in the side window. "Nobody in there or they'd be broiled." She turns the knob and pushes the door open. There's a table and chairs from an old kitchen set, aluminum with a green top and dirty flowered plastic cushions with burn holes. An ashtray is packed with cigarette butts. There are mattresses on each side of the room and a pair of muddy Nikes.

Jules breathes in relief. "I guess they changed their minds."

"Never depend on drug dealers or you're gonna get fucked up."

"Let's go. It's creepy in here – smells like rotten meat." The thought connects and Jules glances around nervously. She stares at Renata in terror. "I almost forgot how this whole thing started."

"Let's wait a while. I don't wanna have to come out here again."

"Please – let's . . ." The sound of a car in the distance makes her stop.

"Out!" Renata says. She leads the way and they close the door and stand on the porch, watching the car as it makes the turn from the road. It drives toward them. There are two men in front.

"Take it easy," Rennie says. "We'll be fine." She has her hands on her hips, fingers under the edge of her shirt, close to the gun.

Jules whispers between her teeth. "Rennie? God!" She grips her purse tighter to stop her hands from shaking.

The car stops and the two guys get out. Jules recognizes them from the night at The Moons. As they walk towards her, they look bigger than she remembers, one really big, with a ponytail and tattoos down his huge bare arms. The other guy has a more compact but muscular body, a row of piercings on one ear, and an eyebrow ring. Their faces are hard, but smiling.

"Hey, girls, right on time." The big one nods to Renata. "Where's your boyfriend? Hospital?"

"Where's yours?"

He sneers. "I hope you were smart enough to leave that cocksucker at home."

"So why the fuck you keep bothering us? We paid for the job – good money – even though you fucked it up."

"Good money, shit. You didn't pay half the price." He looks at Jules. "The job we did for you was $5,000 – with the discount."

Jules gasps. "What? Francisco said –"

"Doesn't matter what that asshole said. We don't take that kind of risk cheap –"

"Don't even bother, Jules," Renata says. She swings her hip out and stands with her legs apart, staring at them, her arms folded. "So what's the deal? Franco's working for you, no?"

"He don't work enough. We have a new deal."

The guy with the earrings walks over to the car and drags out a cooler.

The big guy opens the door of the cabin, and they go inside. The air is stifling. He points to the chairs. Rennie sits and pats the seat next to her for Jules. Jules looks at the stains on the cushion. Rennie takes her hand and Jules sits.

The sound of a generator starts up. Ponytail moves to the air conditioner and turns it on. The door opens and the other guy sets the cooler inside. "Hook us up with a beer, Ray," ponytail says, "while we cool down." Ray reaches into the cooler, sloshing ice. For Jules, the scene loses connection with reality, dusty sunshine slanting through smeared windows, shadows on rough wood, dark brutal men, and beautiful Rennie across the table, glowing. Ray sets four Buds in front of ponytail – Jules realizes ponytail must be Jimmy. He passes the cans around. The men click cans like they're toasting a sports team they've bet on, ready to watch the game. They light cigarettes and sit back as if they're alone in the room.

Jules shudders at the violence under the surface. She and Rennie are not meant to leave here.

Renata hands an open beer to Jules, then cracks the pop top on hers. "Cheers," she says and clicks against Jules' can. Jules puts the beer to her mouth and takes a sip, but she can't swallow. She looks at Rennie, trying with her eyes to make her aware of the danger, but Rennie acts like they're having a picnic.

Rennie takes a long drink of her Bud and looks at Jimmy. "So what do we have to do to get you guys off our backs?"

"Hand over the rest of our five thou."

Renata takes his hand and puts it under the front of her shirt. His mouth opens slightly and his hand lifts the shirt above her bare breasts, his index finger finding her nipple and rubbing it so it comes to life. He licks his bottom lip.

He laughs. "Are you suggesting some kind of payment?"

Renata rolls her eyes. "Isn't that why we're here?"

He rubs his jaw with his other hand, while he cups and massages Rennie's breast. His eyes lower. Rennie tilts back in the chair a little, opening her legs.

Ray turns to Jules and grins. Jules is thinking about the gun in Rennie's waistband, wondering how long Rennie will wait to threaten them.

"What do you think, Ray? It's a start."

"You're gonna stick me with the school teacher – no offense, Julie."

Jules blinks. She wonders how they know about her. She looks at Ray's dirty fingernails and stained shirt. He seemed cleaner when they came to South Beach.

Ray turns to Jules and runs his hand down her thigh and between her legs. "We each get both. How's that for the first payment, girls?" Jules swallows the beer that has warmed in her mouth. The back of her neck goes cold.

"What do you mean, first payment?" Renata asks. "How many times you think we're going to come out here?"

"Haven't got that far yet in my thinking."

He looks at Jules. "Hey, she's got a sweet little pussy, I bet you. We're gonna have a good time." He turns back to Renata and strokes the skin near her crotch with his fingertips.

She closes her eyes and writhes beneath his hand with a look of pleasure on her face. She takes his finger and pushes it under the cut-offs. "We got the whole afternoon to drink and party. You got any weed?"

He smiles, showing many teeth. "We got whatever you want."

Jules is shaking. It would be just like Rennie to take advantage of the offer and spend the day doing coke or something. The sex means nothing to her, and she doesn't seem to sense the violence.

Rennie puts her hand between Jimmy's legs. She rubs her thumb up and down over the bulge. She motions to Jules with her head. "You guys wait here a minute while Julie and me take a pee." She stands up. "We'll be right back."

Jim laughs. "Don't think of taking off. You'll just have to come back out here again. Watch out for the gators."

Rennie puts her hand behind Jules' shoulder and Jules gets up stiffly. Rennie leads Jules out the door and into the tall grass. She pulls the gun out of her waistband. "Hold this." She pulls down her jeans and panties, squats, and begins to pee. "You might want to take this chance, Jul. Could be a long day."

Jules tries not to stare at Rennie's red curly crotch as urine sizzles into the grass. "I can't do it."

"Suit yourself."

"I mean, I can't have sex and do drugs with these guys."

"Honey, you're losing it. There's no way I'm going along with these fuckers. You think they'd give us a five thou credit for a little pussy? Hell, no. Those days are long gone — if they ever existed." She shakes her butt and stands up, yanking up the jeans. "They're just as likely to kill us as fuck us. I'm going to break this up, once and for all. We owe it to Francisco. I'll threaten them with the gun, fire a few shots near their balls — show 'em we're tough and tell 'em we're done with their bullshit. Then we're out of here. If they don't leave us alone from now on, I'll tell the police and we'll take our chances." She points to the cabin. "You have to help me out. I need to catch 'em off guard."

Jules swallows. "You'll call the police?"

"If I have to. C'mon, help me."

Rennie takes Jules' hand and pulls her back toward the building. "I need to get them in a vulnerable position. The problem is there are two of them."

Jules sees a flash in Rennie's eyes, the excitement of taking control.

"Tell ponytail I'm waiting for him on the porch. You start undressing Ray fast."

"Huh? How's that going to work?"

"Trust me. Send ponytail out to the porch with me and just get Ray's pants down. When you've got his crotch down to the knees, knock over a chair or something, for a signal. Then get out of the way —"

"I don't know how to do that! What are you going to do!"

"Shh! Don't worry. Just get his pants down and give me a loud signal."

"I don't know."

Rennie takes Jules' hair and smooths it behind her ears. "It's okay. I'll handle it."

Renata puts her arms around Jules and kisses her hard on the mouth, as if sealing a pledge.

Jim opens the door. "Oh, you girls warming up for us." He looks back at Ray. "Lipstick lesbies. I told you."

Renata whispers to Jules, "You go on inside."

Jules uses her most frightened, pleading look, but Renata angles her chin to motion Jules to keep moving. Jules walks in past Jim. Renata stays on the porch. "Come on out here, Jim. Bring some herb with you. Julie's shy."

Jim takes a drink of his beer. Ray motions him to go on. "You're letting out the cold air."

"A'right. I'm not staying out there all afternoon. It's hot. We're gonna smoke one and then we're coming back in here on the mattress."

He picks up his beer and walks out. He looks to the side and smiles before he shuts the door.

Jules takes hold of herself and walks around the table to Ray. She touches the back of his neck and feels the heat of nausea fill her stomach.

"Let's see whatcha got under the clothes, honey."

Jules steps back and pulls the shirt off over her head. She's thinking of Rennie and how she would do it, relaxed and sexy. It will all be over, as soon as she gets Ray's pants down. He scoots his chair to the side to face her and takes a drag of his cigarette. His mouth goes slack, smoke drifting out the sides. Jules reaches behind her back and undoes the bra hook. She flings the bra onto the table. The cool of the air conditioner touches her nipples and they stiffen. She envisions what Rennie would do and steps forward. Ray puts out a hand toward her breasts, but she moves in until they're rubbing his forehead. It's not easy to go right for his pants. She's never been the aggressor. Ray's hands move down to the button on her waistband.

It occurs to her that if he gets her pants down first, she'll be the one in the vulnerable position. She takes his fingers into her hands and lowers herself to a squatting position in front of him. He bends forward and kisses her, something she's not expecting. His lips are hard and she feels the pressure and warmth of his tongue pushing into her mouth. His breath isn't disgusting like she expected, and the beer taste reminds her of the kisses that Rennie plants on her. Jules lets her mouth stay there and her hands move down to his belt. It's tight and she has to concentrate to undo the buckle, but the zipper slides easily and she breaks with his lips as she moves down farther, taking the jeans to his knees. He's wearing boxer shorts and she puts her fingers inside the waistband and stretches it out and pulls the shorts down, catching them for a second on his cock, suddenly harder and longer than she expected.

Ray reaches for her and she knows it's the moment to signal Renata. She lets out a scream into his face that staggers him against the back of the chair. She steps away against the side wall, watching his eyes open wide and his hand drop the cigarette. It falls with a glint of ash to the wood floor, as an explosion from outside puts time into slow motion. There's another shot and another.

Ray trips and grabs the table as the door flies open. Renata fills the space, her eyes huge, glancing at Jules. Jules jumps farther into the corner as Renata's arm comes up with the gun, a moving flash and explosion, again and again. Ray falls sideways in a spray of blood, taking the chair down with him. Renata points the barrel of the gun toward the sky, catching her breath. Jules looks at Ray. His shirt is smoldering and blood bubbles from a hole in his chest. She shrieks and slides across the wall to the corner and out the door. She throws herself into Renata's arms.

Rennie holds her tight. "Okay, Jules, everything's fine. Take a minute. I need you to calm down so you can help me." Her fingers move upward to Jules' neck, massaging. "We have to get rid of these guys. The longer they're missing, the more chance we have of staying out of it."

Jules nods and steps back, covering her bare breasts with one arm. "I thought you were going to threaten them."

"How well would that have worked, huh? I had to do it. They almost killed Franco, and they would have killed us too. If not today, then another day."

Jules is near losing it. She shakes her head, her hair whipping. Her hands go to her temples to stop the motion. She stares at Rennie. "You didn't tell me because then I couldn't have done my part."

"You would have. I just didn't see a reason to put it on your conscience. You've got a shitload of worthless weight there already."

"I would have failed you."

"You'll never fail me, Jules. That's something I'm fucking sure of. I won't fail you either."

Jules searches Renata's eyes, hoping she means it.

"C'mon. We need to get these fuckers out of here before somebody else shows up. We'll take 'em out in the airboat."

"You know how to drive that?"

"How hard can it be? Just a big lawnmower with the blade on sideways."

Jules nods.

"Okay. Let's get the big guy off the porch first." Rennie takes Jules' shoulders. "Squint your eyes until you get used to it."

Jules squints to blur her vision of the body lying back in a pool of blood even wider than the lawyer's. She focuses gradually until she sees the chest wound and the ragged crater where the penis and balls used to be. She gags and steps back, the little remains in her stomach splattering to the porch. She wipes her mouth and takes a deep breath before she walks inside, grabbing her bra and shirt, without looking at Ray. She steps back out on the porch and concentrates on getting dressed. "How'd you do that without him grabbing the gun?"

"Your scream. That was great. All his attention was focused elsewhere. Besides, he couldn't see anything below his gut." She snorts a sort of laugh. "Bet he hadn't seen his dick in years."

Renata takes Jules' hand and kisses it. "Stick with me, Julie. Everything's gonna be fine." She wraps her close in her arms.

Jules gives herself up to Rennie and rests her head on her

shoulder. She feels Renata's lips slide down to nuzzle the base of her neck. She would be all right if she could press against Rennie forever. It's the one thing that can save her from the insanity her life has become – yet the idea itself is insane.

Renata lifts Jules' chin. "We better get busy. Never know who could show up." Jules nods with her eyes closed. She can feel Renata's breath on her mouth.

"Okay, Julie girl – hello? – we'll dump this one off the side of the porch and drag him around back to the airboat."

She walks side by side with Renata and bends down with her, taking the shoulders as Renata reaches under the lower back. Jules cringes watching Renata's face inch close to the bloody gaping hole and exposed internal organs as she struggles for the leverage to push him over. It takes two tries until the body thumps down into the dry grass. The wood porch is still an obvious place of slaughter.

"There must be a bucket somewhere. Let's look around for something and slosh this off, so it won't be so noticeable if anybody comes down the road."

Jules points toward the inside. "The cooler probably has a lot of water in it. That would be a start."

"Shame to empty out all those beers. They must be nice and cold."

"Rennie!"

"Seriously, let's just take a look for something else. If we can't find anything we'll put the beers in the car. It'll be hard to refill this big cooler and carry it back and forth anyway."

Jules shakes her head, but follows Rennie inside. "Nothing," Rennie says. "Wait here. I'm going to take a look at the airboat."

Before Jules can say anything, Renata is out and down the stairs. Jules looks around the room and shivers. She can still taste the kiss, even with the flavor of bile in her mouth. She recalls those minutes when she undressed him, and wonders how she could do it. Renata clomps up the stairs. "We're set. Two five-gallon buckets. C'mon." She pulls one bucket from inside the other and hands it to Jules.

Jules takes the handle. "Yuck. Smells."

"Bait probably. Let's get moving." Renata walks through the grass and Jules follows. Renata squats on the dock to fill her bucket a little over half. Jules does the same. They carry the water the short distance to the side of the porch, set the buckets on the wood and step up. Renata sloshes hers over the side and takes Jules' and sloshes it. There's still a diluted puddle that's easily identified as blood. "This is stupid. Let's get the other body out. No sense in doing this job twice."

Jules looks at Rennie. She might as well be doing spring cleaning for all the difference it makes to her.

They drag the guy out of the shack and drop him off the side into the bloody grass. Jules picks up the bedding and Nikes and puts them on the table, then sloshes water and pinkish cigarette butts between the slats of the floor, while Renata does the same on the porch. Jules is sweating and feels lightheaded. She hasn't finished when Renata comes in with another bucket and sloshes the rest of the blood away in one last whoosh.

"Done," she says. "Everything will dry fast in this heat. Somebody might figure it out eventually, but they won't know about us — if they even care. Not like they're gonna call the police to find clues." She looks down the road. "I doubt anybody else is coming back here for the night. When everything's dry, it'll look fine — cleaner than usual."

Jules throws the bedding and shoes back on the wet floor. Renata turns off the A.C., and they go outside and shut the door. The sun is low. A mosquito bites Jules on the arm. She swats it and smears the blood with all the rest of the splatters.

"Ouch," says Renata. "We'd better work fast before we're eaten alive."

It takes several more minutes to drag the bodies the few feet to the dock and roll them onto the boat. Mosquitoes are biting every inch of Jules' exposed skin.

"We have to rinse off. Let's get in right here. The wind will dry our clothes while we take these guys for a ride."

Jules looks into the dark water. The incline to the edge looks slippery for getting out. "What about the gators? All this blood in the water?"

"I don't see any. Give me your hand."

"Thanks, but I'll just wash up with the bucket."

Renata shakes her head, but hauls a half-bucket of water for Jules and pours it over her body from the chest down. Jules rubs her arms and clothing. It feels good to get the blood off and cool down, if anything can be good. Renata brings another bucket, and Jules bends down while Renata pours slowly and rubs spots on the back of Jules' shirt and down her thighs.

"Done. I'm going to jump in, so it will be faster. You help me out."

Before Jules can object, Renata has splashed into deep water and sinks under. She swims up swishing her hair back and rubbing her face and down her arms. Jules moves closer to the edge and puts out her hand. Renata staggers a few steps on shallow mud, emerging from the swamp with her shirt clinging tight to her round breasts and jutting nipples, water flowing from her face and hair. Like a mermaid, Jules thinks. Renata takes Jules' hand for the final two steps up the embankment, but the touch is light, and Jules realizes that Renata doesn't really need her help.

"Don't you ever get scared?" Jules asks.

"Not for long. I talk myself out of it."

"How?"

She twists her hair, wringing out water. "Once you learn that you don't have anything to lose — and you are how you are because of what's inside your head — it takes off all the pressure." She motions for Jules to sit on the metal bench. "Let's get this sucker going." She looks at the steering wheel and the starter and points to the key in the ignition. "Okay. It's just like a normal wheel and starter for a car, and there's a speedometer and gas pedal." She hands the set of ear protectors to

Jules. She turns the key and presses the gas, heading straight out from the dock across the open area of water that seems to be a path.

Rennie picks up speed as they glide. The sound is too loud for talk, but the air keeps the mosquitoes from biting, and the warm wind dries their clothes and hair. From the front bench, Jules looks back at Renata's strong stance and confident steering as they tear toward the horizon. Renata flashes a wide smile and a look of triumph, as she veers off into the untouched weeds. Jules feels alive, for however long it lasts.

Renata takes a turn, approaching a shallow bank of scrubby trees. She lets off the gas. They slow and stop. "No sense in going any farther. Gators everywhere."

"Where?" Jules whispers. She looks around and finally recognizes a floating tire treads with eyes.

Renata points, "One, two, three, four . . ."

"God!" Jules moves closer to Rennie. The closest gator is barely two feet from the boat, which sits low in the water.

"Yes, he's a hungry boy!" Renata stoops and Jules bends down to help shove Jim's body over the side. It splashes down into the grass. A gator opens its mouth, drawing attention to its ten-foot length in the cover of thick weeds, but it doesn't move. Renata shoves the other body over the side and dips a bucket of water to swish off the blood. She stands staring at the closest gator.

"Let's just go," Jules tells her. "I don't want to see it."

"Yeah. If they don't eat, there's nothing we can do about it."

Renata slowly turns the boat in a wide arc. She hits the gas, following the compass east, back the way they came. It seems a short ride until the dock is in view. She slows the airboat, managing to get it close to the dock, and hands Jules the rope. "Just tie it up however you can. I don't know how to turn it around in this space."

Jules tries to tie a nautical-looking knot while Renata puts the buckets and ear protectors back. They walk up the slope and pass the shack. Renata stops. "Looks fine to me. Already near dry. Best we can do."

Jules walks toward the car.

"Wait, forgot the beer." Renata turns back to the porch. Jules hears an engine in the distance. "Rennie, leave it. There's somebody . . ."

Renata catches up to Jules and they run the few yards to the car. Jules gets in, slams the door, and starts it up.

Rennie slides in, shutting the door as Jules takes off. She drives fast, trying to get as far away from the cabin as she can.

Renata crouches on the seat, sticking her torso out the window. "I hear the car. Get off the road. Into the weeds. It's dry here."

Jules guns the engine and turns straight into the grass. "Where's the water?" She drives out about 100 yards. "I don't want to get stuck." She turns parallel to the road behind thick high brush.

"Stop. Turn off the engine."

The sound of the other car is loud. Jules holds her breath as it comes into view across the tall grass. It's a red Mustang convertible with a man driving and someone on the passenger side. Renata and Jules duck. It passes by.

Renata sits up. "They didn't see us."

Jules looks. "They had to. We saw them."

"They weren't looking. Headed somewhere fast."

Jules takes in air between her teeth. "They might have seen the car."

"The sun is blinding in this direction. I think we're in luck. Besides, the car's not ours. No connections. Get back to the road in case they decide to turn around."

Jules puts on as much speed as she dares. "Sorry, Rennie, I should have worked faster."

"No *sorrys* allowed, honey. This is a no-fault state."

Jules glances in the rearview and sees nothing but the empty gravel road. "The whole world should be no-fault — there's so much time wasted on pinning blame."

Rennie turns to her and smiles. "We're doin' okay, baby."

She winks and punches Jules lightly on the shoulder. "Can't wait to tell Francisco that it's all over."

Jules nods, her eyes on the road. She's not eager for anything. The numbness will be followed by nights alone, more guilt and fear.

CHAPTER 21

October 6, 3:35 pm, Atlantic Shores University

Richard

It's Wednesday, only halfway through the week, and he'll soon see Renata. He tries to pay attention to what he's reading, five poems, all rhyming, brought to him by a bright, sweet nineteen-year-old brunette waiting for his insight. He's been doing this for too many years to be flattered by the mournful young men and women who consistently flow into his office, desperate to believe that he can enable them to fulfill their lives with recognition. Now all he feels is their suffering.

He looks at his watch. He has to finish up with the girl in ten minutes. Renata's first visit to his office. He feels sweat spring out on his chest as he visualizes her hair spread over the wide black desk beside his computer, her glorious ass presented to him for whatever he desires. It's dangerous. He's been half-hard all day, his cock sometimes tight in his pants, thinking of those moments soon to come. He'll have to tell Rennie to keep the noise down. He should never have asked her to come here, but it's the only way he can fit her in with Linda's cutback in hours. Excuses are hard to come by as things stand.

The girl hands him another poem. "What about this one for the contest? I think it has more of the concrete stuff."

"Imagery?" His hand takes it automatically and his eyes roam down the page, catching the words moon, sea, and stars. He wonders if Renata will dress as sexily when she comes to the university as she does on the beach. It doesn't matter. A bra-less young lady in cut-offs up her ass isn't exactly unusual on campus – notable to his male colleagues, however, especially heading into his office. He hopes she does dress scantily. He'll get his fingers inside the shorts as soon as the door closes.

He looks up from the poem. "Yes, you've used some concrete words here. Good. Why don't you see if you can do a little more with it? Be more concise and try to get a little twist into the last line."

"Yeah?" Her eyes brighten up. "Then I should enter?"

He realizes she's talking about the annual writing contest, which he organizes in order to get material for the university literary magazine. She's not ready, but he hates to tell her. There's nothing he can say to her right now that she will understand – she's starting from scratch. The level of pain she must eventually reach is still far in the future. He knows it well. He has stopped pretending that he will eventually be another Wallace Stevens. "Try taking out the rhyme, and put it away for a month. Then see how it sounds. The contest deadline is still two months away."

She looks at him and frowns.

He glances at the clock, straining to hear a click of heels down the hall. Rennie is due. "Have you ever taken a poetry class?"

"I have to do my requirements first."

He nods. "Take Intro to Poetry Writing next semester. You'll be surprised at how inspiring learning poetic technique can be. Understanding the rules gives you original ideas of how to break them."

He stands, dropping his hands to cover the slight erection,

still in wait for Renata. He learned the rules so long ago, he can't find a single new way to break them.

She leafs through the notebook again. "I have another one —"

He touches her back lightly, urging her to the door. He opens it and glances down the hall — no one. He won't live if Renata doesn't show. "Work on that one for now."

The girl looks up trancelike.

He reads her posture, the downward slope of her shoulders and her open face, and realizes that there's a crush connected with this one, often the case, nothing of his doing. "I have another conference," he says. "I'm sorry."

She walks out, her face flushed, now clearly dissatisfied with the results of the half-hour she's spent in Richard's office. Having submitted her deepest secrets for his reactions. He could mention that he'll never remember her dire admissions from all the rest, but that would be worse. He can't tell her that there are no publishers searching for poetry, no matter how sublime, and that the only magic is in staying up all night in the fever of inspiration, on those rare occasions.

Tammi is hanging for more of his words. "Do you teach the class?"

"No. Yes. Sometimes. Look on the schedule for fall. You'll enjoy yourself. All the poets here are inspiring."

"Thank you, Professor Langley. I'll work on it."

"Richard, if you like. Poets needn't be so formal, Tammi."

She smiles, taking pleasure from being included in his world, even so slightly.

He watches Tammi's back go down the hall in tight little Capri pants, noting what a cute figure she has — and energy. She's bright and in possession of all the social skills she needs. She doesn't need to live in the gloom of the impossible quest in order to be loved and respected. If only she could be told the truth and hear it, forget this obsessive, frustrating, deteriorating need to create.

Richard steps back inside his office, running his fingers

through his short-cropped hair, in pain with the growing anxiety that Renata might not show. It's been two weeks since they've made love, and he has no idea how many other men have had her in between. Had her? She's had them, whoever they are. He's torturing himself. He's way out of control. Nothing matters — not job or family — as much as one lithe young woman. Renata replaces his need for poetry. She *is* poetry. She's like a Florida panther, rare and wild, without reason or purpose of her own, supplying pure primitive beauty to the world. He is a most fortunate man to have found what he'd been looking for all of his life, even if he didn't know it.

He sits back at his desk and lets his eyes go out of focus. He remembers the day on the beach when they met, his rebirth. It was nearly a year earlier, just a short time after his mother passed away. He was running a lot then, trying to escape himself. His mother's death was a relief after her months of suffering, but his pain came from the realization of how unhappy *he* was, how bored with his perfect life, and how selfish that was. His mother had existed on hard work, unable to enjoy herself by the time her business began to pay off, yet she remained grateful and happy, or so it seemed. Something was wrong with him — a cold negativity had crept into his existence. Whether it was learned or chemical, temporary or permanent, he didn't know, but it was grounded in the ridiculous, unshakeable expectation that the world owed him excitement, a reason to get up each day.

Renata, ever-changing, unpredictable, always a challenge. He remembers touching her at that first meeting. She had taken his hand to her chest, asked him to feel the heat of her skin, burnt pink as the sunset, above the tiny white bikini top.

He looks at his watch again. It seems forever since he's touched her. He envisions the indentation of her waist, the spread of her buttocks when she sits naked. Warmth rushes through him, and he puts his hand on his fly and unzips. A fantasy is better than nothing. He drops a little spit into his palm and curls his fingers around his cock.

There's a knock. "Yes?" He fumbles to zip his pants, but he can't. He scoots closer to the desk. The door opens.

Judy, the secretary, sticks her head inside. "There's a student looking for you." He sees by her raised eyebrows that it can only be Renata, wearing something of a size Judy is trying to convey in advance, lest he suffer a stroke. He feels his prick touch the underside of his desk as she smiles and stands aside. The door opens wide for Rennie, the epitome of innocence from the neck up, with hair in pigtails and a clean bright face. From the shoulders down she's nearly all exposed skin, bursting over and from under a yellow cotton halter top with eyelets and ribbon, her barely covered nipples showing through. Inches below her belly button ring, an incredibly short pair of lace-trimmed cut-offs makes him think she must have shaved her pubic hair entirely.

Judy backs out and closes the door with a solid clunk, making it clear that there's no limit to what these young poets will do, and she knows he will handle it. Richard smiles and lets his eyes work slowly up to Rennie's grinning face. "This is what all the cute little sorority chicks wear, right, professor?"

"Not quite. Come over here, lovely miss."

Renata shoves the blotter to the edge of the desk and lifts her ass and legs, turning and scooting toward him across the black Formica desk in true Renata style. She splits her legs wide around him, sitting directly above his cock. The crotch of the cut-offs, less than an inch wide, barely covers her slit, the fringe of white threads blending with carroty pubic hair. She kisses his forehead and he tilts his face up to give her his mouth, and her tongue goes inside. The edge of the desk cuts into his dick, now fully erect and pounding, but the feeling is not pain, more like the severe pleasure that comes from massaging a sore muscle.

He grazes her thighs with his fingers, back and forth from the inside to the knees, and enjoys her light moans of pleasure. There's a scattering of bumps inside both thighs. He looks down and sucks in a breath. His mind swirls with the possibilities. His erection wanes. "What is this?"

She grabs the insides of her thighs and looks them over, as if seeing the red inflammation for the first time. "Oh, mosquito bites. I thought you knew and were scratching them for me."

He lifts her legs one at a time and sees fifty or more bites on each. He looks closely at her arms and finds the same, somewhat camouflaged by makeup. Now that he looks closely, there are some on her neck and face. "Where the hell did you get these? I haven't seen a mosquito near the beach in years."

She pauses and he wonders if she's concocting a lie. He puts his fingers to her lips. "You don't have to tell me. It was a rhetorical question."

"Rhetorical?"

"I'm just shocked by how chewed up you are. I don't expect an answer."

"Maybe I should take one of your classes. I could learn some new words."

"I'd ruin you."

He looks back at her arms and legs. He can't understand how she can sit still and not scratch herself raw. He feels himself getting hard again, looking at her skin, even as bitten and mottled as it is. "Poor baby."

"Everglades," Renata says. "This time of year —"

"God, Rennie. I thought that was over."

"It is now." She kisses him and runs her fingers up the back of his head, tries to keep her mouth plastered over his.

He breaks away and takes her head firmly in his hands. "Those guys are dangerous, for Christsakes." He remembers the door, zips his pants, and gets up to lock it.

"They can't do nothing now."

He ignores the double negative. "You don't know that."

"I sure do." She whispers, "I got rid of them."

"You . . . killed them?"

She takes his hands and puts her face, as sweet as a ten-year-old's, into them. "Jules helped me." She touches his chin. "It's all over."

She remains on the desk, legs dangling at his sides, hands on his shoulders, and gives the details of the events, how it was necessary, self-defense. He touches her delicately muscled arms. How impossible it all seems. How innocent she is of the law and its mercilessness.

"Don't worry, Richard. Professor, should I call you that here?"

He shakes his head at the lunacy, at all the lunacy.

She lifts his chin. "It's done. The bodies are gone. What do you want me to do for you? That's why I'm here."

"I want you to let me help you, get you a place in the Grove, closer to me, where I can take care of you. I know of a cottage for rent behind a house on Kumquat Street."

"You can't afford that."

"I have a little extra coming in right now. Besides, it's cheap because it's small and in need of repair, but it has a shared pool and laundry facilities. I can help you fix it up – paint and get some furniture. We'll put everything in my name and that way you'll be safe, and I can see you every day."

There's no expression on her face. "No, Richard. What can I do for you now? Blow job, regular? Your secretary is gonna start wondering about how long I'm in here."

He feels anger creeping up his neck. "Rennie, sit in a chair. If I have to forgo the sex to talk to you, then I'll do that. You know I want what I can't buy. I love you."

She slides off the desk and sits in the chair across from him. She's so far away that he wishes he hadn't told her to move. "That's the problem, Richard. I don't want to hurt your feelings – I just don't have what you want. Everything here is for sale – or *rent* is the better word. There's nothing to give you for keeps."

"I'm not going to wait until they find you. Something has to be done now."

She puts her arm across the desk and touches his hand with her fingertips. "Nobody's looking for me. Let me make you feel good. That's what I like to do."

Her touch is light, but invisible wires of passion drag him out of his chair and around the desk until he's kneeling in front of her. His head is light with his idea. "No. Let me make you feel good."

Her eyes glaze over, whether in dreaminess or boredom, and he unzips the cut-offs, determined to make her melt. She lifts her hips from the chair and he struggles to pull down the tight shorts, finally slipping them off her feet. She moves to the edge of the chair and he gets on his knees and bends forward to devour her. The scent of her cunt envelops him and he puts his tongue inside her lips to taste her sweetness. It's been a long time since he's done this. He flicks her clit with his tongue and takes it between his tongue and top lip, pinching it lightly and rubbing back and forth with his tongue. He nuzzles his nose into her soft pubic hair and her salty juice runs down his chin. His tongue trembles, near exhaustion, as she rocks against his mouth for minutes that blend into eternity. Finally, she lets out a long sweet moan, soft and childlike. She twitches, shivers, and relaxes like never before. Richard's chest swells. The old dog still has tricks.

Her eyes are slightly out of focus, and he waits while the glaze diminishes. She smiles at him. "What do I owe you?"

The remark stings, even as a joke, but at the same time, it gives him an opportunity. "You owe me your —"

The sound of a key turning the lock shoots a dart of panic through his brain. His body covers Renata's open vagina from view, but he's kneeling in front of her bare thighs, and her shorts are on the floor next to her feet. He looks over his shoulder.

The door swings fast. Judy is holding a sheet of paper, and behind her in the hall is another face — Tammi. He feels drool on his chin, but doesn't wipe it.

Judy's face pales with embarrassment followed by pain. She backs up in slow motion, as if moving slowly might not disturb the atmosphere and they could go back in time. "Oh, oh — I thought you'd left. This student — I'm so sorry — I said I'd put this in here – so it wouldn't get lost –" She backs out and the door shuts with a bang.

Richard turns to Renata. He can't speak. He wonders if Tammi saw Renata go into his office and manipulated Judy to interrupt.

Renata makes no move to close her legs or reach for her clothes. Her eyes are wide, excited. She ruffles his hair. "Is this a problem?"

His mouth opens. Nothing comes out.

"Should I go tell her that I'm not a student, that you pay me?"

"No."

"I'll say whatever you want. Just tell me."

He's trying to imagine the view from the door. Is there any legitimate reason he could have been kneeling between Renata's thighs? He laughs.

"What can I do?"

He knows Judy respects and admires him and won't want to cause him trouble. He'd only have to mention that Renata is not a student at the university – but she can't ignore the incident with Tammi as witness. He wonders what they said to each other after the door closed. What will Tammi do? Christ.

Renata stands, naked from the waist. He looks at his watch. "Let's wait a few minutes in here until it's time for Judy to leave. I'll call her at home. I have to think." He picks up the shorts and hands them to Rennie. He feels unexpectedly serene. "Don't worry." He holds the armrest of the chair. It's painful to straighten his legs after all that time. His right knee cracks loudly.

She stops, one foot not yet into the pants leg. "What was that?"

"Nothing."

"You okay?" She laughs and pulls up the shorts, zips them, and stands in front of him, her freckled arms and legs so bitten that the spots blend together like a rash. He clenches his teeth.

She needs his guidance and support and he needs her. Nothing else matters.

He'll tell Judy the truth. She'll be relieved not to have to deal with the ethical problems of a student/professor relationship. But what about Tammi? Gossip is bound to flow through the poetry classes.

He offers Renata taxi money, but she says she has a ride in a few minutes. Probably that pimp. Richard focuses on her delicate wrist as she pulls the office door closed behind her.

He sits back down. He can't go home until after he calls Judy. He's not sure when he'll be sane enough to go home and face Linda again. He calls. The voice mail picks up. Just what he hoped to avoid. He can be much more convincing in person.

"Hi, honey. I'm covering a class tonight for Patrick. Emergency. Sorry. Don't make me dinner. I'll get soup at the cafeteria. I should be home a little after ten. Sorry."

His mind is a complete blank. He grades papers for half an hour, then picks up the phone to call Judy. He punches in her number. He breaks out in a sweat. He hangs up.

He knows Judy won't call Linda, but if word gets out at the university, it's only a matter of time until she'll hear from someone. He grades several more papers, then picks up the rest of the stack and puts them into his briefcase. If he loses his job, he might never have to finish them. Is that what he's been working toward anyway – without the guts to take the final step? It was insanity to invite Rennie to his office.

He locks his office door and walks down the empty corridor. He knows every stain on the carpet, anticipates the smell of Pine-sol before he passes the men's room, recognizes each outdated notice on the crumbling cork bulletin board. There's something he's been wanting to do. He sets down his briefcase and grabs a sheet of paper, rips it off the board. He grabs another and another – a poetry contest over a year past submission deadline, a blood drive two weeks past, a program put on by the West Indies Club a month ago – serving meat patties and jerk chicken – he had always meant to attend one of those. One by one, he rips off every notice, including two for events in the coming week. He can't stand the thought of them remaining there for months or years to come. Thumbtacks and pins fall to the floor. He crumples the papers into a wad and stuffs them under his arm for the next trash can he passes. Now he can stand to look at the empty board – although staples holding the remaining paper corners make his skin crawl. The sameness is nauseating, twenty years of it behind him. Not so much to lose here. Everything to gain if he uses his imagination.

He stops at the trash and stuffs in the paper. It's not the recycle bin, but fuck it. He leaves the cold air-conditioning, maybe forever, and walks out into the warm humidity. The sun is low and there's a breeze. But the good feeling lasts only a moment. He can't go home yet, or he'll have to make up another lie. He gets into the car and backs out. A beer will help calm him – or maybe a single malt scotch. There's Flamingo Pub right down the street.

He takes a seat at the bar and orders a double shot of Glenfiddich. He would go more expensive, but that's the best they have. His eyes wander around the walls, hesitating on a beer poster, a softball trophy, a punched place in the cheap paneling where somebody demonstrated his strength and intelligence. Shabby. This is another place where he's spent hours of his life, looking like a poet, scribbling ideas and phrases on cocktail napkins – as a poet should do. Those thoughts seemed so important.

He sees two students come in, guys from his Tuesday-Thursday comp class a year or two ago. Maybe a night class was cancelled – or else they live in the neighborhood. They look at him and nod. He can't remember what grade he gave either of them. They don't seem enthusiastic to see him. They go to the other end of the bar. He wonders if they've heard something already. They might be ignoring him to keep from snickering. Impossible.

He picks up the scotch and takes a sip, swirls it and sips again. Maybe he'll just become a drunk. That would fix everything. Live in a crummy room, drink cheap wine, and eat a few meals a week on the $300 a month retirement he is already eligible for. The Charles Bukowski lifestyle — it worked for him. He laughs into his shot glass, almost spills it. A crummy room at The Moons would be just fine. Renata. If he could be near her, he wouldn't need to be a drunk.

Of course, becoming a drunk might be difficult. Lately, after two or three drinks, all he wants to do is sleep. But if things get bad enough, who knows? He's spent most of his life as a model child, an ambitious young man, a loving father and faithful husband — a misspent old age seems beyond allowable, into deserving.

"Another, please," he tells the bartender. "Two more." This time he doesn't feel tired. He feels better. He watches the bartender pour the sparkling liquid above the rim of the shot glass and set it in front of him without spilling. He watches the second one, liquid gold. No need to make a big issue of this. Cunnilingus in the office is frowned upon, certainly, but he hasn't heard of it as cause for automatic dismissal. Actually, he hasn't heard of it at all. He laughs. Surely he isn't the first. He takes another long sip, letting his top lip extend over the glass, dipping it into the divine musty spirits. The liquid no longer tingles on his tongue. It slides down his throat leaving a trail like cream.

Of course, the details would be taken into account — married man, prostitute, oral sex during office hours, a young female student observing. Not the best of circumstances, but surely Tammi is no virgin, no psychological harm. Would oral sex be taken more lightly than penetration? He's not sure about the political climate. Eatin' ain't cheatin'? Not a chance with Linda. He'd have to admit everything and his marriage would be over. Office hours — technically, he was being paid for the time during which his face was buried in Renata's sweet fragrant cunt, but in consideration of all the grading he's done at home and on weekends, he's made up for those few stolen minutes hundreds of times over. He lets the last of the scotch roll into his mouth, holding it, feeling the delicious richness before he swallows. Two doubles makes four drinks, and he doesn't feel sleepy at all.

CHAPTER 22

7:00 pm, Coral Gables

Renata

It's a calm evening. Renata gazes at the sparkling water of the swimming pool outside the bedroom window. The delicate ferns and jungle foliage surrounding it transport her into a private paradise as she slides her head back and forth on Dean's cock. She hears his wife Jeri's groans from a distance, the other side of the king-sized bed, and feels content. From the sounds of it, Francisco is doing his best work. Renata opens her eyes to look at Dean's face. He's watching the other two with his jaw hanging, not worried that his wife might die of pleasure from another man, happy for her. He's already come once earlier inside Jeri, while Renata licked around the edges of the transaction and Francisco brought up the rear. Renata looks for a signal, wondering if Dean wants to fuck. Seems like hours he's had his hands on both sides of her head controlling the rhythm, plastering her hair against the sides of her head. She'll have a saucy poof when he's finished. Nothing like giving a blow job to reshape the coif — and work up an appetite. She thinks about Cuban food, chicken, rice and beans, plantains.

She looks at Dean hopefully. His eyes close. More of the same. He can do this for hours and then come in a second if he hears his wife finish.

Renata thinks about high school, her early mastering of the blow job. It was something you didn't talk about to the other girls, but they knew that's why you had dates every night. She'd been giving hand jobs to her cousin in the basement since she was old enough to pull down a zipper, so blow jobs were the next step. She enjoyed the feeling of silky skin gliding across her lips and never had the tendency to gag. Swallowing the warm mouthfuls of semen used to remind her of eating a salty soft-boiled egg, with something tangy, like lemon, added. That was before she tasted oysters. The high school boys were vulnerable to her from the start, but she never took advantage. They looked like sleepy children while she was doing them, eyes half closed, no cares – regardless of what touchdown wasn't scored or what free throw missed the basket. They could count on her when nothing else could make the pain go away. It was all the same to her to make them feel good.

That was the problem. It was all the same. Everything was. By seventeen she quit school and got her first job rolling joints for a friend's mother. Not really a paid job, but room and board, as long as she had sex with the woman and her boyfriend. They took care of all her needs. There was nothing she wanted then, besides sex and drugs – still the basics.

Dean starts with his huffing noise. Another minute or two and he'll come. Renata glances at Jeri from the corner of her eye. She's on her hands and knees, her head hanging between her shoulders aimed toward the fancy carved headboard that looks like organ pipes from a church, especially by candlelight. Francisco's still working hard behind her, but she's run out of fuel to make any noise. Her salmon-pink nails dig into the pillow, kneading like a cat. She arches her back and goes into another orgasm. Renata looks at her delicate white shoulder blades, the graceful line of her neck shining with sweaty curls.

She's built a lot like Jules. Beautiful, innocent Jules, she has no idea of the pleasures two women can share.

Dean is behind schedule. Renata tightens her lips and uses her fingers like milking a cow. She thinks again of those years living with Lenore, the first woman in her life, and Lenore's boyfriend. What was his name? On Christmas Eve, Lenore would make homemade eggnog and the two of them would sit at the kitchen table in their flannel nightgowns and roll forty or fifty joints with decorated papers, to hang on the tree for the holiday season. It was the happiest of times, knowing you could walk into the living room, grab one of the tight little bundles and light it up, any time of day or night. Everybody was in good spirits. After a few days the decorations got scarce because of all the friends who would drop in and help themselves, and by New Year's the branches were empty, but sometimes, if you looked hard and were real lucky, you'd find one camouflaged by tinsel or hidden near the trunk.

Dean's huffs are getting more regular and Renata is careful to keep the same tension and rhythm with her fingers and tongue. His hands clamp her ears tight and she stops moving her mouth and hand, as he lets loose of that hot oyster into the back of her throat. She holds still while he finishes, then swallows, gathers saliva, and swallows again. "Only for you, sweetie," she says. Making people happy always makes her feel good. She kisses him politely on the cheek and gets up.

Jeri is slumped on the pillow, face to the side, eyes closed. Renata reaches over to catch a few strands of her hair with one finger, moving them away from Jeri's mouth. The corner of Jeri's lip goes up in a half-smile, a thank you, the only gesture she has the strength to make. Francisco sits back on his knees, pulling off the condom, then wiping his balls with an antibacterial towelette. All in a day's work, his job, like any other. Of course, he gets to come in the bargain, but he's barely broken a sweat, only enough to make his perfect toffee skin shine in the candlelight. She expects he'll do her later, when she tells him about the expedition into the swamp.

Dean puts his arm out for Jeri to move over and put her head on his shoulder. She smiles and moves next to him, and his arm goes around her. Renata gets dressed and meets Francisco in the dining room. As always, the money is inside a pretty card on the table.

On the way home they stop on Calle Ocho to pick up Cuban food. Francisco unpacks it on the table at Renata's.

"Check the news," Renata says.

"For what?" He turns on the TV.

Renata pulls off her clothes and throws them into the laundry basket, heading into the shower, her stomach grinding from the delicious smell. "You'll know if you see it," she calls. "It's a secret. I'll tell you when Jules gets home."

"You and Julie have a secret?"

"Uh-uh. We'll tell you, if you're a good boy."

Francisco pokes his head inside the shower curtain, sticks his tongue out and flicks it like a snake. "Oooh, that hurts."

"Huh?"

"The little piece that attaches the tongue. It's sore from so much licking, grating on my bottom teeth. Nothing much on the news. Want a beer?"

"Sure."

As Renata finishes her last plantain, she hears Jules moving around. "I'll have to bring her over. You make her a vodka. She doesn't take orange juice anymore." Renata pulls a long t-shirt over her head and picks up her hairbrush. "Did you ever drink squeeze?"

"Huh?"

She works hard at a clump of tangles. "Squeeze — the only thing worse than straight vodka. Once when my foster parents ran out of money for booze, they got the Sterno out of the hurricane supplies and ran it through slices of white bread — drank it. Said it reminded them of their youth. They always had some way to get high. I tried it — disgusting."

"Don't think I've ever been that desperate."

She puts down the hairbrush. "I give up on this."

She walks out into the hall and knocks on Jules' door. No answer. She opens it. The light is on in the bathroom, the door still closed. "Hey, girlie. What's up? Are you busy in there?"

Jules opens the door and pops her head out. She's fresh from the shower, wrapped in a towel, but her face is puffy and tired, eyes red.

"Wow, sweetie, I guess there's actually enough hot water in this building for two of us to shower on the same night, huh?"

"Yeah, amazing," Jules says, her voice barely audible.

"Hey, I'm here to perk you up. Don't bother getting dressed, just throw on a nightie or something and come on over. Time to tell Francisco about yesterday's adventure. Celebrate."

"No, I don't think so – I'm not feeling that well."

"I hope you haven't been bawling over those dickheads."

"I don't know. Them and other things. I can't stop thinking about – all of it." She sobs and puts her hand over her mouth. "It's so horrible. I don't know what to do."

"What's there to do? It's over. Everything is okay now."

"It can never be okay again."

"I'm not letting you sit here. C'mon." Renata puts her fingers inside the towel at the gap between Jules' tits and gives it a tug toward her. Jules grabs the towel tight to her body, as if Renata seeing her small breasts and curly little snatch would be a problem. "I mean it," Renata says. "I'll wrestle you down and drag you over naked if I have to."

Jules bites her lip. "Okay. It doesn't matter what I do. Get me something out of the dresser? Please? I don't have anything in here. Top drawer."

Renata crosses the room and turns on a light. She digs through the drawer until she finds a thin pale blue cotton nightshirt. It looks like new. "Here, honey. This is pretty. We've got a drink waiting for you." She hands the nightshirt through the door. Jules has stepped back.

"Oh, not this. Sorry. It's too thin. It's for a special occasion."

"How much more special can it get than a night with me

and Francisco? Huh? Put it on, baby." There's no answer. "Julie?" The door closes. She wonders if Jules is having some kind of breakdown. She opens the door glimpsing dark pussy hair, as Jules pulls the shirt down over her hips. It fits her slim body nicely, nipples clearly outlined, dark triangle between her thighs. Renata looks at her face. "Are you okay, Jul? How long have you been here crying and making yourself sick?"

"A while. Besides everything else, I lost my job. I have no money for food or rent."

"Good. I mean, you were wasting your time for the lousy tips over there. She fire you because of the missing cash?"

"She didn't accuse me. It could be, or else it had to do with drinking — and coming in late. I don't blame her, either way."

"Don't worry about a thing. You got me and Francisco to help you out."

"I know. I've been thinking about that. But I'd have a hard time with becoming a . . ."

"Pleasure enabler? Think of all the jobs that cause pain instead of pleasure — dentist, cop, dogcatcher . . . Without people like us and alcohol and drugs, the world would be way out of balance." She tugs at Jules' shirt. "C'mon. Francisco's waiting with the drinks."

Renata takes Jules by the hand and into her apartment. Francisco comes out of the bathroom in fresh shirt and jeans. His hair is wet and curly. "*Hola*, my hot mamas, pajama party?" He points to a plastic cup of vodka on the table next to the bottle, takes his beer, and sits on the bed.

Jules is standing by the door. Renata picks up the cup. "Come here, sit down. We have something to tell Franco."

Jules hesitates and then shrugs and walks over. Renata hands her the cup and sits down with her back to the window, leaving room for Jules to sit between her and Francisco and lean on the pillows against the wall.

Francisco puts his hand on Jules' knee and squeezes. "So what you girls been up to, eh?"

Jules looks at Renata. "You tell. I can't."

Renata picks up one of Francisco's bare feet and massages his toes. "We killed those fuckers."

Francisco's face loses a few shades of tan. "What fuckers?"

"The swamp fuckers." She explains what they did, and Jules nods, paler than usual. "No more problems from those assholes."

Francisco shakes his head, his jaw clenched. He jumps out of the bed. "Fuck. This scares the shit out of me." He looks up at the ceiling, his hands in the air.

"What? They were gonna kill us. That's what this is all about. We got them first."

Francisco's eyes dart around the room. He sits back down. "What if somebody finds out? Then we're really dead meat. I can't believe you did this!"

"We cleaned up and got out of there before anybody saw us."

Jules looks at Renata. "What about —"

"Oh, one minor problem." Renata explains about the red convertible. "But they didn't see us, or didn't care. Besides, we were in the bartender's car."

Francisco drops onto the bed with a groan of defeat. "Fuck. That's not good either. They see the license?"

Renata shakes her head no. "The grass was too high. They didn't even slow down."

"I hope you're right. I know whose car that is, and he ain't sociable. I think he's related to the *pendejo* with the ponytail. Whoever he is, we don't want him around here. I'm thinking they could have mafia connections."

"They don't look like any kind of mafia. Let's have a toast." Renata raises her beer. "To the end of this."

Francisco grits his teeth and touches his bottle against Renata's. His face is still pale.

Jules cringes, but she bucks her plastic cup of vodka against each beer bottle and drinks.

Francisco looks from Renata to Jules and back. "Okay, let's try to forget about it. I brought us a treat." He focuses on

Renata. "X, baby. Wanna?"

"Got enough for Jul?"

"Sure do – two hits each, if we feel like it."

"No, I don't –"

Renata reaches for Jules' arm and strokes it. "Ooh, you'll like it, honey. X is lovely. I guarantee."

Jules pulls her legs up and crosses them under the nightie. "Ecstasy? I read that makes your brain bleed."

"I don't know. Maybe." Renata crosses her eyes. "All of a sudden, you're worried about a little blood?"

"Rennie –" Jules pleads.

"Sorry. Bad joke." She pats her hand. "It doesn't hurt. Promise. It makes everything in you and around you feel good, like one solid orgasm – for hours. You don't even have to take your clothes off to enjoy it."

"I thought it was for having sex."

"Not really – until it's pretty much worn off. Sipping water is so good, I think sex would kill you!" She laughs. "Stroking is nice."

Francisco says, "I'm taking my pants off. It's hot in here."

"Okay by me. Okay, Jules?"

"I might not stay."

"Look. It's really totally fantastic. We'll all be peaceful and rock in each other's arms."

Francisco puts two small tan pills into Renata's hand. He puts one into his mouth and slugs the beer. Rennie downs one with her beer and holds the last pill toward Jules. "Here, baby, you don't want to be behind."

Jules picks up the Ecstasy with her thumb and middle finger and looks at it.

"Go ahead. You need it tonight."

Jules shrugs. "Okay. Hell. My brain hasn't been doing me much good as it is." She puts the pill back on her tongue and swallows it with the vodka.

Renata strokes her neck. "No more vodka. Just water for the rest of the night. It's better that way."

Francisco pulls off his pants and sits on the bed in his box-ers.

"Wow — underwear," Renata says. "A treat."

He waves her remark away and turns to Jules. "No messing with knives or dangerous objects. Nobody will be able to drive you to the hospital."

"You're the only dangerous object, Franco." Renata laughs. "She's not a moron. She'll be fine."

Francisco goes to the TV and changes the channel. "I'll put on some music video while we wait for it to work."

"No news is good news." Renata reaches for a brush from the windowsill. "Would you mind brushing out my hair and braiding it, Jul? It's all tangled."

CHAPTER 23

9:30 pm, Coral Gables

Richard

He looks at his watch. He has a half-hour to kill in order to arrive home at the appropriate time from a three-hour class. The students are within view at the end of the bar. The scotch makes him feel bold, and he thinks about buying them each a beer and telling them the facts. At least then they'd have the truth before gossip distorted every detail. They're young and horny – they'll understand. He finishes the scotch. No. They'd think he was insane.

He might as well head over to South Beach. Rennie is no doubt busy, but he can pick a nice outdoor place on Lincoln Road and have some dinner by himself, take a walk under the stars and let some of the booze wear off. He'll tell Linda he was starving, and it was too late to be banging around in the kitchen. With luck she'll be asleep when he gets home. She might not be looking forward to seeing him either.

He goes out to the car and takes a sweeping glance at the night sky. Can't see many stars with all the lights – no lucky ones. He rolls the windows down and feels the cool breeze as he drives. Never worry about a change. Change is good. No sense in dragging everyone into the pit. If it's gone, then it's meant to be. He pulls into the parking lot on Meridian near the mall. No spots. Even on a Wednesday night, parking is a disaster. Fuck. He drives into a second lot. Still none. Fuck. Always a hassle. He won't pay over ten dollars to valet it. He drives all the way east to Collins without finding a spot. This puts him very near to Renata's. He continues down the next block. There's a parking meter open. Amazing. He takes it.

Richard drops several quarters into the meter and walks toward The Moons. He hasn't brought himself here on purpose. Fate created the space. What does it matter? Renata won't be home and he'll find a restaurant and have dinner. He walks through the bar, glancing to see if she might be having a drink, and continues up the stairs. As he approaches her door, he hears talking inside. He stops. Rennie and a man – probably that Fernando idiot – maybe someone else too. God, who knows? The words are soft and Richard can't pick up anything. They might be having sex. A quiver takes hold of him. He doesn't dare knock. She might tell him never to come back. He wants to tell her that nothing matters about his job anymore. He doesn't want her to worry about him. He goes down to the bar.

He orders a scotch and remembers he's had quite a few. Maybe he can become a drunk after all. He sits facing the stairway so he can see if anyone leaves. How long does she spend with them anyway?

He sips. It wouldn't be a bad life to live here with a bar in the building and the beach a few steps away. He wouldn't need much money, if he kept the drinking to a minimum. He could put in some serious writing time. Have it all, Rennie and a creative life. The thought makes him feel like a kid again. He sips the scotch. Nobody has left upstairs. He can't sit still any longer. The room shifts in his vision. He puts his feet on the floor. The beach will refresh him if he walks through the tide and lets the foam rush across his ankles. He pays the tab and heads south toward the widest part of the beach.

A half-moon creates a sparkling trail across the waves, following at his side — like a faithful dog. The moon is a faithful dog. He wonders if that would work in a poem. Probably not without the scotch. He swerves just in time to avoid a palm.

The air has a thick presence. There's a feeling of swimming in the stickiness of salt and sea life, a strong sensation he enjoys. He passes through barely moving shadows of palms under yellow streetlights that line the beach. What man — or poet — could ask for more than this? He laughs. The men and poets who have met Renata! They live their lives in painful desire.

He feels himself sway as he crosses the street. He cuts across the sand through the obstacle course of rental wooden lounge chairs turned on their sides. He chooses a chair close to the water and rights it, misjudging the height as he drops to sit. The sudden stop would be jarring if he had any feeling. A cool breeze comes up from the ocean, and he stretches out comfortably, his hands behind his head, and looks up at the Big Dipper.

CHAPTER 24

Midnight, Tropical Moons, Room 2-B

Jules

She takes the brush and picks up a handful of Renata's heavy strawberry-blonde curls from her right shoulder and then her left, pulling them back to work on the tangled ends. She can't feel the Ecstasy yet, but she's letting herself drift, as she's been told to. There's nothing left of normal life, after all. She's miserable with the effort of living. The goal of becoming a writer — or anyone her father will be proud of — might as well be abandoned. She's willing to leave the night, and maybe the rest of her life, to chance — and Renata. She begins section-ing and gently separating the voluminous quantity of hair, brushing downward and then upward, until she has three smooth sections. She enjoys the softness as she weaves the thick braid. When she finishes, Jules pulls the heavy hair off Renata's neck, and seeing the damp hairs underneath, blows to cool her delicate white neck. She bends and kisses Rennie on the side of her neck.

Rennie looks up with a slow smile.

Jules stands to reach her drink, but her legs are rubbery. She sits back down on the bed.

Rennie leans against Francisco and puts her hand out to stroke Jules' arm. Her fingers go inside the edge of the nightshirt near the armpit. Jules holds her shoulder back to allow the finger to move in farther, to encourage the tingle rushing down her body. Rennie smiles and draws her finger from Jules' arm up to the collarbone, then continues to stroke from shoulder to palm. The room fades. Only touch is real. It seems that Rennie will stroke her in the same satisfying motion forever.

She finds that Francisco is stroking one thigh and Rennie the other. Jules' knees are crossed and the nightie bunched up so that her pubic hair is exposed. Neither of them is looking. They're staring into her eyes. She thinks that she should be embarrassed, but she's not. She stares back unblinking for a long time, going deeper and deeper into Rennie's large black pupils, fascinated. She can't remember what embarrassment feels like. These are her very best friends who love her and whom she loves. Jules pushes up Rennie's long t-shirt and looks at the beautiful red pubic hair so close to her fingers. Rennie smiles and takes Jules' hand and places it there, rubbing up and down until Jules begins to move her hand herself.

At some point the rocking starts. Jules wonders if she's doing it herself. Forward and back, forward and back, between them, looking into their eyes, feeling the sway of their bodies. She knows they feel the same love for her as she feels for them.

Francisco's watch is on the windowsill. It was 12:30 – hours ago – and now it's five till one. Time is not passing. Jules is rocking, rocking, or is it rolling? Yes. It's smoother than rocking. Smooth as silk, smooth as ice cream. Why did she ever worry about taking drugs?

She looks at Renata and Francisco, rocking or wavering, a little blurred around the edges. Their eyes look like cats'. Their faces are like sweet angels. Jules never has to blink, or move a finger, or her tongue inside her mouth. She can't tell if she's breathing.

Renata begins to stroke down her shoulder and chest and stomach and thigh, long sweeps, the lightest touch through her nightie like butterfly wings. Her body turns into soft rushes of pleasure. Her body is lovely, and she might be having an orgasm, a long, long one, but she might not, and it doesn't matter, just so it never stops.

After hours or days, Renata moves, and there's a glass of water near Jules' lips, Renata offering her a drink. Where did the glass come from? She sips gently. It's not normal tap water – something smoother in her mouth, clinging to her tongue, but not really. She remembers how to swallow. The water shimmers at the edges of the glass, beautiful, like mercury.

It's five a.m. when Jules begins to understand the concept of time. She's lying with her head on Rennie's thigh. She doesn't want to know that the drug is wearing off, but there's no doubt. She tries to savor the feeling, but she can no longer lie paralyzed, and enjoy herself. She sits up. Renata and Francisco are kissing, sucking each other's lips and gasping for air when they let go before locking together again.

Jules realizes they are going to have sex inches away from her. Francisco pushes Rennie down on the bed and climbs on top of her, his dark legs straddling her creamy light ones, her red pubic hair shining in the soft rays from between the curtains. His dark, hard penis pokes at Rennie's pink flesh, and Rennie lifts her hips to help him find the place. It's beautiful to watch their bodies together. She can't move her eyes from Francisco's penis sliding in and coming out of Renata, more shining with her juice every time.

Renata moves her head into view, eyes wild. Her voice is husky. "Julie, you okay?"

"Yes," she says. She can't think of anything else.

"Give me a kiss then, sweetie."

Jules moves up and Francisco sits back on his haunches to give her room. Renata puts her hands out and takes Jules' face, guiding it to her lips, kissing her and letting her tongue go inside, sucking her lips, and entwining her fingers in Jules' hair. "Join us?"

"No."

Renata moves back onto Francisco, and Jules breathes them in, the smell of sex, like the ocean — or like Venice — a place she's never been.

"I love you, Rennie," Jules says.

"I love you too," Rennie says.

"I love women," Francisco says.

Caution is returning, but the world has changed in many ways that Jules never would have dreamed or wished for. She slips off the bed and goes back to her room.

CHAPTER 25

October 7, 6:30 am, South Beach, 78 degrees

Richard

His eyes open to a gray morning sky. The sound of crashing waves tells him that he's on the beach. He raises his head and puts it back down. The wood bench feels like rock pressing directly on his brain. He thinks. Single malt scotch is not supposed to cause a hangover. He moves his arm slowly toward his face and opens one eye a crack to read his watch. What day? Panic rises through the layer of nausea in his stomach. He never went home. He gazes at the clouds. Was it only yesterday that Renata visited his office? Impossible, but correct.

He drags himself up and slumps on the chair, facing the ocean. There isn't a hair on his body that doesn't hurt. A ghost crab skates sideways across his sandy oxford, its eyes on stalks searching his face, as if Richard could move fast enough to grab it. He looks across the road at the hotels and restaurants. Delivery people and early morning runners have appeared. They move quickly, with purpose in life that he has lost. Renata. She's sleeping a few blocks away.

He straightens his collar and brushes sand from his pants.

He's completely out of place on the beach. It's surprising that the police let him sleep there all night. Now in the sunlight, wrinkled and sweating, he has the appearance and smell of a vagrant. There's little traffic and the street looks amazingly wide. He crosses to a café. He needs some water and juice before he dehydrates and dies.

He cleans up as much as possible in the men's room and then forces himself to eat. The eggs are only halfway down his throat as he begins the trek back to the car, feeling worse. He has to feed the meter before he gets towed again. Before he realizes it, his steps have led back to the bar at Rennie's. Led by his dick – the expression applies, but what of it? The goals that propelled him through most of his life have come up short. His dick deserves a chance to lead before it gets too old.

There are two men and one woman already imbibing when he steps inside. The air conditioning is cranking out cool air for a change, since the day hasn't warmed up, and he feels a slight relief as he sinks onto a stool and orders a bloody Mary, the appropriate daybreak drink. The others have beers in cans, no need to appear socially acceptable. He drinks the bloody Mary fast and chases it with a beer. This is his new scene.

He remembers his last trip upstairs and the voices coming from Rennie's door. He finishes the beer, pays the tab, and walks slowly up the steps.

There's no sound. He puts his ear to the door. Nothing. He knocks softly, in case she's sleeping. He waits. He knocks again.

The door opens. Rennie sticks her head around the door. Seeing Richard she steps out. She's naked, and her flaming pussy seems to angle toward his face. He steps in front of her to try to cover her on one side.

"Richard, what are you doing?" she whispers.

He catches the intake of a snore and sees a dark head and shoulders on the bed, the punk pimp. Something explodes inside his chest.

He swallows hard. "I need to talk to you. I waited on the

beach all night."

She shakes her head with a look of disgust. "Waited for what? Go home."

"A kiss? Can I have a good morning kiss to get me through the day?"

She moves forward and fits her naked body into his arms, but he knows her only purpose is to get him out of there fast. He glances at the bed. No movement from the bastard. He runs his hands down her silken back to the heaven of her ass and clutches her delicate frame to him, as he slides his tongue between her lips and works her mouth. Waves of pleasure hot wire his cock.

She pushes him away. "Go home, Richard. I'm busy here."

He realizes his breath might be a problem. He nods toward the bed. "Doesn't look like you're busy. Come out for a wake-up drink."

"I don't get up this early. Go get yourself another one, and you'll be all ready for work." She slides behind the door and it closes.

He stands there for a minute, staring at the grime and fingerprints on the doorframe. He looks down at his shirt and pants. He can't go home and face Linda in this condition. He can't teach his class, His presence is unwanted by everyone he knows – except the students, whom he is preparing to neglect. He looks at his watch – nine – he needs to call Judy.

He walks down the stairs and takes a seat at the bar. The kindness of strangers will have to do. Yes, he can become a drunk after all.

By noon his own bottle of scotch is a comfort before him. He's been involved in one conversation after another, politics, TV, poetry. They drink and leave; he stays. He barely blinks when he looks at his watch and notices that he missed his afternoon class and never called in.

It's dusk when he wakes up on a different bench by the water. He feels scummy but not sick. Must be drunk still, he tells himself, but he can walk fine. Time has flown. He walks closer to the water and strips off his shoes, shirt, and pants, piling them so as to pick up less sand. His arms are bright pink below the lines of his short shirtsleeves, and he can assume his face and neck are also. He strolls into the cool surf in his Calvin Kleins to neck deep and scrubs at his arms and face. In a few minutes he's feeling cleansed and ready to start the night – at Renata's. Surely, she has some spare time at last. He wrings the seat of his shorts and puts his clothes back on. The relief of cool night air gives him energy and he uses it to walk quickly in Renata's direction.

As he passes Jules' door, he hears the TV. On impulse, he knocks. Jules opens the door and frowns.

"Hi. Just in the neighborhood and thought I'd stop. Have a minute?" Voices become loud from next door, and Richard glances in that direction.

"I don't give out that kind of information."

Richard puts his hand up. "No, no. I wasn't going to ask anything like that. I wanted to apologize for last time we spoke. I was upset, and I believe I was rude."

"Yes, you were."

"I'm sorry, really. If you're Rennie's friend, it's important to me to be your friend too. I know you're writing a novel, and I meant to ask you about it until we got on the wrong track. Thought we might have a drink or something and talk – a little literary discussion." He motions downstairs.

"No. Come on in. I don't feel like socializing with the street crowd tonight." She opens the door wider and Richard walks in. "It was partly my fault that you were upset. I wasn't very tactful." She points to a chair at the table. "I have vodka if you want some straight."

"Fine." Richard knows that he's about to mix vodka with a day of beer, scotch, and no lunch, except for some chips. His grandmother's saying comes to him out of the blue – "Beer after wine, just fine; wine after beer, oh dear." Something like that. Vodka and scotch not covered at all. He laughs to himself as he watches Jules take the bottle from the refrigerator and pour a third of a tumbler, which she hands to him. She pours a taller one for herself and brings it to the table. He clinks his glass against hers. "Truce," he says.

Jules nods and takes a sip. "I don't know what we'll talk about. I haven't written anything but shit, and it hardly matters anymore."

Richard is taken aback by the harshness in her tone, but he understands the feeling, and realizes that this isn't her first drink of the day. "You've given up?" He looks around the room and cocks his head at louder voices coming through Renata's wall. He wishes he were alone so he could listen. "It's difficult to work under these conditions."

"These are the conditions I chose. The problem is, I'm no writer. I've failed. I keep hoping that one day a story will roll itself out for me like a red carpet to fame and fortune – but I doubt it, and I won't kill myself over it."

"At least you don't waste your life worrying."

Jules laughs. "Oh, I'll probably be 'wasted' all right. I just won't have to waste myself because I'll have help."

He takes Jules' hand across the table. "What's going on? Something to do with the Everglades affair?"

Jules shakes her head wildly, as if she can't believe his question. "Yeah – I've killed a man and aided in the killing of two others. Think about it. If I were writing this plot, would I be heading for a happy ending?"

He lets go of her hand and sits back in the chair. "No, but truth is stranger than fiction, as you know."

"Lately." Jules looks at him glumly enough to make him hesitate, but he continues with what he tells the students, not surprised that even half drunk he can spout it so easily – "Reward and punishment in life are rarely fair – whereas just deserts are the backbone of good fiction. We create structure, balance, and logic that are lacking in reality. It's the art of fiction that keeps us hopeful – a way of experiencing perfection that has never existed in our world. Poetry helps too, in understanding our –"

"So I might get away with murder because life isn't fair."

"Somewhat dependent on luck, wouldn't you say?"

"I've never been lucky."

He turns his palms toward the ceiling for drama. He can tell it's a drunken movement, but it feels good. "So, what about a reversal?"

Jules laughs and Richard sees that he's finally getting on her good side. It will be helpful to have her influence on Rennie.

"In fiction?" she asks.

"In life. In fiction you'd have to learn your lesson in order to change. The lesson is what you want to avoid right now."

"I don't know. My life is falling apart. I'm a murderer, for God's sake."

He pauses, running low on arguments. "True, you used poor judgment, but there's a gray area —"

"I should have turned myself in right away. I might still. Take my chances and leave Rennie out of it."

Richard puts his glass down hard, thinking the table top was lower than it is. "No. Really. She'd get tied in — go straight to prison. Think about her lifestyle."

Jules rubs her eyes with her fists, rubs and rubs. Richard wonders if she'll ever stop. Then she takes a long, slow drink of the vodka. Finally she looks at him. "So, Professor, what do you suggest?"

"Save a life to replace the one you took — the lawyer's. The others don't count for much."

Jules' eyes are bleary. She starts to laugh wildly. The ice clinks in her glass and vodka sloshes onto her shirt. She chokes out, "Save a whale, save a manatee! What are you talking about?"

Richard sees that she's losing control. He's not sure she'll remember anything he says. He's not sure he will either. He grabs her wrists to make an impression and pulls her down hard into the chair. Her glass goes flying, hits the floor, and breaks.

"I'm talking about Rennie. I know you love her and you know I do. We're the only two people on earth who can save her. Help me do that."

She stands halfway up and strains against Richard's hands that still clutch her wrists. "I already said I would save Rennie. I'll sacrifice myself. Fuck. I just told you that."

"The only way you can save her is to get her out of here. Convince her to come with me —"

Jules sits back down. "With you?" She stares. "What am I supposed to do when she's gone?"

Richard lets go of her wrists and slams the flat of his hand on the table. "I'm telling you how to save her life!"

Jules looks at him and whispers, "I've heard you begging. I know what you're trying to do."

Richard takes a breath and looks into the glass of vodka. "What do you mean, you've heard me begging?"

CHAPTER 26

9:00 pm, Tropical Moons, Room 2-A

Jules

She points to the faded beach scene on the wall. She feels sorry for Richard, but she wants him to understand she's no fool — at least not his fool. "Okay, Professor Dick. Move that picture. See what you hear. See if you can take it."

His mouth drops open, but he stands and walks to the wall, looking at Jules.

"Go ahead." She motions to the picture.

He lifts it off the nail and sets it on the floor. His face has a look of disgust, but he puts the side of his head into the rectangular hole. Jules watches his eyes. She sees them go blank, then widen, then close. He looks at the floor. "Who is it? Who's over there?" he asks.

Jules shakes her head. "It's her work."

"You love her. Don't you want to save her from this? One day she'll die. One way or another. It's dangerous. It's sick."

"If I ran over there with scissors every time I wanted to save her, I'd have a dozen dead men on my hands by now. You'd be one of them."

He reaches to rehang the picture and stops. He groans and finishes the job. "You should seal that hole."

"She likes me to listen."

He drops back into his chair. "You're probably right." He rests his chin on his hand and looks at Jules. She knows he's running scenes through his mind, trying to remember how much he might have revealed, wondering how much Jules has heard of his love-making.

"I understand," she says. "I feel the same way you do – only worse. I'm worried I might be a lesbian – I've never felt this strongly about any man."

Richard looks Jules up and down. He takes her hand lightly. "No. It's Renata. She's supernatural. There's no man or woman alive – probably no mammal, fish, or reptile either – given the chance – who wouldn't fall in love with her."

Jules nods slowly, gets up, and smiles. "You're right. Let's not forget Pepe." She crunches through broken glass to the cabinet, goes to the refrigerator and pours another vodka. There's laughter coming from Renata's. Richard hands his glass over for a refill.

He drinks half of it, the effects becoming obvious even to Jules. "I have no playsh – place – to go," he says, "nothing to do. My job is fucked, and my wife will divorce me, soon as she hears. All I want to do is stay here, close to Renata. End all that. If Renata won't come with me, I'll stay where I can see her every day."

"Where?"

He points into the air. "This hotel."

"Not a good idea."

He ignores her. "There must be a room open here."

Jules looks at the clock. "Go home. Desk is closed. Find out tomorrow."

"I'll stay here."

"Here? No. There's no room."

"I'll just sleep here with my head on the table. In the morning – get my own playsh." He puts his glass aside and rests his face on the table.

Jules stands up. "No, you can't stay. Get out of here." She's panicked at the thought. "Get the hell out!" He doesn't move. She walks to the other side of the table and shakes his shoulder. She yells into his ear, "Get up, asshole! Get up!" She moves his head from side to side roughly, she lifts his hand and lets it thud on the table. "Fuck," she says.

The door opens. "You okay –" Renata steps inside wearing a towel. "I heard a glass break then –" She stops. "Oh, fuck."

Jules tries to walk towards her and hits her hip on the corner of the table. She stops and holds herself up. "Won't go home."

Renata walks to Jules and rubs her hip. "Fuck. You okay, Julie? You all been drinking, huh? He's a goner. Just let him stay there. He'll fall on the floor and be out of your way."

"He's going to cause trouble for you."

"No. Don't worry. Just go to bed. We'll get rid of him in the morning. I don't want you hurting yourself trying to move him, okay?" She starts to guide Jules toward her bed. "Ouch. What's that? Damn."

Jules watches as Renata picks a piece of glass from her heel. Blood is flowing. Jules can't think where she keeps Band-Aids. "Sorry," she says. "Sorry." She's so tired she can hardly move. She feels Renata holding her, backing her up then moving forward. Are they dancing? She doesn't know, but it's nice. She feels herself guided into the bed, a quick kiss on her lips. Rennie is a blurred vision above her. She reaches out and her hands touch cool, soft flesh, lovely, lovely breasts. She's pressed down, Rennie's warm mouth covering hers, colors spinning in her head.

Jules opens her eyes to sunlight. She closes them. Too bright. She reaches for the curtain to pull it closed without looking. Fog is starting to clear from her brain and she recognizes the hangover, headache and a nauseous stomach. She remembers Richard. She props her hand under her head and looks across at the table. Not there. Thank God. He must have gotten up and left. She feels sorry for him and hopes he made it home alive.

Then she remembers Renata. Confusion and fear wash over her. Did they make love? What counts as making love to a woman? She remembers touching Rennie's breasts — and her lips and tongue. Warmth comes over her, becomes nauseating heat. Her head is too heavy to lift, but she reaches under the sheet and finds herself naked.

She hears movement on the floor and glances to the side. Richard is sitting up, rubbing his eyes.

"Jesus! What are you doing here?"

"I'm not Jesus, but I must have been crucified. Do you have a gun?" Using the table leg for support, he climbs to his feet. "I'd really feel a lot better if you would shoot me."

"Christ! Why are you on my floor?"

"I don't know, and I'm not Christ either." He rubs his hand down his face. "I don't have enough sense of humor to keep this going."

Jules is clutching the sheet up to her neck since she has no clothing nearby. "Would you leave so I can go back to sleep? I can't hold my head up much longer."

"I'm thinking this is Friday, right?"

Jules thinks. "Yeah. Pretty sure."

He sits down hard on a chair and looks at the clock. "After ten! Jesus, I missed my comp class."

"I would forgive you," Jules says, her voice hoarse, "but I'm not Jesus either." She starts to laugh, but it hurts.

Richard gives no sign of hearing her. "Can I use your phone?"

She points to it on the dresser. "Local calls only. Make it fast. First, though, I need to get my clothes and go to the bathroom."

He turns his back to Jules and motions for her to go ahead.

She doubts he'd bother to look anyway. His eyes are trained on Renata, past, present, and future. Jules gets up and drags the sheet, covering herself, picking up her shorts and shirt on the way. She passes a section of newspaper on the sink with pieces of broken glass on it. Moments return to her memory. Ugh. She shuts the bathroom door and groans at herself in the mirror.

CHAPTER 27

October 8, 10:10 am, Tropical Moons, Room 2-B

Renata

She hears Richard's voice and decides to go over. She's not in the mood to entertain him this morning, but she has to rescue Jules. She remembers how sweet and earthy Jules smelled when she tucked her in, the caresses and the kiss so natural. She wonders what Jules and Richard had talked about. She'd hoped to go over, but Franco's cousin kept her busy all night — fucking endurance in that family.

She puts on a t-shirt and shorts and drapes Pepe around her neck. "Be a good boy," she tells him as she strokes his yellow and pearl skin. She wraps his tail under her arm and tucks it into her waistband on the other side. "Not too many kisses for Richard this morning, okay, Pepito?" The snake will keep Richard from hanging on her. Although it's likely Richard will be so hungover he won't want to hang on anything but the toilet bowl.

Renata crosses through the hall and opens the door. Richard is on the telephone, facing her. His face is colorless and bloated, yet crushed like a paper bag around the eyes.

When he sees her, she catches a sparkle still alive in there, despite the slump of his shoulders. He keeps talking into the phone, his voice gravelly from the alcohol. "I'll be in for my office hours . . . " He pauses to cough. "I'll see you for a few minutes before class. I . . . " He listens and nods. "Good. See you then." He hangs up and puts out his arms to Rennie.

She leans forward for a peck, holding Pepe's head to the side. "He hasn't been getting enough affection," she tells Richard.

Richard blinks. She knows he wants to say, me either, but he doesn't. He stands and walks toward her.

"Where's Jules?" she asks him.

He motions his head toward the bathroom. Water is running in the shower.

"What about your wife?"

He puts his hand on Renata's hair lightly, avoiding Pepe on the other side. Richard exhales long and hard. "She called the university earlier to see if I'd been in. As far as she knows I could be dead. I might keep it that way."

"What?"

"I could get a place here — near you."

"Really?" Renata has been expecting something like this. He wants 24/7 guard duty so he can protect her — smother her — with love. It'll kill them both. Francisco is probably on his way over at that moment to ask about his cousin and reclaim Renata with a quickie.

"Richard, you can't live here. Look around. This place is toxic. Imagine what goes on."

"I'd rather take you out of here. But you won't go. I have no other choice. I have to stay and protect you."

"The last thing I need is protecting. If you stay here, I'll have to protect *you*. Trust me."

"You'd see."

Renata holds Pepe's head away and kisses Richard on the lips, lingering, then touching his cheek with hers. "It's like you're fifteen." She touches his ear. She has an idea. "If you stayed here, I'd have to lock you up. How would you like that?"

"Lock me up? What do you mean?"

"Are you into it? S and M."

"I never tried it."

"I can get a huge wooden box. These guys I know — for a while they took turns, master and slave, keeping each other in a box — days at a time. The slave would wear cuffs on his ankles and everything. A dog collar." As she makes up the details, she wonders if any of it is true. "They said they'd loan it to me."

"All right. I'll be your slave."

"Fuck. I'm kidding. I don't want a slave, Richard. Besides, you have better things to do. I thought that idea would scare you to death."

"I'd try it for you. I don't have anywhere else to go."

"C'mon. Your wife and children need you — and your students. I saw that girl in the doorway with the look on her face. She thinks you're a fucking god. You can't desert them."

Footsteps pass by in the hall. Renata's door opens and closes. "I have company," she says. "Are you going to wait and listen — or go?"

Richard lets out a growl. "Renata, I can't live like this!"

Jules sticks her head out of the bathroom. Steam rolls toward the ceiling. "Richard, leave. Now! Goodbye!"

He looks from Jules to Renata and back to Jules. They stare unblinking. Pepe raises his head and stares.

"I'll be back. I have nothing else. I'll be back." He throws his hands in the air and stomps out leaving the door open.

Renata watches until he's gone down the stairs.

"Think he'll be okay?"

Renata turns back to Jules and shrugs. "When he gets over his hangover. Thanks, honey. I have to go."

"I'll do anything for you — any time," Jules says — "I mean it."

Renata opens the door farther to look at Jules, wrapped in a white towel, sweat beaded on her chest. Renata holds Pepe's head aside and kisses her on the cheek.

Jules takes her hand. "I can't remember last night. I don't know what happened."

"With Richard? Nothing that I know of. He passed out."

"No, between us – me and you."

"Not a thing. You drifted into vodka dreamland."

Jules looks into Renata's eyes. "I touched you."

"You stroked my tits and ass a little, and kissed me. It was sweet. Don't worry about it."

"I wanted to do more."

"Jules, you know I don't have a problem with that. You're my beautiful, best girlfriend."

Jules stands staring.

"Come on over. Play with me and Franco."

"No. I . . . want to be with you alone, and that means I'm a lesbian."

"Do you think I'm a lesbian?"

"Yes. No. I don't know."

"Neither do I. I don't care either." She runs her finger under the edge of Jules' towel and watches her blush with pleasure. "If somebody told me I had to pick one sex to fuck for the rest of my life, I'd pick a man – I think. But as long as I don't have to choose, why should I?"

"I'd rather have sex with you than Francisco. Doesn't that mean something?"

Renata laughs. "Hot as he is? Makes me feel damn good."

"It makes me a lesbian."

"Fuck. This shit isn't worth talking about. You're behind the times, girl. The more the better, drugs and sex. Girls are fun to cuddle and lick and have warm memories with – they're soft and nice. They feel good. Anybody with half a brain knows that." She smiles. "But it's sort of like playing with yourself, always easy and secure." She takes Jules' hand and tickles her palm with a swirling motion. "There's nothing like a rough hand and a big hard cock, a lot of sweat and a little pain, the things you can count on from a man." She licks the corner of her mouth. "Whatever. It doesn't matter." She holds

Pepe's head and kisses Jules lightly on the lips. "Gotta catch Franco now. We can talk about it – or do it – anytime."

Jules opens her mouth but doesn't say anything.

CHAPTER 28

12:45 PM, Atlantic Shores University

Richard

Sunshine rises off the blacktop and drives splinters of white-hot pain through his head. South Florida is an outrageously horrible climate for hangovers. He pulls into his parking space under the meager shade of a queen palm and tries to gather his thoughts. Judy has told him that she took the liberty of canceling his class on Thursday, when he hadn't picked up his mail and wasn't in his office. He told her he would be there for the Friday afternoon poetry class. He can't disappoint the serious students who live for poetry and look forward to his advice and encouragement. A "class cancelled" sign on the door would depress a few of them for the entire weekend.

So far he's heard of no official action against him, but he needs to see Judy before class to explain. He looks at his watch, takes out his cell phone, and calls Linda. The phone rings until the voice mail picks up. "Honey," he says. "I'm sorry. So sorry . . . I don't know what to say. I've been drinking for two days . . . Honey, I'm in the university lot. I have to teach my class – then I'm coming home. I don't know if you're there. I hope you'll listen to what I have to say. I'll be home in a little while and –" There's a loud clunk, as if the receiver was lifted and set down forcefully in the cradle to cut him off.

He breaks out in a cold sweat. At least she's home, another chance to talk. Maybe he should throw himself on her mercy. He fumbles to take the key out of the ignition. If he's going to leave her, he should do it, just do it. But now that saving the relationship seems almost impossible, he feels the need to fight for it. His brain is foggy with alcohol, and the dizziness and nausea make him want to lie there in the air-conditioned car. He pushes the seat button and leans back, just for a minute.

He opens his eyes to a sharp rapping noise. It's a young guy with dimples, frowning against the glare, a student from his poetry class, tapping on the car window with a metal pen. Richard is covered with sweat. He presses the button and lowers the window. The student steps back. Richard realizes the stench of alcohol must be brutal from his breath and skin.

"Professor Langley, you okay? It's almost time for class."

Richard looks down at his watch. An hour has passed. "Fuck," he says quietly. He looks up at the student and tries to put some optimism into his voice. "I'm fine, thanks. Thank you for waking me. I only meant to rest my eyes for a moment." He gives a little wave, waiting for the boy to move off so he can straighten himself out without anybody watching.

The student doesn't leave. He hunches down and puts his face almost inside the window, his blond buzz cut brushing the seatbelt attachment. Richard struggles to remember the boy's name, but all synapses are dead.

The student gets close to Richard's ear. "I . . . uh . . ."

Richard's eyes are burning and his tongue is dry. He turns to face the student, covering his mouth to be polite. "Yes – what?"

"I heard something – I don't know if it's true. It doesn't matter." He pauses, but Richard doesn't have the energy to interrupt. "I wanted to tell you that I'm on your side. Whatever this fucking institution tries to do – we need you here. You're the only one who cares anything about poetry and poets – and knows how hard it is. I'll get a group together and go to the dean – or the president, if you want. Just let me know. Your personal life is your business. There are lots of students here who will do anything they can for you."

Richard feels his head bobbing. He tries to smile. He knows he should be flattered and grateful, but the only feeling he can identify is an urge to flee – or kill himself. "Thank you. I'll see you in class. I appreciate your support."

"It's not only personal, because you're such a great teacher and human being, but there's an issue here. Like what happened to those high school teachers – Nazis finding out they went to Plato's Retreat, getting them fired. I believe if there's no law broken and you're on your own time, it's none of their business."

Richard keeps nodding. There's no logic in the comparison, but it would seem ungrateful to argue with someone on his side. Besides, his head is throbbing so that it's too painful to speak. He wonders if there has already been talk of firing him.

The student is still talking – and Richard can't sit there a second longer. He's already an hour late to see Judy. Nausea fills him like steam. He grabs his briefcase from the seat and shoves the door open. The student steps back into the car in the next slot. "Sorry," Richard says. He makes a desperate attempt to remember the name, but still comes up blank. "I appreciate all you're saying. I'm very late. Thank everybody for me – or I will in class."

The student looks stunned, but Richard waves and crosses the lot to the building. He tops the stairs, breathing hard, sweat running between his eyebrows, and turns down the hall toward Judy.

She looks sideways from her computer screen as he approaches her desk. He barely slows as he passes by. "Sorry, I'm running late. Can you come down to my office in five minutes?"

"Sure," she says and goes back to typing.

Richard stops at the men's room, urinates, and washes his face. He makes soapy water, by dripping pink dispenser soap into his cupped palms, and swishes out his mouth. The soap tastes sweet in comparison to the cloying alcohol. He can't help glancing in the mirror – his clothes look exactly like he slept in them, and his face has the mottled sheen of rancid hamburger. He's not quite alive.

He barely settles at his desk when there's a knock and Judy sticks her head inside.

"Come in," he tells her. "I need somebody to talk to."

She sits down and winces, and he can see that she's suffering along with him. She's not the type to enjoy his disintegration.

"Before I forget to tell you," she says softly, "your wife called back about an hour ago, and I told her you were on your way in. I said that you didn't want her to worry, but you had some problems to deal with."

"What did she say?"

Judy shakes her head, as if to throw off the memory of Linda's voice and the pain of the whole situation. "She thanked me for delivering the message, but she was very angry. She said she knew what was going on."

He feels bad that he has put Judy in this position, having to talk to Linda under these circumstances and get involved in his personal fucked-up way of handling things. Besides that, the gossipmongers on the staff must be after her every minute. He owes her the complete truth. He gives a brief version of the situation with Rennie, emphasizing that she is not a student, but admitting that it was an insane choice for a rendezvous.

Judy listens without expression. She tells him that she will support him as much as she can – without lying – because she knows he would not want her to do that. However, the Dean of Students has already been involved and that means a meeting must be called with Richard, the English Department chair, the student, and herself so something official can be written up to show that his conduct is being dealt with.

"A letter to be put into my file," he says.

"I suppose so."

Richard takes her hand. "I know you'll do exactly the right thing," he tells her. "You have grace under pressure." It's true. What he doesn't know is how he will handle himself. The thought of the meeting is enough to make his brain implode.

She smiles and thanks him. He hopes he's made her feel a little better. When Judy leaves, he tries Linda once more. Again, the voice message comes on. He hangs up. There's nothing he can record at this point that will make her pick up the phone.

He has five minutes until class and he doesn't want to arrive early. He sits, staring out of focus at the wall of books beside him, immobile in his chair, almost asleep, numb, too depleted to worry. At one minute till, he rises robot-like, feeling a little refreshed, the nausea beginning to fade. He's been doing this for enough years to get through anything. He steps inside the door. The class of twelve students sounds like thirty. Immediately they quiet down. He nods a greeting and takes the empty seat they've left him in the circle. He scans the roll quickly, putting the checkmarks beside each name, no absences.

"Okay, you each have a poem due today. Who would like to go first?"

Deirdre, a small brunette, raises her hand and passes the copies of her poem to the student on her right. Everyone is silent, and no one looks up as the sheets circulate. Richard pulls on the fabric of his shirt to let air inside. His stomach burns, but he forces himself to pay attention. This could be the last time he sees these students. He begins to read the poem. Within a few lines it's already clear that the poem is about him – his ripe peach of desire. He realizes that Deirdre must be a friend of Tammi's to know the story. At this point, he supposes Renata's hair color and freckles are common knowledge among the tight-knit group. He wonders what words the students use to describe what he was doing. The last stanza, so dark, is strange coming from Deirdre, a generally happy soul. Without knowledge of his predicament, the meaning would be obscure. He looks up from reading to see if the others are finished. The students press their lips hard as they read. Unexpectedly Deirdre stands and begins to read the last stanza aloud.

> Pink satin surface, sweet smell, tang of life you
>   can't resist,
> The hallowed halls echo eerily what's passed
>   your lips.
> Tossed into a glowing heap, the crumpled
>   paper, dry ink,
> Now dead ashes poured from vessels you have
>   drained and forgotten
> To fill and refill and never fill,
> The sucking black hole that drags you in.

The class stares at Richard, waiting for his reaction. He picks up the poem. It's heavy as lead, but he has a horrible desire to laugh, despite their concern. He wants to howl and run from the room. He bites his lip to gain control. Then he speaks in his classroom voice. "The line that ends with 'you have drained and forgotten' enjambs nicely with 'To fill and refill and never fill,' concisely adding ambiguity." He points to the sheet and looks up at the class. "Notice that? – the persona is forgetting to fill and refill the vessels and/or trying to fill and refill the black hole. The lack of punctuation at the end of the one line lets the meaning carry over to the next."

Deirdre looks stricken. She frowns down at the poem. "It's not a persona. It's a real person!"

Richard braces himself.

"He can't fill a black hole! Nobody can fill a black hole! It's you, Richard!" She smears her eyes with the back of her hand

and snuffles. Her voice becomes shrill. "We're the empty vessels – the ones you used to fill. The black hole is the whore who's taking you away from us! Tammi told me!"

Richard bites the inside of his cheek. He doesn't have the energy or desire to clarify anything to these students. He wonders if she means *whore* literally. How much could she know? Other girls are snuffling. The guys look nervous. The student – Stan? – who woke him in the parking lot steps over to Deirdre and puts his arm around her, kisses her forehead as she sniffs. He motions to the class. "It's no use. His head is somewhere else. This woman is like a drug."

Richard should demand an apology, respect, at least while he is present in the room, but he can only agree. He should have known there would be something like this. The pain of student devotion twists through his chest. Poets are far too sensitive, even as young as these. He wants to appreciate their sympathy and accept their help, but he's unworthy and incapable.

"I'm sorry. I'm so sorry," he says. Noses are being blown. He feels himself breaking down. "Listen, I can't explain it. I know I'm on dangerous ground, but I can't do anything. My whole life is changing – I don't know –"

"Hey, man, the students are on your side. We want you to stay."

"It's like a drug, you're right, but better – my last chance at fulfillment in life –" He stops. They can't understand, and he's lost his mind to reveal so much personal information. He blinks back tears and forces a smile at the tall Jamaican to belie his emotion. "Let's pass out the rest of the poems and get through as many as we can. I don't know what will happen after today."

The rest of the class goes by in a blur. New day, different poems, wrecked career, but the usual lack of concrete imagery. He wonders if he's ever made a difference except in their desperate minds.

As they pass by on their way out, the girls hug him and the

guys shake hands. "Good luck," he hears several times. "Thanks . . . Thank you . . . " he says. The ordeal will be anti-climactic if nothing happens and he's back at the job the following week. That's unlikely. He can't come back – can't face it anymore. He gathers the leftover poems and walks to the door, dreaming. A job in New England, cold crisp days – Renata in a furry coat. His boys could visit for Christmas and ski. In the summer he'd take them hiking. He shakes his head to clear it. Renata isn't going anywhere, and if there's a letter in his file, his chance of finding another teaching job is basically non-existent. Of course, there's the bed and breakfast . . . As he turns to switch off the light, he sees that someone has sketched a quick picture on the blackboard – an egg in a frying pan, the old TV commercial. This is his brain on drugs. A joke. He chuckles. They're all on their own choice of drugs, just milder ones, compared to that drug called Renata.

He's in his office gathering the few books and notes from his desk when somebody knocks.

"Come in. Door's open," he says.

Judy sticks her head inside. "Dr Roberts would like to see you."

He sees her scanning the room quickly, a new habit learned under duress. He's ready to walk down to her office, when the door opens wide, and the department chair steps in. He can tell she's upset, although she has a strong, determined look on her face. She closes the door behind her and walks toward him.

Richard smiles and stands. "I always wanted to tell you how much you look like Tina Turner. I wasn't sure how you'd take it, but I mean it purely as a compliment. You're a strong, lovely woman, and it's been a pleasure to work for you."

She smiles with her usual warmth. Then her eyelids flutter and she grits her teeth. She's probably decided that he's gone completely insane.

"I'm sorry I have to bring you the news, Richard. The provost and academic dean have informed me that you're to be put on leave from teaching until . . . all this . . . business . . . is straightened out." She shakes her head. "I'm sorry. We have to set up another meeting with the student. There are some complications. Please get your syllabi in order, so somebody can take up where you left off."

"Do I get paid?"

"I . . . don't know. I'm hoping this is all a mistake and you can come back in a week or so." She blinks rapidly a few times, his reaction obviously not what she was expecting. "This is all new. I'll find out."

She's knocked off guard, just like the students, like any normal person. He puts out his hand and takes hers. It's warm. "I'm okay. Don't worry."

"I am worried about you, Richard, but I don't know what to do. This student Tammi indicated that you tried to touch her inappropriately that morning."

He flinches, then lets out a short burst of laughter. He's both angry and amazed.

She shakes her head. "Nobody believes it, but she has some family connections – I don't know – with upper-level administration. It's best to show them something is being done, until things calm down."

He chuckles, feeling insane with the irony of the whole thing. "Fine."

She nods, biting her lip.

He knows she's making a point of not letting his bizarre attitude affect her.

"I'll give Judy everything the sub will need," he says. "I hope you can get a poet – maybe Patrick. Somebody has to take over the contest."

"Thanks. We'll do our best. I'll have Judy put a sign on the door that says you're on personal leave until further notice."

He lunges forward to give her a quick hug, feeling her stiff resolve turn soft as she hugs back. A tear runs down her cheek as she turns and walks out of the office.

He doesn't have the presence of mind to gather his syllabi, notes and books. He'll come back early on Monday and take care of everything. He locks the door and heads to the car. It's already three o'clock.

Halfway down the street he can see that the Volvo is not in the driveway. He walks past the empty garage with a glance through the window. He starts unbuttoning his shirt in the living room, peels it from his hot sticky back and chest, smelling alcohol and sweat, and drops it on the bedroom floor, followed by his pants. He'll throw them directly into the washer later. No need to pollute the hamper with the stinking reminder of his insanity and infidelity – if Linda ever returns and does laundry again. It occurs to him that he spent an entire night out – two nights! – and, ironically, he wasn't unfaithful.

He drops his underwear in the bathroom, steps into the shower, and begins to soap his hair. Linda can tell everyone that he had a mid-life crisis. Maybe he should buy a sports car and take up skydiving to complete the picture. No one will ever understand what has really happened – that he has been engulfed by the essence of raw, unspoiled sensuality. It's overpowering and without boundaries, sublime. He's been given a rare prize. The water pounds at his head. Renata is freedom. With her he could write again, without fear or artifice.

He hears the front door slam as he rinses the last suds from his hair. His chest tightens. He doesn't want to hurt Linda, can't hurt Linda. She'll always be the only person capable of understanding him.

Her footsteps approach from the hall. He shuts off the water, grabs a towel, wraps it around his hips, and steps out of the stall. She stands in front of him in the doorway. Her eyes are black slits. She looks beneath her feet and snags his dirty Calvin Kleins with the pointed toe of one shoe, flinging them in a perfect arc to catch on Richard's hand where he holds the towel in front of his groin.

"Whatever in the fucking universe are you doing in my bathroom?"

"Please. Can we talk?"

"It's too late for talk. I'm making a fresh start, beginning right now. I don't know what I'm going to do, but I've already moved the boys to my mother's."

"Please —"

"Don't bother trying to see them or getting in touch with me. I'll let you know when I can bear to listen to anything you have to say."

"I'm suspended from teaching."

"Then you have nothing left."

"Nothing," he repeats. It doesn't sound as bad as he would have expected.

CHAPTER 29

Saturday, October 9, 1:00 PM, Tropical Moons,
Room 2-A

Jules

She wakes up still lightheaded, but feeling well enough to
be hungry. There's no food, except for a loaf of bread, so she
makes two pieces of toast and uses the last tea bag. This is the
morning she planned to get an early start looking for a job,
before the sun got too hot and the bars too busy.

She decides to take a look at what she's written on the
novel while she drinks her tea. It's been days since she's booted
up the computer. So many writers are famous for their drinking — Hemingway must have done much of his work with a
hangover, but so far it hasn't worked for her. The screen lights
up with the first page, and she winces as she reads. The plot is
going nowhere, just like it was the last time she looked. No
elves or fairies have come to fix it. She remembers that her
goal is to write something to impress her father. Her life has
changed so much that he hardly seems to exist. She hasn't
written or called her parents since her first month on the
beach, and it was always up to her to keep in touch. They don't

want more bad news.

Jules starts and stops and rewrites. It's slow going. An hour passes and she's barely gotten into the scene. Her mind goes blank. She covers her face with her hands. Shit. It isn't working. Jules stops with her fingers above the keys. There's one thing she can do. She'll write the truth, the sex, the murder, the drugs. Why not? It's fiction to everyone but Renata. Police don't read fiction. She can use everything that's happened.

She saves and shuts down. Time for a break. She has to work out the point of view. She should talk to Richard for some tips – now that he owes her for a night on her floor. He must know more than just poetry. She has a novel in her after all, unfolding further each day that she lives. Right now she needs to get out and find temporary work before she has to hock the laptop for grocery money.

There's no sound from Renata's, and Jules shuts the door quietly and tiptoes to the stairs. Rennie would try to talk her out of wasting her time, to take the "easy money" with her and Francisco, and Jules has run out of arguments.

The early drinkers have already taken their seats downstairs out of the glaring heat in the semi-cool lobby. Oliver is standing with his arms crossed, watching the TV screen above him at the end of the bar.

Jules smells coconut suntan oil as she crosses the room and takes a seat in front of him. "Hi, Oliver, how's everything?"

"Not bad. Get you something?"

"No. I'm okay. I was wondering if you know of anybody on the beach looking for a waitress or inexperienced barmaid – within walking distance."

He studies her for a few seconds. "I'll think on it." He frowns and puts his hands on the bar. "I had a detective in here this morning asking about you girls – a P.I."

"What?" Jules bites her lip. She puts her head down and takes a breath. She's going to react calmly. She raises her head. "Sorry – this heat is getting to me. What did he want?"

"Mainly he wanted to know about Renata."

"Did you tell him we borrowed your car?"

"No, never asked. He wanted to know her occupation. I told him to talk to her – none of my business. I get flustered with cops and those types – even the ones without uniforms." He giggles.

"Why would he want to know that?"

"I didn't ask." He frowns. "You girls aren't in trouble, are you?"

"No – no." She clasps her hands below the bar to keep still. "I thought maybe I did something illegal. I'm not used to driving anymore."

"The tires were filthy. Where'd you go?"

"Sorry – the Everglades." The second the word is out she realizes she shouldn't have said it. "We were supposed to meet somebody for an airboat ride, but he never showed."

"P.I.s don't investigate traffic violations, you know? I thought maybe he was working for the lawyer. The blond guy who's been hanging around."

Jules shrugs, unable to talk calmly.

Oliver steps back and looks under the bar on his side. He brings out a card. "Here – this is his name and number. Maybe you or Renata should give him a call. I'd rather not talk to him again." He winks. "He was kinda cute though."

Jules tries a quick smile. "I'll tell Rennie. Thanks."

"Jules – if I hear of a job, I'll let you know."

She smiles the best she can and walks back slowly toward the stairs. Out of sight, she breaks into a run. Fuck. Now Oliver knows they drove to the Everglades. Could the P.I. have already connected the murders? If he comes back to the hotel, he'll find Renata eventually. Maybe Jules should call, like Oliver said. It would seem less suspicious. Or Rennie could handle it better.

Techno is blaring from Rennie's place. Jules is panting as she hits the door with both fists, and gives it a good pounding, just in case there's a customer inside. Nobody answers so she opens it. Francisco comes out of the bathroom zipping his fly.

"Hey, Julie, that you making noise?"

She's caught off balance. She doesn't know whether to tell him before she tells Rennie. "Me? You must be trying to register your bass on the Richter scale."

He laughs and walks over to turn it down. "Cute, babe. Just got a new CD player – warming it up for Rennie."

"That's nice. Where is she?"

"Don't know. I came back here and she was gone." Francisco turns to the counter and gets something from the drawer. Jules watches the muscles in his back and arms as he moves. He walks toward her and opens a metal box. He motions with his head. "Burn one?"

"Huh?"

"Smoke some herb?"

"Uh, I don't know." She's thinking she needs to talk to Rennie before she does anything.

"Up to you. I smoke alone, no problem."

"Sorry, sure. That would be nice. I don't have my head on straight today."

"Why do you need a straight head? This will put it right for you – a little tilt. Good stuff, *mamita*."

Jules sits on the bed and looks out the window while Francisco fills the pipe. There's nothing she can do now anyway. When Rennie gets home, she'll know what has to be done.

Francisco brings the pipe over and lights it, taking a long hit deep into his lungs, and smiles. He hands it to Jules. She sucks lightly, feeling the burn in her throat, and hands it back to him. They pass it back and forth in silence. Jules watches Francisco, looks at his soft lips and high cheekbones. He's a beautiful man. She's feeling better.

"You think I'm a lesbian?" she asks him.

He exhales into his words. "Why would I think that?"

Jules takes a deep breath. "I love Renata. I thought maybe it showed."

Francisco takes another long draw and holds it, looks at her.

"Doesn't it show?"

He exhales slowly. "There's a little opium in this." He picks up her hand and kisses it. "Everybody loves Renata. That's the way it is."

"Do you?"

He bobs his head slightly and wets his lips with his tongue. "Yeah. But I know how to do it."

"How?"

"With reservations."

"You hold back – so you won't get hurt? How can you?"

"No, I mean I make a reservation when I want it – otherwise there will be some other asshole inside her when I get here." He laughs.

Jules can feel the look on her face. She should know Francisco can't talk seriously, especially smoking dope.

He reaches over and grabs her thigh. "Julie, baby, love will kill you. You can't take it serious – no matter with girls or boys. Enjoy what comes your way, and let the rest fly. You watch me. You see how I do it."

She stares at him, searching for the place where his coolness and attitude come from.

"Love is my job, baby. I'm a professional." He widens his eyes at her and nods.

She sees that he's teasing her, laughing at her innocence, yet, at the same time, he's telling her something he believes. This emptiness is his source of recklessness, the same thing Renata has tried to tell her. They have accepted a bitter truth of life.

She reaches for the pipe and takes a long pull. The realization brings a disturbing feeling. She knows so little.

Renata opens the door, sniffs. "Smells like a drug den in here. Got any left?"

Jules remembers the reason she rushed over there in the first place. Fuck. Renata joins Francisco on the bed and takes the pipe. She giggles and whispers something in his ear. Jules doesn't want to disturb the party. She'll handle the P.I. herself.

She might never have to mention him.

"We have room," Rennie says. She pats a spot on the bed for Jules.

"Thanks, Rennie. But if I don't go now, I never will."

Rennie exhales. "Not a good reason."

Jules walks into her room wondering if Francisco will make love to Rennie now. Is Renata in love with him? He certainly takes up a big part of her. Then there's Richard, and how many others? Somehow Jules has to outdo them all, the whole universe of men, to have Rennie for herself.

CHAPTER 30

8:00 pm, South Miami

Richard

He wakes up after a long nap. The lights have not
been turned on and Linda is still gone. It's been years since he
had the time to fall asleep and wake up by himself naturally,
but there's no peaceful feeling like he remembers. He's hot
and jittery. He picks up the phone and dials Renata. No
answer, no machine. He drops the receiver hard. He expected as much, but now he needs a plan so as not to go
insane.

He can't remember eating anything all day. Food, he tells
himself. He'll fix soft-boiled eggs, then try her again. He cooks
the eggs for exactly three minutes and eats them with dry
toast, dipping the points of bread into the runny yellow, not
tasting anything, chewing slowly, barely able to swallow. He
cleans up the dish, fork, and pan, and checks the clock. It's been
fifteen minutes. He rings her phone again. His mood swings
from nausea and desperation over losing his family, to nervous
stress – now he has all the time he needs to see Renata and he's
wasting it.

By midnight he's tried her place eight times and is beginning to worry that Jules will hear the phone ringing and tell Rennie. They'll both know who is calling.

He goes to the mailbox, bringing bills to his desk – electric, trash, water. He takes out the checkbook and starts to write. He throws down the pen. Let them send their warnings until they cut him off. He needs none of their services. He'll move to The Moons where it's all included.

Oddly, he feels inspired to create. He opens the bottom drawer of the file cabinet to look for an old poem in progress, from months or years ago. He remembers that he has one photo of Renata hidden there, taken on the day he borrowed a digital camera from the photography department at school. He'd printed out several shots, but gave the others to Renata.

The black and white photo is hidden somewhere under poems he has never been comfortable enough to let anyone read. He picks up the handful of sheets and shuffles through, reading a stanza here and there, amazed to find the clarity of the images admirable and the concise expression of honest emotion appealing.

Reaching into the back of the drawer, he feels the stiff paper of the photo and pulls it out. She said it was the only clothed picture a man ever took of her since childhood. He supposes you could consider her clothed, though the skirt is hiked to her hips and she's wearing nothing under it. His chest is tight as he studies her model features and the shadowy hollows of her smooth throat. He feels himself harden with the terrible craving to put his lips over her mouth. He studies her delicacy, realizing that her vulnerability touches him more than her beauty. He's drawn to the poetry of her extremes, the unfathomable height and depth of them. The life inside her glows like neon, yet there's a dark private corner of fragility and despair. Her playfulness seems born of pure courage. He doubts that anyone knows her true story, but he senses the depth of suffering in her past.

He sets the photo on the desk in front of him, opens

his belt, and unzips. So crude and physical, but he feels spirituality in his arousal. He pulls out his cock and begins to stroke it. If only she could feel his thoughts touching her body, tightening, squeezing, grasping to become one with her consciousness, if only he could concentrate hard enough to bring her to him through waves of mental passion.

The orgasm builds, a hot focus, blurring all thought, leaving only love and need. He leans into the desk with his thighs so he can see her lovely face beneath his strong straight organ. As he feels the tightness moving through him, he bends slightly over the photo drooling the starchy come over her, giving his only true possession, the substance that contains his life and energy, the symbolism of baptism that makes her his own.

He regains his posture and glances over his shoulder as he zips. This act could be considered disrespectful. Linda would be shocked — and frightened — but Renata would understand the beauty of it, his milk, the thin translucence of a wedding veil across her eyes, evidence of his love.

Still breathing heavily, he sits down and studies the photo. *Milky strands, peach-freckled face, a wedding veil* — imagery begins to stir his imagination, the urge to write a poem. He's crossed many boundaries in the last few days, discovering new freedom and complexities to explore. Fear has almost gone. Laws are for the lawful, and he's so far outside of society in his own mind that nothing can touch him — he'll pay no debts or fines, answer to no one, suffer no consequences until stronger powers force him into submission. He has never felt closer to Renata's world than he does now.

He gets down some ragged lines, the poem building on itself, as in his younger days. Inspiration released by his muse, Renata. It's the first time in years he's sat in a chair so focused, to create. He will need to revisit the poem many times, to invest more meaning and trim needless words, but he feels good, having these lines, the magic reborn. The gnawing in his gut remains — his loss of Linda and the twins — yet there's an exhilaration that can't be ignored.

CHAPTER 31

9:00 pm, Tropical Moons Saloon

Jules

Her vodka bottle has long been empty so she decides to have a drink at the bar and then call the P.I. If he can meet her there, maybe he'll pay the tab. Every dollar counts at this point. She's finished two drinks when she finally has the courage to call. She expects to leave a message, but the phone is picked up.

"Eddie Garcia."

Jules is taken aback by the gruffness of his voice. "I . . . um . . . the bartender said I should call you – the bar where I live . . ."

"Sorry. What's your name?"

"Jules Gregory, a friend of Renata's. The bartender at Tropical Moons Hotel said to call you."

She waits through silence.

"I'm at the bar, if you want to talk. End stool by the TV."

"Sorry. Yeah. Took me a second to think."

Not a mind like a steel trap. Good. "So, we can just let this go?"

He says, no, he'll be there, just give him a half-hour. She'll savor the third drink and then hope he pays the tab. She doesn't want to get too drunk anyway, just enough to be calm and say the right things to get rid of him for good.

She orders a vodka and orange juice this time, for dinner. The Moons doesn't set out little bowls of snacks, but the drinks are much cheaper than in the places that do. She's sucking ice by the time Garcia walks in the door. He's a tall man with a mustache, medium-sized paunch, middle forties. Pleasant. She's nearly forgotten why she called him, but as he stands before her, panic rises to her throat. What was she thinking? Rather than removing suspicion, she'll probably create it.

He puts out his hand. Jules smiles and tries to think what Renata would do, and feel how she would move. She touches his hand in a sensual way, slowly letting her fingers slide against his palm as she pulls back. Her mind is in turmoil. She should never have told Oliver where they took the car.

Jules swallows a small piece of ice. "Oliver told me I should talk to you."

"Yeah, thanks for the call." He sits down. "You're Renata's friend?"

"Yes. We're good friends."

"Mind if I ask – what do you do, Jules, for a living?"

"I'm a writer – working on a novel."

"Oh, I'm a reader. What have you written?"

"Nothing, yet. I'm just starting."

He shifts in his seat. "You get paid in advance?"

"No. I waitress, temporarily."

"I see. Well, I really wanted to talk to Renata. Is she around?"

Jules is fearful that he'll ask about Rennie's line of business. She takes his hand and clasps it in what she feels is a friendly and delicate way. "My friend is out tonight, but we might be able to find her if you want to take a walk down the beach. She's in one of the bars. I need to get up off this stool myself."

Garcia looks at her.

She's trying to suggest an evening together. Bold for her. Terror is building in her chest that he'll refuse, and she won't know what to do with him. She wants so much to give up the old Jules and be fearless and irresistible like Renata, get what she wants from Garcia without even trying.

"I guess we could take a look."

Jules slides off the stool. She has to get him to pay for the drinks. Renata would have slid right onto his groin, and then turned away to light a cigarette, while he gladly ripped bills out of his wallet. "Let's get going then. There are three good possibilities." She motions to Oliver. "How much?"

He brings the tab and Garcia acknowledges his presence, as Jules takes out her wallet and starts to look through the few dollars slowly. She checks all the compartments. She goes through a second time, and Garcia waits, looking off toward the stairway. "I thought I had a fifty in here," she says. "I purposely put it in here for the evening." Oliver's eyebrows lift as he watches her. She's uncomfortable with lies and knows she's doing a terrible job.

Garcia turns with a resigned look on his face. She shrugs. "Sorry."

"No problem," he says, but clearly it is a problem. He studies the tab, then slowly counts out the money to cover the check.

She leads him south on the street, not saying anything, trying to come up with a plan. The drinks have dulled her senses, but not filled her stomach, and she's starved. She juggles the idea of telling him she's hungry, and will owe him the money, with the possibility of simply trading her company for dinner. They get into the first block of crowded sidewalk cafés, and she sees an Italian place that has always appealed to her. She takes his hand and stops. "Let's sit here and watch for her. She'll have to pass by, heading one direction or the other."

Since it's a weeknight in off-season, there are two empty tables, one on the street and one next to the building. She waits for his reply, her mouth filling with saliva as she breathes in the aroma of the pasta and cheese dishes surrounding them. Her stomach is ready to cave in, and she wants to grab his arm and beg for garlic bread. He points to the table by the building. "Okay, let's eat up there. Less car fumes."

Relief is instant. The rules are clear since she has already admitted to having no money. She's learning, but it would be easier if she had more to fill out the sundress.

The waiter brings a menu and Garcia orders a bottle of wine. She's in a nice place, he's a nice man, and she's going to have dinner. With food in her stomach she should be sober enough to deal with his questions.

The salads come and she leads the conversation onto South Beach and what it's like living in a resort when you're not on vacation — constant nightlife outside your window, the lure of the sun and beach. Garcia tells her how he was born in New Jersey and spent fifteen years as a New York homicide detective. He moved to South Florida a year earlier when he was recovering from pneumonia. He couldn't stand the cold up there anymore. But he hasn't adjusted to the heat.

Jules laughs at his anecdotes of roaches and mildew in the tropics. She's happy to let him talk while she shovels in the bread and salad. When the main course comes, she picks at the baked ziti, knowing she will have food for tomorrow.

When the waiter comes to take the plates, Garcia orders cappuccinos. "Have you been watching for your friend?" Garcia asks. "I almost forgot."

"Yes, I imagine she's due by pretty soon."

"Really?"

"Sure. She's probably having dinner, and she'll be looking for some live music or a different place to drink."

"Come on. Gimme a break."

"Huh?" Jules feels the blood leave her face. The food in her stomach expands to her throat. If she hasn't been playing him, he must be playing her. Immediately, the bloody cabin and two bloated bodies fill her head, and she's sure he knows the whole story.

"You don't have the vaguest idea where your friend is. You just wanted somebody — anybody — to buy you dinner."

"No. I know she's on the beach somewhere."

"I don't mind buying you dinner. You're a lovely woman and I didn't have any plans for tonight."

Jules exhales. "Thank you. I'm sorry. I should have asked, but I didn't have the nerve. Next time's my turn."

He reaches across the table for her hand. "The sky's clear and there's a cool breeze. Let's walk off this food and find a place with music to have a couple more drinks."

Jules smiles. She licks the foam from her lips as she takes the last sip of smooth cappuccino. She feels great at the moment.

He pays the bill and leads her onto the sidewalk. She holds his hand on the left and the Styrofoam container of ziti on her right. Crazy thoughts come to her that she might be able to do this again, might be able to do it regularly. Rennie would be happy if Jules had a man to take her out.

Her head floats on the swell of alcohol and a satisfied stomach, high above the roller bladers and dog walkers dodging the two of them on the sidewalk. Jules enjoys the warm looseness of Garcia's hand and relaxes into the idea that she doesn't have to think. She's no Renata, but she's a new Jules, one who takes herself less seriously. She has no idea what's "right." She shakes her head and laughs to herself, tagging along at Garcia's side, insignificant in the universe. Her book comes to mind. She has no training. Where did she get the idea she could write a novel? She'll keep going now that she has a fresh idea, but she resolves to quit punishing herself over things outside her control.

CHAPTER 32

11:00 pm, Tropical Moons, Room 2-B

Renata

She pulls a thin blue nylon top over her head and arranges
her nipples to line up. The thin, low-slung pants that Francisco
gave her expose close to six inches of tanned skin below her
navel, perfect for a night on South Beach. The phone rings and
she ignores it. Instinct tells her it's Richard who's been ringing
eighteen times during the past twenty minutes, and she does-
n't want to make explanations. If she takes the phone off the
hook, he'll know she's home and nothing will stop him from
driving over.

She straps on her sandals and wraps Pepe around her neck.
She's happy for a night to herself – just to wander and have a
few drinks, look at the moon if there is one, and maybe late,
take a tourist down to the beach chairs and have fun, no
money involved. The phone starts ringing again. She wonders
if the guys with the box still have it. She could put Richard in
a box, if he wants to be so close. She'd feed him and let him
touch her now and then. After a couple of days they'd both get
bored with it, and then he would go back to his real life. She

dials the gay couple and leaves a message about the box, asking whether it's transportable.

She passes through the bar and out onto the street. Breezy warm air with salty humidity reminds her why she never left South Beach since the first night she came there. Pepe perks up, holding his head out beside her face, seeming to enjoy the smells or the breeze. People look as they pass by, and she smiles at them, knowing everyone wonders what she does with the snake. She touches the thick coil on her shoulder. The Peps is Rennie's good boy.

She heads for Mangoes where the roof is partially open so there's no cold A.C. It's Pepe's kind of place. There's a jam at the door, but they clear for her, and she goes up to the bar. Brent is the bartender, the blond surfer type she met there with Jules. He slaps a coaster down on the bar. His eyes are round. "Hey, baby doll, where have you been?"

"You remember all your customers?"

"No way. Hey, you didn't have that snake the last time, did you?"

"Sure. He's my true love."

Brent pulls his eyes off her tits. Pepe is keeping her nipples hard with the flicking of his tail. "If I buy you a drink, can I get the show I missed last time?"

Renata searches for the memory – showed her tits probably. "Pepe's my boy tonight," she says. "I'll buy my own drink."

He shakes his head and takes her hand to kiss it. "I'll get the drink. What would you like? We don't want to make Pepe boy unhappy when you're reaching for your money."

The tiny purse hangs around her neck between her tits and under Pepe's tail, and she thinks for a second it might be fun to ask Brent to take the money, just to see what he'd do. But she might as well get a free drink. "Okay, a Kaipuriña. Thanks. It's Pepito's favorite."

"You don't let that snake drink?" Brent says.

Renata makes pouty lips and kisses Pep's nose. "I wouldn't poison my baby with alcohol."

Brent nods, following Pepe's curves down Renata's. "Sure is a beauty." He winks and goes down the bar to a new customer.

Renata strokes Pepe and looks around the crowd. Salsa dancing in back. Moist tan shoulders glisten in the moving colored lights. Tits and ass shimmy like egg white, bouncing off one another in the crowd. She's wondering where Jules is, since she wasn't in her room. Hopefully she hasn't taken some poor-paying job. There's no reason for Jules to kill herself waitressing when she can come into the outcall business for more money, and still have the time to write her book. Renata enjoys having Jules around, so sweet. Julie loves her so much that she sees her flaws as awesome virtues. Richard is like that too, but she doesn't want him around so much. He's always trying to change her for her own good.

She finishes the Kaipuriña and picks out pieces of limes and sucks them. They're sweet with the sugar and *cachaça* from the bottom of the glass. Brent brings a refill and she trades in the empty. It's a wonderful life, however dangerous and pathetic as people might think. Fuck the straight world of nine to five, with TV for entertainment. Nobody can be happy like that. Look at Richard, and he has it better than most – or did.

Some yokel has been staring at her from down the bar. Now he's standing at her side. She tries not to look. She feels him there, hovering, breathing. He touches her arm. "'Scuse me. I can't get the bartender's attention down the other end, but I figure if I stand here, he'll be right over."

Renata lifts her eyebrows and looks at him. Short dark hair and an earring, nice skin up close, but she doesn't like his snotty attitude. There's no time to reply before Brent is in front of her.

"What can I do for you?" he asks the guy.

"A refill for me and a Shirley Temple for the snake."

He looks at the guy. He motions toward the empty seat at the far end. "I'll have your drink down there in a minute."

"Here will be fine," he says.

Renata is slightly amused. For some reason Brent thinks he

has dibs on her and this guy is trying to take over. Like it's between the two of them and she'll be told the outcome. Not tonight. She picks up the Kaipuriña and takes a long drink. Brent is called from the other end of the bar, but shoots a look at the guy.

"Want another?"

Usually she enjoys stirring up some fun, but tonight she feels like moving along. She turns to the guy and gives a quick wave. "*Mañana, pendejo.*"

"I speak English."

"Maybe you should head back up North then."

He looks at her.

She drains the drink, leaving the sweet juicy limes. She can't enjoy them. She reaches under her arms to be sure Pepe is all tucked in.

Brent is watching as he pours a beer, and she gives a wave and a smile with a little pucker to mean a kiss at the end, a kiss off. He shakes his head and winks. She walks out into the cool sweet air.

The streets are crowded, but people make way for her and Pepe. A few stop her so they can ask questions about the snake. Isn't he heavy? Isn't she scared he'll crush her? How old is he? What's his name? A cautious finger now and then grazes his side. She keeps walking until she sees a nice empty corner stool at an outside bar near a pool. Breathing space with a view of the sidewalk. She slides onto the stool.

She enjoys watching the people go by, girls in thin, skimpy tops, their tight ass cheeks under stretch knits or peeking out from short shorts. Focused on the flesh in front of them are the men, their clean, soft necks or thick curls, muscle shirts showing shoulder blades and armpits. South Beach is life she knows how to live. She orders a beer to cut the sweetness of the Kaipuriñas and sips from the bottle. Jules? She glimpses a thin dark-haired woman among the crowd — Jules — holding hands with a tall Latin guy. "Hey, girl. Come up here!"

Jules looks and a smile flashes across her face. Then there's tension, something Renata can't interpret. "Rennie, hey!" Jules turns to the man and they take the three steps up to the bar.

"What are you up to?" Rennie asks. There are no other seats, so they stand in front of her. She can see something in Jules' eyes — fear?

"This is Garcia — sorry, Mr Garcia."

"'S okay. Eddie."

"He's a private eye." She swallows. "We were hoping to find you."

Renata reads the panic. She puts out her hand, her guard up, feeling the strength in Garcia's handshake. "Yeah? Here I am, ready for a party."

"I want to ask you a few questions — but later," Garcia says.

"Yeah, I'm not firing on all cylinders right now, if you know what I mean."

Jules tilts her head to Garcia. "Maybe we should talk about this another time."

He nods. "Let's get a drink."

She takes a little sip on her beer as Jules and Garcia order. She needs to keep her head halfway straight, in case there's a problem.

CHAPTER 33

Midnight, South Beach

Jules

Jules is happy to have Rennie sitting there, beautiful in blue, Pepe languishing across her shoulders, but she needs to talk to her privately before Garcia has a chance to ask questions.

Jules takes a drink of her beer and watches Garcia's eyes. They flicker over Renata's breasts for a second where Pepe's tail is floating, but there's no particular stare.

Jules wonders how she can get Rennie to the ladies' room to talk without making it obvious to Garcia. He's not a cop, after all, and maybe doesn't care much about a couple of nasty drug smugglers or a cheating lawyer. "I need to make a run to the restroom," she tells Rennie. She winks the eye that Garcia can't see.

"I need to rest too," Renata says. "Pepe'll help us clear the crowd — unless you'd like to hold him, Garcia?"

"'S okay." He laughs. "You need him for protection."

Jules wonders at his tone. Sarcastic? Could he be implying that the last thing the two of them need is protection? No, she's paranoid. He's relaxed.

Renata leads the way through the tables and into the back of the restaurant. Heads turn. The two-stall restroom is empty when they enter. Renata stops at the sink and puts her hand on Jules' shoulder. "Honey, do we need to do something about this guy?"

"What? No. Rennie. He's okay. He took me out for a big dinner. He's just doing his job, asking routine questions."

"What kind of questions?"

"He asked Oliver about you, what you do. Oliver saw him talking to a lawyer, a blond guy. I started to worry – but now I don't think it means anything at all. He doesn't seem very concerned."

"He was looking for me?"

"I think."

"We can't give him any information. We don't know what he knows – or who he's working for."

"No."

"We have to find out. Then I'll decide what to do."

"No more killing."

Rennie puts her other hand on Jules' shoulder and pulls her closer, holding her cheek to cheek. Jules feels Pepe's breath near her ear. "We'll figure something out," Rennie whispers. "We're together in this."

Jules swallows, trying not to picture Garcia in a puddle of blood.

"One of us might have to fuck him to get his mind on other things."

"Me? I don't know."

"Let's see what happens." Rennie motions to the stalls. "I really do have to pee." She navigates Pepe around the corner.

Jules goes into the next stall. Her mother always told her never to pass up a chance to go – and never sit on a public toilet seat. She hears the solid stream in the next bowl and wonders if Renata sits. She imagines her perched like a dove. She looks under at the position of Rennie's feet. Pepe's tail flickers below the partition. She must be sitting, smiling, enjoying the release, the way she enjoys every physical pleasure. Jules sits. After you've killed three men there are rules you can give up.

Renata joins Jules at the sink. "I'll decide what we do. What did you tell him?"

"Nothing. He didn't ask me anything."

"Good."

"He only asked where to find you." She chews a fingernail. "I made a mistake – with Oliver. I'm sorry. I told him we took the car out there to the Everglades."

Renata touches Jules' arm above the elbow. "Don't worry about it, sweetheart. It doesn't matter. The red car must have seen the license and reported it."

"Renata – I sort of like Garcia. He's not after us. Maybe I can see him again and find out if he knows anything."

"Maybe. We don't know what's gonna happen."

Jules takes her hand. "You're not thinking of killing him?"

"I'm not thinking anything yet. Let's go back out there and see what's what." She tucks Pepe's tail under her arm and gives Jules a kiss on the cheek. "Come on, honey. Ease up."

Jules follows Rennie back to the bar. Garcia is drinking a beer and watching sidewalk traffic. He looks calm. Jules walks up to him and he hands her a Corona. She thanks him and smiles. She's feeling sober from the food and the walk. She sits on his left and Renata sits on his right, where an empty stool has opened up. Jules notices that he has a soft face and kind eyes.

"So, is your business fun?" Renata asks Garcia. "I always wanted to be a private eye. I've seen enough movies about it."

"It's not so romantic," Garcia says.

"Romantic?" Jules asks. "Usually the detective is a drunk who doesn't make enough money to pay his office rent."

He nods. "Yeah, but he gets the beautiful women. People think it's exciting work, and the drinking loner idea appeals to a lot of men." He raises his eyebrows to Jules and takes a slug of his beer. "None of the women are as beautiful as you ladies." He widens his arms to take in the corner. "This could be a scene for a movie."

Jules smiles. He's a kind man. She can't think that something might have to happen to him.

"Do you get to carry a gun?" Renata asks.

"Sure — not that I really want to." His hand moves behind his back toward his waistband. There's no obvious bulge under his loose shirt, but Jules knows it's there and it scares her. "It's a precaution," he says.

Jules feels her throat tightening. She looks down at her beer. She knows Renata is setting him up.

"I like guns," Renata says. She touches his thigh. "Maybe you can show us yours."

Garcia's head jerks slightly. He's either on guard or just aroused by the sexual innuendo. "Maybe," he says. "Not here."

"Later." She bites her lip and smiles. "What d'you want to know from us?" Renata asks.

Jules throws her a look, begging her not to continue.

Garcia seems surprised. "I don't want to talk business now."

"Jules said you were asking Oliver about our trip to the Everglades."

Jules' head jerks.

Garcia frowns, acting as if he doesn't understand. Jules sees that Renata is trying to catch him off guard. He takes a drink of beer. "I have a few routine questions, but not now."

Jules strains for an idea to change the subject, but her mind is clouded with fear.

Renata takes a swig off her beer. "As good a time as any. Wha'cha wanna know, honey?"

He leans back against the bar. "All right. Whatever you want to tell me."

Renata tosses her hair away from Pepe. "We drove around for a couple of hours that day, saw some birds, then left. We couldn't find the guys we were supposed to meet."

"Oh, uh huh, in the Everglades."

"There was a car that drove by. We tried to get his attention, but he just kept going."

"You and Jules alone?"

"Yeah. Just us."

He takes a long drink of beer. "See anything unusual?"

"Bunch of fucking alligators, nothing I don't see on the beach regularly." She starts to laugh with the crunching in of her belly like she does when she's really having fun. Her shoulders hunch and her chest vibrates with a laughter from deep inside. Jules hopes it means they don't have to kill him. Then again, Rennie could be enjoying the idea.

He laughs along, then turns to Jules. "Interesting, thanks, but not related to my investigation. I'm pretty much finished with that."

"No? What kind of case is it?" Renata asks. "Something juicy, like – a murder?"

Jules fights to get the mouthful of beer down her throat. She widens her eyes at Renata.

Garcia laughs and turns back around. "That's what everybody wants to hear, like in the movies."

"Well, is it?" Jules asks.

He gives Jules a soft look. "No. Sorry. Can't say what it's about."

Renata drains her beer. "Let's blow this hot dog stand. How about a walk by the water?" She puts out her cigarette. "Get some of the smoke out of our hair from all these bars."

Jules feels her hand shaking as she takes a long last gulp from her bottle. Renata has something terrible in mind. Jules has to talk her out of it. She drains her bottle and sets it on the bar. "I'd better make one more pit stop before we head out," she says.

"Me too," says Rennie. She glances at Garcia. "We don't *always* pee together." She laughs as she passes him. "We figure if you're left alone with the tab, you'll pay it."

He smiles halfway and shakes his head slowly. Jules is sure he doesn't have a suspicion in the world, except that they're airheads after free drinks. She follows Rennie into the bathroom. There's a woman washing her hands. They split up and go into the stalls. Jules realizes she really does have to pee. She sits down and lets it rip.

The woman goes out. Renata is brushing her hair at the mirror. Jules steps beside her to wash her hands. "See? He doesn't suspect anything. We don't have to kill him."

Renata puts the brush back into her purse and zips it shut. "Jules, don't you get it? He's working for the lawyer. If he's connected up those two sleazebags, we're dead meat. I think he's waiting just a little longer to be sure."

"If he knew about them, he would have been more interested in your Everglades story. We can't kill him. He's not a scumbag like the others. He's just a regular working guy."

"Regular guy or motherfucker — you can't tell. He could be fooling us completely. I hate this too, but once he puts it all together, it's our asses. There's one witness, remember."

"The red car? They didn't see anything."

"They got our license number! How else could he have found Oliver? They must have suspected something and gone back and found the bodies. Hell, Garcia knows everything. He just wants to get laid before he turns us in."

"No, Rennie. You're mixing this all up." She puts her fingers on her temples to demonstrate exasperation. "I can't sort it out, but I know you're wrong. He would've told the police by now if he knew anything. Maybe he doesn't want to add it up. He doesn't care about the slime. He likes us."

"This isn't the movies, Jules."

"The movies come from real life. We didn't really want to kill anybody and he can figure that out."

"I did — I wanted to kill them all." She uncaps her lip gloss and strokes it across her upper then lower lip.

"I know you don't mean that." Jules watches Renata's lips, fascinated.

Renata presses her lips together. "Come on. We'll go down to the beach and see if we can loosen him up. Feel like getting naked?"

Jules is past any shock at this suggestion. "Okay — if we don't have to kill him."

"Don't worry."

Garcia has paid and waits by the sidewalk. He looks innocent to Jules, like a nice uncle or an older brother.

Renata takes his right arm and motions Jules to the left. They turn back towards Tropical Moons, strolling in the light breeze off the ocean. As they pass the open front of Mangoes, Jules sees Brent the bartender watching them. She waves. Renata flinches, like she's been shocked, but doesn't acknowledge his stare.

Jules and Garcia wait outside The Moons, while Renata takes Pepe to the room. Jules makes small talk about the beauty of the beach, but she can only think about Rennie and hope she's not up there loading the gun. It doesn't take long, and Rennie nearly bounces out the door with childlike energy. Jules sees there can't possibly be a gun concealed anywhere under the tight clothing. Garcia's gun is still enough to worry about.

Renata leads the way toward the other side of the street where the beach is broad and sea oats block the distant view from the street to the surf. It's a cool walk through the dry sand, and Renata breaks off to run into the water in front of them. Jules and Garcia watch her. She unfastens her top and waves it, arms above her head wiggling her chest, then kicking up water.

"She's a lively one," he says.

"She's incredibly beautiful and alive," Jules tells him. "She deserves more in life."

"Doesn't everybody?"

"I don't know."

"You know, she could very easily get herself into a lot of trouble."

Jules feels the air go out of her stomach. "I'm with her all the time. She's fine."

"She's a prostitute."

"Not really. She just has a lot of boyfriends. Men come to her and beg for attention. Sometimes they give her gifts or money."

He clucks his tongue. "Julie, she makes a living off of men. She's a whore."

"You don't need to use that word. It's cruel. You don't know her." He stares into Jules' eyes with meaning that she refuses to acknowledge, and she realizes for him there are no moral questions. Everything is answered. She can't think of anything else to say. "Come on. Let's cool off." She motions and runs past him into the water with her dress on. Rennie has her pants off by now and is planted wide-legged in the surf, leaning backward, arms stretched high to the stars, her laughter peaking when a wave rushes above her knees. "Life is a beach!" she yells. It seems to echo over the water. Rennie grabs Jules and kisses her on the ear. "We can't kill him now anyway," Rennie whispers. "Brent saw us together. We'll just have to hope you're right."

Jules sighs with relief, though she's not quite so trusting in Garcia as before. She nods and kisses Rennie on the cheek, wondering what Garcia is thinking. She's getting more and more used to female love in her life. She feels Rennie's warm hands lifting her dress, sliding up her hips. "Let's entertain him," Rennie whispers. "Suck him in, in case we need him." The dress slips over Jules' head.

Jules cringes, but the feeling washes out to sea with the next pull of tide on her calves as Rennie's fingers slip her panties down to her knees. In a trance almost, Jules lifts one leg and then the other. No one in sight except Garcia, who has stopped to stand above the water line. He taps a cigarette out of a pack and lights it. It must be his first one of the night. Renata tosses Jules' dress and panties to the dry sand and squats on her heels in front of Jules, holding her by the back of the thighs. "You're so beautiful," she says.

Renata's face moves toward her, but Jules jumps backwards across the sand. "Rennie – no."

"What's the matter, sweetheart? I'll make you come."

"I can't." Jules looks at Garcia.

"He'll love it, honey. They all do."

Jules feels the tears welling. "It's not just that. I'm not ready. I want it to be special and perfect between us." She can't move her eyes from Garcia, who takes a long drag on the cigarette, then moves to the right to sit on a wooden beach chair. "I want it to be private." She reaches for Renata's hand. "I love you, Rennie. I mean that."

Renata stands. She shakes her head. "Oh, Jules, you can't love me like that. I'll hurt you. I don't know how to love anybody, any one person."

"I'll teach you. Fresh start for both of us."

"I don't know, sweetie."

Jules moves closer and takes Renata in her arms. She feels the wonderful smoothness of their soft breasts against each other, and her hands feel the thin ribs in Rennie's back. "We can have a wonderful life together."

Rennie puts her head on Jules' shoulder and kisses her neck. The roar of surf is loud as a high wave comes in and breaks. It foams around their calves and brings goosebumps to Jules' legs. "Rennie, we have to go away from here, before something else happens — anywhere you want."

Rennie stands back and looks at Jules. She doesn't say anything, but Jules can read the stare. It's no time to start behaving like Richard.

Jules turns toward Garcia. It's too dark to see his eyes, but he's facing them, perfectly still. The ash of his cigarette glows as he inhales. Rennie takes Jules back into her arms and gives her a quick hard kiss. They drop hands and start gathering up their clothes.

CHAPTER 34

Sunday, October 10, 9:00 am, South Miami

Richard

The sun is bright outside the glass sliding doors and he sees that leaves have accumulated on the surface of the pool. The water is cloudy. Linda must have discontinued the pool service. His lower back aches, but other than that, he can't think of a good reason to get out of bed. There's nothing for breakfast. The boys aren't there to need a ride to church. He has to assume Linda is handling all that. Not a word from her. Of course, he hasn't tried to call her mother's. A shudder runs through him and a hot sweat breaks out on his chest. His mother-in-law was always so proud of him.

Memories of the night before are vague. He wonders how many times he tried to call Renata and how long he let the phone ring. The Jules woman could probably answer those questions. He stares at the ceiling, the finely textured white plaster, so much like frosting. It was worth all the money they paid for professional remodeling. He glances around the room. It's perfect. There is no good reason why he can't live here with his family and do his job like he has done so happily in the past. He just can't. He lifts his head from the pillow. Dizziness and nausea come in waves. He rolls to the side and off the bed. The worst is over.

He puts toothpaste on the brush. The phone rings. He walks back into the bedroom to listen as the machine records. It's Linda. He picks up.

"Richard?"

"Yes."

"Why didn't you say anything? All I heard was the click."

"I don't exist to you anymore, do I? I'm surprised you can hear my voice at all."

There's strength in her pause – or maybe it's confusion. "Richard – I thought you might want to talk. I'm worried about you."

"You weren't worried about me when you took the boys and left."

"I left? You were long gone."

He has nothing to say. It's true.

"Richard, are you doing something else right now? I don't think I have your attention." Her voice becomes shrill. "Is she there with you?"

He wonders how much she knows. "No. I'm ill. *She* doesn't want anything to do with me now that I'm free." He almost chokes on the last word, the knowledge coming clear as he states it.

"Oh, now that you're *free*? Well, what did you expect?"

"It doesn't matter. I'm doing what I have to do."

He hears her breathing hard on the line.

"You sound like you've joined a cult or something. I've been thinking that for a while – that you're living in a trance. I have to tell you something. You might not like it."

"I'm inured to bad news."

"Richard." She clicks her tongue. "I hired a P.I. I know what you've been doing, and I think you should see a psychologist. I would be happy to set up an appointment and go with you."

Richard can't cover the phone in time to hide his laughter, hysterics. "I'm sorry. The thought of a detective tailing me is hilarious. My life is a sordid B movie – and so unoriginal. He probably has video of me passed out on the beach." He laughs brokenly at the vision and the memory that he hasn't even seen Renata for more than a minute since the break-up with Linda. "I hope you aren't giving him a lot of money."

"No. I already paid him off. I don't want any more information about your sad, sorry life, and now I understand that nothing matters to you."

He considers telling her that he's inspired, writing poetry again, good stuff, but it's too late. Neither is it a good time to ask to see the boys. "You're right. I don't care about anything I should. You're wasting your time on me. You deserve a better life."

The phone clunks. That's that – perhaps. Mostly, he hopes that she's given up on him for her own good, but in another way the finality of losing her would be devastating.

His mind turns back to Rennie. There's not much use in trying to get her on the weekend. He decides to take a drive over to the beach, maybe do a run. He can leave her a note. Then he'll come back and write. Spend the afternoon at it.

CHAPTER 35

1:00 pm, Tropical Moons, Room 2-A

Jules

Jules opens her eyes in the glare of a hot afternoon, sunlight streaking the ceiling. She sees a tailless lizard in the corner and wonders how those creatures always get inside. Memories of the night come to her out of order. She recalls stumbling up the stairs of the hotel with Rennie, after Garcia left them. He'd given Jules his arm to keep her steady while she put her clothes back on and – after a few more drinks at some outdoor café – said he had one drink too many. She can't remember what she thought at the time, but now she realizes he meant he couldn't perform sexually. She should have told him it wasn't expected or desired. She thinks of the exhibition she and Rennie gave in the surf. She remembers that they might have to kill him. She yanks herself out of bed and pulls on a robe.

Jules drops ice cubes in a cup. The plastic liter of Smirnoff that Rennie left contains a refreshing mouthful. The perfume of the vodka fills her head as it slides over the ice. She takes two slices of bread from the refrigerator. She's got to make some money, can't keep accepting the presents and cash that Rennie drops on her table. Rennie has said more than once that money is meaningless and as long as she has food and a place to live, so will Jules. But Jules can't accept rent, and it's coming due.

Jules hears Rennie moving around. Low techno starts to pulse on the new CD player. She goes to the wall and takes off the picture to see if there's company. At first voices are mixed with the music, but she soon catches a few of Francisco's syllables. They're likely to be in bed. His voice is cooing, soothing, and Jules knows that he is kissing Rennie, sucking the soft freckled flesh. She reaches inside her robe and touches herself. Her head against the wall, she listens to the whispers as she strokes. She loses herself in the waves, light, lingering ripples of pleasure, and the final shudder. She takes a deep breath and sits down in the chair, reaches across the table for her drink, and sips. Thoughts of the rent are back, and Garcia.

There's a knock, and a key turns. The door opens.

"Hey, Julie. Whassup?" Renata has Pepe across her shoulders. She's wearing a towel as usual. It barely reaches to her thighs.

Jules remembers the framed picture still lying on the table. A blush blooms over her face. "Hi, Rennie."

Rennie bends and gives her a warm kiss on the lips. "Hey, cheer up, missy." She motions to the picture. "I thought you might be listening. You could've crawled in with us – fun's fun."

"No. I couldn't."

Rennie rolls her eyes.

Jules takes a drink of her watery vodka. She passes the cup to Rennie. "Today I have to look for work – and I thought we could see Garcia again tonight, try to figure this whole thing out, see what he knows." She searches Rennie's face for a reaction, but there's none.

Rennie swallows. "This is water." She makes a face. "See him. That's what you should do. Take the dick to bed."

"I thought it might be a good thing to talk some more. Besides, he's a good person. We can't —"

"Kill him?"

Jules bites her lip. "We can't."

"You're right. Francisco says to wait —"

"You told him?"

"Sure. I don't keep secrets from him — not many." She moves Pepe's head out of her armpit. "Francisco's not worried about Garcia." She strokes Pepe. "He thinks Garcia is sniffing around on something else, enjoying our company. So, if you're fucking him, that'll be extra insurance. I doubt he cares about those slime balls out in the Everglades if he does have a whiff of them."

Jules flinches. "That's what I said. But fucking doesn't cure everything, Rennie."

Renata smiles and lifts her eyebrows. "You'd be surprised."

"Maybe if you do it, it does."

"Fuck. Give him a try. If it's lousy, you never have to do it again."

Jules shudders, making the connection to the dead lawyer.

"Pull yourself out of this fucking funk, Julie baby." Rennie drags her up by her wrists from the chair. "Come on. We'll call him up and see if he wants to go out."

Jules puts on a sundress while Rennie waits. Jules sees her eyes slip over her breasts and crotch. She combs her hair. She wishes she would have gone over and crawled in. Hesitancy has always been a problem for her.

"Come on." Rennie takes the comb from her hand. "You have his number?"

Jules points toward the card on the dresser. Rennie grabs it and pulls her out the door.

Francisco is at the table holding a cigarette over the ashtray, reading the *Herald*. Jules thinks how beautiful his hair is damp and tossed in ringlets from the sex. He looks up. "Hi, girlie."

Jules nods. "Good morning."

Rennie goes straight to the phone and dials. Jules crosses

her arms, heart pounding, as Rennie waits for Garcia to answer, and then invites him out for another night with the girls.

"I see. Yeah, we had such a good time. . . Meet in the lobby? . . . Eight? See ya." She hangs up. "He's got his kid for the day, but he's set for tonight."

"He has a child?"

"Yeah, a nine-year-old boy," Renata says. "He said they do kid stuff, like go to comic book stores and magic shops."

"He's a good guy."

"Okay, then," Rennie says. "It's up to you to make sure he doesn't know anything or care to."

Jules looks at Francisco, but he's deep in his paper. She looks back at Rennie, pulls out a chair, and sits down. "But you're going, right?"

"No, no. He's all yours. I was just making it sound more casual. Me and Franco have an appointment. Just tell Garcia I couldn't make it."

A frown takes over Jules' face. "Rennie, I'm not good at this. I don't know what to do. I don't really want to sleep with him."

"I thought you did."

Francisco looks up. "Julie, sweetheart. Close your eyes and let him stick it in. Then he's all yours." He points to a drawer. "Take a condom."

Rennie strokes Jules' hair and gathers it in her hands. "Listen to Franco, baby. He knows men."

Jules tilts her face to plead and Rennie plants a kiss on her forehead. "Let's have breakfast in the morning, and you can tell me all about it."

"Sure," Jules says, feeling dazed.

Renata points to a liter of vodka on the sink. "Yours." Jules smiles her thanks and takes it. Renata places two condoms in Jules' other hand and closes her fingers. They touch lips. Jules turns and heads over to her place. Too many drugs, too much alcohol to trust her brain anymore. If it wasn't for Renata, she'd turn herself in. Let somebody else take control.

CHAPTER 36

7:30 PM, Tropical Moons, Room 2-A

Jules

She sits on the bed and rubs her feet. Time to clean up and get ready. She feels like she spent the whole Sunday going bar to bar, and although nothing was actually offered, it was a solid day's work. Her feet still hurt. Brent mentioned a possible bar-maid job, in between his questions about Renata, but that wouldn't be available until the manager returned from vacation, if it were true. A big *if*, but a nice place to work, and her only hope for the moment.

She showers, combs her hair, and picks the sundresses from the chair. There are two of them, both loose hanging with thin straps over the shoulders, and she isn't sure which one she wore the night before. She doesn't want to look like she slept in her clothes. Both are slightly wrinkled from sitting. She takes a guess and puts on the blue. If she doesn't remember, what are the chances that Garcia will?

She's sipping her beer at the bar when Garcia passes the window and opens the door. He smiles when he sees her. He looks better than she remembers, younger with softer skin.

Maybe he shaved a mustache or something.

He takes the stool next to her. His fingers tap the bar. "Hey, how are you?"

"Pretty well. You okay?"

He puts his hands on his lap. "A little shaky actually. I don't usually drink that much."

Jules nods. She can't get herself to say "me either."

"I had my son since nine this morning."

"Rennie told me. Oh, yeah, she couldn't make it tonight. She said to tell you she's sorry."

"That's fine. I'd rather spend the time talking to you."

She wonders why he's trying to flatter her. She feels herself slipping into her own interior fog, again too much drinking without eating.

He orders a beer then takes her hand. "Hey, honey, I like having you to myself. Rennie was a work connection – too much for me."

Jules feels her chest harden. "Part of a job?"

"Was. It's out of my hands."

Jules panics. "Is she going to be arrested?"

"Huh? Not that I know of. I can't talk about it."

"She's my friend – I guess I don't have to tell you that." She blushes deeply. "I'm scared something will happen to her."

"Jules, you must know that your friend's profession is damn risky. She's into all kinds of stuff that you can't even imagine. I see how you girls are, and that doesn't bother me – much – but be cautious about getting involved in any deals with her. That life isn't for you."

"You don't know me."

"I'd like to . . . Listen to me, okay? Renata is bad news – low life – she's headed for a lot of trouble. I'd advise you to stay away from her – if it's any of my business."

Jules nods slowly, swallowing an angry defense of Rennie's innocence, for fear of revealing her own deceit, as well as the depth of her feelings that are none of his business. His words frighten her, implying that he knows something, and she can't repeat the terrible slurs to Rennie. It comes to Jules that she must have been hallucinating to consider Garcia as a lover. Just being with him, she's aligning herself against the only person she truly loves.

Garcia looks into her eyes. "I'm glad you're thinking seriously about what I said. You should move out of that room as quickly as possible."

She frowns. She can't believe how backward he's got the whole thing. She can only shake her head. A rush of emotion sweeps over her. "I'm in a bad situation. I'll probably be evicted before I can move. Rennie is the only person who has ever helped me out."

He takes her hand. His eyes are soft. "I thought you were a writer?"

"I write. I haven't made a cent on it. Now I can't even find a waitress job. I had nothing to eat yesterday except the dinner you bought me. I'm sorry I let you do that."

She wipes the tears from her eyes, disgusted with herself for her weakness and for carrying on, revealing it to him.

"Hey, take it easy, sweetie. I didn't mean to come on so strong. We can talk about this later. Let me take you for something to eat right now. It's no wonder you're upset. You're starved." He takes her elbow and puts his hand around her waist. "Come on. I enjoy seeing you eat. I'm hungry too."

She resists for a few seconds, thinking she shouldn't accept, but her body has turned against her mind at the offer of food. If she eats she can think more clearly. If he likes to feed her, he might as well have his way.

After dinner, Jules sips coffee, relaxed. The warm taste of garlic is still in her mouth, and her lips feel soft from the olive oil she dipped her bread in. She could sit at the outdoor table all night, gazing across the street at the palms and stars. The world is almost in focus again, at least more so than it's been for months. She looks across the table at Garcia. He's gazing at the moon. He turns, smiles, and reaches for her hand. "I'm sorry I said those things about your friend. I'm worried about you here with this South Beach crowd. You don't fit."

Jules tries not to let the strain come back into her voice. She needs to steer him away from Rennie. "No, I'm not cool enough, true. But it's okay. Let's not talk about it now."

"I didn't mean it like that. Take a walk?"

The walk is toward The Moons, and Garcia stops her in a pocket of darkness at the edge of the building. He puts his arms around her and his mouth over hers, warm and devouring. His hands on her neck and shoulders bring heat into her chest and she braces herself and kisses back hard. This is what she is supposed to do, dissolve any suspicions. She plants herself hard into his groin and puts her arms around his sides. His warm huskiness is overpowering. It's not so bad to be in a man's control. She remembers Rennie telling her, men are good for that – on occasion.

He leads her inside, through the bar, and up the dark stairs. As they come to her place, she sees a huge wooden box past Rennie's door, nearly blocking the hallway. There's a padlock securing the lid. She looks at Garcia and frowns. He shrugs. "Fire hazard."

She shrugs back and opens her door. There's no light or sound from Rennie's, so Jules is on her own. Garcia sweeps her inside, like in the movies. The empty vodka bottle is on the table and the bed is unmade, but Garcia only looks into her eyes. He bends her down onto the rumpled sheets and goes back to kissing her neck. She's thinking that it's nice, enjoying the moment. He pushes her sundress strap aside and moves his lips down her shoulder to her chest. His tongue flicks her nipple. It stings, like a shock running through her. His word – whore – comes back and pierces her mood like a knife. Why did she trust him? He'll use her to get to Rennie. Panic drives away any pleasure. Stiffness comes into her arms, but her dress is tugged over her head fast. His face slides down her abdomen, and his mouth goes between her thighs. She jumps. He lifts his head, and she scoots away. Her feet hit the floor. She stands up breathing hard.

He pulls himself part way up. "What'sa matter, honey?"

She's trembling with the shock of how far she's gone with this stranger. She doesn't want him to touch her anymore, and she knows fucking him isn't going to help anyone. She has to shift the blame off Rennie. She puts her hand on his shoulder to steady herself. "I have something to tell you."

Garcia sits up straight and smooths his hair into place, moving the fine tendrils to the right side of his part. He takes a deep breath. "What?"

"Your investigation —" Her voice is shaking. "The murder . . . I know about it. Rennie had nothing to do with it. I — I think it was to protect her." She stands up and finds the sundress and pulls it over her head. "Wait here." She goes into the hall. No light under Rennie's door, so she walks right in and turns on the light in the bathroom. She gets down on her knees and reaches into the back corner of the cabinet. The bottom is damp and gritty. Finally she feels it, the lawyer's pinkie ring, right where Rennie said she'd put it. She rinses her hands.

Garcia is sitting at the table in front of the empty vodka glass. She holds the ring out to him.

"What's this?" He takes it and turns it over in his palm. A tiny red stone catches the light. "A school ring?"

"Evidence," she says. "One of Renata's boyfriends gave it to her." She thinks of using Richard's name, but holds back. "It's supposed to mean she's safe. The person who intended to harm her is — gone."

"Who?"

"I don't know. You're the detective. I thought it would mean something in the murder investigation."

"Murder?" The complete blank on Garcia's face stops her. "I'm not investigating a murder. I told you that."

Jules covers her mouth and tries to stay focused. She knows she's made a huge mistake. Her voice comes out tiny and weak. "You're not? I thought you said . . . you said all those things about Rennie, how dangerous she is."

He shakes his head and his lips form the word *no*.

"I thought . . . ?"

"Is she involved in a murder?" he asks.

"No, that's what I was trying to tell you. She's not. I thought you were after her by mistake."

"Somebody was killed to protect Renata?"

"I'm not sure. Probably just scared away. I was going to make it seem like murder to get your mind off Renata."

Garcia stands up. He has a deep crease between his eyebrows. "Which boyfriend gave her this?"

"I don't know. Maybe it was just a present – I probably misunderstood, listening through the wall. I enhance things. I'm a writer – trying to be." She takes his hand. "I couldn't stand what you were saying about Rennie, and I thought the ring would put you on a different track. I'm sorry." She holds out an open hand.

Garcia nods, but closes his fingers around the ring. He pauses. He nods again. "I shouldn't say – but now that the job's over – I was doing surveillance on one of Renata's married boyfriends – that's all. If there's a murder investigation, it's being handled by the police."

Jules drops into the chair. Good thing she didn't give Richard's name. She tries for a laugh. "Too much TV." Immediately she realizes that there's no TV in the room and her face starts to burn. She puts out her hand again to take the ring.

He drops it into his pocket. "I'll see if I can find out anything about this – to set your mind at ease." He looks hard into her eyes. "I better go." He motions next door. "Tell your friend that I'll take care of this." He tucks his shirt neatly into the sides of his pants, avoiding the back where Jules imagines the gun is.

"I don't think she cares. It wasn't really the big deal I made it out to be."

"Remember what I told you – you're asking for a lot of trouble hanging around here. Maybe I can find out something to convince you of that."

She smiles and nods as if she's tired of hearing it, but her legs are so shaky, she can barely walk him out the door. He bends and kisses her forehead. "Take care, Jules."

He turns and walks, and she closes the door behind him, with little relief. She listens as his footsteps go down the stairs. Her knees turn to rubber and she clenches the doorknob for support. There's no telling what she might have triggered.

CHAPTER 37

Monday, October 11, 6:30 am, Tropical Moons

Renata

She gets in just before dawn and tiptoes down the hall, wondering if Garcia is at Jules' place and if Julie had a good time. Julie deserves a good time – and a man to feed her regularly, since she won't let Renata do it. She feels a twinge of hurt for Jules, thinking how she suffers from fear and loneliness. She wants to barge in and give Julie a hug. It's almost like love, as she remembers it, the cause of much pain. She holds up her half-finger to remind herself. Fuck you, it's saying to her. She's allowed herself to get closer than she realized.

She passes Jules' door and stops outside of her own. In the dim light of the bulb, an enormous rectangular shape looms a few steps beyond from the darkness. "Fuck – the box," she says aloud. "Fuck." She almost forgot about the slave idea. She's avoided Richard pretty well for a few days. She hopes he got lonely and went back to his family. She walks around the box. It's almost as tall as she is, over six feet long, and fancier than she would have thought – gothic style, and built like a fortress. The paint is a rich glossy black, highlighted with gold and silver chains and stained glass inserts. There are rollers on the bottom, and inlaid screws where it's put together almost seamlessly. David must have got his buff gym buddies to carry the pieces up the stairs. Amazing. Beautiful.

There's a hole on top where a head and shoulders can stick through with bolted trap doors, front and back, out of reach of the occupant. No escape. One side has a hole cut out for a face, with flowing blond hair painted around it, and down lower is a smaller hole – no doubt measured to be just the right height and size for David's lover's cock and balls. They thought of everything. Various holes, for other positions. She opens the door to her apartment and sees a white envelope someone slid under the door, even though it was unlocked. She takes out a note and a key, and sets the envelope on the table. David is as good as his word. She pictures Richard's bare neck and shoulders atop the castle. Crazy, but intriguing.

She thinks about the closet where she was held captive. It took her almost a week before she fought to be let out – but a man couldn't last that long in a box, no matter how much he loves her. She hopes.

She opens the refrigerator for a little light, throws her purse on a chair, and strips off her black stretch cotton dress. It's always better to be naked, no matter how comfortable the clothes. She takes the envelope and reads the card:

So happy to get this monster out of our place!
Hope you have as much fun as we did.
Love you, David

Rennie wonders. She'll have to feed Richard. How will she do that? Lots of pizza delivery. She's never really been into S and M. Too many problems. She shuts the refrigerator door and throws herself onto the bed. "Ahh." The lusciousness of cool sheets and some sleep alone. She'll have to move the box inside the apartment, and there will hardly be room to walk around. Richard will hear her every word. What about

Francisco? He'll soon be back from the Bahamas and there's bound to be overlap. Will Richard consider it sweet torture to witness them fucking? Not a chance.

She rolls onto her back and looks up at the ceiling, thin amber light creeping across it. Still, it's something new – an experiment. She's never tried to take total control over a man before, although she's been controlled – if not by the man, then by her own feelings. That's the secret to making the system work, isolation and brainwashing. She learned that first hand. She doesn't have enough meanness to stick it out for long, but then she only wants to scare him away, not bind him to her forever. Just give him a taste of her lifestyle from a place on the sidelines where he can't interfere. That should send him back to his wife and kids – where he can be happy again. She stretches and yawns and curls on her side. It'll be painful for both of them – but a few days ought to do it.

She wakes up to the phone ringing and ringing. The message machine is turned off. Pepe is curled around her leg and she's hot and sweaty in the sunlight from the half-open curtain. She doesn't move to answer. Probably Richard. She's not ready for him yet. She closes her eyes and holds still until the ringing stops, as if he might sense that she's in the room and come right over.

It feels late when her eyes open and she remembers the box in the hall. She needs to get it inside before somebody steals it. She props herself on her elbow and looks at Pep, so peaceful. She unwraps him from her leg, holding his head near her thigh and unwinding him tail first with her foot. If she's lucky Garcia will still be there with Jules and he can help move the box.

Renata pulls on shorts and a t-shirt and walks next door. Maybe Jules will have some coffee. Fat chance. In case of Garcia, she knocks.

Jules opens the door. She's wearing a stained robe and her face looks puffy. "Hi, Rennie."

Renata steps inside. No Garcia. She takes Jules by the

shoulders and stares into her eyes. "That bastard do something to you?"

"No, no. He left last night. I couldn't have sex with him. It didn't feel right."

Renata lays her head on Jules' shoulder and hugs her. "You silly sweetie. You're my sweetie, huh?" She takes her head and kisses her. She feels Jules clinging. Renata pulls back. "Hey, what's wrong?"

Jules shakes her head to mean nothing, but her eyes are watery. "Need to talk."

"In a sec. You gotta help me move this thing out of the hall first."

Jules sniffs and wipes her nose. "What is that? A house for Pepe?"

Renata laughs. "A dungeon for Richard. He wants to be my slave. I figure I'll let him try it. What the hell?"

Jules' face puckers up. "You want Richard here all the time?"

"He won't last long."

Jules frowns.

Rennie takes her hand. "Let's push the thing into the apartment before management gets after me." She leads Jules into the hall and watches her reaction as she walks around it.

"Richard's crazy if he gets into that thing," Jules says.

"Duh."

"I mean certifiable."

"Wanna bet on it?"

"No. I'd never bet against you." Jules smiles. "Maybe it's a good place for him."

Renata opens her door and goes behind the box. "Help me do this."

Jules pushes beside her and they roll the box over the painted concrete onto the linoleum of the apartment. Renata moves the chair and they push the box next to the wall. Rennie sits down on the chair. "He better not last long. No space to breathe in this room."

Jules points at the box. "Pepe will like that," she says. She giggles.

"You're right. I'll never be able to keep him out of there." Renata's laughter joins Jules' as she pictures Pepe wound for warmth around Richard's thigh. Jules slumps down on the bed, jerking with uncontrolled giggles, and Rennie walks over and drops onto the bed next to her, hugging her side and vibrating with laughter.

Renata settles down and props her head on her elbow. She hears a sob from Jules. "What's the matter, honey?"

Jules turns away, weeping into her hands. "I'm scared. I made a big mistake."

Renata climbs over her to see her face. She caresses Jules' arm and watches the tears run between her fingers. "Come on, tell me. It can't be that bad. Garcia's a moron to leave."

Jules gets out the words, telling Renata how she tried to throw him off track, admitting that she gave him the ring and used the word *murder* when Garcia hadn't known anything about it.

Renata gets her some toilet paper so she can blow her nose. "It's okay, honey. It's not your fault. You did your best to help."

"He was investigating Richard, I guess — unless you have another married boyfriend."

"Fuck! I'm so stupid! Richard's wife hired Garcia. He's not after us at all."

"What if he starts another investigation?"

"I don't know. He's probably only interested in stuff he's paid for. The cops handle the murders. We don't even know if he took you seriously."

"He did — but he still seems to like me," Jules says.

"Yeah. He wouldn't want to cause you any trouble."

"He wants to cause you trouble, Rennie."

"Why? Think he feels sorry for Richard's wife? He sees this stuff all the time."

"I don't know. He's sort of judgmental."

Rennie shrugs. "Let's not worry about it. We can handle

him." She massages Jules' thigh and squeezes it. "They're all just dicks, professor dick, private dick – except Franco. He's a cock. Frankencock, huh? If he fucked the holes in the mattress they'd come."

Jules smiles. "If you say so."

"Go, get your shower. We'll eat a late breakfast – I feel like eggs." Jules starts for the door, and Renata remembers the news. "Hey, Julie, we need to go by Mangoes. I saw Brent last night and he said for you to stop in. Maybe some part-time work." Renata smiles her biggest and brightest. "Things are looking up, girl!"

The phone rings. Renata has a feeling she'd better answer. At this point Richard might come over with the excuse that he was worried. She picks up.

"Rennie – I was giving you one more ring before I drove over there. I thought something must have happened."

"Sorry, Richard. I've been really busy. In fact, I'm just heading out the door. What if you come over tomorrow? That's Tuesday, right? Say four or so? Is that okay?" She giggles. "I have a surprise for you."

There's a pause. Renata waits. Richard really has no choice, and she knows he's struggling not to sound disappointed.

"Okay. That'll work fine. A surprise?"

"Yeah, baby. An amazing surprise."

"What?"

She clucks her tongue. "I'm not going to tell you, silly."

"A hint?"

"Mmm. It's something you and Pepe will both like."

She hears the air go out of him. "I thought you were serious. How can a snake and I like the same thing?"

Renata laughs. "Quit fishing for compliments! You'll see. I have to go. Bye, hon." She hangs up before he can start on another chain of thought. Poor Richard.

CHAPTER 38

12:30 pm, Tropical Moons, Room 2-A

Jules

She saves to a disk and closes the laptop. Time to meet Rennie and head down to Mangoes.

"Cute dress, honey. Nice nips," Rennie says, as they walk along the strip.

Rennie's words, warm sun, the smell of coconut oil and the sound of the surf. If Jules gets the job her money worries will be over, and after a few months maybe she can sell her book. She takes a deep breath and makes a silent pledge to herself: lose the fear and guilt, drink less, eat more, love Rennie. A gust catches her dress and cool air rushes between her thighs.

Brent is pouring beer with a dreamy look toward the waves as they step into the bar. It's nearly empty with a few men having something pink and frozen at a table close by and a few farther down having beers. A spark comes into Brent's eyes when he spots Rennie.

"Hi, there, baby," Renata says. She stretches toward him over the bar.

Jules watches, understanding his pleasure, as Brent touches

his lips to Rennie's and lingers. She thinks of Rennie's sweet scent and the soft moistness of her mouth. There's a slight sting of jealousy, but she pushes it away.

"Julie is here to go to work."

Brent turns to Jules. "As a matter of fact, I gave the manager a recommendation based on what Rennie told me about you. He said you could train with me for a couple of hours anytime and see how it goes. You've worked behind a bar before, right?"

Jules is caught between the truth and what Rennie would expect her to say. She doesn't want to make Rennie a liar. "Sure, I know my way around a bar." All the way around it to the ladies' room, she thinks.

Rennie waves and throws a kiss. "Francisco gets back from the Bahamas in a few minutes. See you later."

Brent takes Jules behind the bar explaining the contents of cabinets and coolers, and the glass washing routine. He puts Jules to work cutting up fruit and then heads to the back for a break. She gets a slicing rhythm going on the oranges, making thin zests, inhaling the fresh tangy aroma.

Brent is in back a long time, but no new customers come in. The guys with the pink drinks finish and switch to Red Stripe, bottled. Jules finds the opener, the beers, and flips off the tops. She wipes up the rings of water and tosses their plastic cups into the garbage. So far so good.

Soon the fruit is all cut and stored in the container of separate plastic sections. Brent is still in back. She starts moving liquor bottles and wiping the shelf. It needs it. She looks up just in time to catch the glance of a tall Latin walking by – Garcia. She looks down, but too late. He's walking toward her. She straightens herself, thinking how Renata would stand, how she would handle the situation.

"Hi, Julie." He bends to brush his lips against her cheek.

"Back on the beach so soon? Would you like something to drink?"

"You didn't say you'd found a job."

"First day. Do you want something?" She wishes Brent would come back out. She looks at the other customers, hoping for a distraction.

"No thanks. I'm working."

"Oh," Jules says. She'd noticed his direction was toward The Moons, but she doesn't want to ask about it. She begins wiping the second shelf of bottles, trying not to let him see her trembling hands.

"Yeah. There's always business around here." He moves closer. "I can't help reminding you to watch out for yourself. Understand?"

Jules lifts her shoulders and makes her eyes big, knowing that's exactly what Rennie would do. "I'm fine. I really don't know why you're so worried."

Garcia raises an eyebrow. "Think about it, honey."

CHAPTER 39

Tuesday, October 12, 6:45 am, Atlantic Shores
University

Richard

The halls are dim and silent in the early morning, hollow.
What could be lonely, he now finds refreshing. Despite the
headache from a late-night pint of scotch, he plans to be in
and out before the students and other instructors start arriv-
ing. He turns the knob and steps inside, shutting the door
lightly behind him in case Patrick – so young and enthusiastic – is in the adjacent office already working.

Richard sets his briefcase on the desk and looks around.
He used to arrive at work before six, in his first few years, fin-
ishing a poem a week sometimes, starting many. He often
jumped out of bed at five after making love to his sleepy wife
– the sweet, passionate Linda he remembers. She'd get up with
him to have coffee and cinnamon toast before he left for his
office. She was proud of her poet-professor husband.

Those days have been over for many years, the inevit-
able boredom seeping in to replace them. He's sure that
Linda will soon find interesting substitutes for his whining,

over-explored, middle-aged presence around the house.

He opens a file and flips to the contest entries, pulls out a thick folder. He's sure Patrick will be glad to take over the job, no matter how many extra hours are involved. Just like Richard – and all of them – used to feel, before their enthusiasm was lost over time, worn away by consistent disappointment.

He sees Tammi's name on the top sheet as he sets the stack of papers on the desk. He should frame it, the piece of paper that changed his life. Yet more accurately, he set the odds against himself. He might be able to change it back if he had the motivation. As it is, he feels philosophical, not inclined to judge his actions.

There's a knock outside. It's so light he's not sure it's his door. "Come in," he says. He holds his breath, waiting to see who it might be, how long it will take. The knock comes again. "Come in," he yells.

Still nothing. He goes to the door and opens it. Tammi stands there. Her eyes are at his chest level and she talks into it without looking up. "I saw your car in the parking lot – and I wanted to tell you that I didn't mean to get you in trouble."

He bends and tilts his head to catch her eye. She's holding back tears, except for one. She looks up slightly. "I was so shocked – I had to tell Deirdre. She told her boyfriend and then all kinds of stuff started to happen. Somebody went to an administrator and I had to tell the whole story. I'm so sorry."

Heat rises under his collar. "You said I touched you."

She puts her hand over her eyes. "No. I mean, I didn't mean to. I said it by mistake. Your hand – it was accidental. The dean confused me."

Richard tries to think back again to a time his hand touched anything beyond Tammi's shoulder or arm. Never. He takes a breath and opens his mouth to give her a harsh lecture, but he stops. This event is much less devastating than he would have imagined. He's tired of the subject already. He just wants out of there. He doesn't need to watch her cry. "I see," he says.

"I didn't know what would happen – that you would lose your job." She snuffles and wipes her hand under her nose. Her eyes are dazzling blue under the shine.

He lets out a breath. "I could probably come back, if I wanted."

"We want you back. We love you. You'll see."

Before he can say anything, she pecks the side of his face with a kiss, turns, and runs down the hall. She's out the door to the stairs, a flash of beauty and innocence that keeps him standing there wondering until her steps die away. He makes himself concentrate on gathering his syllabi, grade book, and contest entries into a clean file folder, along with an envelope of keys. He doesn't know if he'll come back here. He looks around the office and sees many souvenirs, photos of his family, and gift items he's collected over the years. He'd like to take some of it, and the artwork, but it's too much to carry.

He puts the materials for Patrick in the box on his door, and continues down the hall. His briefcase is full, and he has a plastic bag bursting with poetry journals of his poems that were published over the years, the plastic cutting into his fingers with the weight of all that work. He shakes his head, half amused, but still grieving over the sad truth – that right now it all means nothing.

He needs fresh air fast. He runs down the stairs and outside. Up ahead, in the parking lot, there's a commotion, the bass turned up loud on someone's car stereo – or a drumbeat. A number of students sit among the trees on the grassy strips between rows. He slows his pace. This must have been planned. About a dozen students are marching in a slow circle around his car. Tammi is among them. The two Jamaicans from his creative writing are sitting on his hood playing drums. Tammi must have gone to the dorms and spread the word that he was on campus. Thank God that it's too early to draw much of a crowd.

As he gets close enough to read, he sees his name on a computer-printed banner. When had they planned this? Panic springs into his chest. He feels his escape route closing off. He turns into the next row, thinking maybe he can hide until they're gone. He can't stand sympathy and heartfelt pleas. Someone in the circle spots him and the group starts marching to the beat in a sort of ragged conga line toward him. He recognizes students from his current classes and a few from the past semester. Headache and fatigue press him into the pavement. He stops. A brilliant thought comes to him. He could sprint all the way home if he didn't have tons of paper weighing him down. He could come back later for the car – or have it towed. Energy builds in his legs with the contrariness of the whole idea. Leave the stack of mildewed journals and yellowing manuscripts, the briefcase of lecture notes he can't imagine he'll ever use again. The symbolism of his work, deserted on the blacktop, will not be missed by the English department. There will be more than one who will envy him deep down in their guts – wishing that they could take the challenge, do the unthinkable and find what they've been seeking in their writing all their lives – Truth. He feels it now – hovering near him in the form of pure feeling, his personal Truth, almost within reach.

The conga line is only fifty yards away, moving slowly in time to the drum. They're chanting something out of sync and he can't get the words, except for his name. His heart breaks for them, with their golden aspirations, but the bags hit the ground and his leg muscles ignite in the passion of escape. He turns away, toward the empty field, without a glance back, and picks up speed. In Olympic style he hurdles a curbstone and a small bush in one stride, crosses the last row of cars and blacktop, and strikes a path through palmetto scrub and grass. There's an open horizon in the distance, glowing with the vision of his freedom and Renata, and he races toward it.

He's across the field, and onto the pavement bordering the west side of the campus before he looks back. No one has followed. He's not sure whether anyone tried. He runs about a quarter of a mile farther, just in case. He slows to a brisk walk, noticing the discomfort of his dress shoes, the sting of blisters already forming on his heels. He lifts his pants legs to see burrs covering his socks, as expected. He laughs. It's a high trill that comes to his ears. They'll be putting him in the nut house.

The wind is with him when he makes a turn onto the jogging path near his house, and he glides toward home, feeling light and loose, eager to get to his computer. The flicker of inspiration in his chest, the start of a poem, and in a few hours his muse will replenish the inferno of his desires.

CHAPTER 40

1:00 pm, Tropical Moons, Room 2-B

Renata

She wakes and smiles, seeing Francisco's shining face next to her on the pillow. His features brighten the room, even with his mouth partly open and a heavy dose of beer on his breath. The touch of his hand resting in sleep on her bare hip is soft. The night before, he asked her if she'd missed him. He wasn't gone long enough, but she said, "Yes, I missed your huge pulsating member." She worried that he would say he loved her. But she sensed him draw back, knowing even through the alcohol not to change the way things were. Now she thinks of Julie, the slender body and beautiful face, the woman who loves her. Can she ever love anyone back?

She pokes Francisco. He rouses and kisses her.

"Hey, buddy, Richard's headed this way."

"Professor Dick?" He yawns and stretches. "Time for me to leave." He gets up and starts picking clothes off the floor. "Where's the snake this morning?"

She directs her eyes to the box. "Pepe loves the new house. I should pull him out and check for snake shit."

He looks up at her while he steps into his jeans. "Dickhead is really gonna let you lock him in there?"

"Wait and see."

"Rather not."

Francisco leaves and Renata goes into the shower. She hasn't really talked to Richard since he left his wife. Maybe she can charm him into going back without having to lock him up. Fat chance. She knows what he wants — her to run away with him, to a new life where he can tow her around among his poet friends, safe and far away from everything she knows. She pictures herself next to professor types and their wives, sipping red wine and eating raw vegetables. She knows how they live — poetry to improve their minds and fitness clubs to make their boring lives last forever.

CHAPTER 41

3:00 pm, South Miami

Richard

The blisters on his heels sting as he takes a shower in preparation to see Renata. He lathers up his hair and wonders what kind of clothes he'll need. He should take a small bag with shorts, t-shirt, and swimming trunks – maybe a good shirt and slacks, shaving gear and toothbrush in case the surprise involves going to dinner and the theater or some other dressy occasion. Not really Renata's style, but she might have thought of something with his tastes in mind.

Surprise, surprise. What can it be? He'll be prepared for any occasion, and if it turns out as only a "special blow job," he'll take her to dinner at Tantra or Touch, one of the dark sensuous restaurants on Lincoln Road. Now that his wife has left him, there's no reason for them to hide out in the stuffy hotel room. Thoughts of his sons come into his mind, wrenching his gut, but he takes a breath and puts his brain into searching for his small nylon overnight bag. He rolls his clothes neatly – pants, shirt, bathing suit, socks, underwear.

He takes the bag into the living room and sets it by the

door. He'll stay as long as he's invited. He'd stay indefinitely, if she'd let him, buy beach clothes, and maybe new towels and sheets. He looks at his swords, sheathed, blades up, the graceful *katana*, used for battle, mounted above the sturdy *wakizashi*, symbol of an honorable death. They're valuable, his treasures for many reasons, and he'll worry about them being stolen if he doesn't return for days or weeks. He takes them carefully off the wall and wraps them in a blanket, setting the bundle by his small bag.

He takes a taxi to school and gets the car. No students around. His life is his own.

Traffic is light, and he finds a parking spot in a lot where the car can stay all night. Truly his luck has changed. He looks inside the bar as he crosses the street. There she is, raising a glass of beer to her lips — elevating it, he might say. The sunlight seems to concentrate within the yellow liquid, splitting into a thousand rays, spreading out to greet him, so that it's not apparent whether her glass is the focus or the source of the heavenly light. He stops to watch as she drinks and sets the glass on the bar. There's no free will here. Her radiance would take any man against his wishes.

He can't tame his smile as he walks toward her. She turns to face him, stunning in the brightness of her hair and a white dress. He floats across the room, holding his things in one hand, and takes her chin with his fingertips, stooping to kiss her lips. They've grown softer.

"Hey, baby," she says. The sound of her voice sucks the strength from his legs, and he sits on the stool next to her. He orders a beer and tells her how much he's missed her and how he's inspired, feeling young and creative again with every thought of her. He mouths the words, but his attention is on her skin, her eyes, her lovely fingers stroking the side of the glass. "You usually drink from the bottle, don't you?" he asks.

She nods. "Mostly. So, you ready for your surprise?"

"If you weren't so beautiful, I couldn't sit here a second."

She stands up. "It's upstairs. Let's go."

He throws a ten on the bar and waves off the change to Oliver. He picks up his bundles and she leads him upstairs. A familiar scene for those watching? Richard wonders.

Rennie opens the door to the apartment and Richard stares. "What is it?" Immediately he knows, but the breath has gone out of him.

Rennie prances to the side and makes a showy gesture toward the box. "It's for you. Just what you wanted. To be my sex slave."

Richard walks past it to stand next to her. He puts his bag and the bundle of swords on the floor. "I never saw anything like this."

"Nobody did. This is custom made."

"For me?"

"No, it's pre-owned, but low mileage, and the inside is immaculate." She laughs.

Richard cringes with the image of a previous owner that sweeps through his head, but he quickly lets it go. He tugs on the heavy lock. "That'll hold me all right."

Renata puts her arms around his neck and pulls his face down to hers. Her breath is warm and beery, enough to make his cock move firmly against her hip. "Wait till you see what I'm gonna do to you," she says.

He pulls her against him as a heavy wave of passion tightens his pants further. God, she feels good, better than he ever deserved.

She pulls at the back of his hair and looks into his eyes. "Ready to climb in?"

"Why do you ask? You don't think I'm up to it?" He pauses, letting her beauty bloom over him. "I'm always ready to experiment – this looks to me like a challenge." He drags himself back to some sliver of reality. "Maybe I should use the bathroom first."

"Yeah. I haven't figured out that part. Do slaves get bathroom privileges?"

"Definitely." He moves her thick curls aside and kisses her neck, then licks once at her soft hairline, tasting the light salt of perspiration. Her hand goes down to massage his cock tight inside his pants. He takes a breath to get the initiative to move. "I'll step into the bathroom for a minute. Then you can enslave me. I want to take it slow and easy."

"Don't worry, baby. It's going to be a long night."

He feels his eyebrows go up, and for an instant he wants to change his mind. She has total control, complete power over him. He couldn't do this with anyone but Renata. He closes the bathroom door, glancing into the vanity mirror as he passes by. His strong jaw is prominent, yet the fine skin ruffles slightly beneath it. He knows the lines of character under his eyes and around his mouth will eventually deepen to signs of weakness in old age, but he doesn't feel weak. He unhooks his pants and lets a strong stream flow. Time has been good to him, but life is ever changing.

As he walks into the room, Renata is pulling the snake through a hole in the front of the box. "He loves the dark," she says, "but there's not a lot of room for the two of you."

Richard nods broadly. "Thanks. My body parts thank you."

She lays the snake on the bed and walks toward Richard, one slow step at a time, hair blazing, hips rolling, tantalizing him with the curved indentation between her thighs. He remembers the Brazilian phrase for it, *pasa gato*, from a student's poem, the space a cat can pass through. It was a fine poem, unusually fine. These are unusually fine legs.

Renata stops in front of him, unzips her dress and lifts it over her head revealing nothing but smooth skin and red curls. A heavy wash of arousal puts Richard down on one knee. He cups her right breast, sucking and licking at her abdomen, rubbing with his cheeks and nose, getting all of her he can against his skin. It's been so long, way too long in this short life. He remembers the baby softness he noticed the first time he touched her, the peachy freckling and smooth pink nipples that made him a prisoner.

She moans and braces herself on his shoulders and he lowers his face to the target. She splits her legs and a thin trickle of juice rolls down her inside thigh as he goes forward with his tongue and pulls back her labia to find her clit, hot pink and hard. His knees ache and the seam of his pants is cutting him in two. He puts a finger inside her and breathes through his nose, never breaking the rhythm of the licking until she shudders and subsides. She kisses his forehead and takes his hand, guiding him up. He pushes on one knee to stand, enjoying the vivid blush of orgasm from her thighs to her chest and feeling his cock ready to burst through the double seam of his Levi's.

"I've been waiting a long time for you to finish that," she says, breathing hard.

The vision that Judy and the student witnessed, his dripping mouth, Renata's bright open crotch against the dark leather chair, comes back to him. He laughs. "That glowing bush of yours lit up my office forever in my memory. I don't regret it."

She stretches up to give him a kiss, then takes his hands off her hips. "Now it's time you listen to your mistress."

He bows.

"Take off your clothes." She crosses her arms and stares, looking stern despite her nakedness.

He's twitchy with nerves and excitement, but hides it as he slips off his shoes and socks and pushes them under a chair. With relief he unhooks his belt and pulls down his zipper, dragging the jeans and boxers to his knees in one grab, letting his penis spring from between his legs, taut and alive. He steps out of the pants and creases them over the back of the chair, locking his eyes on Renata's firm, enticing face. He's never seen this act before, but the boldness and excitement pique his interest beyond the physical.

Her eyes flash and her hair whips with a "No." She flips the pants to the dark linoleum. "Neatness is out. Clothes go on the floor – for Pep."

He groans, thinking of the stinking snake body sweating in

his clean pressed shirt, but it's all or nothing from here. He flings the shirt in a wad to her feet. He spreads his arms, showing everything he's got, muscled and furred, naked, tingling, taut. "Whatever you desire, my love, always."

"Mistress, to you now — mistress of all cunts and cocks, everything that throbs in the night — mistress of your body and soul. You'll do what I say, and it won't be easy. You won't complain. Isn't that right?" She moves closer and curls her fingers around his cock.

This sounds like an act she's done before, but the electricity stuns him. He breathes, "Yes. I promise."

She leads him by his cock to the box where she's placed a chair for him to step on. He follows the pressure of her hand upward and stands looking through the hole on top. By the light spilling from various cut-outs he can see what must be a padded seat. She throws back the lid with one hand and motions to the steps that lead downward like a ladder into a boat. He puts his foot inside and tests the first step.

"Move it, slave."

He looks down at her still holding his erect cock with her outstretched arm.

She lets go.

"I'll take your dare, mistress!"

He puts more weight on the step, testing the strength and, holding the side, lifts his other leg over the top to find the lower rung, climbing backward. Renata smiles at him. He bends to make sure of clearing the side with his still erect cock and turns and sits down on the stool looking out. His shoulders are just below the level of the sides if he sits up straight.

"Perfect fit." She swings the top half over and he positions himself so that his head is in line with the hole. She closes the lid all the way and snaps the padlock closed.

He's relieved to drop the act, but a sweat breaks out on his forehead. "Where did you get this?"

"My friend David. I think it's a gay fad on South Beach."

Richard frowns, but he's happy not to hear the name of yet

another lover.

Renata moves to the front, facing him. "So, do you like it?"

She stands on the chair and leans into him, her chin on his head and fingers around his neck, immersing him in the soft scent of her skin and soap, her breasts firm against his eyes and cheeks. He can feel her rapid breathing and hear her heart. He could luxuriate there forever, but his cock strains outward as if on a leash.

He speaks into her rib cage. "It's unique, but how are we going to make love like this?"

"Huh?" She laughs. "Make love with a slave? Moi?"

He knows she doesn't mean it, but this foreplay could get tedious.

She pulls back and looks into his eyes. "I was locked up once, in a dark place."

He thinks he sees tears and settles himself down. "When you were a child?"

"No, a few years ago. I never told anybody this – except Jules."

"Tell me. You can tell me anything, sweetheart." He wishes he could hold her.

"I don't need any cry-baby sympathy. I learned plenty about myself in there – and about the world. I had time to think."

"Tell me. I want to know everything about you." He would rather hear it while he's holding her, but with Renata there's often only one chance.

She nods, gets a chair, and sits down facing Richard, below him, as he sits inside the box. "It's not really that interesting." She crosses her arms under her tits and spreads her legs so he can see her clit through the trimmed pubic hair. "I married this guy, Ace, and the marriage sucked. No use going into detail. After a few months, I fell in love with someone else – by accident. Maybe my true love. I believed in it at the time –"

"That's okay. I don't need details." He rests his feet on the lower stool and gets comfortable. His cock relaxes between his thighs.

"I knew I had to leave Ace, and he figured it out before I got up the nerve. He wasn't the kind who believed you have to let go of the things you love."

"So he locked you up?"

"Yeah — in the hall closet every morning before he left for work. He let me have my cigarettes and a lighter, and a flashlight. Oh, yeah, and my vibrator. I played with myself for eight or nine hours a day."

He watches the sadness leave her face and amusement begin to flicker in her eyes. She rubs her clit with the halffinger as demonstration, then looks up at him, biting her lower lip. "It wasn't so bad."

"You could go crazy doing that." He feels the flicker of his cock on his thigh. "What about food and water?"

"I had a bottle of water and an apple a day — then dinner when he got home and watched me cook it. There was something pure about it. My only decision in life was whether to eat the apple all at once so it wouldn't get brown or to space it out in tiny bites. I usually ate it all for lunch, even though I couldn't see the brown part in the dark. I even ate the seeds, one by one." She throws Richard a kiss across the short space. "They were magic seeds that kept me happy." She goes back to her clit, pulling up the skin to expose it further, looking up at him with round eyes.

Again he's hard enough to burst. He pulls at himself inside the box, not wanting to orgasm, but unable to keep his hand away. He doesn't want to interrupt her story. "How long did it go on? I can't believe you didn't go crazy."

She waves off his concern and laughs. "I still have 20/20 vision too — it was only for a couple weeks. Oh, he gave me an Etch-a-Sketch. He picked it out at the toy store because he thought I would draw some interesting stuff in the dark. He wasn't all bad, just couldn't bear to lose me."

"What happened to him?"

"Killed."

Richard feels his cock retract a little. He hesitates. "Who killed him?"

"My lover. It was a crime of passion, to save me – my fault. He's still in prison."

"How do you know?"

"I would've heard something if he got out." She stops rubbing her clit and slides to her feet. She thinks of a version of the story he'll like better than the real one. "I cut off my finger as penance. It was all my fault." She steps close to the box, holding her half-finger out toward his face, and grins with all her teeth showing, a dazzling wicked look. Juice runs down her leg.

"My God! Why? That's senseless. You can't take responsibility for his actions."

"If you were put in prison on my account, I would do it for you, and you could write it into a poem – or Julie could write it into her book."

"Nobody's going to prison. Don't even think of it. How did you – cut it?"

"I don't remember. With a knife I guess."

"You don't remember? You must have nearly bled to death."

"No, not even close. No more stories." Her face changes. "Now it's time for punishment."

He can't think of an appropriate response.

"Get down on your knees, slave. Use your imagination." She points at the box. "Figure out how to fuck in this thing."

He frowns and moves down into the dark on the bottom. There's a hole for his face and a slot for his arms, and if he kneels straight up, his cock and balls are within the area of the correct cut-out. He works himself into place. The feeling is unusual with the outside air cool on his genitals.

Renata's face comes close to his, but a piece of wood on a hinge is swung into place, covering the hole, and he hears a latch. "What are you doing?"

She leans over the top so he can just see her eyes. "You want to experiment, don't you?"

"Let's get to it." His voice is muffled. He wonders if she can hear. "Maybe you should let me out," he yells, "since I haven't seen you for so long."

She drops out of sight. "What?" Her voice comes as a whisper from down low. "Let you out? You wanna go home already?"

"No, no. I just thought . . ."

"Well, alrighty then. You keep quiet."

"Do me one favor," he calls. "Put my swords away for safe keeping. They're in the blanket on the floor."

"A slave with his own swords? Yes, I'll put them away." She giggles. "They're mine now."

"Everything of mine is yours." He hears a clang, and then a drawer opens and closes, then footsteps as if she's walking away. His arms are outside the box and he waves them. The wood edges grate into his armpits. "Where are you?" There's no answer and he pulls his arms inside. He must do what she wants with vigor, all of it, pass every test.

Metal handles, like large drawer pulls, are at shoulder height at each side of the arm slot. He takes one in each hand and presses himself against the front, getting a little more height so as to press his cock and balls completely through the hole. He feels exposed, but strong, his cock extending hard and long outside the box.

Warm fingers grab him and a hot, wet mouth engulfs him. He grips the handles tighter, straining against the wall. She sucks hard and he feels the edges of her teeth. Pain blends with pleasure, sensitivity heightened with the slight burning and warm saliva. He's hard and helpless. He grits his teeth as he goes over the edge of pain into bliss or madness, his cock taking control. The orgasm builds fast, the concentrated hardening, the tightening so far removed from his body, surging with such intensity, that the man who thought he'd outgrown every possibility of sexual surprise slides into another universe. He comes and comes, sighing and pumping, slumping against the

side of the box, weakened by pleasure. She pulls free and he
drops to the seat.

"How was that?"

He's breathing hard. "Strange. New."

"You didn't like it?"

"It was better than I could have dreamed. Now I want to
see you, touch you."

"Well, it's getting late. I'm going down the street to get us
some dinner. What do you feel like, Italian, Cuban, Mexican?"

"First, I need to go to the bathroom again."

She goes to a box on the table, gets a key, and opens the top.
He's thinking he should run while he has the chance. But he
said he'd give this a try, something he hadn't quite thought
through. When he comes back, she's already put on a sundress.

She turns to him. "Like it?"

"You're a glimmer of heaven. Let's go together."

"No, you get comfortable in there. I'll be right back with
the food." She smiles. "I know what. Let's think of this like a
test for when you get older. I'll have to take care of you in the
box like I would then – feed you, bathe you, help you go to
the bathroom. See if you like it."

"You mean you'd take care of me if I got old and feeble?"

"I don't know. See how I do."

"Okay, I'm sure you'll do fine." He climbs in. "You don't
have to lock me in. I won't leave."

"We want it to be realistic." She snaps the lock. "How's
Cuban then?"

"Food? Fine, sweetie. Just, no *vaca frita,* too much choles-
terol. Please hurry back."

She looks around. "If I had any paper you could do poetry."
She blows him a kiss and winks. "I'll get some."

"Just food for now," he says. He loses sight of her as she
walks behind him and out the door. For a few seconds he looks
over the room, noticing that nothing has changed since his last
visit – even the same clothes seem to be thrown on the floor,
but that can't be. The snake is curled under the sheet on the

bed. He realizes that Renata didn't lock the door. It's not a particularly good position to be in, but a few minutes won't kill him.

The phone rings several times and stops. He wonders if it was a business call. At least she's not going to be able to set up appointments with him right there, listening. He remembers that she said it would be a long night – surely she didn't mean a long night alone? He kneels down on the floor in front of the built-in seat and finds a pillow. It smells like patchouli, a scent from his hippy days, surely not put there by Renata. Slaves can't be choosers. There's just enough room to stretch out. He closes his eyes, and without reason, starts counting. Now he understands why prisoners scratch the days onto walls.

His thoughts go back to the strange mixture of pleasure and pain, the unexplored territory inside himself – a possibility of rich inspiration – but he's not sure if he wants to mine that deeply.

CHAPTER 42

7:00 pm, South Beach

Renata

It is her intention to go straight to the Cuban place for some *vaca frita*, but as she steps outside the hotel, Garcia is coming toward her on the sidewalk.

"Renata," he says. "I was hoping to catch you. You never answer your phone."

"I have to get food for a starving friend."

"I have a few questions to ask you."

"Do I have to answer them now?"

"You don't have to, but I'd appreciate it."

She wants to tell him to fuck off – and let Julie alone too – but decides she'd better talk sweet and send him on a different track. "Okay, let's have a drink inside."

They go in and Renata takes a table at the opposite end of the room from the bar, so the bartender can't hear. It's Jorge, the late-night guy, and she wonders where Oliver is. She insists on getting the beers herself and leaves Garcia seated, telling him it's her turn to buy.

"*Dos cervezas* – Buds. How you doin'?"

"Hanging in."

"Where's Oliver?"

"Dunno. Boss called me in early." He nods toward Garcia at the back table. "That's a P.I. you're talking to. He was here a couple of nights ago, looking for you."

"Yeah, new customer. Don't tell anybody. It's probably not good for his reputation."

Jorge smirks. "I should have guessed." He puts the beers on the bar.

"He's a nice guy. Lonely type, like in the movies."

"And you're the hot mamma with the money? You don't need those lonely guys." He winks.

Renata laughs and takes the beers. She used to believe she'd be a movie star, like every teenage girl. She walks smiling to Garcia and sets the beers on the table. She's had plenty of acting experience. Time for more. She sits, clicks her glass against his, and sips.

He takes a long drink. "Thanks. Hot one tonight."

"Hot and moist. That's why we live here."

He's looking at her, thinking. "I wanted to talk to you about Julie."

"Jules? She's doin' great. Working at Mangoes now."

"I know." He takes a sip of beer. "She said something about a murder."

Renata screws her face into pure disbelief. "Murder?"

"She tried to say she was making up a story to protect you —"

"Huh? I don't need protecting."

"Look, she gave me a ring —"

Renata feels her heart thump. "Oh that. It's from a client. She thought he was going to hurt me — all a mistake. She's trying to help me get rid of him."

Garcia frowns. "This guy still comes around?"

"No. I haven't seen him for weeks."

"I need his name."

"John."

Garcia takes a drink of beer, shaking his head. "Okay. John what?"

"Seriously, men don't give me their names."

"Jules wouldn't tell me either."

"She wouldn't know. Whatever Jules said, she was confused."

Garcia clears his throat. "Listen, there's something else I have to tell you. Bad news." He takes her hand on the table. "The bartender – Oliver – he was murdered Sunday night on Key Biscayne."

"What?" Renata glances up at the bar.

"I saw the police report. He was beat up. His penis was cut off."

A cold shock passes through her and she has to concentrate to hold back tears. She's surprised by the sudden painful emotion. She can't shrug it off. "A hate crime, you mean."

"Possible. I realized he was the bartender at this hotel, the one whose car you and Julie borrowed to go to the Glades –" He takes a drink of his beer. He shakes his head. "I've been keeping an eye out, but I can't do much alone. I'm wondering if there's a connection between all this and if I should talk to the police."

"I don't see how a hate crime against Oliver could have anything to do with me and Julie."

He stares at her without blinking. "I don't know what's going on, but it's too coincidental." He takes a long drink. "Maybe you witnessed something and you don't realize it. They could have gone after Oliver to get to you."

"And cut his dick off?"

"It's missing. He had a stud in it, according to his . . . friend – a piercing – but I don't think the jewelry was valuable." Garcia cringes. "Maybe they just wanted to hurt him. Or maybe he didn't cooperate."

Renata feels a shiver roll down her shoulder blades. "Yeah, I think he had a Prince Albert."

She drinks and stares into her beer, hoping Garcia believes

what he says about them being witnesses, because it lets her and Jules off the hook. But it's still a problem if he takes the lawyer's ring to the cops. She needs time to talk to Julie — and Francisco. "Don't go to the police, please. They'll drag me down there for no reason and then they'll make one up. Besides that, Jules will be questioned, and she'll get so nervous it will make her sick."

He looks at her like she's insane. "I'm trying to protect you both."

She wonders how she can stop him. She can't kill him at this point, and he's not the type to silence with a blow job. "You're mistaken. We don't know anything and we're fine."

"Tell you what. I'll see what else I can find out before I go to the police. I don't have much to tell yet. But you and Julie have to be careful."

"I'll talk to her. We'll be careful. I have a man staying at my place right now, so we're really safe."

"Yeah, I know. I wouldn't count on him much."

"What do you mean?"

"I saw him go up there and not come down. I saw that box too. No explanations necessary."

Renata is frantic about Richard by the time she steps out on the street. She orders a sandwich from a café on the next block rather than make him wait any longer. The news about Oliver has taken away her appetite. The place is busy and it seems to take forever. She thinks about Pepe. He'll need to be fed a rat in the next week. Feeding Pepe, feeding herself — that used to be all she had to worry about.

CHAPTER 43

Wednesday, October 13, 9:00 am, Tropical Moons

Jules

It's full light when Jules is awakened by a pounding noise coming from next door. It takes her a second to figure it out. The banging gets louder.

"Jules, are you there?"

"Okay, Richard. Coming," she yells. She gets up and puts on her robe, annoyed. She thought she heard Rennie earlier, but maybe she dreamed it.

She pads through the hall in her slippers and opens the door.

"Have you been in there all night?"

"No, Renata left early with Francisco. I locked myself in."

"For spite?"

"No. I chose to do this. Jules, I know all about her life. I can't change it in one day."

"Or one decade. I don't know what you're doing here –"

"That's between me and Renata."

"So why'd you lock yourself in?"

"I decided to spend some box time – for inspiration. I

know you can't understand that. Most people couldn't."

"Richard, I'd beat myself with a stick if I thought I'd be inspired."

"Oh. Well, the problem is I threw the key on the bed so I wouldn't be tempted to get out. Now I need to use the bathroom."

Jules can't quite stifle a laugh. "Aren't you afraid of fire?"

"All I have to do is yell, and you'll come over."

"Fuck. I should leave you in there for that." She finds the key easily on top of the sheet and unlocks him. He steps up and over the top of the box onto the chair.

He's wearing shorts and Jules is surprised at how muscular his legs are. If only he'd use them to run on home. "Should I wait and lock you in again?"

He glances back from the bathroom. "No thanks. I'll use willpower this time."

The bathroom door closes. Jules looks around for Pepe, but doesn't see him. Renata is surely out early. Sparing Richard from one of her sexfests with Francisco probably. She looks out the window. Another glaring sunny day. She needs a day of rain, a little cool breeze. The shower goes on. He seems to be settling in. Not good. She hardly gets a chance to see Rennie on a normal basis. Now with Richard taking up residence, he'll force himself into every minute of their time.

Back in her room, she hooks the laptop up to the printer. She's got an idea to show Richard the pages she's written. As much as she dislikes him, he's a writing instructor, and he has plenty of time on his hands.

When it finishes printing, Jules takes the forty pages in to Richard. He looks surprised and flattered, standing with his head and shoulders through the opening. "I'll give you my honest opinion," he says.

"Thanks. I need the truth."

She's pounding out another page when she hears someone on the stairs. She opens the door. It's Rennie holding a paper bag with a grease spot.

Jules puts her finger to her lips and motions her inside. "Richard is looking for you," she whispers.

"I had to go over to Francisco's place. Franco won't come in with Richard there."

Jules notices Rennie's red eyes.

"Are you okay?"

"Yeah. Rough night."

"You know, I was thinking I could talk to Richard's wife. Maybe it's not too late for him to go back," Jules says. "If I could get them together —"

Rennie leans against the door. "I doubt it would work."

"Would you care if I asked her to come over here? It's worth a try. A little more time in that box and he might be ready to go."

"She must know where he is already. Garcia would tell her."

"But she hasn't been invited here. Do you have her number?"

"She moved out of the house, but she works downtown — Miami Mutual."

"Linda, right? I've heard Richard talk about her."

"Linda Langley. The perfect wife for him. He's just lost his mind lately." She takes Jules' arm. "Let's go down to the bar and get a drink. I have something I better tell you. I can't keep whispering."

Jules grips her glass of juice, and tears fill her eyes as Renata tells her that Oliver is dead. She looks at the bar, hardly able to believe he won't be there again. She covers her mouth when Renata gets to the mutilation. Jules' whole body is shaking. "This is my fault. I started it."

"If anybody started it, I did," Renata tells her. "The main problem is that Garcia thinks we're in danger. He was here last night, and he's keeping an eye out."

"Oh, God." Jules takes a long drink of her juice.

"Besides that, Francisco says there are other guys — foreigners or Mafia — in on this, making it rough. Francisco did some deliveries – trying to make up the money. Now they won't let him quit."

"Who's after us, the police or the drug dealers?"

"Maybe nobody, maybe both."

"What are we going to do?"

"Nothing. It seems like Oliver paid the price for now. Francisco thinks this is a sick joke, something about Oliver and an anonymous tip."

"Oh! Poor, poor man. What about Garcia?"

"He's on the wrong track. We just have to make sure he doesn't get on the right one. I don't think there's any evidence of a connection or we'd be locked up by now." Renata leans toward Jules and takes her face in her hands. "Don't worry." She kisses her softly, her open lips moving around on Jules' mouth. Jules closes her eyes and feels the sensation run through her. She doesn't check to see if anyone is looking.

"It'll be fine, honey. Rennie will take care of Julie." She picks up the greasy bag. "Right now Rennie better take care of Richard."

CHAPTER 44

2:00 pm, Tropical Moons, Room 2-A

Jules

She takes a break from the writing. She's been at it for hours, probably all a waste of time, but it makes her feel good. Time to call Linda at her office. There's no problem getting her extension. When Linda answers, the sound of her voice is crisp and assertive.

Jules takes a deep breath. "You don't know me, Mrs Langley, but I would like to talk about your husband. He needs help –"

"Listen – I'm very busy here. I can't do anything for him. I'm not sure I would want to."

"Sorry, I'll make it short. He's being kept like a slave inside a box –"

"Where does he shit?"

Jules pauses. "I –"

There's a whimper and then muffled sniffing. Jules senses that Linda is torn into ragged pieces, and her bravado is a façade she can't keep up.

Jules waits. She can't hear anything. "Linda, I'm sorry to tell you this. I thought maybe if you knew —"

"I have to think of my boys, and myself. I know all about her — that redhead and the filthy place where she lives — disgusting. She can go to hell and take Richard with her!"

The phone clicks.

Fear and guilt come over Jules. It was a terrible move. She sits back down to read what she's written. She's rewriting when she hears a knock.

It's Richard. "I want to talk to you about your manuscript."

"You read it? Not much to do in that box, huh?"

"Can I come in?"

He sits at the table and grins. "It's fantastic!"

"What?"

"Excellent! — interesting characters, fast-paced plot, clean and vivid prose. In all my years teaching I haven't seen anything better."

"You mean it?" Her mind soars instantly to the pride she might finally share with her father.

"Yes. I can't wait to read more. I can help you with a few technical points if you want — some point-of-view errors."

"You think I might get it published?"

"I do. It's always a gamble, but I know an agent who might be able to help you."

"God. That would be wonderful."

"Our feelings about Renata cause conflict between us — but we can be civilized. I would enjoy talking to you about writing."

"Really?"

"Writing has always been my life. I can never leave it completely."

Jules takes a deep breath. "If I could write and make money, I would take Renata away from this place so fast —" She stops.

Richard shrugs. He stares at Jules. "Maybe between the two of us we can get her out of here. It might be worth the compromise."

Jules nods, wondering what he has in mind, not sure she wants to share.

Richard goes back to Rennie's room and Jules sits down on the bed. She has a trial night of bartending for Brent at Mangoes and it's almost time to get ready. She looks out the window at the street. Her heart flutters. What if she was really able to support herself and Rennie — and they could go wherever they wanted? With Garcia hanging around, and all the problems with Francisco, Rennie might have no choice but to leave.

CHAPTER 45

6:00 pm, South Beach

Renata

She waits for Francisco at the diner, holding off on a drink.
He's always on Cuban time, no matter that he was born in
New Jersey. She gasps as he opens the door. His hair hangs in
his face, he's not shaved, and he's wearing shades. She can see
swelling and bruises on the side of his face that glasses and hair
can't cover. He doesn't smile as he sits down next to her.

She touches his cheek lightly with her lips. "Poor sweetie,
what happened? It hurts to look at you."

He takes a long time to answer. "We have to get out of
here. There's all kinds of hell coming down. These guys are
tough. They have nothing to lose."

"Fucking insane. How'd we get mixed up with them?"

The waitress is standing by the table with her pad.

"Chocolate icebox pie," Renata says. She looks at the bottles glinting behind the bar. "And a double Cuervo, please."

"Same," says Francisco, "no pie."

Renata runs her hand through the back of his hair, lightly
massaging his neck. "How'd we get into this, *papi*?"

He whispers, "My fault. I thought I was doing a transaction with Miami boys and some Glades locals. Seems now there's connections with some big-shot Colombians. We'll get blamed for any trouble with the cops."

"I thought you said it was Mafia?"

"Not Italian Mafia."

"The red Mustang. Was that them?"

"Yeah, that guy. He's a key motivator behind all the shit. Any heat on them, we're the cause — we're dead. I'm doing a little job for them tonight, but I think they're just playing with me. We gotta leave."

"Leave? Where would we go?"

"I have friends on a cruise ship — it's all set. Some labor involved at first, until we get things going our way. New names and passports — new opportunities, *mi amor*." He tries to smile. A crack in his lip widens.

"What about Jules? We can't leave her."

He nods. "Yeah, Julie. They'd grind her into little pieces. I can get her on, if she doesn't mind the work."

"She's better at it than we are."

"True, true. It's been a long time since this boy served soup."

Renata makes a face. "Waiting tables? That's what we'd be doing?"

"If we're lucky. Cleaning bathrooms if we're not."

The waitress comes with the drinks. Renata slugs hers.

Francisco picks his up and toasts her empty glass. "Yeah, babe, enjoy the night, because we're outta here tomorrow."

"Is it worth it to live like that?"

"Like what? Rather let them kill us? You'll have a nicer room on the ship than here at The Moons. Smaller, I guess. Better view of the ocean."

"I mean doing things we don't want to all day long, just for money."

He chuckles.

"How can you laugh?"

He touches the cut in his lip. "It ain't easy." He tosses down his shot. "Listen, Renata — it's not forever. If you got another plan, fine, but leaving here is the only way I know to stay alive."

Richard is the only other plan she can think of. It would make him the happiest man on earth. The thought makes a hard fist in her stomach. "I'll talk to Jules when she gets off work."

"I'll pick you up as soon as I'm done — in the bar. I'm not coming up while that prick's in the box."

"He'll probably be gone."

"Just meet me in the bar around 3:00 am. We'll go to a hotel in Miami. My place isn't safe. We'll pick up Jules in the morning."

Renata takes a forkful of pie and drops it back on the plate. "I can't live like that —"

"Like what? It's not the end of the world, *mamita*. Just the end of this world." He gestures to include the surroundings. The movement makes him groan, but he smiles. "We can get tequila anywhere."

CHAPTER 46

8:00 pm, Tropical Moons, Room 2-B

Richard

He sits on the bed scratching at the words of his poem, feeling much better after a shower, but wondering where Rennie is. Rennie, impossible to predict, as wild and rare as a Florida panther – more dangerous. There is no limit to the pain that he would go through for her sake, but the waiting while she keeps her "appointments" has to stop.

The door opens. "Richard, my samurai!"

"Rennie, back so soon."

"Are you being sarcastic? Or would you rather I left you alone?"

"No, heavens no."

She moves close and pats his cheek. He stands to kiss her, but she waves him off. "I'm sorry I've been gone so long. I had to get a snack for Pepe."

She holds out the bag in her hand and takes a carton from it. She opens it and dumps. A brown rat scrambles down the side of the laundry hamper. She turns the hamper on its side, pulls Pepe off the bed, and loops him into it. She closes the lid.

"Hope he goes for it – hasn't eaten since I got him."

Richard moves close and kisses her, moving his hand in her soft hair.

She breaks away. "You can't stay here much longer, Richard." She looks into his eyes. "I can't either. We have to say goodbye."

"Goodbye? What do you mean?"

"Some things came up. I don't want to talk about it. How about if we have a fantastic night, and you go home real early in the morning?"

He winces. "Renata, I'm not leaving and you're not leaving me. I'll take you wherever you want to go."

Her hands are on her hips.

"Renata, I won't leave unless you go with me. You'll have to get the police to drag me out."

"There's a good chance of that." She stops and her face softens. "Look, Richard, I don't know what's going to happen. You want to get as far away as you can, as fast as you can, if you don't want to die."

"Die?" He reaches out to her, but she moves back farther. "I can help you. We can go right now. Listen to me, Renata. Right now!"

"Leave Jules by herself? No. Not a chance. Run out on Francisco?"

"Francisco? Leaving him would be the best choice you ever made. He's the one who dragged you into this slime pit. This is all his fault."

She points at him with her half-finger. "No. Look, it's nobody's fault. Saying things like that – you really make me mad." She starts unzipping, turns her back.

"I'm sorry. You must know how other men in your life affect me. I love you. If I didn't, I wouldn't care."

She strips and tosses her dress on the bed, her tapered back and toned ass bringing a tingle into his cock. "You're not too crazy about other women in my life either."

"Jules? That's not true. I just didn't know her. We had a talk today. I read her manuscript, and I believe it can be published. I offered to be her mentor."

"Really? That's awesome."

"It changes everything, doesn't it? Would you go, if Jules came along? I have some money saved – I'll be getting part of the house sale also. We could create an amazing life together somewhere else – Jules too, for a while anyway. Nobody has to die, for Christsakes."

"We don't?" She laughs and throws her head back, sounding hysterical. There's a thump from the laundry hamper. "Good boy, Pep," she says. "They told me to kill the rat and dip it in chicken broth, but I figured he'd eat it live." She peers into the hamper. "Boy's got a rat down his throat."

"So what do you say? Will you go?"

"Let me think. We need to talk it over when Jules gets home, and I have to see Francisco later tonight."

Richard makes a noise in his throat. "I have a huge deficit of caressing and kissing. I'm tired of thinking and talking. Let me hold you."

"I could use it." She sits on his lap and burrows her naked body into his arms. The softness of her shoulders and hair, the heat of her mouth and tongue, the smoothness of her ass, take him beyond all problems. She pulls him close, and he pushes deep into the most luscious moment in the world, the splendor more inside his mind and surrounding him, than in any one part of his body he can name or feel.

He can only lie still afterward, slightly moving his lips to kiss and kiss, murmuring "I love you," not able to open his eyes, in a paralyzing comfort so deep that he imagines it might be similar to death.

It's dark when he awakens. Someone is calling Renata. Wind whips the palms outside and whistles through the canvas awnings, slapping loose edges against the building. Renata sits up beside him and calls out into the darkness, "Jules, you're early."

"What?" Richard pulls up the sheet.

Jules opens the refrigerator, making light. "There's a hurricane coming – a small one. We don't have to leave the beach. They closed Mangoes to board up. It was supposed to hit farther up the coast, but changed course."

"A hurricane," Richard says. "Great. Nobody told me anything about a hurricane."

"That's all I've heard at the bar. It's all over the TV and radio."

"I've been slightly disconnected from the world."

"When does it get here?" Renata asks.

"About eight hours from now, I think. Four or five am, Irene, 70 mph."

Richard can see the excitement in Jules' nervous movement. He looks at Renata. "I'm glad you didn't leave me locked up."

"Oh, it's only a little one." Renata stands naked and clicks on a lamp, Jules closes the refrigerator, and Richard tugs the sheet to cover himself. Renata turns to Richard. "We should prepare – get some booze before the liquor store closes. Richard, you get the ice. This will be Jules' first hurricane."

"What about leaving? All the trouble?"

"More trouble?" Jules asks.

Renata throws Richard a look. "Same stuff."

He resigns himself to the celebration, despite his whirling mind. "Okay. We need cups and snacks – wine too. I'll go to the little grocery."

"Get us a pizza – and I need some money, please."

Jules nods. "I have money," she says. "Let me pay."

Richard waits until Jules has gone next door to get her money to climb out of bed and put on his pants. Renata steps into shorts and pulls on a t-shirt.

Richard kisses her neck. "I thought we had to leave."

"Tomorrow. Not now."

Richard takes a breath, afraid of what he has to ask. "Does that mean you're coming with me?" He puts his arms around her.

She pulls back. "We'll talk about it later."

This is the closest he's ever gotten to a yes. He can feel it. She needs him now and his life is ready to bloom into the luscious days he's dreamed of ever since he met her.

Renata places her hand so the half-finger and thumb go on each side of his mouth. She jiggles his cheeks. "Don't smile so hard — you'll break your face."

CHAPTER 47

11:00 pm, Tropical Moons, Room 2-B

Renata

On the beach the breeze has gathered energy, and white-caps catch the glint of streetlights as the ocean charges up. Inside, Renata sets down a brown bag and pulls the wet strands of hair off her face and out of her mouth. She concentrates on unpacking the bag on the table. Her usual calmness is difficult to maintain. Indulgence will help.

"I've got the rum, vodka, and limes – and a carton of cig-arettes. We could use some weed. Maybe Franco has his cell turned on."

Jules sets another bag next to her. "Here's the beer and orange juice. We have enough to drink. Let's not do any drugs. Just in case."

"This is barely a hurricane, no time to strengthen –"

"I just –"

"Okay, it's your first." She pushes the curtain aside and looks out at the street. "Richard better hurry up with that ice."

Jules opens a beer and hands it to Renata.

"I called Linda — she wouldn't even consider talking to Richard. She was extremely angry — and broken up."

"Told you."

"He's nearly destroyed her. He'll have to work it out himself."

"You know, it might not be a bad idea to take him up on his offer, sweetie."

"What offer?"

"To take us away. Both of us. You and me would be friends and lovers, and I'd just have to sleep with him once in a while. He's got some money." She kisses Jules' lips and pulls back her hair. She puts her hand on Jules' cheek.

Jules doesn't move. Her cheeks are baby pink.

"You're delicious, little Julie." Renata fluffs her hair. "Think about it. I am. He'd be there to help you with your book."

"He said both of us?"

Renata nods. "I wouldn't go without you." She lights up a cigarette.

Jules is silent.

Renata exhales and holds her beer out for a toast. She clanks against Jules' bottle. "*Salut y dinero.*"

As they drink, there's a noise at the door. Renata opens it. Richard has his hands full, a bag of dripping ice in one hand, a wet pizza box in the other, a plastic bag under his arm. He goes straight to the table. "Long walk with all this stuff. Starting to rain."

"Good job, sweetie." Renata kisses his cheek and digs into the bag. "Hey, this is going to be a nice party. I should call Franco for some weed — or some X. We can stay up all night and watch the storm."

"Don't call," says Richard. "We've got plenty of alcohol. My drug days are over."

"You had drug days?" Renata asks. "I can't even imagine you smoking."

"I never smoked cigarettes." He points to her carton and makes a face. "I quit the drugs when I realized I was becoming self-destructive. I don't regret it – I opened myself up in some creative ways – then I stopped. I've always had good sense." He arches his eyebrows. "That's why I'm so healthy."

Renata laughs. "Hand me a cup. I'm ready for the hard stuff." She pours half a cup of vodka and a splash of orange juice, takes a long drink.

The phone rings. She puts up the half-bird finger. "Telemarketing. Fuck. Grab it, Richard. Tell them we've got everything."

He walks toward the phone and pauses. "What if it's a customer? Or that Francisco?" It keeps ringing.

"Just grab it, huh?"

He picks it up and says hello. From the look on his face, Renata expects him to hand over the receiver, but he leans against the wall listening. Renata and Jules watch.

His face pales. "Take it easy. Settle down. The boys will never know."

Renata looks at Jules. "Linda," she whispers.

Jules puts her hand over her mouth to cover a shriek. "Linda? Fuck. This is my fault."

Richard is talking softly. "I'm hoping to go away – out of state. Very soon." He stops. His voice gets louder. "What's the matter?" He listens again and lets out a long sigh. "I'll call the college. They won't bother you again. Nobody at your office needs to know anything."

Renata and Jules watch as Richard tries to calm her down, but he's repeating himself, getting nowhere. Renata gets up from the table and walks toward him, extending her hand. "Let me talk."

Richard shakes his head no, but Renata stands firm. "Calm down," he says. He repeats it. Finally, he gives up and lets the receiver go into Renata's hand. "Hello," she says. No sound. "Hello?"

"Is this the famoush Renata?"

"Is this the famous Linda?"

"I know it's you, you fuck . . . fucking whore."

"We're trying to have a party here for my friend's first hurricane. Richard is fine. He's not locked in the box anymore, and he can call you tomorrow."

"It's not Richard's firsht hurricane."

"No. He'll call you tomorrow."

"No. He can't." Linda whispers something too low for Renata to hear.

"We need to hang up now. Goodbye." Renata hangs up and takes the phone back off the hook. "I have the feeling she'll be calling again."

Richard is sitting on the bed drinking his beer, eyes glazed and turned to the ceiling. Pepe is coiled next to him, a tennis-ball-sized distention about a quarter of the way down his length.

"Hey, you got a buddy there." Renata points to the snake. "He must have opened his hamper."

At first Richard looks at Pepe as if he doesn't see. Then he snaps to life, moves his hand away. "Oh, Pepito. I guess I should get used to you." He reaches back slowly and slides his hand across the creamy skin behind the head. "Nice boy."

"That's a good start," Renata says. The more she thinks about it, the more she begins to see that a life with Richard might work – with drugs – and especially with Jules around. There's no better choice.

They sit at the table with their drinks and Richard asks Jules about her plan for the rest of the novel.

"I'm not sure," she says. "So far I've been following real life. Now I'm almost caught up to the present. I guess it depends where we all go from here. You'll help me, right?"

Richard laughs. "If I'm the one responsible to keep life interesting so you have a plot, we'll have to make it up."

There's a whack on the door. Two more, like a hammer. "Hey, it's open!" Renata yells. "You don't need to knock it down!"

Footsteps diminish down the hall. Renata makes a face and

pushes her chair out.

"Wait," says Richard. "Let me go." He walks over to the door and flings it wide. He stands looking around. Renata comes to stand beside him. Jules follows.

Renata turns to go back inside. "Fuck, here's something." She looks over her shoulder at the door. "A baggie of something – nailed onto the door."

Jules and Richard stare at it.

Renata yanks it off the nail and unseals the ziplock. Inside there's a folded piece of paper and something wrapped in white cotton knit, like men's underwear fabric. She sticks two fingers into the bag and opens the fold of fabric to see. She jerks her hand back. "It's . . . " She gags, sucks in a breath between her teeth. "Let's sit down." She walks slowly toward the table and sits waiting while Jules and Richard take their seats.

She reaches for Jules and squeezes her hand. "It's Oliver's –"

"Oliver's?" Jules covers her mouth.

"His . . . Prince Albert – and . . . some skin." Renata looks at Richard. "The bartender." She points toward downstairs.

"Prince Albert?" Jules asks.

"The tip of his cock – and jewelry. I guess the cops never found it."

Renata opens the baggie again and pulls out the piece of paper, unfolds it. She swallows and reads: "A tip from Oliver for your *amigo* Francisco."

Jules and Richard stand looking at Renata, Richard frozen stiff and Jules white, chewing her lip. Renata holds the bag out from her body by the top edge. "I'll flush this. We don't need to unwrap it."

Richard puts out his hand and takes it. "There's no blood – surely it's not real –"

"It's real. Trust me – maybe it's been frozen or something – it's shriveled, like a dried apricot. I wouldn't know what it was without the stud. Let's just flush it."

"No, we'd better save it. I don't know. We need to give it to the police."

"No police," says Renata.

Richard takes the bag from the table, seals the zip, and walks toward the refrigerator. "I'll put it in the bottom drawer until we're thinking more clearly."

"Let's just shut up about it," Jules says.

Renata stares at the door, thinking of Oliver's pain, how they must have handled him. Richard comes back and puts his arms around her shoulders. He kisses her head and turns to the door, still ajar. "Time to lock that door."

"No worries," Rennie says, not wanting to scare Julie. "They're playing games, trying to freak out Francisco."

"Lock the door. I'd feel better," Jules says.

"It's your door, Renata. They want to scare you too or they wouldn't have sent it here." Richard points to Renata's hands. "Wash with soap."

Richard locks the door. "Who killed the bartender? Do you know?"

Renata walks to the table and picks up her cup. "Fuck, no. Some drug network, I think." She looks at Jules. "It's looking more and more like Oliver took the blame for us." She takes a drink. "The shit's hitting the fan — Francisco said it would. He's not sure, but it could be some kind of Mafia after us. Sounds like lots of foreigners are in on this."

"Renata, for Christ's sake, what are we doing here?" Richard asks.

"We have to leave. I know. I told Francisco I'd give him my decision later tonight —" She turns to Jules. "Whether I'd go with him or not. We all have to decide what to do."

Richard looks at Renata. "Surely, you're not considering —"

"Let's not answer any more phones or doors," says Jules.

Renata rinses her hands at the sink. "They must enjoy scaring people."

"We'd all better leave right now," Jules says.

"Not tonight," says Renata. "Cops will be all over the roads with the hurricane coming. There's no place to go anyway. We can leave in the morning."

"I thought you — you'll be leaving with me in the morning? Both of you, right?" Richard's voice is high with anticipation.

Jules looks at Renata for an answer. Renata's chest feels heavy. A dry cough comes out when she tries to speak. The thought of leaving Francisco is more painful than she expected. Maybe he will agree to move north with them. Not.

Richard is standing behind her with his hand on her shoulder. She puts her hand over his. "I'm thinking about it," she says. She tells herself it doesn't have to mean forever, another phase of life, a practical phase. It will be good for Julie — and herself, maybe. She squeezes Richard's hand. It's warm and firm, loving. He offers pure love and never asks for much. His unbelievable happiness, if she answers yes, might make it all feel worthwhile. She's already taken more from him than anyone should give.

She gulps her drink. Her eyes focus out the window on the sliver of black clouds and dark crashing water she can see between the lighted buildings. "You really want me, Richard? After I ruined you, slimed you out of your family and job into this mess?"

"That's ridiculous."

"I did it for nothing, without thinking or caring, just let it happen. I thought nothing in the world mattered." She laughs. "I still don't know what matters — but I owe it to you — and Julie — to try a new way. I'll give you a chance to save me, if that's what you both want. If you think I'm worth it."

She takes Jules' hand on the other side and squeezes Richard's on her shoulder. She looks at Richard. "I don't love you — but maybe I will sometime. You deserve it."

"I've already given up everything for this one chance." He hugs her and she feels the strength in his words. "No matter what, if I died tomorrow I would already have had my share of happiness tonight." He kisses her forehead. "We'll get your puppy – you can do whatever you want – and Jules and I will work on her novel. I'll spend time writing poetry again. My impossible dream has come true." He stands up. "Where are my swords?"

"What?" Jules asks.

"I just remembered. I don't want to leave them behind."

Renata looks around. "The short sword is in the top drawer of the dresser. The long one is under the bed."

"Where's the snake?"

"He's under the covers. Don't worry."

Richard gets to his knees and peers under the bed from a distance. He moves closer and pulls out the long sword, unsheathes it, and holds it straight up in front of him. "I can't forget this. It's symbolic of my protection of you." He puts it on the table and goes to the dresser for the short sword, laying it beside the long one. He sits down again next to Renata, stretching his arm around both women.

"That feels nice," Renata says.

Jules lays her head on Renata's shoulder. "It's nice, Rennie, our little family." She lifts her head. "Now when do we get out of here?"

Renata gets up and goes to Pepe on the bed, then turns to face them. "Where should we go? Do you have a map, Julie? I'll close my eyes and point."

"No, sorry. But you can choose."

Richard reaches to touch Renata's knee. "I had been thinking north – the bed and breakfast with my brother –"

"I have family up north," says Jules.

Renata wrinkles her nose.

Jules shrugs. "I really only need to make a visit – to show my dad the book when it's finished."

Richard puts his hand on the back of Renata's head. "Okay. You can't live in the cold. I don't know why I ever thought it would work." He looks at her. "The thing to do is to sell my share and buy a new place. How about California? Cool and dry."

Renata's eyes brighten. "Maybe a little town on the beach. I heard about one where lots of musicians live. No cops — probably lots of drugs."

"Bolinas?" Richard says. "I've heard of it. Jefferson Airplane lives there — or used to."

"What?" Renata asks.

"A band," he says. "Before your time, I guess."

"That would be fucking cool."

"It's the most expensive area in the country."

"Oh — well, we can start somewhere else, until Julie's book brings in the major cash."

Jules laughs. "I can't guarantee that, you know!"

"Don't worry." Richard kisses Renata's cheek. "I'll have some money coming in, and we'll be able to find jobs. Maybe I could open a little bookstore."

"Jobs?" Renata reaches for the bottle of vodka. "Let's not talk about that. We're going to California and find gold!" She pours a double shot of vodka for each of them. Richard winks. They all drink it down.

"I — I —" says Jules. She puts her hand over her forehead.

"What's the problem, sweetie?" asks Renata.

"I —" she stops. "I have a confession — something I just remembered." She looks at Richard.

"Tell me. Getting the truth out is always the best," Richard says.

"We know whatever you did, Julie, it was for a good reason. Everything has changed."

"It wasn't for a good reason. It was purely selfish, and I'm so sorry. I don't think it matters now, but it could."

Renata puts her hand on Jules' thigh. "It's okay, girlie, tell us, you're driving me nuts."

"Go ahead," says Richard.

Jules turns to Richard. "I gave the ring to Garcia. I tried to shift the blame to you."

Richard pushes his chair back and stands up. "What ring?"

"Oh." Renata remembers and takes a drink. "The lawyer's."

Jules twists her fingers as she explains the details. "It was before I knew you, Richard. I was afraid of what you might do. You were so intense. I wanted to get you out of the way for a while and keep Garcia busy to take his suspicions off Rennie." She reaches toward Richard's hand, but he doesn't lift it from his side. "I know it was terrible. I'm so sorry."

"No big deal," Renata says. "The cops would've been here by now if Garcia made the connection." She tugs on Richard's arm and laughs. "That's the least of your worries, babe. Now that you're hanging with us, there are guys who'll chop you into stringy little pieces before the cops ever figure it out."

Richard is rubbing his chin. "Nice."

"Don't be pissed. Julie is sorry. Forgive her. Let's party and be happy."

"Please?" Jules grits her teeth. "There's one more problem. The $1,000 I stole. I have to get it to Patty at the restaurant. I never intended to keep her money."

"Send her double when your book money comes in. If she's the nice person you say, she'll forgive you," says Renata.

Jules nods and wipes her eyes. "I guess I can hope for that."

Richard finishes his drink. "I'm so happy right now, if I had a thousand to spare, I'd give it to you."

"You're sweet." Jules smiles and kisses him on the cheek.

He sets his glass down hard. "I need another one of these." He reaches for the bottle, pours half a glass, and tosses down a gulp. "All right, we're past all that. Are there any more details I should know about the two of you?"

Jules looks at Renata. Renata shakes her head and turns to Richard. "Nope. We're all in this together. Off we go in the morning, to live happily ever after."

"This is a big responsibility for me," Richard says.

Renata moves over to his lap and he buries his face in her hair. Jules puts her head on his shoulder, and Renata feels him tense, then relax.

CHAPTER 48

Thursday, October 14, 1:00 am, Tropical Moons

Jules

She gets up and goes into the bathroom to give Richard and Renata a few minutes alone. She wonders if this arrangement is really going to work. She's ecstatic nonetheless. She even begins to hope that with Richard's guidance she might dare to show the manuscript to her father. It's her art, her creation, and she should be proud of it, no matter what.

Soon they'll be safe in another part of the country. South Beach was never her style anyway, although she couldn't admit it to herself. Someday she hopes to be so separated by time and space, and being in love with Rennie, that she'll think the whole gruesome mess was the product of her imagination. Already the details have started to blend with the fiction.

She takes a step into the room. The two of them are on the bed cuddling. This is a good time to leave and make some notes on the computer. She's too drunk to write scenes, but she wants to capture the freshness of the moment, the wonderful feeling of companionship, release, and anticipation of days on the road to come.

She can hear Richard and Rennie through the wall, their drunkenness turning up the volume. It's all right. She'll be Rennie's true love, and Richard can fill her need for masculine attention. They'll all be good for each other. Jules imagines herself in the role of housekeeper. That's fine too. She'll write and cook and hardly need to leave the house once things get settled. She thinks of Francisco. She'll have to tell Rennie to say goodbye for her.

The door opens. Damn. Jules raises her head. She should remember to lock. Richard walks in slowly. His shirt is unbuttoned and his hair tossed in all directions, eyes tired and happy.

Richard puts his hand lightly on her head. "Sweetheart – sorry, you were working. Rennie wants you to go back over and drink with her. Okay? I've had it – after that box. Do you mind if I get a few hours of sleep over here?"

"Of course not." She smiles. "Wouldn't be the first time." She hits the shut-down and closes the laptop. "I'll get you some clean sheets."

Richard chuckles. "Don't bother. Do you think I worry about that? You forget how long I've been visiting Rennie." He keeps laughing as he drops onto the bed in his clothes. "Ooh, I don't want to think about it."

Jules laughs with him. "Things have changed for all of us," she says. "I feel pretty good with everything."

"That's because you're drunk!" He laughs. "Me too. The best bet is to stay this way – at least till morning."

She takes her glass and tiptoes out. He's sort of a lovable fool.

She opens the door to find Rennie in a long cotton robe sitting at the table with a drink and a lit candle, fingering the blade of the short sword.

Jules points at the candle. "Think the electricity will go out?"

"Probably." Renata moves the blade so it throws glints on the wall. "I guess Richard can protect us," she says.

"He has no idea how well you protect yourself – and your

friends."

"What about you, Julie? You wield a mean scissors."

She winces. "All that blood. Then at the cabin. It really happened, didn't it? You know, I almost feel like I made it up."

"It never seemed real, even while it was happening. I feel like that a lot – like I'm in a movie and everything's in slow motion. I never know what's real." She chuckles. "Too much drugs and alcohol." She stands up holding the sword with both hands and points it at an invisible target, slashing air in the dark corner of the room, jabbing right and left. "There's energy in the atmosphere. We're ready for action." Her eyes flash. She thrusts into the air and holds steady, as if waiting for an attacker. She clangs the sword down on the dresser and falls into the chair. "Julie, Julie, what are we thinking?"

She starts the laugh, the sound of her whole body coming to a slow bubbling boil, as she tilts in the chair, her shoulders quivering, back arching, the high sound tickling Jules' ears as something unwinds in the universe that will never again be wound as tightly.

Jules moves to Renata's side, dragging her from the chair, sweeping her to the bed where she lies down and pulls Renata next to her. She puts her arm across Renata's waist, looking into the gap of the robe at the shadowy softness of freckled skin and pink nipples barely visible in the candlelight, bouncing as her laughter trickles away.

Jules runs her finger down the inside curve of Renata's breast. "I'm not thinking anymore, Rennie. Let's not think. In the morning, when the hurricane has passed, we'll get a few clothes together – and Pepe – and we'll all hit the road."

Rennie takes Jules' hand and guides it back under the robe to cup her breast. Heat moves into Jules' chest and she strokes the nipple and puts her mouth into Rennie's hair at her ear. Her voice is low and breathless. "Now, Rennie. Take me somewhere now – away from myself and everything I know."

Renata rolls toward her, mouth open and gasping, one hand yanking her robe wide, sliding her arms around Jules' hips, then moving close to hold her. Their faces are close, the sweet smell of Rennie's skin and hair blocking out everything in the room. Jules has feared and dreamed of this moment. Now it's so simple. Her mouth opens to accept Rennie's. They grab at each other's necks and shoulders, fighting to hold everything at once, need lashing them tight together.

Jules lets go as Renata lifts herself on both hands and pushes her down on the bed, stripping off the robe, dropping it to the floor, and positioning her knees on each side of Jules' legs. Renata reaches into her lips, opening her, exposing her internal wetness to the cool air as she inserts the special finger, the stub, and works it against her clit. The sensation turns Jules' vision to a blur, until her eyes close and she recreates the chiseled face and satin skin of Renata inside her mind.

The finger stops, and Jules opens her eyes. Renata moves forward, shining in candlelight, straddling Jules' hips, pressing her pubic bone hard against Jules', the two clits massaging each other, grinding, pressure radiating heat and vibration through Jules' body. The climax comes easily, a feeling of giving smooth painless birth, as the hardening sensation moves through her, numbing her clit with tightness, an icy pause, then flooding her with a warm rush that takes the strength out of every muscle. She shudders into the delicious, less-conscious world of love. She barely feels Rennie move beside her, a kiss on the cheek, slowing breath in her ear.

"Julie."

She's awakened by the whisper, but keeps her eyes closed. A hand smooths back her hair, then runs down her arm in a long caress. "Julie, honey."

She opens her eyes. Rennie's hair glows in the streetlights, her sweet face above the bed, a tight t-shirt with Mickey Mouse. "Honey, I have to go. Can you get a twenty for me? I don't have a cent, and I'm not sure what Franco's got."

Jules rubs her eyes. "Sure. My purse — in my room."

"Can you get it? I don't want Richard to know I'm headed out. If he wakes up, tell him you're going downstairs for a drink because you don't want to disturb me."

"The bar's open?"

"Doubt it, but he'll be groggy." She holds out the white robe.

"Don't go. Please."

"I have to."

Jules pulls herself up, slides into the robe, and tiptoes to the door. "I think I can get it without waking him."

Fuck. Richard has locked the door so she has to knock. As much as he drank, she wonders if she'll have to wake the whole floor. She knocks loud and hard. Finally the light goes on. The door opens. His face is puffy.

"Go back to bed. I just need something from my purse."

"Huh? Where's Rennie?"

"Shh! She's sound asleep. I'm going downstairs to read so I don't wake her." She guides him to the bed. "Go back to sleep. You need your rest for tomorrow."

He nods, looking unconvinced, but gets back into bed. Jules turns out the light and grabs her purse from the dresser. She stops to listen as his breathing deepens. She tiptoes out.

Rennie is sitting on the bed.

"Here, take sixty, just in case."

Rennie takes it, but returns a twenty. "I'll be back in a few hours."

Jules puts her hand on Rennie's arm. "Just cuddle with me for a minute, so I can go back to sleep."

"Okay, just for a minute, honey."

Jules pulls the robe off, but Renata stays dressed and pulls the sheet over Jules before lying next to her. Jules begins to drift, the howl of the wind soothing in its regularity.

Renata sits up.

"Don't go."

"Sorry, sweetie. Francisco is waiting. The wind is picking up."

"We're still leaving together in the morning, right?"

"For better or worse, the three of us." She bends and gives

Jules a long kiss on the mouth. "Don't step on Pepe when you get up – he's in my robe on the floor."

"I'm not getting out of bed until you come back."

"Okay, my love." She strokes Jules' thigh. "Hope you don't have to pee."

"Rennie, you'll be back soon, right?"

"I have to stay a little – say goodbye. I'll leave at dawn, promise – as soon as the hurricane is past."

Jules grabs her shoulders and hugs as tight as she can. "I love you. Be careful."

"I will." Renata walks around the robe. "Go back to sleep. Big day tomorrow."

The door closes and Jules realizes that Rennie didn't lock it. She should get up, but she said she wouldn't. It was a pledge, however silly, and if she gets up, Rennie might never return. She lifts her head and looks out the window. Lights still on, but nobody on the street. Heavy rain. The wind and waves are loud, and she's never seen the palms so near to horizontal. It's amazing that the roots hold in the sand. She lies back down, rolls on her side away from the door, and tries to relax. Her life is finally ready to begin, just a few more hours to wait.

CHAPTER 49

4:00 am, Tropical Moons bar, Hurricane Irene
approaches, outer bands 45 mph, seas rough

Renata

The front is boarded up and the lobby and bar are
deserted. Francisco is sitting on a stool under one burning
bulb. He finishes the last swallow of a beer and sets the bottle
down. Renata steps into his arms and gives him a hard kiss.
"Finally. I thought you changed your mind."

She gives him another kiss, sliding her hands over his
smooth shoulders and down his forearms. "Where'd you get
the beer?"

"Brought my own." Francisco picks up a cigarette from the
ashtray, takes a puff, and puts it out as Renata watches. The
compact fit of his jeans, the trim waist and thighs, the bulge –
hard to give up.

"Come on. The road's covered with water already. We gotta
get off the beach before we're stuck."

"Hey, we can go right upstairs. Richard is sleeping at Julie's."

"Too close for comfort. I can't leave the car here anyway." They step outside. The whistle of gusts between the

buildings and the slapping of fronds and awnings create a flapping whir. The wind and rain plaster Renata's hair to her face, and sand stings her arms, and she has to fight to keep her balance and make forward progress. Her sandals are sloshed by a wavelet that washes over the curb. The car is a few steps from the building, but she's drenched and gritty by the time she hurls herself inside and slams the door.

The beach is deserted. There is only one car on the side street, parked a couple of car lengths behind Francisco's. Renata points at a woman with her arms and head down on the steering wheel. Francisco shrugs. "Asleep. The cops will move her."

Francisco starts the engine. "Plenty of good parking tonight." He wrings his hair back and wipes his hands on his jeans. "You should've brought your clothes. But I guess we'll be back to pick up Jules."

Renata nods. She still feels confused over the choice she has to make.

Water extends over the beach and across the road, making it look like they're driving through the ocean. The progress is slow. Renata thinks of telling him about the threat left for him on the door, but she doesn't want to add to his problems. After a while she realizes they've gone a long way past Francisco's apartment.

"I thought we were going to your place?"

"I got us a room. My stuff is there – the little I'm taking. I moved out of my apartment yesterday."

"I guess you've already gotten the message then." Renata tells him about the baggie.

He shakes his head and grips the wheel. "Fucking cocksuckers."

"What about Julie? Think she'll be safe up there?"

"Yeah. Since he couldn't find me, he left you the message to deliver."

"Who's he?"

"A major psycho."

"I wonder why they didn't wait for us to answer the door."

"Not ready to kill us yet, I guess, but they don't like being out of touch."

CHAPTER 50

4:30 am, Tropical Moons, Room 2-B

Jules

She awakens to the click of footsteps in the hall. It's still dark and she's surprised, but relieved and happy, that Renata has come back so soon. The door opens with a light creak and closes quietly.

"Honey, it's okay. I'm awake. Come and curl up with me. We can sleep until it gets light. I waited in bed for you, like I said."

There's no answer. Jules sits up. "What's the matter?"

A female voice answers. "Eddie told me you never lock."

"Who? Who are you?"

"Who are you expecting? – that bastard husband of mine? Where is he?"

Jules pulls open the curtain to let in light from outside. The streetlights are still working. A tall woman is standing in the room, her hair and clothes dripping. She sways and leans back to brace herself on the wall. Jules realizes she's drunk. "Wrong apartment. Your husband isn't here."

"Oh, no? There's his box!" She walks slowly toward it. The

sheen of its thick paint is visible from the light outside. She stares at the dark pattern and the padlock. Her head drops and she begins to sob.

Jules watches from the bed, feeling her anguish. "Can I help you?" she says. "Linda?"

Linda's head snaps up. She wipes her eyes and nose on her hand and sniffs. She looks at the box again, touches it, and her hand springs off like it's burned. "Are you in there, Dicky?"

Jules takes a deep breath. "He's not here," she says. She pulls the sheet to her chin.

"So you're that conniving whore."

"No – I'm –"

"I heard you were – thought you'd be – such a beauty – pouty lips, thick auburn curls, face like a movie star – and bigger tits." Linda stares. "You don't look that hot without your make-up, do you? Miss your beauty parlor appointment?" She breaks her gaze and glances around the room. "So where is Richard?"

Jules shrugs.

Linda bends and looks inside the box, losing her balance, and catching herself. "You in there, you pitiful dick?"

Jules decides it's better to let Linda believe she's Renata and get rid of her before Rennie gets home – or Richard wakes up. No need to start complications that might prevent them from leaving in the morning. She wraps the sheet around herself and scoots to the edge of the bed. "I didn't want Richard here. I tried everything to send him back home."

Linda holds the box to steady herself. "You know, there's something wrong with him. Really. He's been a good guy all his life – a husband and father . . . responsible – until now. I keep thinking if I could just talk to him nice – but I can't. I'm so angry and he's so . . .his brain chemistry is – I don't know – fucked up . . . ."

Linda's face changes. She stares at Jules. "You're lying. I know what goes on – I paid for all the sordid details."

Jules nods. "Garcia. Nice guy."

Linda clamps her lips in disgust. "Yeah, Eddie. You fuck him too?"

Jules doesn't answer.

"I left him a message to meet me downstairs – him and my lawyer friend – the blond airhead. They're always so worried that I'd come to thish ... this shit hole alone – but I'm not surprised he's late – either of them."

"There's a hurricane –"

"So what? I made it. Right? Men. I've had it with them. Supposed to be here to help me talk sense – or kick ass. I got tired of waiting." She leans on the box. "Easy for a Florida girl to get here. So where is he?"

"Garcia?"

"Richard. Don't play the stupid whore. I know better. You're smart. You ruined his job and took him away from us." Her face contorts and she starts to cry. "Richard and I were best friends, better than husband and wife. We have two boys. Did you know that? He has twins at home – crying because he broke their little hearts!"

"I know. I'm sorry."

"They're at my mother's, heartbroken." Linda starts to cry again. She whispers, "You know?" She leans forward, pleading, then her passion boiling into a snarl. "You know that? You do? You know about the little boys crying their little eyes out, and you still keep him here? Why the fuck did you bring him here?"

"I didn't. He insisted on staying here. I'm sorry."

"You played with his mind, you fucking freak!"

Jules feels her anger building. She's heard enough insults aimed at Rennie, and she's finished saying she's sorry. She wants to scream, but she controls it, still hoping Richard is dead-drunk asleep and she can save all the trouble. "Look, he's gone up north to his brother's. I made him go this afternoon. I couldn't stand him hanging around here whining anymore."

Jules watches while Linda digests the information. She hits

the box with a glancing, weak-fisted punch, frustration over-flowing. Her eyes flash at Jules, then shift focus to the samurai swords, catching light from the street.

"Liar. These are his most prized possessions. He wouldn't leave them." She goes to the dresser and strokes the ornate etching on the blade of the short sword, then picks up the long sword, tears streaming down her cheeks. She stretches the sword toward Jules and steps closer. She smiles, flat and menacing.

"That's sharp," Jules says. She tries to move, but her legs are wrapped in the bedclothes. She freezes. The sheet drops from her fingers. Linda's eyes rove down her breasts and anger flashes on her face again.

Linda steps forward, holding the sword with both hands. She stares straight into Jules' eyes, and the blade moves closer slowly, pointed toward Jules' left breast, inches away.

"If I only had the guts – I would kill you for the pain you caused my boys." Linda takes a step to sneer into Jules' face. Her foot comes down on the robe, and the fabric moves. With a jerk, Pepe's head appears through the sleeve, his body writhing to escape Linda's heel.

Jules watches in the slow motion of fear, as Linda loses her balance, tilting, wavering, stumbling forward. The tensile blade trickles down Jules' ribs, its tip dragging a thick crimson wake. She watches, dazed, as the blade hesitates at the bend of her thigh, to slip inches inside her, cleanly, as if into baked custard.

Linda falls to her knees, screaming. The blade clangs to the linoleum with a gush of darker blood. Jules grabs her groin feeling the burning tear of pain for only a moment as her head lightens and she falls. Linda's face . . . bloody robe . . . blood . . . The room darkens . . .

CHAPTER 51

4:45 am, Tropical Moons, Room 2-A

Richard

He wakes to the sound of rain hitting the windowpane and the flapping of a broken awning. The wind howls loudly on a long high note. Was there a scream or did he dream it? Where is he? He looks around, realizing he's in Jules' apartment, and Jules and Rennie are next door. No, Rennie is next door alone. Jules is down at the bar. He sits up, becoming frantic, and reaches around the floor for his jeans. "Rennie?" he yells. His head is spinning and he can't locate any clothing. He tries to stand up and sits back down, dizzy. He's got to move fast, now certain that it was a scream. "Rennie, I'm coming!"

He leans on the bed and finds his tangled jeans, tries to straighten them, gives up. He goes to the bathroom and grabs a towel, wraps it around his waist, and runs into the hall. Rennie's door is ajar. He pushes it open just far enough to slide through. He peers ahead of him, the light from the street revealing a naked figure on the floor.

The sight takes the air out of him and the towel drops. She's crumpled, face down, her arms and one leg crimped under her, hair sopping in the puddle of blood. The snake is curled partially on her shoulder, its eyes like magnetic beads following Richard's face. Its head rises, defiant, the lump of rat still visible. "Rennie, Rennie —" His voice fades as he realizes there will be no answer. The long samurai sword lies near her, the tip of the blade under her. He glances around the room, his blood boiling to find the killer — but there's no one. Suicide? Could that be why she fed the snake? She'd have the courage to kill herself, but not the motivation.

He squats down, his legs weak, vision wavering with tears, and reaches toward her, slowly, not knowing what to do. She looks so thin and pale from the blood loss — he can't even see the freckles on her back. He reaches to move her hair for one last look at her beautiful face —

A sound comes from behind him.

He turns. A chair is next to the box and the lid is open. He can see a dark form through the two lower holes on his side. He bends slowly and slides the blade of the *katana* from beneath Renata. Holding the blade upward at his side, he creeps quietly toward the box in a crouched position. It doesn't make sense — a street criminal, using the sword? No matter. Whoever it is, he will kill him. He hopes it's the pimp.

As he steps softly, he sizes up his target, seeing that he'll be able to run the sword through the largest hole, like a magician, inflicting less suffering than the demon deserves. He drops down in a crouch, close, and bends his sword arm backward to aim the point into the hole. He straightens his arm, gathering strength to ram the sword, and the front trap door flies open. He sees into the blackness, her face . . .

His arm drops to his side, empty. The *katana* remains horizontal. He has plunged it inside the box, through Linda's chest, and the point is stuck into the wood on the other side. He watches horrified as her body slumps and her face falls out of view.

He drags himself away, holding onto the chair. He staggers across the floor to the towel, picks it up, and wraps it around his waist. He can't think. The room is filling with blood. Renata is dead and he has killed the mother of his children.

There's only one choice now. He walks wide around the box to the dresser. The *wakizashi* is there where he put it. He picks it up and unsheathes the short blade. He should have realized its purpose long ago, to save him from the wasted nothing he called a life, before he caused so much damage. It has waited, gathering dust, for the poet with an impossible dream, many stupid dreams. He should kneel to commit traditional suicide, *hara-kiri*, the slow, honorable death, but the thought of torturous disembowelment keeps him on his feet. He is a coward. He grips the handle of the *wakizashi*, caressing the fish roe pattern of the polished, carved bone with his thumb, focusing on the ridged blade.

He must leave a note – to explain – for his sons. His paper and pen are in the box, but he can't make himself get them. Linda's blood is seeping from one edge where the wood is not seamed tightly. Soon it will join Renata's blood, and ironically, the river of his blood will complete the unholy trinity, a cruel symbol to haunt a poet's last thoughts.

The streetlights go out and the room is pitch black. He'll never find paper and pen. To die without explanation is what he deserves. He has spent most of his life failing to clarify his deepest emotions, even to himself.

He lifts the *wakizashi*. Upward and left from below the rib cage is the target for a quick death, straight to the heart. He moves the sword to his right hand, using the left as a guide. He blinks, trying to see Renata with the snake curled over her. He wants his last vision to be of this rare and exquisite woman, but the room is too dark. He tightens his hand, breathes in deeply, and plunges the point under his ribs, feeling the searing pain and puncturing of his organs, a draining from inside. His head becomes light. Blackness narrows his vision to nothing. He slumps down.

CHAPTER 52

5:15 am, South Beach, winds at 55 mph

Renata

The water on the road covers the tires. All lights have gone out. Francisco drives slowly, cursing in a whisper as a car passes by, causing a wake. Two police cars sit with lights flashing at the next intersection.

"Fuck!"

One police car makes a slow U-turn and pulls parallel on Francisco's side. He rolls down the window.

"A-1-A is closed except to residents. Where are you headed?"

"We're staying at a motel north of here. A couple blocks off the beach."

"Let me see your license." Francisco hands it over with no comment, his bare arm instantly drenched. The rain beats on the plastic sleeve of the policeman's raincoat as he reaches across. Renata leans toward her side of the car to avoid the water blowing in, holding her breath in hope that Francisco doesn't have anything outstanding on his record. Francisco closes the window while they wait. He looks across at Renata.

The policeman taps on the glass and hands the license back. "Okay, make your turn here and go down the side street. It's clear. I can't let you go any farther on the beach. Too much water and debris."

Francisco nods and says thanks. He makes the left turn.

"For once I don't mind the cops checking people out," Renata says.

"Takes up our time."

"Yeah. You know, Franco, I can't leave Julie by herself the rest of the night — all alone in a hurricane, with no lights, and ... murderers. Take me home. Come back in the morning."

"It's going to take forever to get back there. The cop is going to think we're up to something."

"Go through the back streets. It might be faster anyway. Sorry. I shouldn't have left her in the first place."

Francisco grunts and starts another U-turn. A heavy palm frond smashes down grazing the right front.

"See, we're doing the right thing," Renata says. "That would have smashed the windshield if we kept on going straight."

Francisco looks at her and shakes his head. "If water gets in the engine, we're done."

The streets of the neighborhoods have formed flowing lakes on the sides, but by driving in the middle of both lanes, they are able to get back to The Moons in a short time. Francisco pulls up at the side of the building. "Get Jules. We'll all go to the new motel. It'll be safer."

"Good idea." As she opens the door Renata is blasted with wet sand. She throws herself to the side of the building to make her way around front. Pieces of wood and unidentifiable objects fly past her and she flattens herself and slides sideways to the entrance. The door is flung back against the wall as she opens it. She feels her way around to the stairs and runs up.

The second floor hall is black. She runs the few steps to her apartment and feels the partially open door. She edges along the wall until she reaches the table with the matches and candle. She lights the candle.

"Richard!"

As she moves toward him, past the box, she sees Jules in a puddle of blood near the bed, Pepe half on her back. Renata stops. She holds her mouth shut tight and makes herself walk slowly. She passes Richard, knowing he's dead. She stoops to Jules and raises her head. Pepe slides away.

"Julie? Julie?" She turns Jules on her side. As her leg straightens out, a gush of blood flows from her groin. Her body looks drenched in scarlet paint, but she's warm. Renata pulls the sheet free from under her legs and winds it tightly around the wound, once, twice. She ties one end to the leg of the bed and twists the other around Jules' thigh and twirls it tight, two more times above the wound, tucking the end under Jules' hip so the weight of her body will keep it secure.

"Julie? Sweetheart? Can you hear me?"

She presses her hand on the side of Jules' throat. She can feel something, but it might be her own pulse beating hard. "Julie. Julie." The blood seems to have stopped.

She stands and grabs the phone. It's still working. She punches 911. It rings for a long time. "I need an ambulance. Someone is bleeding to death, stabbed. Two people." She gives the address and the woman tells her that help is coming. She looks back at Richard on his side, the short sword visible between his ribs. "Oh, Richard . . . "

She closes her eyes to clear them and stoops again to Jules, taking her head in her arms. She can't tell if the blood is still seeping.

She strokes Jules' forehead, without response, until sirens can be heard. She wants to stay with Jules, but she's afraid of being arrested. She's got to get back out to Francisco – if he's still waiting. Tell him what happened. Figure out what to do. She looks around for Pepe, but he's hidden in the dark. No time to search.

She gives Jules a kiss on the forehead, lowers her head to the robe, and runs out of the room and down the stairs. A pile of sand has accumulated at the bottom from the door being open. She hears the sirens close by and lurches back into the gusts, grabbing the corner of the door to drag herself outside. Francisco has eased the car onto the road far enough to see her and pulls across the sidewalk, angling the car to block the wind.

He helps push open the door, and Renata falls in. He reverses and accelerates, pulling into a driveway in time for an ambulance and two police cars to pass by.

Renata sits shaking, breathing hard, her eyes closed.

Francisco hits the gas, swerving, then gaining control, as they head slowly west up the side street through water and waves of trash. He glances at Renata, seeing the blood still on her wet clothes. "Christ! Where's Jules?"

Renata points back to the hotel. "She's up there. I think . . . I think . . . dead. Richard . . . stabbed her."

"Richard? Richard stabbed Jules?"

"Then himself. I called the ambulance."

"Richard killed her?"

Renata holds her hand over her mouth and whispers, swallowing between the phrases. "With his sword. I think. But she might be alive. I stopped the blood."

Francisco swallows. "If she was still bleeding when you found her, that means she's got a chance." He squeezes Renata's bloody knee. "We'll call the hospital in the morning. I bet you saved her. I bet she'll be okay."

"I don't know."

Francisco drives slowly through the streaming water, north and west off the beach. After a few miles there's light ahead. The road is deserted, but the streetlights are glowing and the traffic signals working.

"Civilization," Renata says.

Francisco pulls under the awning of an old one-story motel, brightly painted in coral. Renata drags herself out. She tries the lobby door, but it's locked. The outside lights are off. She waits by the boarded-up window while he parks and comes running back, his hair shiny and dripping, the white shirt translucent on his body and his jeans soaked. "Closed," she says.

He pulls out a key and unlocks. "Friends of my parents own this place."

Renata looks at him in shock. "You have parents?"

"Yeah, even me. They can be a pain in the ass, but I'll miss them when we're gone."

Francisco flips on the lights. The room is bright in matching floral print curtains and bedspread. Francisco's suitcases are in the corner, a pipe and a plastic bag of dope on the dresser next to a used ashtray. He turns on the air-conditioner.

"Just like home," Renata says. The word *home* makes her think of a home with Richard and Jules, and the dog she'd been promised. She sobs. Now she'd do anything to have that chance back.

"There's a couple beers in the bathroom sink. Get us one."

She goes in and dries her face, feeling pain in her stomach. She flings a towel around her neck, takes two beers from the icy water, and twists them open. Francisco has the bed turned down and his shirt on the floor. He pulls off his pants and sits. Renata stands trancelike, holding the beers. He pats the clean pink sheet next to him. "Bring those over here."

She hands him a beer and puts hers on the nightstand and strips off her wet and bloody t-shirt and jeans. She rubs her body and her hair with the towel and wraps herself in it. She sits down and lets him take her into his arms. He kisses her neck, and tears gather in her eyes.

He takes the soft towel and blots her cheeks, then kisses her lips and holds her by the chin, tilting her face and looking into her eyes, his other arm around her, holding her tight by the hip. "It'll all be okay, *mamita*. We just have to get away from this place."

He holds her as she shakes with internal sobs. "We'll find a private charter. It'll be fine."

"I'm one of those kind of people that if I love somebody — they die."

He holds her tighter. "I'll take the risk."

"What are we going to do? Poor Jules."

"Think positive — Jules will be okay. We'll write her letters, and when she's healed up, she can come live with us. On a boat or — if you don't like that — an island. How 'bout it? An island in the Bahamas, where all the nice people live." He kisses her ear and whispers in it. "We've got the whole world."

"No —"

"Wide deserted beaches where we can walk naked and drink rum. I know where we can live cheap and you don't ever have to work — you or Julie."

"If only . . ." Renata lets go into the wave of grief, unable to muffle her cries. She lets Francisco cuddle her, like the child she never was, and she goes deeper into the warmth of the moment.

CHAPTER 53

8:00 am, South Beach motel, 78 degrees, cloudy,
6-foot seas

Renata

She must have slept, because it's hot and light. Her eyes
open to yellow and pink flowered curtains and two full beers
on the table. The night comes back to her as a sharp pain in
her chest. Francisco is on his back completely uncovered, one
arm bent under his head, his black hair and tan skin shocking
against the pink sheets. Renata looks at him without feeling,
thinking of Jules, hoping. She reaches for the phone and picks
up the receiver. No dial tone.

She gets up and goes into the bathroom, shutting the door
to be alone. She sits on the toilet, staring at the shower curtain. It's all pastels like the rest of the place. Schools of coral
and yellow fish overlap and blend on the clear plastic above a
border of oyster and scallop shells. The fish look like snappers
with eyelashes. Cartoonish little faces. They're smiling in a sick
way, like they have gas. One fish is smiling more than the
others, swimming in a clear space, all by itself. She knows this
lonely joker and her fake smile. She always thought she was

such hot shit. Stupid. She pushes the curtain to the wall.

The shower is strong and the water still warm. She washes slowly, knowing that her hopes might end as soon as she gets to the hospital. She notices the fluffy thickness of the towels as she dries. It's the luxury of laundry service — the service she might be doing on the cruise ship.

Francisco yawns as she comes back into the room. "You're up, *mamita*?"

"The phone's out. We have to drive to the hospital."

"We can't go there — the police —"

"Just hurry. I don't care! Drop me off."

The rain has stopped, but it's cloudy, and water is still deep on the sides of the streets as they head back south. Only one car passes them. Places of business seem abandoned with odds and ends nailed across windows. Palm fronds and other plants are scattered across parking lots and lawns, and there's a line of sticks and finer particles where the water has receded from the sidewalk. A few palms lie on the sand. Traffic signals are still out. "It's like another planet," Renata says.

"I've got a passport for you."

"What about Julie?"

"No problem."

Renata closes her eyes, hoping.

They approach the hotel on the way to the hospital. Police cars are parked in every direction. A crowd is gathered on the sidewalk, and yellow tape closes off the entrance. A stretcher holding a covered figure is being loaded into an ambulance.

"It must be Richard," Francisco says.

"I thought they'd be gone."

"Probably needed the light to gather evidence."

He drives past as Garcia walks through the door, gesturing to a cop and a guy in plainclothes. Renata drops down, then grabs Francisco's arm and sits up.

"Stop! Maybe I can find out about Julie."

He parks around the corner, and Renata leaps out of the car. She runs to The Moons, stopping at the edge of the crowd.

She takes a deep breath. She recognizes the guy talking to Garcia. He's the blond lawyer, not a cop. Another stretcher is being brought out. Another covered body. Smaller maybe. No! No! Tears gather in her eyes.

In the crowd, she sees the bartender who replaced Oliver and walks slowly toward him, staying out of Garcia's line of vision. The bartender takes her hand, squeezes it. "You live here, right?"

She nods.

"I didn't know them." He looks down at his feet. "It's tragic."

"What happened?"

"Not sure. A woman and her husband killed – I think – in 2-B, but they didn't live there. I heard another woman was taken to the hospital."

"Another woman?"

"There was a Burmese python in there too – alive. I heard they had to fight him off the bodies."

She grabs his arm. "Two dead? One woman alive?" Her voice is mostly breath.

"Yeah. Weird. Somebody called 911, put a tourniquet on her, and left – in the middle of the hurricane."

She crushes his hand. "Thank you! Thank you!"

Renata runs toward the car, glancing through The Moons' doorway as she passes. A man in a gray uniform is carrying out a canvas drawstring bag with something heavy inside. It moves.

Francisco pulls forward for her to get in. "Those stretchers –"

Tears stream down her face. "Jules is alive! Take me to the hospital!"

Francisco starts the car. "Who – ?"

"Richard and his wife."

"His wife? Why?"

She shakes her head. "I don't know. Jules always said he was crazy."

"If you show up at the hospital, you could get arrested."

"I have to take the chance."

Francisco pulls over and parks on the edge of the beach.

"Why are you stopping here?"

"Let's walk down to the water. Take a look."

"Julie —"

He opens his door and walks around the car, takes Renata's arm. "Just give me a minute."

The ocean is rough, crashing, with high rolling waves. Steep cliffs have been cut in the sand, much of the beach washed away. They take off their shoes and walk into the surf. Renata looks out at the ocean. The clouds are low and heavy, blending gray into dark blue. No ships on the water, a dark, deep, opaque sheen all the way to the horizon. Without the sound of traffic, there's silence between the crashes of the waves.

"The ship leaves at five, and we have to be there by four. If the cops take you to the station for questioning —"

Renata keeps walking. "I'll be fast. Garcia is busy at The Moons. Nobody else knows me."

"Maybe not. I don't know."

"I have to go."

"Okay, I'll get us some food while you're up there."

She stops to face him. "No. Don't. I've changed my mind. I'm staying. You go ahead to the ship. I have to take care of Julie, at least until she's well. I'll take her somewhere far away from your pals — the Colombians or Mafia, whoever you said. I'm sorry."

He grabs her around the waist and pulls her against him. She knows he's crying and she bites her lip, holding back her own tears. In a few seconds he lets go and wipes his face on the bottom edge of his shirt. His eyes are red and watery when he raises his head. "You're not coming with me?"

"I can't. Not now."

He rubs his nose on his hand. "I might as well confess."

"Huh?"

"You know, the guy I said was looking for you and Jules?

He was the same asshole causing me all the shit."

"Yeah?"

"He killed Oliver. But now he's dead. There's nobody else after us."

"No?"

"Shot." He points to himself. "Last night. He was a psycho."

"You shot him?"

"Self-defense. I was ready for him. I knew sooner or later it would be him or us."

"You okay?"

"Yeah." He accepts a hug. "There was never any kind of Mafia, or Colombians – we're both off the hook."

She looks up at him. "You were going to trick me into leaving?"

"I just upped the odds in my favor." He looks at her, dark eyes gleaming. "I love you. What else could I do?"

"I know." She knows he wants her to say she loves him too. "You don't have to leave then, do you?" She shrugs. "The police? Mafia? Colombians? We were so scared of them, and it was ourselves we should've been afraid of. Jules said it – I should have been afraid of what I was doing to Richard."

Francisco gazes out toward the horizon. "You never loved me, did you? You never will."

Renata looks down into the sand. Francisco brushes back her hair and she puts her head on his shoulder. She steps back and tucks her hair behind her ears.

"I've been thinking for a long time that I'm so smart, doing just what I want, instead of the boring, disgusting shit everybody else does to live. Fuck. It was a stupid lie. I was fucked up more ways than I'll ever figure out, just different ways than most people. Now I've got a responsibility, to stay and help Julie."

He nods slowly. "I think the ship is the best place for me right now."

His lips come close to hers, but if they touch, she doesn't

know it. Her mind is on Jules, poor Julie in the hospital.

They move along toward the car, his hand on the small of her back, fingers underneath her jeans, but she doesn't feel anything. She can only wonder how her life will change.